When the Light Returns

OTHER TITLES BY JOANNA RUTH MEYER

The Winter Dark Series

While the Dark Remains

The Endahr Chronicles

Beneath the Haunting Sea

Beyond the Shadowed Earth

The Oldest Magic Series

Echo North

Wind Daughter

Into the Heartless Wood

Praise for Joanna Ruth Meyer

"A compelling, satisfying romantic adventure."

—*Publishers Weekly* on *Echo North* (starred review)

"Epic and engrossing. Magic pulsates through every page . . . a lush, captivating new twist on beloved fairy tales."

—*Kirkus Reviews* on *Echo North* (starred review)

"A fantasy novel that packs an emotional punch as it explores how doing the right, kind, and gentle thing can require far more courage than waging war."

—*BookPage* on *Into the Heartless Wood* (starred review)

"Brimming with lush prose, endearing characters, and soul-stirring stakes . . . completely irresistible."

—Rebecca Ross, #1 *New York Times* bestselling author of *Divine Rivals* on *Into the Heartless Wood*

"Breathtaking and beautiful."

—*Booklist* on *Wind Daughter* (starred review)

"Weaves a powerful, beautiful spell in a storyline threaded with fairy-tale magic and heartwarming romance. A rich, romantic tale of identity, agency, and love."

—*Kirkus Reviews* on *Wind Daughter* (starred review)

When the Light Returns

JOANNA RUTH MEYER

47NORTH

This is a work of fiction. Names, characters, organizations, places, events, and incidents are either products of the author's imagination or are used fictitiously. Otherwise, any resemblance to actual persons, living or dead, is purely coincidental.

Published by 47North, Seattle

www.apub.com

EU product safety contact:
Amazon Media EU S. à r.l.
38, avenue John F. Kennedy, L-1855 Luxembourg
amazonpublishing-gpsr@amazon.com

ISBN-13: 9781662532771 (paperback)
ISBN-13: 9781662530708 (digital)

Cover design and illustration by David Curtis

Printed in the United States of America

For my mother-in-law, Joanie, who lit up not only every room she was in but every street and neighborhood, too. She is profoundly missed.

And to my readers: In a world filled with darkness, reach for the light.

And men loved darkness rather than light, because their deeds were evil.

—*John 3:19*

The light shineth in darkness; and the darkness comprehended it not.

—*John 1:5*

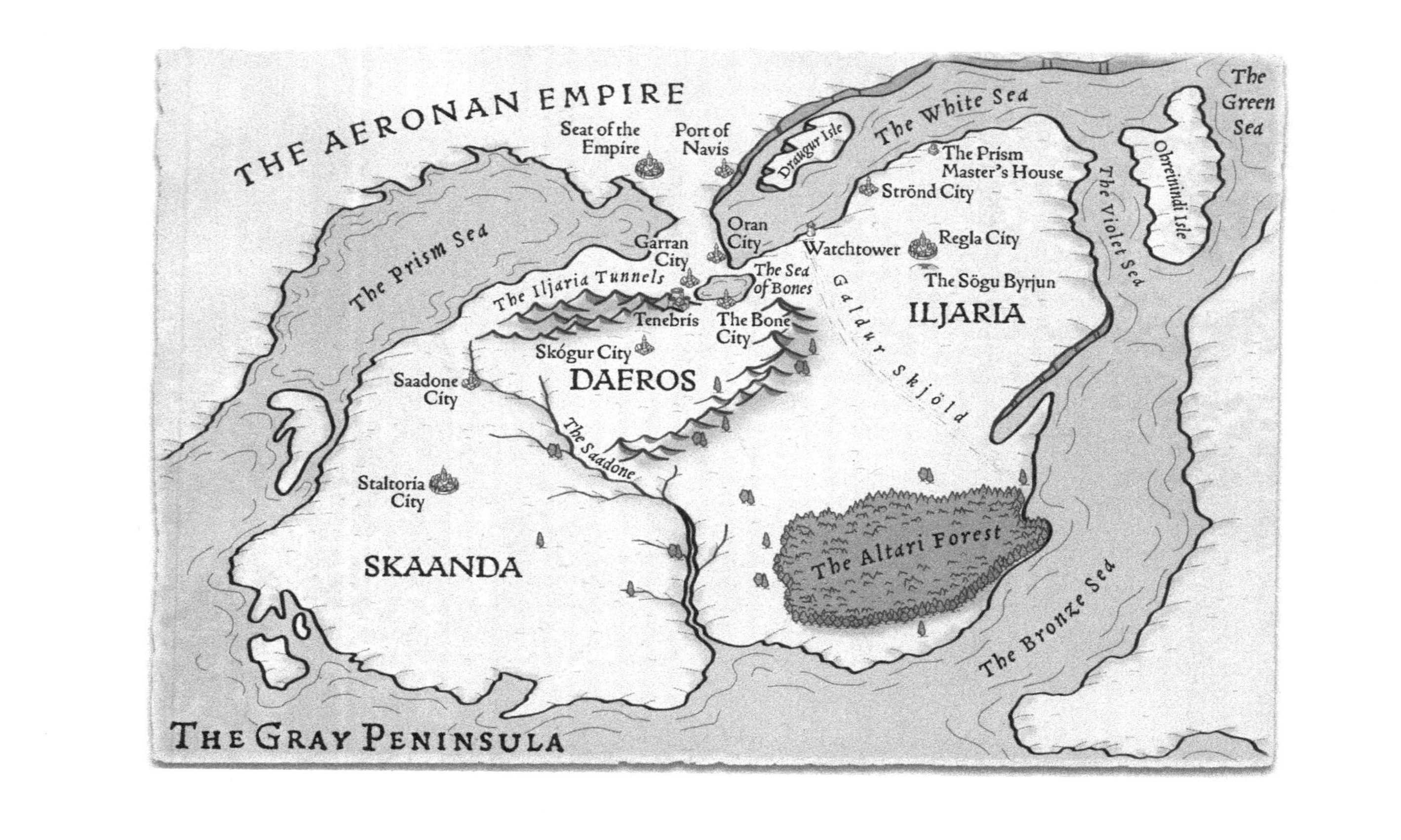

The Aeronan Empire
Seat of the Empire
Port of Navis
Draugur Isle
The White Sea
The Green Sea
Obreinindi Isle
The Violet Sea
The Prism Master's House
Strönd City
Oran City
Watchtower
Regla City
The Sögu Byrjun
Garran City
The Sea of Bones
The Prism Sea
The Iljaria Tunnels
Tenebris
The Bone City
Iljaria
Galdur Skjöld
Skógur City
Daeros
Saadone City
The Saadone
Staltoria City
The Altari Forest
Skaanda
The Bronze Sea
The Gray Peninsula

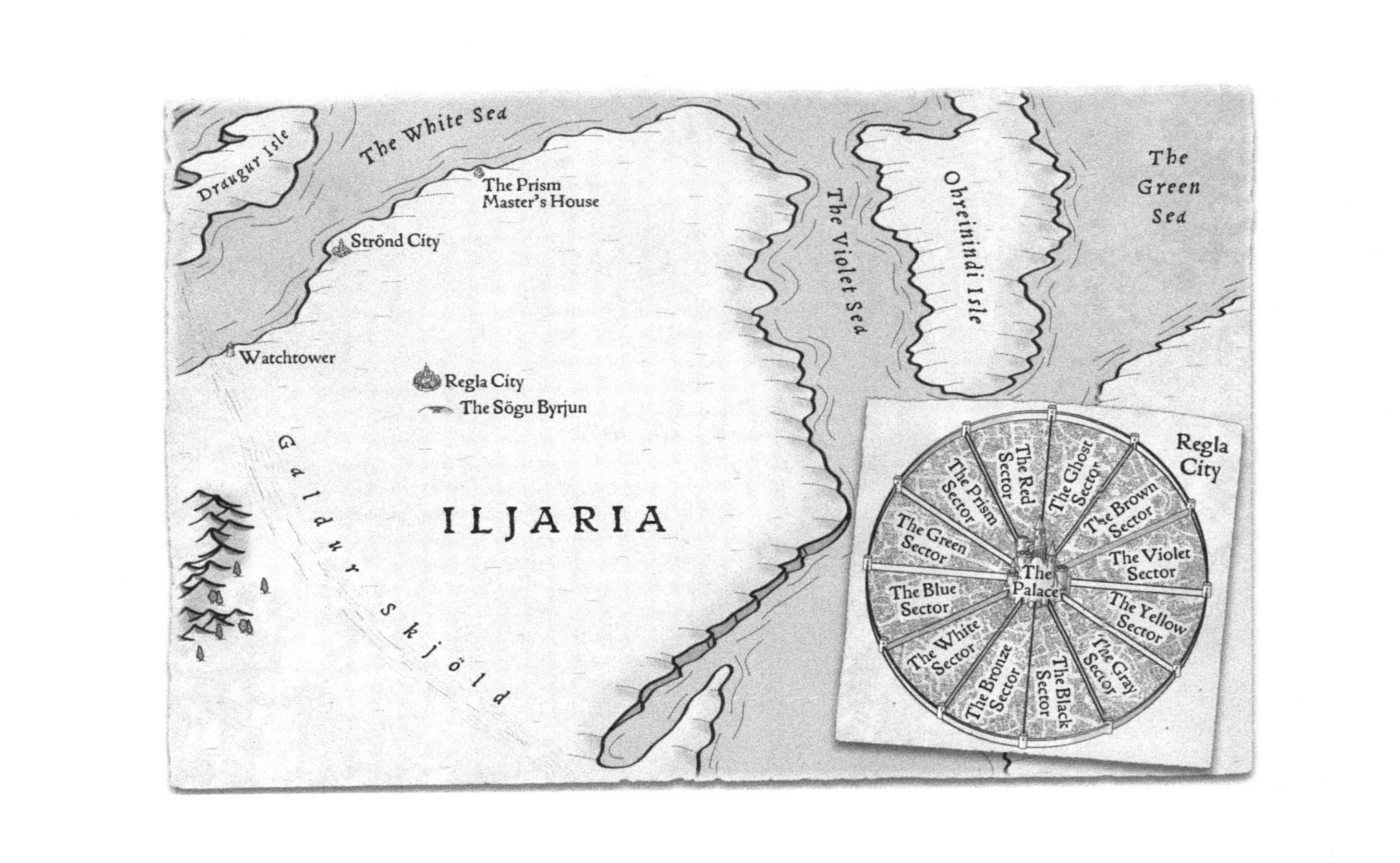

Draugur Isle
The White Sea
The Prism Master's House
Strönd City
Watchtower
Regla City
The Sögu Byrjun
Galdur Skjöld
ILJARIA
The Violet Sea
Ohreinindi Isle
The Green Sea
Regla City
The Palace
The Red Sector
The Ghost Sector
The Brown Sector
The Violet Sector
The Yellow Sector
The Gray Sector
The Black Sector
The Bronze Sector
The White Sector
The Blue Sector
The Green Sector
The Prism Sector

TWELVE YEARS AGO

BALLAST

YEAR 4189, Month of the White Lady

Daeros—Tenebris

There is a viper in the box at my father's feet.

I can feel its anger, its fear, can sense the shape of it, no matter that the box is latched tight: the coils of its sinuous body, the pattern on its hood.

The great hall is lit with lamps and candles, so many and so bright they make my eyes blear. I sit quiet in a row with my three brothers, my feet dangling some inches above the floor. My pulse jumps in my throat, too quick, too hard. I feel like the viper: trapped, waiting.

My father sits in the midst of the hall, two of his four wives perched on either arm of his throne. Neither of them is my mother.

My brothers fidget in their seats, restless to get back to their toys and their games. But I am still, because it is different for me than for them.

There are others here besides us, summoned to watch my father's show: a few of his nobles, his general, an ambassador from Aerona, and a man and woman from Iljaria who arrived with their two daughters yesterday, though the daughters are not here now. The man is the Prism Master, the most powerful magic wielder in the world. His white hair is tied neatly at the nape of his neck, and there is a prismatic gem bound to his forehead. Tattoos in every color swirl around his arms, and his eyes are clear and dark.

The woman, his wife, has a small, slight frame. She wears her white hair in long braids that reach to her ankles. She has a brown jewel on her forehead and delicate brown tattoos swirling up her arms. These two fascinate me. Besides my mother, I have never seen another Iljaria in all of my nine years. But I am too focused on the viper to do much more than steal occasional glances at them.

The Collection performs while my father looks lazily on, his hands in the hair of the wives who are not my mother. If he were to move his feet, just a little, he would nudge the viper's box, maybe tip it over. The latches are too strong, I think, for the serpent to break free, to strike my father before I can stop it. I wonder if it is wrong to ask the First Ones to allow this to happen.

There is a singer about my age or a little younger, whose voice is as clear and bright as a bell. Then a contortionist, a boy of eleven who twists his body into boneless shapes and swallows swords and fire. Then a teen girl so skilled with a bow and arrow she can hit a target across the wide room blindfolded, which she does, seven times.

The viper writhes in its box. Sweat makes my hands slick, though the room is cool.

The archer finishes her display and is relieved of her bow, my father's steward escorting her off to her cage, out of the audience's sight.

Then my father's eyes fix on me.

"Ballast," he commands. "Come here."

For a moment I don't move, the fear holding me fast in my seat. It is only the knowledge that my mother is watching from the outskirts of the hall that gives me the courage to rise and pace toward my father. I bow before him deeply, as I have been painfully taught.

He waves at the box. "Amaze us," he says.

I crouch and unlatch it with shaking hands, holding the viper's will fast with my magic so it won't strike me or, Ghost Lord forbid, my father.

The viper is angry. I release it just enough that it rears up in the box, hood flaring, tongue flicking. A few people in the audience gasp, but I don't turn to see who. I can sense my father's impatience as easily as I sense the viper's rage.

"Ballast," he says, voice dark with disapproval.

I knew he wouldn't be content with the viper waving about, knew I wouldn't get out of this so easily. Sweat pricks the back of my neck. I hold out my arm and compel the viper, bracing myself as it crawls up my arm and wraps, hissing, around my neck. Its tongue glances across my cheek, and I can hardly hold back my scream. The viper is deadly. If it bites me, that will be the end.

I should make more of a show, have the viper dance all up and down my arms, send it toward the audience to make them gasp in fear, then call it back just before it has the chance to strike.

But I am weary, and in this moment I fear the viper more than my father.

So I send it crawling into the box again and latch the lid tight.

My father scowls, rising from his throne and shaking off his wives in favor of grabbing me hard by the shoulder and hauling me out of the room.

I don't know how I forgot, even for a second, that the most dangerous creature in the world will always, always, be safer than my father.

He hits me hard across the face, and one of his rings slices into my cheek. The cut throbs with pain and heat, and I am lucky, I suppose, that my father has guests, that he strikes me only once more before stalking back into the great hall.

My mother is there moments later, pulling me gently to my feet, sitting with me in one of the little parlors by a window that looks out into darkness. She has a cool compress for my cheek, a tray of cakes to tempt me. But I am not hungry, so she sends the cakes away and brings out her colorful deck of cards instead.

She shuffles them and we begin our game, playing in silence, always silence. She can only speak to me with her fingers, because before I was born, my father cut out her tongue.

We play our game as the sting of my cut lessens, as I think about how I am just a viper in a box, held fast by my father's will. But someday I will learn how to break his hold on me. Someday I will strike him, and then I will take my mother, and we will go far, far away from this place.

And we'll never come back.

CHAPTER ONE

BALLAST

YEAR 4201, Month of the Prism Lady

Daeros—Tenebris

"Ballast. Bal. *Bal.*"

I wake to a hand, gentle and cool on my cheek, and for a moment I'm locked in my terror, a scream caught on my lips, a white, blinding agony spearing through my left eye.

Then I remember that he is gone, that the pain and terror both are only echoes, strong though they may be.

I breathe in, ragged and slow. The bed creaks as she slips out of it, then again when she returns, pressing a cold glass into my hands.

"Drink," she says softly, at my ear, and I obey her. The glass cools my lips; the water cools my throat, my belly.

It's only then that I open my eyes.

My eye. I still forget, sometimes.

She sits close to me in my bed, her curly white hair mussed from sleeping, her loose shift slipped down to reveal one scarred and freckled shoulder.

"You took my turn," she says lightly. But she folds her hand into mine, and I know she isn't angry.

I am not the only one haunted by nightmares of my father. Sometimes it's me, waking her. But not these last few nights.

I lie back on the pillow and she lies facing me, close enough her breath is warm on my face. I drink in the sight of her, study the familiar pattern of her freckles, count her eyelashes, which never did quite turn wholly white again, leaving them a mix of dark and light, like mine.

She kisses my brow, the ridge just above the eye that is no longer there.

"You're safe, Bal," she breathes against me. "You're safe."

I fall back asleep, cradling her tight in my arms.

But when I wake again, in the pale light of morning, she is gone.

"Ballast?"

I jump at Finnur's voice, and turn.

He peers through the doorway to my antechamber, where I have been sitting staring blankly into the heating grate, trying to steel myself for what is about to happen. Asvaldr, the enormous arctic bear who befriended me in my exile, lounges at my feet like a ridiculously oversized hound. He takes up nearly half the room. I spent months continually coaxing him outside, where he belongs, but he always came back. So eventually I gave up, and now he stays or goes as he pleases. Mostly, he stays.

"Is it time?" I ask Finnur, who wears a gem on his brow in the Iljaria style, a multicolored one to mark his Prism magic. He's grown in the half year since my father has been gone, and has begun to tattoo his arms, making up for the time he lost as a captive. There is one prismatic swirl on his left arm, two on his right; they contrast neatly with his dark-brown skin.

"Yes," he confirms. "Everyone is waiting."

I stand and Asvaldr opens one black eye, yawns hugely, then shuts it again. I smooth the wrinkles from my robe, adjust the ribbon on my eye patch. I don't always wear it, but I will today; the scarred and empty socket makes others uneasy, and I want the emperor to feel that he is strong. But not too strong. I flick a thought toward Asvaldr, reminding him to come and find me when I call. He doesn't answer me in words—animals don't have that sort of precise language—but I feel his assent all the same.

I join Finnur in the hall, and he hands me my crown, which I shove unceremoniously onto my white and dark hair. I don't like wearing the crown; it was my father's.

You could have a new one made, you know, she's told me more than once. *You* are *the king.* But it seems a waste of precious resources, so I haven't done it yet.

I had the rings made instead.

I rub mine, an etched silver band on the first finger of my left hand, set with a blue stone that looks like a polished pebble because that's what it is. I blink and see a handful of them down in the dark of the tunnels, pulled from the underground river; I see them again in her outstretched palm out on the frozen tundra, the newly risen sun tracing her in gold.

"Ballast," Finnur presses, eyeing me. "They're waiting." At sixteen he's the same height as me, and I expect he'll far outpace me by the time he stops growing. Magic sparks along his skin like static shocks; he's nervous, too.

"Let's go then," I say.

We stride to the great hall together.

Finnur appointed himself my steward when I became king of Daeros. I objected, at first, but he insisted, saying he had nothing else to do here, and no family to go back to in Iljaria that he knew of. He was a far more desirable choice than any of my father's men or, First Ones forbid, my brothers, so in the end I gave up dissuading him, just like I'd done with Asvaldr. Perhaps my favorite thing about Finnur is, despite being absolutely meticulous in his role, he refuses to call me "Your Majesty."

When we reach the great hall, Finnur steps aside and lets me walk in ahead of him, following along behind like a proper steward.

Despite the changes I made to this room practically the instant I became king, just being here makes my heart pound, my hands sweat, my breath stick in my throat. My father's presence lingers more strongly here than anywhere else.

"I can have it bricked up, if you like," I told her, though if I'm being wholly honest, it was more for my benefit than hers. But she said he would win, that way. That we should defy him by making it beautiful again.

I ordered the cages dismantled first. Smashed to pieces and hauled away. The acrobatic apparatuses came down next. We made a great bonfire of them, out on the edge of the Sea of Bones. She stood next to me, tucked close under my arm, and we watched them burn together.

I didn't destroy the ivory throne, but only because it had not originally been my father's; it had belonged to generations of Daerosian kings. I still had no wish to sit in it, though. I shoved it into one of the storage rooms. The mice can sit there, if they like. They can be tiny mouse kings.

I brought in large, lush carpets to spread over the frigid marble floor and lend warmth to the space. There are long, padded benches set against the back wall, which is entirely glass. There are reading lamps and shelves for books, intricate tapestries covering the stone walls, and plants, lots of plants: miniature trees and flowering shrubs and little baskets of herbs and viny things in hanging pots that trail vibrant leafy fingers to the floor.

The hall is meant to be a place of sanctuary instead of torment.

There is no sanctuary here today.

Junius Valens Aelius Cloelius Naeus, emperor of Aerona, stands with his retinue at the back of the room, his form silhouetted against the brightness of the daylight that spills through the glass. He's a tall man, muscular in the way of a sleek cat. His bronze-brown skin gleams with scented oil, and his dark hair, which he wears a little longer than his shoulders, is braided back from his face. He must be forty-five or so, but as yet there is no hint of silver in his hair. He's dressed richly, in drapes of deep-purple velvet, and gold adorns his wrists and neck and ankles. At his hip he has a short sword, worn on a highly decorated belt.

His daughter Aelia stands beside him, along with his generals and his personal guard—I count ten of them.

To his left are the Skaandans, Vilhjalmur and half a dozen of his soldiers.

To his right are the Daerosians, including my three half brothers and Lysandra, one of my half sisters—she thinks herself a courtier and can never bear to be left out of anything. Ten of my own soldiers are with them, as well as the Daerosian nobles—the three governors, the overseers of the mines and greenhouses, and the head arborist. All of them are carefully not looking at me.

My mother, Gulla, and my father's other three wives stand in a little group away from the main one with the rest of my half sisters: Rhode, Xenia, and six-month-old Charis, whom Rhode cradles in her arms. I have little love for the elder set of siblings, but I would rip the world apart for the younger three.

Every step across the hall toward the waiting mass of people is a new agony. My pulse is heavy in my chest, and I wish Asvaldr were beside me.

There's a glimmer of movement among the Daerosians, and I see her at last, standing just behind my brother Zopyros: the sheen of her white hair, the hem of her gown, a light blue, brushing the floor. I find I can breathe again.

And then I'm standing before the emperor, and all thoughts, even of her, go right out of my head.

I fear Junius in a different way than I feared my father, but the feeling overpowers me just the same.

"Well," says Junius, his voice as rich as his velvet clothes. "You certainly took your time. We have been waiting nearly half an hour."

I don't apologize. I bow to him, but not deeply. He is the only person in the room who outranks me, but he is in *my* country, so I don't feel I owe him any more deference than that.

"Get on with it," says Junius. "What is your answer?"

I am aware of Vil standing over to my right—looming, really. He will benefit the most from what happens here today, no matter which way it goes. I sense his satisfaction radiating off him like heat, and I shove down the urge to whirl about and slug him in the jaw.

I take courage from the light-blue hem, though I don't dare look directly at her.

"Your Imperial Majesty," says Finnur, stepping up beside me and bowing to the emperor very low and properly, "as His Majesty Ballast Heron Vallin's steward, I must ask that you formally restate your demands in the hearing of all gathered today, so the legality of these proceedings will not be called into question."

The emperor's lips thin. Technically, the highest authority in Daeros right now is mine, despite the thousands of imperial soldiers camped outside Tenebris. That's the whole point of this pomp and circumstance.

"Very well." Junius's tone turns clipped. "In accordance with the treaties signed by Kallias Vallin, late king of Daeros, the Aeronan Empire lays claim to Daeros, as consequence of unfulfilled contractual obligations and war crimes. As Kallias's chosen heir, you, Ballast Vallin, are held to account for his actions, and are bound by them. Because I am merciful, I offer you a choice: Relinquish your crown and aid in a peaceful transition of power, upon which I will allow you to live. Or face my army in battle and, upon your inevitable defeat, be publicly executed for your father's crimes."

The thud of my heart in my ears makes me almost dizzy. I am faintly aware of Finnur tucking himself under my arm to steady me.

I fight to hold on to the words I am supposed to say: *I will never relinquish my throne, will never abandon my country. I will face your army in battle and see who it is the First Ones favor there!*

But I just stare at the emperor and say nothing.

Even now, though he is dead and gone, I can almost hear my father laughing at me.

Vil shifts where he stands, and irritation flicks along my skin. Vil has all but sold his own country to Aerona—despite not having the actual authority to do so—on the strength of Junius's promise that he will be the one to govern Daeros when it is absorbed into the empire. Red Lord, I despise him.

"Ballast," says Junius, "you try my patience. Make your choice, or I will make it for you."

The light-blue hem shifts on the carpet, and I take a breath. I fix my eyes on the emperor's face.

"I will never . . ." The words, for a moment, slip away from me. My tongue feels heavy, slow, the air strangely charged around me. But then I find my voice again; the words reassemble themselves in my mind, trip easily from my lips: "I will never forget your mercy, Your Imperial Majesty, and in the presence of all gathered here, I humbly accept it. I, Ballast Heron Vallin, relinquish my crown and all claim to Daeros, and will support Your Imperial Majesty in the peaceful transition of my authority to the person you choose to govern Daeros in my stead."

For an instant the room is utterly silent.

Then one of my brothers—Theron, I think—curses loudly while Lysandra shrieks that this is not what we agreed on.

My heart beats, beats. My mind clears.

"A wise choice, boy," says Junius, folding his arms across his chest. "You are less of a fool than I took you for."

"That isn't what I meant to say," I whisper, though no one seems to hear.

My brothers shift aside, and then I see her, fully.

She stares at me: Brynja Eldingar, only living daughter of the late Prism Master, bronze gem flashing from her forehead. Her curly white hair brushes her shoulders, unbound, and her pale-blue gown is ornamented with gold braid.

The horror in her eyes matches the horror in my gut.

She's been in my mind, twisting my words from planned defiance to pathetic consent.

"Wait," I say.

But Junius is already striding toward me. In one swift motion he plucks the crown off my head. He snaps his fingers, and a pair of Aeronan soldiers step up on either side of me, shoving past Finnur, who curses under his breath.

"Escort the former king of Daeros to his rooms," says Junius. "He is to stay there, under guard, until I send for him."

"Wait."

One of the soldiers grabs me by the arm. I swear and wrench out of his grasp, but he just seizes me again, his fellow clamping a hand around my other arm so that I'm caught fast between them.

They haul me ignobly toward the door.

"That isn't my answer!" I cry, feet dragging along the carpet. "I defy you, Junius Naeus! I will meet you in battle, and let the First Ones choose between us!"

He just laughs. "That isn't what you said a moment ago. Save your breath, boy. Lie in the grave you have dug."

"She changed my answer!" I holler. "She used her magic to slip into my mind and make me say all those things!"

"Then she did you a favor," says Junius.

The emperor of Aerona turns his back on me, and his soldiers pull me out into the corridor. I make them drag me the entire way to my rooms, refusing to help them by walking. They're visibly sweating under the effort by the time we get there. They shove me into my antechamber and pull the door shut.

Asvaldr is waiting for me by the heating grate. I forgot to call him, but it wouldn't have mattered.

She meddled in my mind.

I can feel the echo of her magic still lingering there, slippery, dark, cold.

She wielded me like a pawn on a Lords and Ladies board, played me like the Ghost God card in our childhood games of War.

Mind magic is feared and mistrusted in Iljaria, she told me.

Now I know why.

She betrayed me once, down in the heart of the mountain, when she handed control of Daeros to her brother, the Prism Master, and revealed who she really was: not Brynja from Skaanda, whom my father had held captive against her will, but Brynja from Iljaria, a spy for her people, there of her own accord.

Her magic was locked away then, deep inside her. I helped her find it again, helped her return wholly to herself. Her power astounded me, her magic fiercer and stronger than I ever could have guessed. But I didn't fear it.

Despite everything, I never really thought she would use it on me.

CHAPTER TWO

BRYNJA

Year 4201, Month of the Bronze Lord

The White Sea

The air smells of salt and magic.

Sunlight dazzles on the sea, and the wooden deck of the Daerosian ship creaks beneath my feet. The rail I grip with both hands is smooth, no rough texture to ground my wheeling mind.

I shut my eyes and will the ship to cut faster through the waves, command the sea to part for us, to bear us swiftly to the shores of my homeland. I'm not sure what's waiting for me there, but I know what I left behind. Both things unsettle me.

"You shouldn't do that," says Finnur, coming up beside me. He's dressed in trousers and a long linen shirt that has no sleeves, his prismatic tattoos seeming to catch and bend the light.

I never got my own tattoos; I left my father's house too young for them, and I haven't been back since. It's been eleven years now.

"Do what?" I ask absently, opening my eyes again to peer out over the sea. I rub the ring I wear on the first finger of my left hand; it's silver, set with a bright-blue stone that's had all its rough edges smoothed away. Ballast gave it to me.

A lump sticks in my throat and I remind myself, firmly, that this was all my idea, that I have set my feet on this path, and I must follow it to its ending.

"Use your magic to hurry the ship," says Finnur. He runs one hand through his mop of white hair. "The Daerosians don't like it—the Aeronans, either."

In addition to ten Daerosian soldiers, the emperor thought it best to send twenty of his own along on this voyage to make certain I got where I said I was going. It still amuses me that he assumed that number would be sufficient to keep me in line if I got it into my head to be troublesome.

"I don't care what they like."

"But it alters the pattern of the sea, too," Finnur goes on. "Disturbs the pathways of the fish and the other creatures who live in deep places. The waves could come and crash too hard on a shore far from here. Drown a whole village, maybe."

My eyes prick, and I dig my fingernails into the railing hard enough to leave marks in the varnish. "How did you get to be so wise?"

He shrugs. The multicolored gem on his forehead flashes in the sun. "I can feel it," he says simply. "I can feel everything."

Finnur's Prism magic—which means he wields every form of magic except for the power of the Ghost Lord—is the strongest I've seen, and it's only grown stronger in the seven months Kallias has been dead. With proper training, he could easily become the most powerful Iljaria in centuries.

"You're every bit as powerful as me," says Finnur. He quirks an apologetic smile for inadvertently reading my mind.

I laugh, though my gut clenches.

There is a glimmer on the water far in the distance.

Finnur sees it, too. He stiffens beside me, his magic jittering along his skin in prismatic sparks. "Is that it?" he says softly.

"I think so," I reply. "I only saw it a few times. It amazed me when I first went to Daeros with my parents and sister. I don't really remember seeing it on the return trip. Honestly, I don't remember that return trip at all." I take a breath. That was after Lilja was murdered, and I almost ripped the world apart by accident. "The last time was when . . ."

"When your father sent you back," Finnur says.

I nod. I've done a lot of healing in the last half year, but I haven't forgiven my dead father for sacrificing me on the altar of Kallias's cruelty. I don't know if I can.

"All of those times were by land, though," I say, recovering myself. "I've never seen it by sea."

The ship slides on through the waves. Ahead, the glimmer grows brighter. It's the Iljaria's magical barrier, the Galdur Skjöld, which marks the border between Iljaria and Daeros, and extends across the sea all the way to Draugur Isle, just off the coast of Aerona.

The Galdur Skjöld was erected by my people centuries ago to keep the nonmagical Daerosians and Skaandans out of Iljaria and, if you ascribe to my friend Saga's view, to remove themselves from the need to participate in any conflict that arose on the peninsula. Historically, the Iljaria are pacifists.

Or at least that's what I was taught as a child. My brother's attempt to commit widespread genocide on Skaanda and Daeros alike told rather a different story, but I'd still like to believe that it's true.

If it is, though, I'm not sure where that leaves me. I killed Kallias, stabbed him right through the heart, and looked him in the eyes while I did it. Sometimes I can still feel his blood, warm and sticky, on my hand.

That's what most of my nightmares are about.

The ship's captain steers us east, away from the open sea toward Iljaria's coastline and the watchtower that awaits us there, a shining white spire against the broad blue of the sky. A pair or more of the queen's own Skapari—trained magic wielders—will be stationed in the watchtower, powerful enough to part the Galdur Skjöld and let the ship pass through. They will have Green, White, or Brown magic, if I were to guess: the powers of growth, song, and earth.

Finnur and I could probably rip a hole in the barrier ourselves, if we put our minds to it, but that is not the sort of impression I wish to make with my homecoming.

We won't land at the watchtower; there isn't a dock. We'll sail on past the barrier, following the coastline until we reach Strönd City. If we continued on around the coastline, we would come to the house I lived in as a child, but our path doesn't lie that way, and I'm not sure if I'm relieved, or sad. From Strönd City, Finnur and I will travel some miles inland to reach Regla City and the palace of Valrún Solstrøm, the Iljaria queen. My report on the mission my father sent me on as a child has been long delayed, and of course my father is dead, so I will give it to Valrún instead of him.

I shiver a little where I stand. I saw the queen only a few times before I became a captive in Tenebris. My child's impression of her was of one aloof, uncaring, perhaps even a little hostile. But she was young then, for an Iljaria and especially for a queen. My father easily had two centuries on her. I am sure she felt threatened by him, by his power.

I am uncertain if the plot to reclaim Tenebris and the First One bound in its heart originated with Valrún or with my father. I am uncertain if Brandr's violent interpretation of that plan was his own, or the queen's.

And so I am a little uncertain of my reception in the homeland I last set foot in more than half my lifetime ago.

The Galdur Skjöld grows broader and brighter as the ship nears the shore. It ripples like water, translucent, hundreds of feet up into the air, and stretches out of my sight line to the left, across the sea, and to the right, across the land.

My heart stutters.

Iljaria.

Home.

The shore is made all of white sand that gives way to vibrant green grass as the ground rises to meet the rolling hills. The watchtower gleams the same white as the sand, and I wonder if a Skapari wielding Brown magic—earth magic—raised the tower right out of the ground where it stands. It seems likely. Perhaps it was even my mother who did it.

I have not thought about my mother in a very long while. I am not sure what I feel for her. I am not sure I feel anything.

We are very near the shore now.

A door in the base of the tower opens, and two Skapari step out, both women. They are dressed in white gowns and intricately detailed silver breastplates, and wear white gems on their brows that signify their song magic. One has dark skin and the other light, and each wears her white hair in a single plait down her back. It is impossible to guess their ages; they could be thirty, they could be a hundred. That is the way of my people.

The ship's captain, a Daerosian man with dark hair and pale skin named Kyrillos, steps up to the railing to address the Skapari. I don't miss the shake in his knees, the trembling of his hands, which he shoves in his pockets. He's terrified of the Iljaria.

"Hail!" he calls through the rippling Galdur Skjöld. "Requesting passage to Strönd City by the command of His Imperial Majesty Junius Naeus of Aerona."

"What is your reason for requesting passage?" asks the Skapari with dark skin. She doesn't shout to be heard, but nonetheless her voice reaches us clearly.

Kyrillos swallows. "We bear with us Brynja Eldingar, daughter of Hinrik Eldingar, the former Prism Master. She is returning home."

The Skapari's eyes fix on mine through the barrier, and I flick words into her mind with my magic: *He speaks the truth. I am Brynja Eldingar. Let us pass.*

She frowns at me.

"What of the other Iljaria with you?" asks the second Skapari, the one with light skin.

Kyrillos glances uneasily at Finnur.

"I, too, am returning home," Finnur says, "though I have been adrift in Daeros all my life, and do not know who my family is, or my proper name."

"You bear powerful magic," she says.

"In which I have yet to be formally trained," he tells her. "Let us pass."

She presses her lips together. "We will allow you passage and send word ahead to Strönd City, where you will be expected. But when Eldingar and the nameless boy come ashore, this ship is to turn around at once and return to Daeros."

"Yes, my lady," says Kyrillos with a deep bow.

The two Skapari turn their attention to the Galdur Skjöld and lift their hands. The gems flash on their brows. In unison they shut their eyes and open their mouths. Music pours from their lips, and the magical barrier begins to shake.

The song magic swells until it fills the earth, rattling down to my bones, seething through my skin. I can see it, pouring out from them, in ribbons of rippling white.

A rift appears in the Galdur Skjöld, just large enough for the ship.

Finnur doesn't reprimand me as I use my magic to hurl our vessel through the tear and into the boundless sea beyond.

The Skapari cease their singing; the magical barrier seals swiftly shut again behind us.

Kyrillos curses and strides quickly away from the railing to resume his place at the helm.

I keep my eyes fixed on the watchtower as the ship picks up speed, a driving wind filling the sails.

"Do you really not know your name?" I ask Finnur.

The sea draws us on while the watchtower rapidly diminishes until it is the barest prick of a white needle piercing the distant sky.

"Not my surname," he says.

"We'll have to find you one, then."

He shifts his weight from one foot to the other. "I'm not sure there will be time for that."

"We'll make time."

He doesn't answer. He, too, peers behind us. "They weren't happy to see you," he says. "Those Iljaria wielders."

"They're called Skapari," I correct him. "And no. They weren't."

"They weren't surprised, either."

My heart beats overly quick. "No," I repeat. "They weren't."

Finnur looks aside at me. *Is this a fool's errand?* he asks into my mind, because the soldiers are always listening.

We won't let it be, I return. *This is going to work. We'll make it work.*

He sighs. *He said you'd be stubborn.*

I scowl, though my gut twists. *If I wasn't stubborn, I'd be dead.*

I suppose that's true. He quirks a smile at me.

A headache crawls behind my eyes, and I find I don't want to be out here anymore.

I shut myself in the ship's only cabin, which ordinarily would belong to the captain but has been mine for the entirety of the voyage. Kyrillos bunks belowdecks with the sailors and soldiers. Finnur stays in here with me, sleeping on the floor between the door and the bed, the bodyguard I didn't ask for.

I sit on the bed now, knees tucked up to my chin, and stare out the porthole into the wide glittering sea. I twist the ring around my finger, over and over again.

Gods, I miss him.

Lords, I suppose I should say, now that my true heritage is no longer a secret. But I played at being Skaandan for half my life, and I find it isn't entirely easy to shed all the trappings of my false identity.

"Brynja?" says Finnur quietly, slipping in through the cabin door.

I don't turn to look back at him, wallowing a bit in my misery. "How long until we reach Strönd City?"

"Another day, Kyrillos says, as long as the wind stays strong."

The knot in my gut pulls tight and foul. "Why didn't you stay with Ballast?"

I hear the creak of the cabin's single chair as Finnur sinks into it. "Ballast . . . didn't need me anymore."

I catch his thought, which I'm not sure he really means to send to me: *Ballast asked me to protect you.*

Tears prick hot. I blink them away. Out across the waves a seabird glides, the sunlight touching his wings and turning him all to silver.

"And I've always wanted to see Iljaria," Finnur adds. "I've always wanted to come home."

Home. For such a long time *home* meant my father's house by the sea, my sister in her workshop, my brother bent over his books, my country, my people. Those were the things I clung to all the long years I was a captive in Kallias's Collection.

But now?

Now, I'm startled to realize, *home* means Ballast's black-and-white hair splayed out on the pillow next to mine, his warm arms pulling me close, the humor and sorrow and wanting and love blazing from his single blue eye.

I hope to the gods he doesn't hate me for what I did to him.

I hope to the gods I haven't ruined everything.

CHAPTER THREE

BALLAST

Year 4201, Month of the Bronze Lord

Daeros—Tenebris

It takes a single moment to sign away my country.

We're in the great hall again, standing in front of the glass wall, where sunset shadows stretch long over the Sea of Bones.

The paper is stiff, the ink silver. It flows smoothly from the pen.

I stare at my signature. After everything I sacrificed to become king of Daeros, I was only king for half a year.

And now?

Now my country belongs to the twelve-times-damned Aeronan Empire.

Vil doesn't wait for me to lay the pen down before snatching it out of my hand. He adds his signature under mine.

I'm momentarily distracted by the presence of a spider, hidden somewhere in the corners of the room; I can feel the points of its legs against the floor and the slight heat of its body, can see its many-eyed view of the world. I could lose myself for a while in the spider's mind—if its spark of life can be thought to have a mind. But I don't let that happen.

I shove my awareness of the spider away with an effort and realize that Junius has signed the document, too, that everyone in the room is waiting for my next part in this horrific charade.

This time, she isn't here to draw courage from.

I turn to Junius and Vil. I jerk my back in a low bow, the proper show of obeisance to an emperor from an absolute nobody, because that's what I am now.

Then I straighten, aware of the eyes of the Daerosian governors on me. Lady Eudocia, who governs the Bone City, looks at me coldly, her face less schooled than the others'. I have a healthy respect for her, for all of them. They did everything they could to help the Daerosian people under my father's volatile rule. I can only hope they will carry on in that same vein under Aeronan occupation. But it guts me to think they despise me for being weak, for abandoning the country I swore seven months ago I'd protect with my life. Now I have to persuade them all to play nice with Vil. Ugh.

Vil smirks—does he have any other expression?—as Junius formally names him viceroy of Daeros, and then there's another round of papers to sign, these requiring the governors' signatures but not mine. I don't have any authority anymore. None of the governors looks happy about it, but they don't have another choice, because I didn't leave them one. *Blue Lady give me strength.*

After that, the emperor's steward seals the documents and secures them in a leather case. I assume they will be brought to Aerona and filed in the records office there. I have a pang of regret because I sent Finnur away, and so I have no steward to stand with me. Then I remember that I'm not a king anymore. I have no need of a steward.

Attendants bring in refreshments on trays. I accept a glass of wine but don't drink any. I feel dull. Heavy. Ghost Lord, I miss her. I clench my jaw.

I circle the room, making sure to stop and speak briefly with each of my governors—no, my former governors.

Lord Seleukos, who governs Garran City, taps his thumb against his own wineglass and takes a long draught. He's a bear of a man, standing a head taller than me and nearly twice as broad. His dark hair has a streak of silver in it, and his eyes glitter as he glares at me. "We won't stand for cruelty," he says in an undertone. "We won't stand for injustice. Our first duty is to the Daerosian people, and if the emperor and his new viceroy"—he shifts his glare to Vil, who is talking to Aelia a few steps away—"if they change anything for the worse, if the consequences of their actions fall to the people—"

"I know," I say, staring into my glass. "I know. But the people are in good hands. I trust you, Seleukos. And I'll be here for as long as I can, making sure the transition goes smoothly."

He shakes his head. "The good thing about your father was that he mostly left us alone."

Seleukos sees the effect of this comment written all over my face, and he grimaces. "Forgive me, Your Majesty," he says quietly.

I give him a tight smile and move on to speak with Lord Damianus, who oversees the mines. After him is Lord Phaedrus, who is in charge of the greenhouses, then Lord Galenos, who governs Skógur City, and Lady Thais, the head arborist. All the conversations are similar to the one I had with Seleukos; none of the governors are particularly pleased with me, and I don't blame them. I step up to Lady Eudocia, governor of the Bone City, last of all. She stands near the glass wall, sipping her wine. She is in her mid-thirties and wears her dark hair in two long plaits down her back.

"You're a fool," she tells me frankly.

I remember the feeling of Brynja's magic, dark and oily in my mind, the strangeness of her words spilling out of my mouth. "The greatest of fools," I agree.

I would say more, except Vil slinks up to us, earrings glittering in the light that spills in through the glass.

He's come to gloat, and I don't feel like giving him the satisfaction.

"My lady," I say to Eudocia, giving her a little half bow. I don't acknowledge Vil at all, just sweep past him, and stride from the great hall. I can't bear to be here any longer.

I slip from Tenebris and out onto the waving autumn grass. Spring and summer were long this year, warm enough to melt all the snow, to let weeds and flowers burst out of the ground. Even the glaciers in the Sea of Bones have shrunk a little, though it will take more than a few summers, I think, for them to disappear entirely.

It's strange that the days still stretch so long, that the light isn't rapidly dwindling in preparation for three months of winter darkness. We will never have that again, now that the Yellow Lord is no longer bound in the heart of Tenebris but wields his power from his dwelling place in the sun.

I had hoped to share this winter with her, the first winter bathed in light. I don't think that can happen now.

I take the path that winds down to Garran City, letting the sun warm my shoulders and the wind cool my face. Asvaldr joins me after a while, lumbering beside me, bits of grass and wildflowers snagged in his thick white fur.

The guard at the gate bows when he sees me, because he hasn't heard I'm not a king anymore. I don't have the heart to inform him otherwise. He tosses Asvaldr a piece of salted fish kept in a barrel just for our visits, and the bear gulps it down in one bite.

"How is your wife, Dion?" I ask. She broke her arm a month or so ago, and I set the bone and healed her as well as I could with my magic.

"Recovering well, thanks to you, Your Majesty," Dion says. "You'll come for dinner some night soon, won't you? When I'm not on duty? She'd like to thank you properly."

"Of course I will," I say, ignoring the twinge of guilt that I might not be here long enough to keep that engagement.

Dion waves Asvaldr and me through the gate, and we wind through the city, past the central fountain made long ago with Iljaria magic; colored streams of water leap up from the basin, twisting and dancing in impossible shapes. Before the Yellow Lord went to his home in the sun, the water was frozen and still. Now it lives again, like so many other things.

Asvaldr and I go directly to the orphan house to speak with the women who run it. They are newly appointed since my father's death—the man who was in charge previously abused his position, to put it mildly. Asvaldr and I are welcomed inside, and he plays with the children in the main gathering hall, to their profound and utter delight. I have a cup of tea with Zenobia and Rute, the former a Daerosian woman of about fifty who has curly gray hair and the kindest smile I have ever seen, and the latter a dark-haired teenager my father kept in a cage and forced to perform acrobatic routines after Brynja escaped.

It's extremely awkward, explaining to them that I have been deposed and Brynja's been shipped off to Iljaria and that, despite my pledging to "aid in a peaceful transition of power," I'm not at all sure how long I'll be out of danger of any repercussions. Vil sure as hell doesn't want my aid, and I doubt Junius even cares, so long as his cartographers can redraw his maps to include Daeros as part of the empire.

"But I'll do everything I can," I promise, "to protect the orphan house and make sure the children—and the two of you—stay safe."

Zenobia nods solemnly and pours me another cup of tea. Rute regards me with suspicion and no small amount of hostility. I know she sees my father when she looks at me, and I can't do anything about that.

"And Brynja just *left*?" Rute demands. "I thought the two of you were . . ." She trails off, because of course she has no idea what Brynja and I were. Nobody does. Uneasiness coils in my gut like a viper.

"Brynja was sent away," I correct, shifting in my seat. "I just wanted to . . . warn you. I don't know how heavy-handed the emperor and his new viceroy"—I can't say Vil's new title without scowling—"will be. And I—I apologize for putting you in this position, after everything else."

Rute sobers and stares at the table. She jiggles her knee because she, like Brynja, has a hard time being still.

"I'm sure the emperor will leave the orphan house alone," says Zenobia, rising from her seat. "What would he want with a bunch of children?"

There is an uncomfortable silence as Rute and I exchange glances, momentarily unified by our shared trauma.

"In any case," says Zenobia, looking a little embarrassed. "It was kind of you to visit, Your Majesty."

I know a dismissal when I've heard one. I collect Asvaldr, bid Rute and Zenobia farewell, and continue on through the city. We stop at the butcher's, which is by far Asvaldr's favorite place in Garran City. The father and son who run the place express concern about the southern pastures. Much of the grass has been destroyed by gut worms, the butcher says, and there isn't enough for the herds to eat.

"Can you do anything about the worms, Your Majesty?" he asks me. "A worm is sort of an animal, isn't it?" He gestures at the magic-evidencing white in my hair.

Gut worms in the southern pastures, I repeat to myself. Lords, I wish Brynja were here. She's better at remembering things than I am. "I will try and save the pastures," I promise.

"And if it's not too much trouble, Your Majesty," pipes up the son, "there's rumors a military draft is on, or will be soon. I—I don't want to go to war."

His pale face flushes red, like he doesn't want me to think him a coward.

"I've called for no draft," I say, momentarily forgetting my demotion to a nobody.

"Not a Daerosian draft," says the butcher. "An Aeronan one."

I frown. "I will try and stop it, then, if there is any truth to the rumors."

The butcher and his son thank me, and Asvaldr and I go on.

We stop at the inn. The proprietor begs me to come and help her laboring goat. I tell Asvaldr to stay out of trouble and follow the proprietor to the animal pen, where I send soothing magic to the mama goat and aid her in delivering twins.

We visit the hospital, where I lend what aid and magic I can to the patients who need it most. I am still awkward with healing magic, but I've worked to improve it since I became king. Usually my mother and Brynja are with me, and the three of us do far more healing together than I am able to do on my own. But the physicians still thank me sincerely, and I'm relieved I've been at least a little help.

I ought to have come to the city earlier—there are far more people and places to visit than I have time to today. I'm nearly out of time already. But before I return to the mountain palace, I make sure to stop in at the greenhouses, the mines, and the barracks. I'm able to have a more thorough chat with Lord Phaedrus, Lord Damianus, and my generals Demetria, Nereus, and Iason, than I could have in the great hall. I feel a little lighter when Asvaldr and I at last take the path back up toward Tenebris. The sun is setting, great shafts of orange and yellow light slanting over the autumn grass.

Asvaldr flicks a thought toward me: wind and ground and joy.

I am more than happy to oblige him.

I climb onto his back and lean close against his great white head. I hold on tight.

He gallops over the earth, and I let the wind wash over me, let the setting sun dazzle my eye.

My heart kicks and my eye blears, and I try to remember the point of all this.

My siblings and my mother and my father's three other wives crowd into my receiving room, unwilling, it seems, to let me wallow in abject misery alone.

It's evening, an hour past the dinner I declined to attend, even though Asvaldr brought me back from our ramble in time.

"I'm not king anymore," I grumble at the lot of them from my place on the low couch facing the heating grate. "I don't know what you want from me."

Asvaldr went off to his den, for once, which is the only reason they can all fit.

My fourteen-year-old sister, Rhode, cradling baby Charis, is the last to come in. She pulls the door shut with a click and, padding over to me, sets Charis in my arms. My infant sister is heavy and soft, staring up at me with a pair of bright-blue eyes. My father gave his eyes to nearly all of us; I suppose that's why he felt justified in taking one of mine back.

I sigh, then stand and pace to the back of the room and turn so I can look at everyone at once. Charis's warmth and weight ground me, and I shift her in my arms so she can see everyone, too. She likes that, burbling in approval.

"You have to do something for us," says Theron, who stands with his twin, Alcaeus, by the door. At twenty-one, Theron and Alcaeus are the same age as me and are full siblings with eighteen-year-old Lysandra, who takes my place on the couch, scowling deeply. They're the children of my father's wife Elpis.

"All of us," Alcaeus adds. "Or that Skaandan bastard will kill us, now that the damned emperor has transferred power to him."

I've had more than I can stomach of "that Skaandan bastard" myself, but Theron is right. If I don't take care of my haphazard family, such as it is, nobody will. Not even a year ago, I wouldn't have given a damn about the fates of Theron, Alcaeus, Lysandra, or Zopyros—who is a year older than me and the only child of my father's Skaandan wife, Unnur. They tormented me when I was my father's magical dancing bear. Though they mended their ways when I became king, there is still not a lot of love lost between us. For the sake of Rhode, Xenia, and Charis, though, I mean to protect the whole parcel of my siblings. Lucky for the older four.

My attention is drawn briefly outside, where there is a fox not far away, hunting a hare in the gathering dark. I can feel the shape of both of them, the fox's hunger, the hare's quick-pulsing fear. There's a falcon winging his way home in the last of the light, a mouse scurrying for its hole. If I were to let my power loose, I would be able to sense every animal within a hundred miles, farther if I really wanted to. Animals are easier than people. At least, most people.

For a moment I reach out with my magic, past the mountain and past Garran City, out into the waters of the White Sea. But though I feel the wavery whispers of fish, of leviathans slumbering in the depths, I can't feel her.

"Ballast," says Rhode, gently bringing my awareness back to my receiving room, to Charis whimpering in my arms, to the watching eyes of my siblings and my mother and my father's wives.

"I put it in writing," I tell them, shifting my hold on Charis. "You are all pardoned along with me; none of us are to bear the guilt of his—his sins."

It was in the papers I signed today; I made sure of that.

The heat hums in the grate, overly loud in the silence that follows. I look down at Charis, give her my finger to wrap her tiny hand around. She holds on fiercely tight and I am so glad that she, alone among all of us, will know nothing of her father. He will never touch her, never shadow her life with darkness.

I take a breath. "But pardon aside, I don't think any of you should stay in Tenebris."

"Where will we go?" asks Zopyros. He stands with his mother, Unnur, by the door, and from the way he ducks his head and won't quite meet my eye, I know he's thinking of all the ways he mistreated me during our childhood.

I glance at my mother, who gives me a little nod; we've discussed this, at length, since I became king. For a while, my mother and my father's other wives—Elpis, Pelagia, and Unnur—kept busy bringing all the children my father stole for his Collection back home, or finding them new homes if they had none. I was surprised that the three of them wanted to remain living in Tenebris after that.

"You could try your luck staying in the garrison with the Daerosian army," I tell Zopyros. "But I don't know what Junius and Vil mean to do with them, and it isn't likely there would be a place for your mother." I offer Unnur a respectful nod. "I suggest the two of you move to Skógur City; you will have to find work when you get there, but it shouldn't be hard, and the money I've set aside for you ought to finance a few months' lodging."

Zopyros blinks at me in shock.

"Mother?" I say quietly.

She smiles and kneels down to the trunk butted up against the wall. She opens it. Inside, beneath a folded blanket, is my carefully hoarded stash of coins, divided into four pouches. I had Brynja filch them for me from the royal treasury, little by little, so that Vil—when he inevitably takes stock of the treasury—won't know anything is missing.

My mother pulls out one of the pouches and tosses it to Zopyros. She gives another pouch each to Elpis and Pelagia, keeping the last one for herself, while I expound on the rest of my plans:

Elpis, along with Theron, Alcaeus, and Lysandra, are to move to the Bone City. Lysandra is to tutor a wealthy family's children, while Theron and Alcaeus apprentice with a swordsmith and a baker, respectively. I have arranged lodging for Elpis and Lysandra, if Elpis will agree to cleaning the landlord's house once a week. Theron and Alcaeus will board with the smith and baker.

I ignore Lysandra's loud, horrified objections, and turn to Pelagia, then stride across the room to lay Charis gently in her arms.

I've found a place for Pelagia, Rhode, Xenia, and Charis in Garran City. Rhode and Xenia will attend school there, while Pelagia looks after Charis and does seamstress work as she is able. If Pelagia's pouch of coins is rather larger than the others, her situation a little easier, no one protests.

Everyone is quiet after I've finished explaining. The heat hums in the grate, and Charis makes her happy burbly noise as she tugs on one of her mother's curls. Xenia asks Rhode in what she thinks is a whisper but really isn't—eight-year-olds are not gifted in whispering—if she can take her doll to school with her, and if there will be sword training at school. My gut clenches; I've been teaching Xenia and Rhode to fence in spare moments. There will be no more of that now.

"When are we to leave?" asks Unnur, when the silence has become unbearable.

"As soon as possible," I say heavily. "I am sure Vilhjalmur will be occupied for a few days as he learns what Junius will and will not allow him to do, but he understands the workings of Tenebris well enough already that when he acts, it will be swiftly. I suggest you all leave by the morning."

This sets Lysandra off again; we are all subjected to a long and impassioned speech about how she is a *princess* and a *lady* and a *member of the nobility* and *she would have made a good queen* and *perhaps she'll just marry Vilhjalmur and seize back control that way.*

"Honestly, Ballast," she says, glaring at me. "It isn't like you to expose your throat and hand your enemy a knife. Why don't you just attack the Aeronan army with lions?"

I sigh. She isn't the only one to hold this opinion, and I know I need to tread carefully.

"There aren't enough lions on the whole peninsula to defeat the imperial army, Lysandra. If Skaanda stood with us, perhaps we would have a chance, but why would Skaanda shed blood to protect Daeros when they can have it for free? If we faced the emperor's army, he would slaughter us all. You included."

Lysandra sets her chin, blue eyes sparking defiance. "But that's what you were going to do. That's what we *all agreed on*: Face the Aeronans. Drive them into the sea. Secure Daeros's freedom. Of course, that was before your Iljaria lover weaseled her way into your mind just like she weaseled her way into your bed, and made you change your answer. Betrayed you. Made you look a fool. Again."

I fight to keep hold of my temper. "Meeting the Aeronans in battle was always a reckless gamble," I say through gritted teeth. "A fool's desperate attempt to try and hold on to his crown."

"She turned you into a coward," Lysandra spits at me. "And you let her."

My pulse throbs in my neck as I flick my eye to the heating vent. That's how she would come and see me—she didn't believe in doors. It was not uncommon, in the half year I was king, for the attendants to find her in my bed in the mornings, instead of hers. But they must have heard our argument the night before I was to give Junius my answer: The whole palace must have heard it. She begged me to accept Junius's demand to relinquish my crown and in so doing prevent a war that, in her mind, Daeros had no hope of winning. I told her I would rather die the free king of Daeros than live as the coward who bared his neck to Junius. We were both angry and didn't even try to keep our voices low.

Clearly, Lysandra heard a full account of the argument.

"What's done is done," says Pelagia, gently extricating her hair from Charis's fist. "We cannot change the past, but we can choose how to move into the future. Ballast's plans are sound. I think we all should trust him, this last time."

Elpis and Unnur nod in agreement, and after a moment, the elder four of my siblings mumble their begrudging acceptance.

"Then it's decided," I say. "I will . . . miss you all." I realize that I almost entirely mean it.

"Good riddance," huffs Lysandra. She turns and leaves the room.

Theron and Alcaeus approach me and bow, very low, before following their sister.

Zopyros and Unnur leave next, Unnur thanking me sincerely while Zopyros bows and avoids my eye.

Elpis—Theron, Alcaeus, and Lysandra's mother—kneels before me and presses her face to the floor. "Thank you for your kindness to my children," she whispers. "I know it isn't what they deserve."

My eye goes a little blurry as I gently draw Elpis to her feet again. "I am sorry for the cruelty you bore on my father's account," I tell her.

She leaves the room with tears running down her cheeks, tightly clutching her pouch of coins.

Rhode hugs me, her own tears wet on my shirt, while Xenia wraps herself around my legs.

Pelagia watches quietly, Charis having fallen asleep in her arms.

"You'll come visit us, won't you?" says Xenia. "At our new house?"

"If I can," I promise.

Rhode looks at me reproachfully. "Xenia will be expecting you now," she reprimands. "She'll be watching for you every day."

I crouch down to look Xenia in the eyes. "It might not be for a long while, Xenni," I tell her. "But I *will* come and see you, as soon as I'm able. You have my word."

Pelagia brings Charis up to me, and I gently kiss my tiniest sister's brow. Her eyelids twitch in her sleep.

"Look after them," I charge Pelagia. "Keep them safe and healthy."

"Always, Your Majesty," says Pelagia. "Thank you."

Then she herds Rhode and Xenia from the room, and it's just my mother and me.

We sink onto the couch together, and I try unsuccessfully to ease the tension from my shoulders. I'm not sure I will be able to fully relax ever again.

My mother taps my leg and I turn to face her.

What are you up to, Ballast? she asks me with her fingers.

"Nothing," I say, rather petulantly.

Her lips thin, and I know without her having to tell me that she doesn't like it when I sulk, because it reminds her of my father.

I gnaw on the inside of my cheek.

I know you are not as calm as you appear. What really happened? Between you and Brynja?

I shift uneasily, remembering the heat of her body pressed against mine in the dark.

"She was right," I say. "My pride would have left my entire country to be needlessly slaughtered. It's better this way."

Is that what you really think?

I shrug. "Whatever I think, it's what happened."

Why do you keep secrets from me, Ballast?

A headache sparks in the hollow where my left eye used to be. I have grown more or less used to my half vision of the world but am ever keenly aware of what I lost. *In Iljaria,* Brynja told me once, her skin hot as lightning against mine, *there are healers blessed by the Green Lady. They could grow you a new eye, if you wanted. Come to Iljaria. Come home. With me. Be whole again.*

But then she slid her magic into my mind and went to Iljaria alone.

My mother sighs. Her fingers move quickly in the room's half-light. *What are you going to do now?*

"Try and keep Vil from wholly destroying my country, if I can."

And then?

I feel the memory of her lips, soft and fiery against my own, and for a moment all the air leaves my lungs. "Then I'll go after her."

Why?

"Because I need to know that she's safe."

Even after what she did to you?

The headache sharpens, so painful I shut my eye. Colors dance in my vision, and I feel her magic twisting through me, powerful, controlling, dark.

"Yes," I whisper.

My mother touches my arm, and I open my eye again so I can see what else she wants to tell me.

She takes a breath. I realize with a jolt that she's nervous, a muscle jumping in her cheek.

You are not the only one keeping secrets, she says with her fingers. *But I am ready to tell you mine.*

TWELVE YEARS AGO

BALLAST

YEAR 4189, Month of the White Lady

Daeros—the Sea of Bones

I am uneasy, on the edge of the cliff. The wind is bitter, and my cheek still hurts from the cut made by my father's ring. My brothers are here, tugging their coats about them: Zopyros and Alcaeus and Theron. They stomp their feet to keep themselves warm and curse under their breath, not brave enough to speak any louder because they are afraid of our father, too.

I am not sure why he has called us out here, but I see his sharp smile and my stomach goes sour.

The Iljaria come to join us, then the Prism Master and his wife and their two daughters. The younger one looks to be about my age, her curly white hair a mess of tangles about her shoulders, her face spattered with freckles like spray from a paintbrush. She has eyes to match her father's: fierce and dark. I wonder what sort of magic she has. I wonder how long she and her family will stay in Tenebris. I wonder if I am brave enough to befriend her, like I want to.

I catch her name, Brynja, spoken as a quiet reprimand from her mother. And her sister's name, Lilja, uttered with pride from her father. I shift my glance to Lilja. She is the same height as the girls' mother, and skinny as a spear. Her white hair is tied back in two long braids, and there are green tattoos on her arms, meaning she is blessed with the growing and life-giving magic of the Green Lady.

Everything becomes clear when attendants bring out a contraption made of canvas and wood. Lilja is an inventor and is to make a display for my father, who is considering purchasing her inventions for Tenebris. But his glittering eyes tell a different story, and dread washes over me, sharper than the wind.

The contraption is a pair of wings infused with Lilja's magic. They will make her soar like a bird, she says. My father nods eagerly. Brynja watches her sister with a sort of breathless pride.

The wings are strapped on. Lilja flashes a brilliant smile and leaps off the edge of the cliff into the Sea of Bones.

For a moment the wings glitter, and Lilja rises into the air.

Then she drops like a stone.

There is a sudden, awful stillness. The faint yet unmistakable thud of a body slamming against the frozen ground.

And then all the earth is shaking, and shards of ice and rock break off the mountain, flying through the air like knives. I cover my head with my arms.

Someone is screaming.

"Brynja!" comes the Prism Master's voice. "Brynja, STOP!"

The earth grows still again, and I lower my arms to see Brynja bowed over her sister's broken body. It's her, screaming. Just as it was her who nearly tore the world apart. I am staggered by her magic. The feral, raw power of it. I don't understand how such a small person can even hold so much.

I glance at my father. He is not unaffected by this wild display of magic—there is a line of blood on his forehead where he was cut by an ice shard. But he regards Lilja, her body twisted and dead in the wreck of her wings, and he smiles and I know that he did it on purpose. That he *killed her* on purpose.

I look at Brynja; she is watching my father, her face a storm of grief and fury. She sees him smile.

And I see his death written in her eyes.

CHAPTER FOUR

BRYNJA

Year 4201, Month of the Bronze Lord

Iljaria—Strönd City

There are four Skapari waiting for us at the dock in Strönd City.

It's been three days since the watchtower, the ship delayed by contrary winds and torrential rains. I can't even see the city through the sheeting rain, just the dock and the four Skapari, protected from the elements by a magical canopy. Red light flickers on their faces. I peer at them through the window of the ship's cabin, anxiety jittering through me.

Lightning fragments the sky, thunder rattles the sea.

"Are you ready, Brynja?" Finnur asks.

"Gods," I tell him. "No."

He gives me a sympathetic smile and opens the cabin door, snapping his fingers to form a canopy of his own before stepping out into the rain.

I didn't bring much with me from Daeros: one trunk, bound in brass, and a leather pack, which I adjust on my shoulders. Finnur has even less, a single leather bag that is stiff and shiny with newness; I think Ballast must have given it to him.

I shove thoughts of Ballast away with an effort and command the trunk to come along behind as I follow Finnur from the cabin and head toward the gangplank. His rain canopy keeps both of us dry, which I appreciate greatly. The trunk ghosts at my heels like a loyal hound.

Kyrillos doesn't come with us; neither do any of the soldiers. They watch from the relative safety of the deck, drenched to the skin. They're not sorry to see us go, and I'm not sorry to leave them.

The moment Finnur and I step onto the dock, the gangplank is snatched back onto the ship, and Kyrillos shouts orders for his men to set sail.

We're left to face the four Skapari: two men and two women. I can't quite discern the colors of the gems bound on their foreheads in the flickering red light, but clearly one of them has fire magic, like my cousin Indridi. My stomach roils at the memory of her death.

"Brynja Eldingar?" says one of the male Skapari. He looks about my age, but I get the sense he's much older. He has dark skin, and he wears his white hair cut short against his scalp. He's muscular and tall—a little taller than Ballast, maybe. I can't sense any power in him, which is peculiar.

"I am Brynja Eldingar," I assert. "I have come to speak with our queen and would appreciate an escort to Regla City."

The Skapari frowns and flicks his eyes toward his companions.

One of the women comes forward. She's young, Finnur's age, if I were to guess. Her curly hair is bound in two plaits that touch her shoulders, and her skin is a warm brown. I sense her magic easily; it's dark and strong. Her power is from the Black Lord, the lord of darkness.

"Brynja Eldingar," says the young Skapari woman, "you are hereby charged with high treason, assault against the Prism Master, illicit use of Bronze magic, warmongering, halting the just purge of Daeros and Skaanda, and meddling with the fate of a First One."

I blink at her, stupid and slow, reaching out with my magic, only to realize with a jolt that all four of them have shielded their minds from me; I will not be able to manipulate them.

"You are under arrest," adds the male Skapari who spoke first. He draws something from the folds of his robe and I take a step back, bumping into the trunk.

"Wait," I say.

But he isn't listening. "You are stripped of your power until Her Majesty sees fit to restore it to you."

I tell the dock to shift for me and it does, but not fast enough.

The Skapari comes with it and locks a cold iron collar around my neck.

I scream and leap away from him, my vision going white. The iron *burns.* I claw at the collar with both hands, but I can't find the latch. Panic overwhelms me. The breath chokes out of my lungs.

Finnur pulls me gently to my feet again, but I hardly know it's him.

I can't feel my magic.

I can't feel my magic.

The other male Skapari, who has dark skin and keeps his long white locks tied back at the nape of his neck, steps up beside me and solemnly tugs me out of Finnur's grasp. The gem on his brow glints violet.

I stumble, dazed.

Finnur gives a shout and flings out his hands, multicolored light sparking from his fingertips. A wall made entirely of Prism magic rises out of the ground, bending around me, cutting me off from the Skapari.

The man with Violet magic sighs and makes a little motion with one hand. I feel myself wrenched backward in time, to the moment the iron collar is locked around my neck, and then I'm on the ground screaming and Finnur is pulling me to my feet and *goddess of death am I going mad?*

I don't know that I have ever witnessed an Iljaria blessed by the Lord of Time using their power. I have no desire to repeat the experience.

"Enough." The second lady Skapari's hands are full of fire, which she flings up, hissing, into the rain. She has a strong, square face, lightly freckled skin, and fierce, dark eyes. Her gem is red, as is her gown, both hem and sleeves dragging along the wooden dock.

I gasp because I know her, because I didn't expect to see her here, like this. "Aunt Dagfinna?" I whisper.

Her mouth goes hard, but she doesn't otherwise acknowledge my address. She's my father's sister. Indridi's mother. The happiest moments of my childhood were spent running wild with Indridi through Aunt Dagfinna's rambling gardens, made by my uncle Kár with his Green magic. But that was before my father sent Indridi away to be a spy.

"You wished to be brought before Valrún," Dagfinna says, not meeting my eyes. "And so you shall. But until the charges laid against you are disproved or dismissed, the queen commands you be bound in iron."

"Who levels these charges against me?" I ask, trying hard to keep my voice from shaking.

My aunt still won't look at me, and I don't need access to my magic to sense her anger—or understand the reason for it. *Indridi.* My gut kicks.

"The Prism Master," says Dagfinna. "The brother you tried so hard to destroy."

Assault against the Prism Master was one of my charges. Hell. I've tried my best not to think about Brandr since I locked away his magic and told his scribe and steward that he murdered our father. He went home with his hands bound. I'd assumed he would stand trial or go to prison or *something.* I had felt a little guilty about it; he's my twin, after all. Evidently, I needn't have.

"Does Brandr have his magic back?" I ask with dawning horror.

"No thanks to you," Dagfinna snaps.

I glance frantically at Finnur. It seems we've come far, far too late.

Finnur steps up beside me, facing the four Iljaria undaunted. "I am Skapari Eldingar's personal guard," he says. "I insist on accompanying her wherever you mean to take her."

The first male Skapari glowers at him. "She is not a Skapari, and neither are you. We have no charge concerning you. We're leaving now. Don't follow us."

He gives a sharp nod, and the Violet and Black Skapari take me by either arm and draw me down the dock to the quay, which is all but hidden in the rain.

I look back at Finnur, hissing at the touch of the iron collar as it shifts with my skin. I think he's trying to speak into my mind, but with my magic cut off, I can't hear him. I shake my head. The Skapari holding my arms tug me on, and I face forward again.

A coach emerges from the rain and my heart stutters. I haven't seen an Iljaria coach in eleven years; I had forgotten them. The coach is made of sleek, polished wood, the bottom curved like the hull of a ship, the top all domed, prismatic glass.

Dagfinna claps her hands and a door opens, steps folding down.

I am shoved in first, settling on one of the brown velvet seats. I peer through the glass—I can't see Finnur anymore.

"Please let my friend come," I beg the male Skapari who looks young but I am certain is not. "He's alone here."

The Skapari doesn't deign to answer me as he and the other three take their seats. Dagfinna claps her hands to shut the door again. The Violet Skapari speaks a lazy word, and the coach slides into motion.

The coach moves *fast*, the rainy world a blur outside. It would take over a week to get to Regla City from Strönd by nonmagical means; in the coach, it will take a single afternoon.

I look behind us and see a glimmer of light through the rain, sparking different colors. The knot in my gut eases a little. Finnur is coming after me.

The coach hums along, and the collar burns, and I try to remember what I am without my magic.

My aunt refuses to look at me, and after a while I can't bear the silence.

"At least tell me your names," I say to the three Skapari I don't know.

There is a row of five seats against the long sides of the coach, with single, wider seats at the front and back. I am alone on one set of five seats; Dagfinna and the Black and Violet Skapari sit facing me, while the fourth—the Yellow Skapari who looks younger than he is—sits with his back to us at the front of the coach, staring out into the whizzing darkness.

The young woman with the black gem on her brow is the first to speak, tendrils of darkness hanging from her shoulders like satin ribbons. "I am Salin Norodahl," she says. "It seems you know Dagfinna Aarhus."

"Aunt," I say to Dagfinna. "I'm glad to see you."

She jerks her face to mine then, eyes flashing. "I am shocked you have the audacity to show your face here. You let Indridi *die*."

My gut twists. "I couldn't save her," I whisper.

Dagfinna sets her jaw and turns away again.

Salin shifts uncomfortably and indicates the young man on her left, the one who wields Violet magic. "This is Adriel Tong."

Adriel gives me a short nod.

"And that"—Salin gestures to the man at the front of the coach—"is Jóvin Reynir."

Jóvin flicks his gaze to me at the sound of his name, and I don't like the sharp glitter of his eyes. He gets out of his seat and settles in the one next to mine, close enough I can count the dozens of tiny, pockmarked scars all over his face. The gem on his brow is yellow, but I still don't sense any magic in him.

I feel uneasy and very, very alone.

Jóvin leans even closer, his breath hot on my cheek. I realize he is angry—wildly, all-consumingly angry.

At me.

My heart stutters, and I try desperately to figure out what I could have done to so enrage him.

Outside the coach the rain stops, or we at last pass through the storm. It is not as dark now, but we are moving too fast for my eyes to catch on any of the scenery. We pass cities, forests, fields; all are no more than a blur of light and color. It guts me that I can't slow the coach and drink in the sights of the homeland that I longed for so fiercely during the years of my imprisonment.

Inside, Jóvin studies me, and I do my best to sit utterly still.

But when he cups my face with one hand and rubs his thumb along the line of my jaw, I recoil, scrabbling sideways and falling to the floor of the coach.

"Don't touch me!" I snarl up at him.

He lounges in the seat, stretching out his legs. "Why not? You let the Daerosian king touch you." He considers. "*Both* of them, in fact, I hear."

He watches me with a sly smile playing about his lips. It amuses him to bait me when I am powerless.

I am beyond weary of men playing games with me.

I pick myself up, slowly, as to not jostle the damn collar. My aunt and the other Skapari look on in tense silence, like they don't want to—or don't dare to—interfere, though as far as I can tell, all the real power in this coach belongs to them, not Jóvin.

"Who even are you?" I demand, leaning against the side of the coach. I wonder if it's the collar making me feel sick, or my aunt's accusations, or the too-quick motion of our magical transport.

"I am Her Majesty's most powerful Stjarna," says Jóvin coolly. "Or I was."

My blank expression makes him roll his eyes. "A Stjarna—a trained wielder of Yellow magic. Did you truly forget everything about the Iljaria when you went off to play at being Skaandan? Or maybe you never knew it to begin with. Your parents didn't send you to be trained because they were afraid of your mind magic, after all."

I am seething inside but don't let myself show it. "What do you mean you *were* Her Majesty's most powerful Stjarna?"

"Don't feign ignorance, Brynja."

My pulse beats erratically in my neck and my head is spinning. "I truly don't know what you mean."

"Why would she know, Jóvin?" asks Salin quietly. "How would she know?"

I glance at the young Skapari, the tendrils of darkness dancing all down her arms now. She meets my eyes. "When you bound the Yellow Lord into the sun—"

"It wasn't *me*," I protest. "It was the Prism Lady and the Blue Lady, the Ghost and Bronze Lords. I was just *there*."

"When you bound the Yellow Lord into the sun," Salin repeats, ignoring me, "Yellow magic—light magic—was bound with him."

I blink at her in utter horror. "Light magic is *gone*?"

Salin looks uneasily at Jóvin and nods.

I glance over at the former wielder of Yellow magic. I understand his rage now. I know what it feels like to be powerless when you have been immensely power*ful*. But an entire *branch* of magic eradicated? It's unthinkable. The Iljaria have no use for members of our race who don't have any magic. That's where the entire country of Skaanda came from—centuries ago, powerless Iljaria fled west to escape genocide and formed their own nation. There is little love lost between Iljaria and Skaanda, even now. I pity the Yellow wielders.

But I also know that meddling in the affairs of the First Ones cannot be without cost.

"If the Yellow Lord had been allowed to wield the full of his power against all of Daeros and Skaanda," I say slowly, thinking aloud, "it would have killed him, which I suspect would *also* have nullified light magic. Either way, you're out that branch of power. But that doesn't have to be the end."

I settle in the wide seat at the back of the coach, tucking my feet up underneath me. "A friend told me once that although all Iljaria have one form of magic that comes easiest to them, with training and practice they can learn the others. You might not be as powerful in the other disciplines, but you needn't let yourself be *entirely* powerless." I look hard at Jóvin. Just because I sympathize with his loss of magic doesn't mean I like him. "I don't suppose you've tried another discipline."

He jerks to his feet, practically spitting in anger, and snatching me by the arm, he hauls me across the coach and flings me, hard, back into my original seat.

"He told me you'd be difficult," says Jóvin through gritted teeth.

I know whom he means, but I ask anyway. "Who told you?"

"The Prism Master. Your brother. The one you tried to kill."

"I did *not* try to kill him."

Jóvin sets his jaw. "You locked away his magic and accused him of murder."

I glance across at the other three Skapari, who seem absolutely determined to stay out of this, my aunt especially. I sigh. "I'd rather hoped that locking away his magic would be more permanent."

"It was neatly done, Eldingar," says Adriel unexpectedly, weaving strands of time magic between his fingers like yarn. "It took a dozen Skapari two months to restore your brother's magic to him, and his power hasn't been quite as strong since then."

"He is *pissed*," adds Salin.

Gods, gods, gods. This is not going at all like I planned.

"He did, though," I tell Jóvin. "Murder our father."

Jóvin gives me a sharp smile. "No one believes that. And no one blames him for what happened in Daeros."

"Everyone blames *you*," says Adriel, rather unnecessarily. "You utterly ruined a plan more than a decade in the making."

Bile churns in my belly. He means the plan that sent me, as a child, into the hands of my enemy to be caged, tormented. Forgotten.

I gave everything I was for a country that does not care about me at all.

I've known this, wrestled with this.

But I hoped it was just my father, just my brother.

I hoped that all the glorious and noble things I always believed about Iljaria were still true.

I hoped that I was not once more treading knowingly into a viper's den, giving myself up to be devoured.

The coach hurtles on toward Regla City, and I think I've made a horrible mistake.

CHAPTER FIVE

BALLAST

Year 4201, Month of the Bronze Lord

Daeros—Tenebris

I sit in my father's council chamber—I will always think of it as his, not mine—and clamp my jaw shut to keep from screaming.

Vil and Aelia sit with their heads together on the opposite side of the table, their advisers—Rafn and Talan, respectively—next to them. Junius isn't here, at least, but I know if I get out of line, he'll be informed in a hurry.

Red Lord's balls, I hate this.

"You can't do any of that," I say, jiggling my knee.

All four of them look across at me. The only person in this room who has any kind of respect for my opinion is Aelia, but even she seems to be growing weary of my constant remonstrations.

"The Daerosian soldiers will not thank you for forcing them to work in the mines," I say frankly. "You should either draft them into the Skaandan-Aeronan army or discharge them with a year or two's pension. And it's no good dismissing the work of Lord Phaedrus—just because the sunlight will remain all winter doesn't mean you should abandon the greenhouses entirely. That would be beyond foolish. The greenhouses employ hundreds of people and feed hundreds more. Lord

Seleukos, Lady Eudocia, and Lord Galenos will balk at the insane tax you mean to levy on their cities. Do you *want* the entire country to come hunting for your blood?" My nobles—former nobles—were banned from this meeting, on Vil's orders, and I'm beginning to see exactly why.

"Daeros is not a country anymore," says Vil coldly. "It's a province of Aerona."

"So it is," I agree. "And you are not a king."

Hatred lights in his eyes, and I give him my best imitation of my father's self-satisfied smile.

Aelia puts one hand on Vil's arm. To stop him from leaping across the table and punching me in the face, probably.

That's what Brynja used to do for me.

"Why are you even still here?" Vil grouses.

"'To aid in a peaceful transition of power,'" I remind him.

"The fact remains," says Aelia, "that the increase in ore must be met somehow. Who would *you* send to the mines, Ballast?"

"Well-paid workers."

Vil rolls his eyes. "Where is the money going to come from to pay them?"

"Why can't Aerona finance the mining project?"

Aelia frowns. "The empire's finances are neither your business nor your concern. One of the stipulations of Aerona making Daeros a province is the mining of this ore."

I fix my one eye on her. "And you really think stripping trained soldiers of their weapons and forcing them to labor without compensation is the answer?"

"Not wholly unpaid," says Rafn, Vil's adviser. He's some sort of cousin to Vil, with similar dark skin, though he wears his coily black hair braided tight against his scalp. He's about thirty. "There is whatever remains in Daeros's treasury, as well as the tribute that will be coming from Skaanda."

Vil looks aside at Aelia. "I thought we had eliminated the tribute."

"Not unless Skaanda also becomes a province of Aerona," Aelia tells him quietly.

Vil goes all tense. I would bet the remainder of Daeros's treasury that he has yet to send word to his sister, Saga, of how deeply he's entangled himself with the Aeronans. All to become viceroy of the empire's newest province—not even a king.

I keep jiggling my knee. I alone of all my family remain in Tenebris. I even found my mother a tiny room in Garran City near my youngest siblings, because I don't trust Vil not to use her as leverage against me. My own days here are numbered. It's only a matter of time before Vil decides my "aid in a peaceful transition of power" is no longer needed and makes a move to get rid of me. I mean to use every second I have left to keep him from destroying my country and ruining the lives of my people. The thought of explaining all of Vil's horrible decisions to my governors is giving me a stomachache. I promised every one of them I wouldn't let him shake things up too badly, wouldn't let Aerona radically change what Daeros is. Here I am, already failing. Some king I turned out to be.

No. Ex-king. Lords, I want to tear all my hair out. But damn it, I'm not giving up.

"Why doesn't the Skaandan army work in the mines?" I say in what I hope is a completely offhanded manner. "They will do as they're told to earn the salary they are already being paid, and they're not needed for battle at present. The emperor will leave a regiment here to protect his new province, and it isn't like you need to guard against Skaanda."

Aelia nods thoughtfully while Vil glares at me like he wants to rip my head off. He probably does.

"What about Iljaria?" asks Talan.

I shrug. "What about them?"

"Don't we need to protect against them?"

I rub at the edge of the table and wonder if her ship has landed yet. It must have. "Several hundred spears, less or more, would make no difference against a legion of Iljaria magic wielders."

Aelia leans over and whispers in Talan's ear. I watch her sharply; I know what she's telling him.

"In that case," says Talan, "I think it an excellent plan."

"My soldiers are *soldiers*," Vil says viciously. "They're not *laborers*."

I fix him with my eye. "You didn't think the same about the Daerosians."

"Damn it, Ballast."

I smile again and show my teeth.

"It's a good plan, Vil," says Aelia. Her hand goes to his shoulder this time, massaging it with strong fingers.

He relaxes a little under her touch.

"Remember what all of this is for," she tells him quietly.

"Fine," he grinds out. "Rafn?"

"I'll see it done at once, Your Highness," says his adviser. He rises and quits the room.

Vil stands with a scrape of his chair. "This council is over."

Talan and Aelia get up, too, Aelia slipping her arm about Vil's waist.

To annoy Vil, I stay in my seat a few moments longer, rising belatedly like an indolent cat.

I step past him, toward the door, and he grabs my arm.

"Watch yourself, you one-eyed bastard," he says to me, very low.

I hate the fear that races through me because of all the times my father grabbed me in exactly the same way. But I am not powerless here. I wrench out of his grasp.

"Go to hell," I tell him, and leave the room.

The last time I saw my father, he was in the heart of the mountain, red running down his throat from the prick of Brynja's knife. He was bewildered, confused, an arrogant child losing suddenly at the game he thought he was winning, the one he assumed he knew all the rules to.

The last time my father touched me was a little while before that, when he smeared honey on my cheek and locked an iron collar around my neck, then agitated a wasp until it stung me.

My father was cruel. There is not a part of me, I don't think, that he did not hurt.

Now he's been dead for over half a year.

It's newly night when I ask my owls to fly me into the glacier valley, the first of the stars appearing in the vast dark sky.

They threw his corpse down here, after Brynja put a knife in his heart, just as he discarded the bodies of so many children he murdered according to his whims.

I don't know why I want to find his bones. Not to mourn him, certainly. Perhaps just to assure myself that he is truly dead.

But there are many bones down here. I don't know how to find his.

I walk awhile, along the ice, as the stars look down and the owls fly above, waiting for me to call them back.

It isn't the first time I've looked for him down here. But it feels like it might be the last.

I roam farther and farther out onto the ice, not noticing the prick of the wind because I have my magic to warm me. There are creatures dwelling even in this frozen wilderness, and I let myself feel them all: tiny spiders and a family of arctic hares; a lone white wolf and a half-grown deer, separated from his herd; fish under the ice and, deep, deep where the water still flows, an ancient beast I have no name for, long and spined and slumbering.

"You were a fool," I say aloud, kicking little bits of frozen ground so they skitter like pebbles across the ice. "You were a wicked, conniving, twisted, arrogant fool. I hated you. Every second of my life, I hated you."

Grief and rage stick in my throat.

"I'm glad you're dead," I say. "I'm glad you have no grave, glad that no one mourns you. I'm going to forget you. I'm not going to let you have a hold over me anymore."

Tears well in my good eye and pool in the socket of the missing one.

"I HATE YOU!" I scream.

The wind rips my voice away, causes my words to bounce and echo between the cold obelisks of the glaciers.

I twist the ring set with the blue stone around my finger, again and again. I miss her so much I want to claw my own skin off. I hate that my last memory of her is her magic in my mind, controlling me. Wielding me.

I hate that I'm alone down here, not knowing if the sacrifices I've made will be worth it, or if it will all come to nothing, and my people and my country to ruin.

I curse and rip the ring off, hurling it into the dark.

But the next moment I'm scrabbling after it, frantic, desperate, not resting until I find it again, wedged in a crack in the ice.

I slip it back on my finger, willing my wild pulse to slow, then sit on the frozen ground and hug my knees to my chest. I let myself miss her.

It's some while later that I at last call the owls and bid them bear me up to high ground again.

I return to Tenebris, and my childhood bedroom, where I retreated after giving up my throne. This is the place I first spoke to her, when I caught her peering down at me from the heating vent.

I don't know how much longer I can stay here, fighting to protect my people, playing nice with Vil while I try to keep his claws out of all the things I've worked for.

Damn Vil. I can't believe they were together, at least sort of, for a long time. And they *kissed.* More than *once.*

I lie back on my bed and scowl up at the ceiling.

"You are making a nuisance of yourself."

We're back in the great hall, where Junius sits on a padded chair looking out the glass wall toward the swiftly rising sun. I think of the Yellow Lord, of my dreamlike memory of the beautiful house the Prism

Lady made for him. I wonder how he fares, bound forever to the heart of that star, as he was once bound in the heart of this mountain.

I stand before the emperor with my hands clasped behind my back and tell myself there is nothing to fear.

"Why do you insist on antagonizing my new viceroy?" asks Junius.

"I don't like him," I answer frankly.

The emperor gives a huff of laughter. "Your honesty is refreshing, if no less foolish than your father's countless lies."

I grimace.

"I spared your life," Junius goes on, "when I needn't have, for all I don't truly think it right to make you bear the cost of your father's sins. But there is always a reckoning when one plays at being king."

I clench my jaw. I wasn't playing.

"Vilhjalmur thinks the people of the former country of Daeros will not accept him as viceroy while you remain in Tenebris, crown upon your head or no."

My pulse stutters, but I keep my expression perfectly blank.

Junius settles deeper into his chair and puts his hands behind his head as he continues to study me. "Vilhjalmur suggests I execute you after all, or throw you in prison, or, at the very least, put an iron collar round your neck to keep you from using your magic. He's afraid of you, of course."

The emperor means to convey with this speech that *he* is not afraid of me. He must not know that if I wanted to, I could compel a venomous spider to bite him, or ask a mouse to slip poison into his mouth while he sleeps, or have Asvaldr storm into Tenebris this very moment and rip him to pieces.

Junius's brow twitches and I feel some little satisfaction in the realization that he *does* understand the threat I pose, that he *is* afraid of me. But I'm careful not to smile. I have no interest in him enacting any of his threats because he feels I am mocking him.

"What is it you require of me, Your Imperial Majesty?"

His eyes go hard, not fooled by my show of humility. "It was wise of you to send your family away, Ballast. Less wise for you not to leave yourself. You've done all you can with the transition in power—I consider that part of the contract fulfilled."

"I care about my country."

"It isn't yours to care about. Not anymore." He rises from his seat and steps up to the glass wall, staring out over the Sea of Bones. The sunlight turns the glaciers all to red and gold.

Uneasily, I go and stand beside him. I sense one of the owls, winging home late to its nest on the cliffside. The horses in the stables, impatient for their morning grain. The cats in the palace, curling up to sleep after a night of good hunting. Spiders in their hidden corners, spinning masterpieces no one will ever see. Asvaldr, seeking his breakfast.

"Your father left a bad taste in my mouth, with his cages and collars," says Junius to the glass. "And I have no real wish to see you dead. There's no point to it." He turns his head and looks hard at me. "But you can't stay here, Ballast. I am embarking for Aerona this morning—I have been gone too long—and I am leaving Vilhjalmur in charge, viceroy in truth as well as name. Not even Aelia, I don't think, can save you from him forever."

I manage an acknowledging nod and jump as Junius claps one hand on my shoulder.

"You did all you could, boy. Time to put your tail between your legs and slink away now. Daeros is no longer your concern."

"Yes, sir," I say, trying not to think about Garran City and the orphan house and the hospital and all the people who trusted me to lead them.

"Goodbye, Ballast." He gives me a grim smile and strides away across the hall, four of his guards falling in step behind him.

For a little while longer I stay where I am, trying to catch hold of my fragmented thoughts, put them in order, turn them to actions.

When the sun is high enough to slant overbright through the window, making my eye tear, I go one last time to my childhood bedroom, where I grab the pack that's waiting for me. I've had it ready for a few weeks now.

I take a breath and heft the pack onto my shoulders.

I leave Tenebris through a side door.

I don't look back.

ELEVEN YEARS AGO

BALLAST

YEAR 4190, Month of the Gray Lady

Daeros—Tenebris

My father has acquired two new victims for his Collection. He went all the way to Skaanda to get them, and were it not for my brothers, the mountain would have been peaceful in his long absence. My brothers played at being kings while he was gone. They made the children perform, and when I refused, they locked me in an empty cage and poked swords through the bars, cackling as I was forced into a merry dance to avoid being skewered. I didn't avoid it completely. I'm still nursing a long, deep scratch on my left side. At least when they saw the blood, they got scared and ran off in a hurry.

But my father is back now. He's brought a harpsichordist with him, and an acrobat, whom he keeps in a cage that dangles from the ceiling as if she's a parrot. I don't get more than brief glimpses of her until the first night she's called out to perform, and even then I can't see her very well.

She's a blur above our heads, making death-defying leaps, swinging on bars and silks and doing cartwheels on a wire that's thinner than my hand. Every single time she jumps, my stomach drops to my boots, and I'm terrified she will fall and dash her head open on the marble floor. But she doesn't. She lands every jump, executes every skill with precision. She ends her routine by launching herself into empty air and grabbing fistfuls of silks at the last moment, sliding down the length of them and ending in a bow at the foot of my father's throne. She is small and bony and gulping air like she's starved for it, but that's not what makes me stare at her.

She looks like the Iljaria girl who almost brought down the mountain.

She's not, of course. She can't be. She's clearly Skaandan, no white in her hair, no magic in her veins. But she has those same fierce, dark eyes, a similar distinctive spray of freckles across her face. I feel sick at the thought of that day, at the memory of Lilja's body, broken on the snow, a scream frozen on her lips.

Then the acrobat is shoved back into her cage, and my father bids me control the pair of wild white wolves he had hunted alive just for me, and I forget everything but the taste of my own sour fear.

CHAPTER SIX

BRYNJA

Year 4201, Month of the Bronze Lord

Iljaria—Regla City—the palace

I jolt awake as the coach comes to a stop.

The iron collar is cold and stifling at my throat. My body feels impossibly heavy, and I want nothing more than to fall back asleep. I hadn't realized how tired I was.

I creak bleary eyes open and look out through the glass dome of our transport.

The coach has docked just outside the palace, a massive stone-and-steel tower crowned with spires of glass that pierce the sky like blades, shimmering with prismatic color where the sun touches them just right. A forty-foot-high wall made of prismatic glass circles the palace, impenetrable except through the twelve gates that open out onto each sector of the city.

I was a child when I came here last, but staring at the palace now, I don't feel as if I have grown any. I almost feel smaller than I did then.

"Brynja."

I startle at Adriel's voice, the violet gem on his forehead glittering.

"She's waiting," he says, almost apologetically.

"Get up," adds Jóvin.

Aunt Dagfinna and Salin step out first. I follow, stumbling on solid ground after the long, constant motion of the coach. Salin catches me before I can fall, her dark eyes filled with what I can only read as pity.

Adriel and Jóvin come after me.

"Let's *go*," says Jóvin, prodding me hard between the shoulder blades.

It takes everything in me to not whirl around and slam my fist into his face. I don't need magic for that.

"Come on," says Salin quietly. "You will walk more easily after a little while."

Salin and my aunt lead the way toward the palace, me just behind them, with Adriel and Jóvin bringing up the rear. I feel very much like a prisoner being escorted to their execution.

I hope that's not actually what's happening. Do the Iljaria even believe in execution? My childhood memories have no answer for me. I suppose I'll just have to go and find out.

I pray fervently that Finnur is here somewhere, though I don't dare look around for him. I'm not sure what he could do against an entire country of Iljaria, even with his powerful magic, but it would make me feel a lot better if I knew I wasn't completely alone.

We wind up from the docking station, feet clacking on the lacquered tiles that pave Regla City's streets in elaborate, interlocking patterns. As our coach docked in the Brown Sector—the part of the city dedicated to earth magic—the tiles here are brown.

Regla City is built as a vast circle, with the palace in the exact center, and its twelve sectors spanning out from it like spokes in a wheel or slices of a pie—narrower by the palace, widening out as each sector reaches the city's circumference. Each of the twelve branches of magic, from Prism to Ghost, has its own sector, with shops and housing and conservatories catering to each particular magic, with colored tiles to match. The only exception is Ghost—wielding that power is banned, so there is no school in that sector. I remember my father saying offhandedly once that the Ghost Sector was filled mostly with cheap housing for the weakly powered Iljaria who couldn't afford anything more. If it's true, it rankles me in a way it didn't as a child.

As we near the center of the city, our brown-paved way narrowing, we come to one of the twelve gates in the prismatic glass wall. Two Iljaria stand guard there, gray stones on their brows. They carry no weapons because they do not need to; they are blessed by the Gray Lady and wield death magic. They bow to the queen's Skapari and open the gate for us, eyeing me curiously as I pass through.

My heart is a wild thing in my throat; the collar burns and burns.

Past the gate is a courtyard paved in a spiral pattern of different-colored tiles. Founts of blue and green and white water dance impossibly in the air, connected to nothing, while an apple tree, heavy with fruit, grows suspended upside down, its roots waving gently in the breeze. Glass globes filled with fire bob about like soap bubbles, and a leopard lounges in one corner, seemingly playing a Lords and Ladies game with a little white-haired boy who has a kestrel sitting on one shoulder.

I blink and I am in an iron cage at the peak of the great hall in Tenebris, looking down at ten-year-old Ballast as Kallias forces him to control a host of venomous snakes, first to slither all around Ballast, then to hang around Kallias. But it isn't enough. It's never enough. After, when everyone else has filed out of the hall, Kallias strikes him hard across the face.

I'm still staring toward the boy and the kestrel and the leopard when Salin and Aunt Dagfinna step through an archway and onto a narrow stair. I trip and fall, tearing a gash in the knee of my trousers. Blood wells bright, but it is another moment before I register the pain.

Jóvin hauls me to my feet again and shoves me up the stair.

I curse at him, shake him off.

The stair is steep and long, and I've lost my breath by the time I get to the top of it.

We come into a wide, airy hall, the floor a glimmering, polished gold. The walls and supporting arches are carved in intricate patterns and painted in swirls of bright colors. There are plants . . . everywhere. Trees in all seasons and stages of life, berry bushes, trailing vines, hundreds of flowers. None of them are in pots. They either drift about like clouds or have their roots splayed out over the floor.

Valrún has Green magic, I remember. Seems messy.

The Skapari walk on either side of me now, Adriel and Salin on my right, Dagfinna and Jóvin on my left.

Nothing looks familiar from my childhood visit to the palace; either it's changed a whole lot or I was in a different part of it, or I wasn't paying attention back then. I was here just once with my whole family: my parents, my older sister, Lilja, and my twin brother, Brandr. As Prism Master, my father often went to wait attendance on the queen. For whatever reason, on that occasion he brought all of us with him. I remember Aunt Dagfinna and Uncle Kár and Indridi were there, too.

My feet echo along the gleaming floor, and the iron collar burns, and *twelve gods*, I hope Finnur isn't too far behind.

The cut on my knee pulses with pain; there's a trickle of red running all down my leg and smearing the perfect golden floor.

We come into a narrower corridor. The Skapari fall in behind me.

"Straight ahead," murmurs Adriel.

A pair of arched doors wait at the end of the hall. They're carved and painted in swirls of green, and there's a sudden scent of deep earth and growing things.

The doors swing open soundlessly as I near them, revealing the throne room just beyond.

It's a round room, the very center of the palace, with the queen's throne set on a high white dais in the middle, like the hub of a wheel, echoing the city's design. Vines trail all along the wide white steps that lead to the dais. The ceiling, which stretches thirty feet above my head, is made all of glass. Sunlight shines in and puddles on the floor, refracting off the golden tiles and making the whole room hazy and overbright.

I squint and try to steady my breathing as I walk toward the dais, my aunt and the other three Skapari once again flanking me.

The dais has twelve steps, one for each of the First Ones. I climb slowly, head spinning with fear and uncertainty.

At first all I see are Valrún's slippers—pale green and embroidered with flowers—and the sweeping hem of her gown, heavy with glittering jewels. As I climb a little higher, the whole of her comes into focus, and I vaguely register that there are three other people standing on the dais beside her: two women and a man.

The Iljaria queen ascended to the throne at the shockingly young age of twenty. She is twice that now but doesn't look it. My people live for three centuries at least, and so the marks of aging touch us rather more slowly than they do for others.

But I am still awestruck when I reach the top of the dais. I stand there, staring.

Valrún's smooth dark skin gleams in the falling sunlight. She wears a sleeveless, leaf-green gown with a neckline that plunges deep between her breasts. Her long white hair hangs in gentle waves past her bare shoulders, and there are swirls of green tattooed on her arms and wrists and hands. Instead of the customary gem on her brow, she wears a crown heavy with emeralds. Her eyelashes are dusted in green powder, and vines hang all around her throne, moving like snakes across her lap. Her earrings are real, living lilies that strain up toward the light.

"Well, sister. I see your years away have worked all sense of decorum out of you. Will you not bow before our queen?"

I turn my head slightly to see Brandr looming on the queen's left side, clothed in his prismatic robes with his multicolored gem flashing on his brow.

"You've cut your hair," I say stupidly.

Last I saw him, he wore it in long braids, the ends crimped with metal. It's cropped short behind his ears now.

"You will *bow* before Queen Valrún and the Prism Master," snaps Jóvin behind me. He kicks me in the back of the knees so I topple forward, putting out my hands to catch myself.

I look up at Valrún, who regards me with an expression I can't read.

"Rise," she says. The word is clipped, cool.

I stand, feeling a little dizzy.

"My queen," I say, ducking my head. "There has been a misunderstanding."

"No," says Valrún, playing with one of the vines in her lap. At her touch, flowers bloom, pink and fragrant. "You have betrayed your country. I am astonished you dared to return."

I blink at her, fear sliding down my spine, the cut on my knee stiffening as it begins to clot.

I catch Brandr's smile out of the corner of my eye.

Gods, my brother really *does* hate me.

"Forgive me, my queen, but . . . how have I betrayed Iljaria?"

Her eyes narrow, and Brandr steps closer to her, trailing idle fingers along her collarbone.

I look at him sharply, but he just smiles and begins to massage Valrún's shoulder.

The queen doesn't seem to notice him at all. "The Iljaria have been waiting to return to Myrkur for eight centuries," she says, referring to Tenebris by its Iljaria name. "And what do you do? Lead Daeros and Skaanda right to the Yellow Lord—"

"I didn't—"

"Un*bind* the Yellow Lord—"

"That was Brandr, actually."

"—stop the just purging of two wicked nations—"

"It was genocide, not justice."

Valrún halts her list of my crimes to stare hard at me. She makes a careless motion with one hand and a vine slides off her lap, wraps around my ankle, and pulls me toward her until we are face-to-face, eye to eye.

This close I see that her dark skin really is smooth and flawless, not the barest scratch or freckle to mar it, like she is made of blown glass. She uses her magic, I realize, to keep herself looking this way.

I have a vague memory of my mother traveling to Regla City for beautician appointments with an Iljaria wielding Green magic—a Vaxandi. I wonder if my mother has changed at all in the eleven years since I saw her last, or if she has continued seeking out Vaxandi to eradicate any evidence of aging.

I think of my own body and Ballast's, riddled with scars. Would erasing the physical presence of them erase the memory of the trauma that created them?

"You are very small," says Valrún.

I clench my jaw, aware that Brandr is laughing at me but refusing to look at him.

"Since my father is dead," I tell her, "I came to Iljaria to give my report to you."

"Your report." Valrún waves her hand again and the vines pull me back a little, putting relieving space between us. "I have already heard it in full from your brother."

"You have heard *his* report," I correct her. "Not mine."

"Very well. Give it."

I resist the urge to tug at the iron collar. "Eleven years ago, I was sent as a spy to Tenebris."

Valrún frowns.

"To Myrkur," I correct myself. "I posed as an acrobat in Kallias's court, and I watched and listened for any activity around the Yellow Lord bound in the heart of the mountain, as I was bidden. I was there for eight years before I finally heard Kallias discussing his digging project, and his engineer explaining that they would reach the heart of the mountain in another two years. I escaped from Myrkur that evening, to come and bring word."

"That is not what you did," says Valrún. "You went to Skaanda to spill our secrets."

"No," I say fiercely. "I brought another captive home—the crown princess of Skaanda. Once there, I conferred with Indridi, who advised me to wait. We met Brandr on our way back to Myrkur."

Brandr's hand tightens on Valrún's shoulder. "And then you stood by as Indridi took her own life."

Dagfinna curses behind me.

Grief slams into me anew. "I had no choice. I couldn't save her."

My brother shakes his head in utter disgust.

"In Myrkur," I go on, "I delayed Kallias's digging progress with the help of an Iljaria captive. I aided Brandr when he came. I betrayed my friends into his hands, gave him control of the mountain. It was Brandr who released the Yellow Lord."

"But after that," says Valrún, "you changed your loyalties rather quickly."

"I couldn't let Brandr slaughter half the world. I didn't believe that my father orchestrated such a plan, especially after I read Brandr's mind and learned that he murdered our father. So I stopped him."

"With the help of a half-blooded Iljaria bastard prince, and the Skaandan and Daerosian armies," says Valrún. Anger sparks in her eyes. "Iljaria were *killed* that day. Because of you. Then you illicitly used your mind magic to take Brandr's Prism magic away, and bound the Yellow Lord into the sun, eradicating light magic entirely."

"I didn't know that would happen. But I couldn't let the Yellow Lord destroy millions of innocent people."

Valrún shakes her head, dumbfounded. "Do you admit so freely to your own guilt?"

My stomach is roiling. "I committed no sin."

The queen laughs. "You committed many. You were a fool to come back here."

I stand before her and see my death written in her face. I was a fool. I *am* a fool.

I think of Ballast, holding me tight against him in the dark, his fingers tracing the scars on my shoulders, his mouth warm on mine. I think of the angry words we shouted at each other in his bedchamber, the way they gutted me despite the tears in his eye. He told me Iljaria might not be what I thought. I didn't want to believe him.

But he was right.

And now I'll never see him again.

Valrún stands abruptly from her throne, stepping past me to the edge of the dais. I turn to see that a crowd has gathered in the room, colored gems flashing from foreheads, shoes and hems whispering along the golden floor. I look out into the sea of faces, but apart from the four Skapari who brought me here, none are familiar.

The queen glides along the dais, leafy vines trailing in her wake. I watch her, uneasy.

"My queen," I say. "The Aeronan emperor will not be content with his newly made province of Daeros. He will shift his attention to Iljaria soon."

Valrún turns to look at me. She throws back her head and laughs. Leaves rain through the air, settling on the dais in piles of green and gold and silver. "The emperor has grown very arrogant indeed if he thinks himself strong enough to conquer an entire nation of people who, to him, might as well be gods."

She strides toward me, stoops down, and grabs my chin with one hand. Her nails press deep, green sparking off them. "I have not yet decided what to do with you, Brynja Eldingar. It has been centuries since there was a traitor in our midst."

It is fruitless, but still I protest. "I am not a traitor."

Her nails dig harder into my chin, and I clench my fists at the pain of it.

"Loose my collar," I whisper. "Loose it, and let me prove my loyalty. Make me a Skapari. I will serve you."

Her eyes glitter.

Behind me, Brandr says, "Don't trust her, my queen. She is incapable of anything but lies."

"He *murdered* our father and stole his power," I say through gritted teeth. "Brandr isn't blessed by the Prism Lady but the Ghost Lord."

The twist of Valrún's lips tells me this is not news to her, and yet still my brother is allowed to wear the multicolored jewel on his brow and call himself the Prism Master.

"What would you have me do with your twin, Brandr?" Valrún asks without looking past me. "Her sins were against you, more than anyone else."

My heart thumps heavy and dull. My breaths come ragged. Fear weaves itself into my very bones.

"My sister does not deserve to live after all of the things she has done," he says.

Valrún smiles but still doesn't look at him.

"But I am the Prism Master," my brother goes on. "I will be merciful. Bind her in the spire. Perhaps, at some later date, she will be of use to us. If not, let her die in her prison, when the years of her life are spent."

I feel numb at this pronouncement of my fate.

Brandr grabs me by the shoulder, tugs me around. I keep my gaze fixed firmly on the floor.

"Look at me," he commands. "Look at me, and thank me for my mercy."

Bile burns acrid in my throat.

"Look at me!" Brandr shouts.

I lift my eyes and peer into his. They're mirrors of mine, piercing and dark. The freckles on his face mimic the pattern on my own. Even the shapes of his nose, his lips, his ears, match mine. We shared a womb, he and I. I wonder if he hated me even then.

"Thank me," Brandr says, low and cold, "or I will kill you right now."

I shake my head. "I'm not sure what game it is you're playing, Brandr, but I'm an expert at games, and I'll find a way to beat you at this one."

He laughs. "Goodbye, Brynja." He looks at me as he snaps his fingers.

The iron collar tightens around my neck so at every point it's touching my skin, almost but not quite choking me. It burns me, and I fight to keep from screaming.

"Take her to the spire," he snaps.

Jóvin and Adriel, the former vindictive and the latter regretful, climb the dais and seize me by either arm.

"Wait," I whisper. "Please wait."

But no one hears, or no one listens.

I think about Ballast, digging in his heels while he was dragged out of the great hall after I meddled in his mind.

I wonder if Adriel is strong enough in his time magic to bring me back to that moment, so I could stand with Ballast, make a different choice. Keep all of this from happening.

But I'm not sure even the Violet Lord himself could do that.

I go quiet and numb.

I let the Skapari take me to my new prison.

THIRTEEN YEARS AGO

BRYNJA

YEAR 4188, Month of the Prism Lady

Iljaria—the Prism Master's house

I hesitate outside of the door to my sister Lilja's workshop, holding tight to a bundle of flowers in one hand and a glimmering green stone in the other. She's been holed up in there for days now, deep in the throes of her latest project. She hasn't even come out for meals.

I found the stone in a sea cave, washed smooth and bright by the tide. The flowers were growing wild in the hills—they're lilies, like her name. I thought she could wear the stone on her brow and use her Green magic on the flowers to keep them thriving in the oily gloom of her workshop.

But somehow I don't quite have the courage to go in and show her my gifts. So I do it with my mind instead. I nudge open the door, unfold my hands, and send the lilies and the green stone to float inside and settle on one of my sister's worktables.

"Brynjaaaaa—" comes Lilja's voice a heartbeat later.

She appears at the door, Green magic sparking off her skin, grease smeared on her nose, her face tight with irritation. "What are you *doing*?" she demands, shoving the lilies and the stone back at me.

I gnaw on my lip and try not to cry. *I brought you presents,* I say into her mind.

She scowls at me. "You know I hate it when you talk like that. Open your mouth and use it, Brynja. The First Ones gave it to you for a reason."

I nod in utter misery.

Lilja sighs. "Your presents came barreling in and knocked apart the machine I've been building all week."

"I'm sorry!" I cry freely now, a drippy, sniveling mess.

Lilja puts a hand on my shoulder. "What's wrong, Brynja?"

I stare at her helplessly through the veil of my tears, because I don't really know.

She softens and tucks a stray curl behind my ear. "Father and Mother are at the palace attending the queen, and Brandr—I'm sure—hasn't looked up from his books since he fell ill last week, and I've been in my workshop and you're tired of being alone. Is that it?"

"Yes," I whisper, my chin wobbling.

Lilja offers me a handkerchief to wipe my eyes and squeezes my arm. "Come on, then. You can help me put the machine back together, just this once."

I follow her into the workshop, where she sets the lilies to bob in the air, roots coiling as they grow. I work beside the sister I idolize, and in this moment I feel happy. I feel whole.

FOUR MONTHS AGO

SAGA

Year 4201, Month of the Green Goddess

Skaanda—Staltoria City

It's raining when we reach Staltoria City.

I'm disappointed. I wanted to see the guard tower and the golden points of the spears decorating the walls shine in the sunlight. Instead, my city looks gloomy and dull, the banners drooping like mourners at a burial.

I am wrung out with anger and grief; the only thing that's left is weariness.

But gods above, I'm glad to be home.

We wind our way through the cobbled streets, our horses as exhausted as we are. I left most of the army in Tenebris with Vil—I took only two dozen soldiers back with me, among them Pala and Leifur. I don't trust Daeros or Aerona to abide by the verbal truce we made on the battlefield, and I wanted Vil to have all the military backup he needs as he works to hash out the stipulations of an actual peace treaty with Ballast and Brynja and Aelia. I feel a pang of some emotion caught between hurt and loss at the thought of Brynja. I have yet to come to terms with her betrayal, no matter that she set herself against her brother in the end. I thought she was my best friend, but she lied to me about who she was for *three years*. I don't know how to get past that. I don't know if I even want to.

I force myself to relax my too-tight hold on the reins.

The city is quiet, our horses' hooves echoing on wet cobblestones. I expected more of a welcome than this—I expected any welcome at all.

But it's been nine months since I left Staltoria with Pala and Leifur and Vil and Indridi and—and Brynja. Perhaps we were forgotten.

Or perhaps not. Faces peer out through rain-blurred windows, through slivers in cracked-open doors.

We are nearly halfway through the city before I notice the gray banners draped in every doorway, the ashes smeared on windowsills turned to paste in the rain.

Gray.

The color of the Goddess of Death.

I glance at Leifur, who rides alongside me, his form tall and strong in his saddle. His mouth presses into a grim line, and he shakes his head. He doesn't like this, either.

Dread grips me.

We ride through the far city gates and wind up the hill to the palace. Spears line the path, gray cloth draped between them. It signifies only one thing:

Death.

This is why no one came out to greet us.

It feels as if my mind is separating from my body, like I'm looking at myself from somewhere far above, removed from the dawning horror of this moment.

"Do you want me to ride ahead, Saga?" asks Leifur quietly beside me. Rain drips from his helm and into his eyes. "Your Highness," he corrects himself. He knows as well as I do that my parents do not permit the informality I have encouraged on our long journey together.

I'm not sure that's going to matter anymore.

"No," I tell him. "I want you with me." Leifur has been a steadying presence in a world that is constantly changing its shape and its rules around me. I can rely on him.

He nods. "I'll stay."

The rain seeps under the collar of my cloak. I shudder and wind my free hand into my horse's mane.

Leifur dismounts first at the palace gates, then offers his hand to help me down after him. His grip is strong and warm.

The guards at the gates open them and usher us through, though neither looks me in the eye.

We step into the rain-soaked courtyard. Stable hands dash up to take our mounts.

I can't help but compare this homecoming with the last one: me, back from the dead in the triumphant light of day, with a person at my side I thought was my friend.

I square my jaw and cross the courtyard, Pala and Leifur flanking me.

We pass through the aviary and into the palace through a side door. Elíndis, my parents' top adviser, meets us there.

Elíndis is nearly sixty, older than my parents, her body straight as a spear shaft. She was a decorated soldier in her time, then a brilliant commander, then promoted at last to head of the royal council. Her skin is darker than mine, her black hair only just beginning to silver.

She's dressed all in gray, from her robes to her shoes to the veil draped over her face. She folds it back at our approach, revealing the tearstains on her cheeks.

I stumble a little, and Leifur grabs my arm to steady me.

I almost stop Elíndis from telling me what I already know. If she doesn't speak the words aloud, perhaps the truth of them will be undone.

Elíndis looks at me with a deep, all-consuming grief.

Then she drops to her knees and bows before me and tells me that my parents are dead and I am queen of Skaanda.

CHAPTER SEVEN

BALLAST

Year 4201, Month of the Bronze Lord

Daeros—Garran City

My mother is expecting me.

I approach the tiny room I secured for her above a bakery in Garran City, and the door opens before I have a chance to knock.

I step in and try not to feel dismayed at this shabby place I put her, no matter it was the safest lodging I knew of.

She taps my shoulder, and I turn my attention to her hands.

I saw you from the window, she says in her finger speech. *And I have been very comfortable here, so stop fretting about me.*

I grimace. "You're not supposed to be able to read minds."

She gives a soundless laugh, and I hate my father all over again.

"Are you ready?" I ask her.

She nods, bustling about to gather up the three large packs waiting on the narrow cot that serves as a bed.

I take two of the packs from her, leaving her one at her own insistence.

Having no tongue doesn't make me infirm, she tells me, rolling her eyes.

We pocket two Iljaria light globes, the Yellow magic inside them strangely faint, and leave the little apartment together. I lock the door behind us and hand the keys off to the baker, Melitta, once we're downstairs. She's about my mother's age and has been impossibly kind to me since I was a boy. Every time I visited Garran City, she always insisted I come into the bakery and sit by her fire and pet her cats and eat cinnamon buns or honey cakes with loads and loads of jam until I was full near to bursting. Sometimes Melitta even patched me up after an encounter with my father. I knew my mother would be safe here, and I can trust the baker to keep our departure a secret.

"I've asked the rats and weevils in Daeros—as many as I could reach, anyway—to stay out of your cellar and your flour sacks," I tell Melitta. "And Nutmeg is going to have nine kittens." I nod to the heavily pregnant cat curled up on the rug behind the bakery case.

Melitta laughs. "Send a few rats back so those kittens have something to do, then, won't you? And take this." She presses a paper sack into my arms that smells of yeast and sugar. My mouth waters.

"Thanks, Melitta," I say. "For everything."

She smiles, reaching up to clap her hands on my shoulders—I'm a good deal taller than her. "Be well, Your Majesty," she says.

Then my mother and I step out into the night.

Garran City is never fully dark, lamps on tall poles illuminating the streets, tin lanterns shining from windows and above doorways. It is a city used to three months of winter darkness, and it hasn't changed since the Yellow Lord was bound into the sun.

The city is crawling with Aeronan soldiers, so my mother and I keep to the shadows. I haven't gone to visit Rhode and Xenia and little Charis since they left Tenebris—I know I'm being watched—but I did send a few messages via animals so they wouldn't think I'd forgotten them. First Ones willing, when all of this is over, I will no longer have to worry about their safety and can see my sisters whenever I wish.

We slip quietly through the streets toward a small gate in the city wall, where an Aeronan guard stands watch. We crouch in an alley by the gate, and I take my mother's hand and, with my fingers, slowly spell words into it. She spells words back into my hand.

I close my eyes and reach out with my magic. There is a stray dog near, sniffling about for scraps in the street. He's harmless but will serve my purpose. I compel him to charge, snarling, at the guard.

The Aeronan yelps and fumbles for his sword while the dog drives him away from the gate, long enough for my mother and me to rush up to it and slip through. Once we're safely on the other side, I send the dog dashing out of harm's way and leave the guard to resume his post, cursing.

We run, then, over the waving autumn grass, the packs making us clumsy.

Asvaldr is waiting at the base of a hill. He yawns and plods up to greet us, pressing his nose against my outstretched palm.

The enormous bear lowers himself to the ground, and I help my mother clamber onto his back. I made a sort of saddle for him, which he's been a bit grumpy about, but there was no other way to secure our luggage and make sure my mother would be as comfortable as possible on our journey. I tie the packs onto the saddle, then climb up behind my mother.

Asvaldr flicks his thought into my mind: earth and stars and wind and motion.

"Yes," I tell him. "We're ready."

He bounds into the night.

East.

Toward Iljaria.

Asvaldr runs all night, and partway into the morning. My mother and I make camp at the base of a hill while the arctic bear goes off to find himself some breakfast. I build a fire, smoke wisping up into the pale light of the new day.

My mother makes porridge in the small pot she pulls out of the packs. Birds wing overhead, and for a while I let my mind trace their paths, feel the lightning-quick beats of their little hearts and the wind in their feathers. I'm startled when my mother presses a bowl into my hands and touches my shoulder so I look up at her.

Daydreaming, she says with her fingers. She smiles at me.

We eat the porridge and two of Melitta's sweet rolls each. Afterward, I unfold the well-creased map I keep in my pocket and plot out our path for the hundredth time.

My mother pokes me. *Stop worrying.*

"I don't know how."

All will be well. She closes her eyes and tilts her face to the sun. She spreads her arms wide. A guttural noise comes out of her throat and magic spools from her fingers, floating like ribbons on the breeze. My father thought he severed her access to her song magic when he cut out her tongue.

He was wrong.

I have seen her use her power only a few times in my life, and never this freely, this *joyfully*.

She dances in the grass, spinning and dipping and singing, her magic dancing with her, in shimmers and whorls of white.

It's because she *is* free, for the first time since my father caught her and put her in a cage. Free, and at long, long last, going home.

I weep, watching her. My father deserved to die a thousand times over for all the things he did to my mother.

All at once she turns toward me, grabs my hand, pulls me into the dance with her. I catch her joy, and then I'm laughing with her, though tears still pour down my face.

We sleep in the shadow of the hill, wrapped in our coats with the packs for pillows. Sometime during the day, Asvaldr comes to join us;

when I wake, on toward evening, he's there, his fur washed red in the light of the setting sun.

After a quick supper we pack up and climb back onto Asvaldr. The great bear bounds over the earth as the moon rises, a sickle of silver in a sky full of stars. He races it until it sets again, and dawn shows rosy on the horizon.

We travel ever east, between the northern edge of the Sea of Bones and the White Sea, sleeping during the day and riding Asvaldr at night. I don't know that this part of Daeros is watched, but I don't want to risk it. I tell myself that even if my mother and I were seen leaving Garran City, no one could predict *where* we are going.

Probably.

Every few days I send a bird or a mouse on ahead of us to scout out how much farther it is to the Galdur Skjöld, which my mother tells me is the Iljaria name for their magical barrier. She assures me that between the two of us, we have enough power to rip a hole in it. That's what she and her sister did, all those years ago. I hope she's right.

Unless things have changed, my mother says, the Iljaria don't patrol every inch of the Galdur Skjöld—they couldn't; it stretches for miles and miles, across the peninsula and on out into the sea. And, really, that's the entire point of the magical barrier: to take the place of a patrolling army. There are watchtowers here and there along the length of it—those are the usual points of entry into Iljaria. But we don't want our arrival trumpeted from the rooftops.

We turn northeast when we've passed the eastern edge of the Sea of Bones, and for a while travel parallel to the Galdur Skjöld, though it is yet too far away for us to see.

We've been journeying this way for about a week when an ermine wanders into our camp just as I'm scraping the last of my breakfast porridge from my bowl. The little creature crawls up into my lap and puts its paws on my chest, squeaking insistently in my face until I notice the white cord around its neck, easy to miss amid the white of its fur.

I loose the cord, on which hangs a tiny glass bead.

The instant I weigh the bead in my hand, images unfold behind my eyes, and I know I'm seeing memories, captured and preserved for me by someone capable of wielding more than one form of magic at a time.

Finnur.

My heart races as the memories reach their end. I tap the bead and they repeat themselves. Then I hand it to my mother.

What will you do? she asks me, a wariness in her face because we both know I haven't told her everything.

"What we planned," I say, and taking the bead back from her, I grind it under my heel.

She waits for me to elaborate, but when I don't, she turns away from me and stretches herself out to sleep.

The ermine is still waiting in my lap. I close my eyes and send thoughts into it, an answer to the memories in the glass bead. I feed the little creature a few grains of my porridge, and it darts off happily, carrying my message back toward Regla City.

My mother sleeps easily, but I do not, peering up into the sky as scudding clouds pass over the sun. I try to tamp down my fear, but there's nowhere for it to go. Black Lord's *bastard.*

I wish she were here. I wish I could pull her against me, tuck her head under my chin, hold her until I fall asleep.

She is too far away, and I can't speak into her mind as easily as she can speak into mine, but I try anyway:

Brynja. Be safe. Please, please. Be safe.

I wake to the setting sun and another animal messenger, a kestrel I sent out two evenings ago. It lights on my shoulder and sends images into my mind: the shimmer of the Galdur Skjöld in an empty stretch of land far from the watchtowers on either side. If we turn straight east, we will be there before morning.

I shake my mother awake, hoping she's not still angry with me.
"It's time," I tell her. "We're going east. Tonight."
To breach the Galdur Skjöld? she asks.
I nod. "To breach the Galdur Skjöld."
She smiles, her eyes sharp. *I'm ready.*

TEN YEARS AGO

BALLAST

YEAR 4191, Month of the Bronze Lord

Daeros—Tenebris

I shuffle the deck of Iljaria playing cards again and again, using the upturned tray on my bed as a makeshift table. I flick my eyes up to the heating vent, anxious for her to come.

She doesn't visit every night, but it's been nearly a week since she last did, and as my father didn't make either of us perform for him tonight, chances are high that she'll be here. I filched two meat skewers, dripping with spicy-sweet sauce, from the kitchen for her. I would have grabbed more, but the cook caught me at it and threatened to tell my father, so I darted out in a hurry. It's later, though, than the time she usually visits. I'm beginning to lose hope.

I shuffle the cards again.

The heating grate makes only the slightest squeak as it swings open, held by a single screw.

My heart leaps, and I can hardly keep from grinning like a fool as she hops down from the ceiling and settles herself cross-legged onto my bed, the overturned tray between us.

"Hey, Brynja," I say, trying not to sound overly eager.

"Hey, Bal." Her voice is quiet; her eyes won't meet mine. She keeps her shoulders hunched.

She's shaved her head again, her dark hair mere prickles along her pale scalp, a nick just behind her left ear, already scabbing over. She doesn't cry—she never cries—but she looks close to it now.

My gut twists. I don't ask her if my father did something to her, or if she ran afoul of his steward, Nicanor. We don't talk about that stuff when she visits. It would ruin this fragile, hallowed thing between us. For a couple of hours every few nights, my father doesn't exist; she is not his captive and I am not his son. We are simply ourselves, two friends playing cards. She is really, really good at cards. I suspect I win occasionally only because she lets me.

"Hungry?" I say, and put the plate of skewers on her lap, careful not to touch her.

She nods and wolfs down the meat, licking her fingers while I shuffle the deck of cards yet again. She seems a little better when she's finished and sets the plate to the side. She taps the overturned tray. "What are we playing tonight?"

I smile and deal out the cards. "War. What else?"

She smiles, too.

We both study our cards for a few moments, and then we begin to play, alternating turns. We fall into our normal easy rhythm, Brynja laying her cards down fast and fierce while I do my best to keep up.

She wins the first game, and the second, wielding the wild Ghost Lord card both rounds to make my points count against me, her smile as sharp as her eyes. After that, I put the cards back in their box and we settle into our usual places on opposite ends of the bed, books on our laps. I try to have new ones for her to read every week—she devours them like she's as starved for knowledge as she is for food. And she must be. I have my lessons with the tutors every day; all she has is the damned iron cage in the great hall.

Tonight she absorbs herself in a volume of the history of the peninsula, lips moving soundlessly as she reads. I don't even open my own book, too caught up in watching her.

I'm seized by a sudden, reckless desire to grab her hand and pull her out of Tenebris. We could figure out a way to evade my father's soldiers, and then—and then, I don't know. Dig lichen out from under the snow to eat—that's what the reindeer do, right? We could live in some city far away where my father would never find us, and I could apprentice myself to the horse-master and she could apprentice herself to, well, whomever she liked, and we would be happy. We would be free, and we would be away from him, and we would be happy. We would be so, so happy.

But there's my mother. And the other children in the Collection, and the baker in Garran City, and my little sister Rhode, and the palace physician who is so kind to me—

How could I leave them all?

"Ballast," says Brynja without looking up from her book, "did you know that the peninsula doesn't have a name because Iljaria and Skaanda and Daeros couldn't agree on what it ought to be called? Daeros came centuries late to the debate, really, but ever since Skaanda was formed, it's been a point of contention." She grips the book tight and glances up at me, suddenly self-conscious. "I'm sure you know that."

I shake my head. "Nope. What did Skaanda and Iljaria and Daeros want to call it?"

Her eyes light up and she bends back over the book. "Skaanda wanted to name it 'Lifandi,' which means 'living,' and Iljaria wanted to name it 'Galdur,' which means 'magic.'"

"What about Daeros?" Her eagerness is contagious, and I find myself hanging on to her every word.

"Daeros wanted to call it 'Xiphos.'"

"'Sword,'" I say, recognizing the word.

She nods. "Why would you want to call an entire peninsula 'sword'? That's ridiculous. It's like begging the gods for eternal war or something." She flashes a grin at me, and I have a sense she's just this side of laughter.

I grin back.

"But in maps drawn in other parts of the world," Brynja goes on, her eyes scanning the rest of the page, "it's labeled 'the Gray Peninsula' because it has to be called *something*, and it's not exactly the only peninsula in the world."

She sobers then, and I do, too.

Gray is the color of death.

"What would you call the peninsula?" I ask her after a little while. "Would you side with Skaanda or Iljaria? Magic or life?"

"Neither," she says. "I'd call it Sólarljós. Sunlight."

"Even though there is none for the whole of winter?"

"Yes," she says. "Because even when there is no light, there is the memory of it. The hope of it."

She looks at me, and I look at her, and I feel utterly *known*, in a way I never have before. I wonder if she realizes how much her company has meant to me, these last few months. I wonder if she would think me pathetic if I told her I've never had a friend before.

It's late, past the twenty-first hour, and she doesn't stay much longer. She helps me stuff the books and the deck of cards back onto my tiny shelf, and smooths away the wrinkles in my comforter. She stands for a moment in the middle of the room, her hands in her pockets, her head tilted to one side as if she's debating whether to tell me something.

But in the end she just gives me half a smile and scrambles up into my heating vent like a squirrel, pulling the grate back into place after her, one hand darting through the decorative metal covering to tighten the screws.

"See you later, Bal," comes her muffled voice. "Sleep well."

"See you, Brynja," I say softly.

And then I stretch out on my back and shut my eyes and listen to the faint sounds of her scampering away in the ceiling and tell myself severely that I'm eleven, and that is far too old to cry because I'm lonely.

CHAPTER EIGHT

BRYNJA

Year 4201, Month of the Bronze Lord

Iljaria—Regla City—the palace

Jóvin and Adriel usher me out of the great hall and down a long, straight corridor walled with mirrors. Globes encasing Red magic bob along the ceiling, and the mirrors and the light dazzle my eyes so that even though I look straight ahead, I am half blinded. Jóvin's nails dig into my arm, and I want to shake him off but don't dare. Adriel's grip is not painful but still firm.

I glance at the wielder of Violet magic, but he won't meet my eyes.

At the end of the corridor is a glass door, which Adriel opens with a snap of his fingers. Beyond is a stair, too narrow for us to walk three abreast. Adriel leads us and Jóvin hauls me along behind, fast enough that I trip on the shallow steps and fall on my already injured knee.

We climb and climb, and I picture those knife-blade-like spires I saw from outside of the city.

Just as I think we will be climbing forever, we reach the top of the stair, and another glass door. This one evidently requires a key, which Jóvin fishes from his pocket.

Now Adriel does look at me, and his gem flashes bright. For a split second his form goes faint at the edges, but when I blink, he is perfectly solid again.

Jóvin unlocks the door and shoves me into the chamber beyond: a narrow room illuminated poorly with a single light globe, mere sparks of its Yellow magic left. The glass walls are opaque, the room largely in shadow. There is a low shelf that is perhaps meant to be a bed, also made out of glass.

There is nothing else.

I didn't come all this way just to be locked in another cage.

In the iron one, in Tenebris, I could see through the bars into the hall below. There was not a sense of suffocation, mirrored back at me in endless reflections.

"Wait," I beg, lunging at Jóvin as he moves to close the door again. "Please wait."

But Jóvin just sneers at me, yanking the door shut hard enough to rattle the spire. The key grates, and the outline of the door vanishes entirely, folding into the smooth glass of the wall. Two sets of footsteps sound on the stair, quickly fading.

I pound on the place where the door was, half mad with terror.

"Brynja."

I whirl around, blinking in confusion to see Adriel.

"The queen won't leave you to die," he says nonchalantly. He walks the short length of the room before settling on the glass bed, crossing his legs at the ankles.

"She needs you for something," he adds. "Or she would have killed you. Do you have any idea what?"

"How are you here?"

He rolls his eyes in exasperation and wiggles his fingers. Violet sparks dance between them.

Oh. Time magic.

"You came in here when we were out on the stairs?"

"*Yes*, Brynja. Please try and keep up. Do you know what Valrún wants from you?"

"No."

Adriel scratches at his jaw, the beginnings of white stubble showing against his dark skin. "You're *really* powerful. Everyone knows that, even the Prism Master, though it took him a while to admit it was you who locked his magic away. Valrún doesn't have a Huga among her Skapari."

I reach into the recesses of my memory: Huga are wielders of mind magic, like me.

"How many Skapari does she have?"

"Seven, at present. Eight, if you count the Prism Master. She has Black, Red, Green, Gray, Brown, my Violet, and Jóvin's Yellow, or lack thereof."

"Brown?" I ask him quietly.

His eyes snap to mine. "I forget she's your mother."

I take a breath. "She's still the queen's architect, then."

"Yes."

My heart beats hot and frantic.

"Why did you come back, Brynja?" he asks me then.

I feel the power radiating off him, see him start to fade around the edges.

"White Lady's tongue," he curses. "You want something from Valrún."

"I wanted to come home," I correct him. "I thought I'd be welcome."

"You were a child when you left," he says. "You need to grow up now. Beware, Brynja. You're in over your head. Don't cross Valrún."

"Adriel—"

But he's gone, and I am alone in my glass prison, beating my fists against the wall.

I spend a long while sitting on the floor.

I try not to think about how narrow the walls are. I try not to look at them. It doesn't work. Panic crawls into my mind, and it's all I can do to breathe, breathe, to keep from throwing myself against the place where the door should be until my body is a bloody pulp.

It's maddening in here.

Eventually I get up and pace the length of my prison—seven steps from one wall to the other—and then the breadth—only three. It's more coffin than cage.

I touch every inch of the walls. I find nothing but a chamber pot, tucked under the glass bed. I hurl it at the place where the door was with all the strength I possess, but it doesn't shatter the glass, just bounces back and hits the side of my head so hard that for a moment my vision goes white.

I sit back down then, pressing one hand against my throbbing temple and blinking tears from my eyes.

Gray Goddess take me—whether Valrún means to kill me or not, I'm not certain I'll last more than a day or two in here.

The soft touch of a hand on my shoulder and the rattle of the iron collar falling to the floor make me scream.

I jump to my feet and turn to see my mother standing just inside the room, regarding me coolly.

I stare at her.

She's short, like me. I might even be a little bit taller. How did I not realize how small she was, when I was a child? Her pale skin is smooth but not quite as flawless as Valrún's. She has a dusting of freckles on her nose, the tiniest wrinkles in the corners of her eyes, a crease in her forehead. Her white hair is loose, the curls brushing her shoulders. A polished brown gem glitters from her brow. She wears a flowy white gown embroidered with brown whorls, cinched with a tooled leather breastplate.

Except for her clothing and her gem, it's like looking in a mirror. This shocks me. I never knew I looked anything like my mother.

"How are you here?" I whisper. I glance to the iron collar, overwhelmed with the sensation of my magic flooding back, like the tingling you get when the blood starts flowing to a foot that fell asleep. It hurts, but it's a relief, too, because it means you can feel again.

"Valrún forgets I am her chief architect," says my mother, stepping past me to the back wall. She traces the outline of a square in the glass with one finger, and suddenly I can see out over Regla City, to the sky and the sun beckoning beyond.

"I *raised* this spire," my mother goes on. "I *made* that collar. Of course I can manipulate them."

I blink at her and the world goes blurry.

I'm surprised when she pulls me into her, when she presses my head to her shoulder and strokes my hair and holds me while I sob and sob and sob.

I can't seem to stop. My body convulses with crying. I sputter and choke, I shake, shake.

She smooths my hair; she whispers nonsense words into my ear. She holds me while I cry and doesn't let me go.

It's been eleven years since I've seen my mother. I didn't know how much I needed her to hold me.

She seemed indifferent to my leaving for Daeros on the mission from my father; she seemed indifferent to my existence. Lilja was the child to be proud of, Brandr the one to pity. I was the one to fear, or ignore, by turns.

I am overwhelmed by the thought that maybe one member of my family loves me, after all, by the realization that *this* is part of what I longed for from my homecoming: acceptance, comfort. Remembrance. I don't want to feel alone in the one place I am supposed to belong.

All those long years I spent in Tenebris, I dreamed of home. I thought I would be welcomed with trumpets and singing, with a great banquet spread out on the field behind my father's house. I thought I would be honored, celebrated. I thought there would be rejoicing, in a world where darkness has been driven away.

I forgot that there are some who love the darkness, because it hides the things they do not wish others to see.

It seems an eternity before the storm passes, but at long last, it does.

I lift my head, and my mother offers me a handkerchief without a word. I wipe my eyes and blow my nose.

She walks around the tiny glass room, muttering to herself. Sparks of brown the color of newly tilled earth leap and dance around her, and the room *expands* to four times its original size. A rich red carpet spreads out over the floor. The glass bed turns to one made of wood, with a mattress and quilts and pillows. The window she traced in the wall grows a frame, and beside it appears a shelf, stacked with books and a Lords and Ladies game set.

A little round table and two chairs grow up out of the floor. My mother frowns and waves her hand, making seat cushions appear.

She sits in one of the chairs, and I settle into the other, my cheeks stiff with salt.

"I'm sorry I can't take you out of here entirely," says my mother. "But at least now it should take longer for you to go completely mad." She quirks a smile at me.

It's a joke. My mother made a joke. Did she do that when I was a child? I don't know. I realize I don't know anything about her at all.

"I'm glad to see you, Brynja," she says then. Her voice catches.

I swallow, afraid I'm going to start crying again. I want to ask her so many things, but it's too much, it's all too much, and I'm terrified I might discover that she never really cared about me, that she just wants something from me, like everyone else in my life except Ballast and Saga.

"Do you know about Brandr?" I say at last, my voice hoarse.

Her mouth goes grim. "That his true patron is the Ghost Lord? That he murdered your father? Yes. I know."

I rub at the edge of the table my mother made out of nothing.

"I cannot go against him," she tells me quietly. "I cannot go against Valrún."

"Why?" I say to the table.

I expect her to spout a platitude about Iljaria's pacifism, or give some other excuse.

Instead, she says, "Because I'm afraid."

I look up at her, surprised.

Her eyes are wet, and I find I do not want my mother to cry.

"It was too late for Hinrik by the time I realized what was happening," she tells me. "Brandr had absorbed all of Hinrik's power and your father . . . had a *lot* of power."

I nod. "I remember."

"When Hinrik died, I felt adrift. First Lilja, then you"—she looks away—"then my husband. Brandr would have killed me, too, if I'd had the guts to stand against him. He finally had the magic that he wanted. I hoped that would be enough."

I take a breath, try to keep from shaking. "Did you think I was dead?"

She turns away from me and puts her head in her hands. I suppose that is my answer. "I trusted Hinrik," she says miserably. "I trusted Valrún and Iljaria. I trusted in the Yellow Lord bound in the heart of that cursed mountain. I trusted it was right and just, sending you there. But I didn't realize how it would feel." Her eyes find mine again, tears trembling on her white lashes. "To sacrifice a daughter," she whispers.

I gnaw on the inside of my cheek until it's raw and bleeding. "You didn't expect me to come back."

She shakes her head.

"You planned for me to not come back."

She nods.

I curse quietly.

"Come, Brynja, I deserve far more than that. Aren't you angry with me?"

I look across at her and realize that I pity this woman, trapped as I was trapped, but with no way out that she can see.

"I have spent all my anger," I say. "There is none left for you. It wasn't you who sent me. It was Father."

She rubs a hand over her brow, knocking carelessly against the gem. "I could have stopped him."

"Would he have let you?"

She grows solemn, thinking about this. "No," she says. "But I still should have tried."

My eyes are caught by motion outside the window: a kestrel winging past the spire. I try to read its mind, but I was never good with animals. That's Ballast's domain.

"What was meant to happen with the Yellow Lord?" I ask. "What did Valrún want with him?"

"I'm not certain. I think your brother went his own way in Myrkur. Valrún was . . . not pleased when he returned."

"It seems she's since forgiven him."

My mother gives me a knowing look. "It seems she has."

"Are they . . ." I trail off, a little too horrified by the idea to speak it out loud.

"Lovers?" she says frankly. "Yes, although I think the infatuation is largely on his side."

"She's using him," I say.

"She uses everyone."

"But why?"

My mother shakes her head. "I don't know. Your father did, I think, but he never told me. Brandr is partially if not wholly in her confidence." She looks at me sharply. "What about you, Brynja?"

"What about me?"

"The most powerful mind magic I have ever heard of, blazing out of a nine-year-old girl."

She means the moment on the edge of the Sea of Bones, when my shock and rage and grief about Lilja's death nearly tore the whole world apart.

"Is it still as strong as it was back then?" she asks.

Yes, I say into her mind, *though I am still relearning how to use it.*

My mother rises from her chair, shuttering her thoughts from me, but not before I accidentally read the loudest ones: She did not come here of her own accord; she was sent to garner this exact information from me; I have fallen neatly into her trap.

Hurt bites sharp as swords. For a few moments I thought she cared for me, thought she regretted sending me away. I thought we could build a relationship, find what we lost, be family for each other. But I'm a fool. She's only here because Valrún wants something from her Bronze magic–wielding bear. It turns out that the Iljaria court is no different from the Daerosian one, and I have walked blindly into another collection.

"You're in Valrún's pocket," I say sharply.

She shrugs, stooping to pick up the iron collar with the handkerchief she gave me. She winces, the thin cloth not enough to wholly shield her from the metal. "Everyone is in Valrún's pocket. You will be too, soon, if you choose the right cards to play."

I stand from the chair, backing away from her.

"Why don't you stand up to Valrún?" I demand. "Your magic is every bit as powerful as hers, if not more so."

"Oh, Brynja"—she sighs, stepping forward and locking the iron collar around my neck again—"the sooner you accept that Iljaria owns you and Valrún is Iljaria, the easier it will be for you."

"Mother."

She looks at me, and I don't know if the regret in her eyes is real, or if I just want it to be.

"I'm sorry, Brynja," she says. And then she leaves the glass prison, using her magic to pass through the wall.

At least the room stays the way she altered it. At least I can look out over the city while I contemplate my mother's betrayal and realize I have not wholly run out of anger, after all.

TWO HOURS AGO

VALRÚN

Year 4201, Month of the Bronze Lord

Iljaria—Regla City—the palace

I am enraged when my Skapari pull me from the bath before I am quite finished, and vines with spear-sharp thorns sprout from my fingers. I will eviscerate these women for their ineptitude. But their blood would pollute my bathwater, and I would have to find Skapari to replace them, and that would be an inconvenience. So I shake the thorned vines from my fingers and step carefully over them, then allow my Skapari to attend me.

The younger, Malen, apologizes as she wraps me in my robe of silk and winds up my dripping hair. Malen wields Green magic far stronger than mine. It is why I chose her as a Skapari, and it is why I revile her.

The elder, Osa, wields death magic. Her life has spun on for two centuries thus far, and though she has yet to go to the Gray Lady herself, she has helped many others along on that final meeting.

"There is a boy," Osa explains, while Malen sets her fingers to my face, her magic cool on my skin as it smooths away every imperfection.

"What do I care for a boy?" I snap.

Malen finishes with my face and moves on to my hair, whispering her power into every strand.

Osa brings me a gown, the skirts heavy with beading, the neckline dipping low.

"He has Prism magic," Osa tells me. "*Powerful* Prism magic. He caused such a disturbance at the gate that the guards tried to collar him in iron, but they couldn't catch him."

My heart is a spear beneath my breastbone. "Why is he here? Who is he?"

Osa laces up the back of the gown. "He wouldn't say."

Malen sets my crown upon my head.

"He wants an audience with you, Your Majesty."

"That is why you pulled me out of my bath?"

"Yes, Your Majesty," says Osa.

I curse. "Where is he now?"

"We thought it best to put him in a private audience chamber to wait for you," Osa tells me.

This means they think him a danger and are hiding him from the rest of the palace.

"Very well. Bring me there."

"At once, Your Majesty," says Osa.

Malen clasps a heavy necklace with a green pendant around my throat, and then I stride from my dressing chamber, the two Skapari at my heels.

Brandr lurks in my antechamber and attaches himself to my side as I go out into the corridor. He slips his arm round my waist, playing with the beading on my gown and slipping his hand down lower than is decorous outside the privacy of my bedchamber. I find him diverting enough that I allow this behavior, and even when he no longer diverts me, I will continue to allow it, because I need his Ghost Lord power.

The Green Lady did not bless me with strong magic, but she did bless me with a crown, and continues throwing foolish men into my path to help me keep it.

The private audience chamber is a small room with a high ceiling tucked away in the back of the palace. It has a single plain window that looks out over Regla City, and a handful of potless trees bobbing about. They look a little wilty; I will command Malen to come and tend them.

A fire burns without fuel or hearth in the center of the room, and the boy stands near it, a prismatic gem winking from his forehead.

"Your Majesty," he says at once, bowing low before me. He flicks his eyes to Brandr and adds, tightly, "High Master."

"Finnur," says Brandr. "What the hell are you doing here?"

I take a step back from my Prism Master, eyeing him sharply. "You know this boy?"

"We met in Tenebris, Your Majesty," says Finnur.

Brandr's jaw goes tight. "He was one of Kallias's . . . captives."

Pets, he means. "You are the one she was talking about," I say to Finnur, "the captive who helped delay the digging."

"I am, Your Majesty."

"Your magic is powerful?"

"So I am told, Your Majesty. But I am not Iljaria trained."

I circle this boy. He is lanky and tall, not quite grown into himself. His skin is a single shade lighter brown than mine, and his eyes—his eyes are somehow familiar.

"How old are you?" I ask him sharply.

"Sixteen," he says.

My heart falters. "What is your surname?"

"I don't have one."

Red Lord's burning heart. "Why?" I demand.

"Because I was found as a baby," he tells me, "in a glass boat that washed up on the shore of the White Sea."

Brandr is suddenly under my elbow, keeping me from collapsing to the floor.

"Your Majesty?" he says low in my ear.

I take a short, sharp breath. I pull myself very straight.

"What is it you want, Finnur?" I ask as coldly as I can manage.

I can hardly look at him, hardly *keep* myself from looking at him.

"I want you to make me one of your Skapari," he says, bold as a First One.

Brandr laughs. "You just told us you aren't Iljaria trained."

"Train me then," says Finnur fiercely, not cowed by Brandr's derision.

"I already have a Prism Master," I say.

Finnur shrugs. "Maybe you need a new one."

I nearly laugh at the anger that twists Brandr's face.

"Peace, Brandr," I tell him, one hand on his arm. "I am not about to replace you. But as the office of Prism Master supersedes that of a queen's Skapari—meaning you are *not* a Skapari—I have that place yet to fill, to reach my twelve. Find him a room with the other Skapari, and see that he is trained."

Brandr isn't placated. "May I ask why, Your Majesty?"

"No," I say, "you may not. Obey me at once. That is an order."

Brandr jerks an angry bow in my direction and turns to deal with Finnur, while I sweep from the room and call for Osa and Dagfinna and Jóvin, the three Skapari who have served the crown the longest. I would have called the former Prism Master with them, but of course I can't, because the current one murdered him.

I ask them question after question until I wring from them the answers that I need.

CHAPTER NINE

BALLAST

Year 4201, Month of the Bronze Lord

Iljaria/Daeros Border—the Galdur Skjöld

It's still dark when we reach the border.

The Galdur Skjöld shimmers in the starlight, far larger than I expected, larger even than I can properly comprehend. I had thought that I could call my owls to bear us over the top of it, or ask an army of badgers to dig us a tunnel underneath it.

Now I see that both of those things would be impossible.

The barrier stretches up what appears to be infinitely into the night sky, and I can sense it extends similarly far underground. There is no over, or under, or around.

There is only through.

The Galdur Skjöld seems to be made either of Prism magic, or all magics together, which amounts to the same thing. It hums with an almost watchful power.

We clamber off Asvaldr, and I loose the bear from his harness. For a moment I stand with my head pressed against his great one, sending my thanks and warmth and love into his mind. He nudges his cold nose against my cheek, his emotions pulsing back at me, bright with joy. Then he lumbers off the way we came, and I have a sharp sensation of loss.

I turn back to my mother, who is attempting to carry all three packs, and relieve her of two of them.

"How are we going to get through?" I ask her quietly.

I squint in the pulsing light of the Galdur Skjöld to see my mother's answer:

I will call all the bits of White magic that live in this piece of the wall; I will ask them to join together and make a doorway, and then I will step through. You must do the same with your Blue magic.

I blink at her. "I don't know how to do that. Can't I use your doorway?"

Her smile is rueful. *White magic will notice your Blue and will sound the alarm all down the country. The Galdur Skjöld might even trap you in the wall until the Skapari come.*

I grimace. "That's a no, then."

She steps up to the barrier, raising both of her hands. Her song magic pours out of her throat, garbled by her missing tongue but still shockingly beautiful, and immensely powerful.

The wall hums and rearranges itself, sparks of color fleeing from glints of white. Then, before I'm ready for it, my mother steps through. The Galdur Skjöld seals behind her, and I'm left alone on the Daerosian side.

Panic spikes. My mother can't call instructions to me, and I don't even know where to begin. My connection with animals has always come easily to me, but to manipulate the magic itself?

I step up to the Galdur Skjöld, close enough I can feel the power radiating off it, pricking my skin like needles. I don't dare touch the barrier. My heart thrums through me, anxious, hot, and I have a sudden fear that my mother is already gone, that she means to leave me trapped here, that she never wanted me to come with her and only used me to get this far.

Something pulses in my mind, not words, like Brynja could send me, not even images or emotions like how I communicate with the animals. It's music, a thread of song that brims with love and power.

I take a breath. My mother hasn't left me. She isn't going to.

I consider the barrier. I flick my magic toward it, trying to find the elements of Blue, trying to call them. The Galdur Skjöld pulses before me, but it does not change.

I ponder the animals I have sent across the border multiple times. They work no magic to cross; they are not allowed through by the Iljaria at the watchtowers. They simply pass the Galdur Skjöld unnoticed and unharmed.

That's it, then. I simply need to become an animal.

I laugh at myself and utter a vicious curse.

Become an animal. Simple.

It isn't unheard of. I saw Iljaria wielding Blue magic shift into winged creatures during the battle for Tenebris. And it's possible, likely even, that the cave demons we fought in the tunnels beneath the mountains were Iljaria who changed themselves into animals, and didn't know how to turn back again. The thought sours my stomach.

My mother tells me that if I had grown up in Iljaria, I would have been trained in Blue magic from the age of ten or so to sixteen. I would have lived in the Blue section of Regla City, been schooled with others who shared my affinity. And when I finished my schooling, I would've taken a job that required Blue magic somewhere in Iljaria. Or I could've joined Regla City's Skapari, perhaps be assigned to a watchtower or some other role in the city guard. In the very rarest of cases, I would have been selected by the queen to join her personal circle of Skapari and live in the palace. These Skapari were servants and guards and advisers and nobility, all at once. There was no higher honor an Iljaria could attain, unless it was the position of Prism Master.

I did not grow up in Iljaria. I have not been formally trained in Blue magic.

But I have to try.

There is no other way back to her.

The song in my head grows louder, more insistent. My mother wants me to come through as quickly as I can.

I kneel in the grass before the Galdur Skjöld. I close my eyes, press my hands against the earth.

I need to be something small, I reason, small and quick. Or maybe I should attempt to become a creature that is more the size I already am, so my body will not have to change so much.

The music in my head is nearly deafening. I reach past it, through it. I dig down into the deepest part of myself, to the magic that blazes in my soul.

I ask it to fill me up.

To change me.

The world bursts apart, or perhaps it is my body.

Light and darkness.

Warmth.

Pain.

I am crushed. Distorted.

My heart beats a different pattern, quick, quick, quick. My lungs are strange and small. There is too much air. There is not enough.

The world bobs about.

The Galdur Skjöld blazes bright before me.

There is a song in my mind, calling me.

Something glimmers in the grass, a metal circle set with a blue stone. A ring. It seems terribly important, so I dart down, grab it with my beak. It's *heavy*, but I don't drop it.

I flap my wings and fly with the ring into the Galdur Skjöld, a starling no bigger than the palm of my mother's hand.

The magic of the barrier doesn't touch me, doesn't even know I am there. It is thicker than I thought it would be. I am inside it for what feels like an eternity.

But then I am through and lighting on my mother's shoulder.

She strokes my tiny head with one finger and gently takes the ring from my beak.

I realize several things at once:

Even as a starling, I have only one eye; I see still half a world.

I should have given all the packs to my mother, because the ones I had with me didn't come through.

I don't know how to change myself back.

THREE YEARS AGO

BALLAST

YEAR 4198, Month of the Black Lord

The Iljaria Tunnels

A distant commotion in one of the tunnels shakes me from my sleep. I open my eyes to the familiar blear of magical torchlight, Asvaldr warm and slumbering next to me.

"Asvaldr, do you hear that?" I whisper.

He lifts his head at the sound of my voice and sends images into my mind of winged shadows, teeth and claws dripping blood.

The cave demons. But they don't normally fight among themselves—is there something else down here? Uneasiness shivers through me.

"We'd better go and check." I send Asvaldr an image of *his* teeth and claws, wielded against the demons.

The great bear gets up, stretches and shakes himself, then lumbers out of the cavern we slept in, toward the noise. I loose my sword from its sheath, grab the torch with my free hand, and follow him.

I have been living in the labyrinth of these tunnels for over a year now. In the beginning, when my mind was darkest, when I couldn't shake away the sight of Hilf's death or muffle the never-ending echoes of his screams, I thought I would stay here forever. It was more than I deserved. But no matter how I try, no matter how many demons I slay down here, I can't forget the demon who is my father. Someone has to take him off his throne and rescue the country he seems so determined to destroy. Whether it is madness or clarity, I've realized that someone is me. And the thought of my mother, left to his mercy, eats me alive. I was a coward to leave. So I'm going back now. To try to atone for my sins, and to put an end to his.

I lose sight of Asvaldr around a bend in the tunnel. The cacophony of the cave demons is louder now, and I swear I hear other human noises among the monsters' shrieks: shouts, oaths, prayers. Somewhere ahead of me, Asvaldr roars, and I break into a run.

The tunnels down here are deceiving, and Asvaldr was farther ahead than I thought.

By the time I reach him, coming into a large, echoing cavern scattered with bones, the battle is already over, all the demons slain or fleeing. Asvaldr rears on his hind legs, roaring after them, and my eyes snag on two women, huddled together among the bones and the cave demons' dark bodies.

"Peace, Asvaldr," I say to the great bear. "They have gone."

Asvaldr drops down to all fours again, sending pulses of regret into my mind: He would have liked to kill every last one of them.

I take a step toward the two women, shock radiating through me because I know them.

One is the Skaandan singer my father took from the battlefield; she is clearly unwell, her eyes glassy with fever. The other is—

The other is Brynja. My heart stutters. I haven't spoken to her in years, not since my mother discovered her visits and told me to put an end to them, because if my father found out, he'd kill Brynja without a second thought. So I lied to the only friend I'd ever had. I told her I never wanted to see her again, that she was using me, that we weren't friends, that I would drag her right to my father if she dared to come back. She didn't.

I look at her now, feeling anew the agony of that encounter. Her face is creased with pain and there is black demons' blood smeared across her cheek. The scarf she wears on her head has slid partway off, making visible the dark stubble of her hair. First Ones above, I have never seen anything more beautiful.

I take a breath and go to help her.

CHAPTER TEN

BRYNJA

Year 4201, Month of the Red Lord

Iljaria—Regla City—the palace

I try not to let the boredom or the bitterness drive me mad.

At least my mother left me with the expanded prison, the view out over the city, the six books and the Lords and Ladies game set.

Several times a day, food appears on the table she made for me, so I know I'm not wholly forgotten, but no one comes to see me.

I page through the books, which I can't figure out if my mother meant as insult or comfort or education. Perhaps all of the above. One is a detailed textbook about mind magic, another a history of Iljaria magical education. There's a book of children's stories I recognize with a jolt as having been mine as a child, a two-volume history of the First Ones, and what appears to be one of my father's journals, a slim book that is written with magic, and so indecipherable to someone currently lacking magic.

But I am too impatient to sit and read for long stretches of time.

I pace the glass prison. I stretch, like I used to do in Kallias's iron cage. I do a few flips and some handsprings. I attempt climbing up the wall like a spider.

But the glass is sheer, and there are no footholds, and no heating vents to crawl into even if there were.

I am well and truly trapped.

I play Lords and Ladies with myself, which feels boring and stupid, as I can't use my magic to make the pieces slide about by themselves. I turn it into a challenge after a few abandoned games, trying to balance my strategy equally between both sides.

The game ends in a stalemate.

I wish I had my and Ballast's deck of cards instead. Card games are easier to play solo.

I spend a lot of time standing at the window, looking out. The city is distant below me, the people smaller than ants. Still I watch their patterns, their ways of coming and going, the life and activity of this city that should feel as if it belongs to me but doesn't.

It's been four days of this madness when I turn from the window halfway through the afternoon to see Finnur lounging in one of my chairs.

He reminds me of Ballast sometimes, the way he holds himself, the lanky form of him.

I try not to miss Ballast. My efforts are in vain.

"Finally," I say to Finnur, taking the seat across from him. "What took you so long?"

"I have been ingratiating myself to Valrún," he tells me, "and settling into the palace wing that houses her Skapari."

I'm impressed. "You got her to make you a Skapari?"

He grins. "The best part is how much it irritates your brother."

I grimace. "Don't cross him, Finnur."

"Brandr likes to think he holds all the power, but he doesn't. Don't worry, Brynja."

We're quiet for a little while.

"I'm sorry I dragged you into this," I say then. "This isn't what you agreed to."

Finnur shakes his head, tapping his finger on the table and leaving little swirls of prismatic color in its wake. "Please stop apologizing. I came of my own free will, and we always knew this might be more complicated than we hoped."

"Gods, that's putting it mildly."

He eyes me. "Are you all right, Brynja?"

"Hell no. I want to get out of here."

"I think you will soon. Valrún is up to something. And I think she needs you for whatever it is."

"What do you mean?"

"She had me attend a private dinner with her. Not even Brandr was there, just me and her. She asked me a lot of questions, like if I had ever met the Prism Lady, and if I knew where the Prism Lady was, and if I'd ever heard of the Prism Stone and if I knew where *that* was."

"The Prism Stone?" I echo. "Isn't that just a story?" Supposedly the stone holds a piece of every First One's power, and anyone who bears it wields magic strong enough to break the world, or reshape it according to their will.

"Any story I ever heard about the First Ones has turned out to be true," says Finnur.

I grimace, because he's absolutely right.

"Valrún wanted to know all about my magic, too," Finnur goes on. "I showed off for her a little so she would know that making me a Skapari wasn't a mistake."

"Showed off for her how?"

Finnur shrugs. "I grew a tree out of nothing and had it pass through all four seasons. I made it bear diamonds instead of fruit. I made the whole room catch fire but not burn us. I made it snow, but the snow was sugar and formed into little cakes when it touched the table."

"Finnur!"

"She was impressed."

"Has she asked you to do anything for her?"

"Not yet. I'm with tutors most of every day, catching up on my education."

"Are they teaching you anything you don't already know how to do?"

He gives me a wry smile. "No, but I'm learning all the proper terms for things."

I snort. "That sounds about right. But you *will* be careful, Finnur, won't you?"

"I promise, Brynja."

We fall quiet again.

"I don't know if I'll be able to come see you very often," says Finnur after a little while. "I will try and get her to free you. It's just—" His mouth pinches unhappily.

"Just what?"

"I think it might be worse when she calls you down from here."

"It can't be." I take a breath, flick my eyes around the room. "It can't possibly be."

He shakes his head. "I hope you're right, Brynja."

And then he vanishes just like Adriel, and I realize he used Violet magic to get in here.

I spend the rest of the day trying to read volume one of the history of the First Ones. It's written in an extremely dry and distant style, and the author has described them all wrong. I've *seen* the Bronze Lord and the Ghost Lord, the Prism Lady and the Blue Lady. They are not how he depicts them.

He goes on and on about his theory of magic, how all power stems from the First Ones, that the Iljaria who seem to be more powerful than others have simply learned how to harness more of a particular First One's magic. He goes on to say that if there was a way to harness a First One, it would be possible to take all their magic and absorb it into oneself. This would cut off that particular thread of magic from any others who wielded that discipline.

The only unfortunate thing about this process, the author continues, *is it would most likely kill the First One subjected to it, making the Iljaria who absorbed this power, in essence, the First One. I theorize, however, that this has happened, and will continue to happen, throughout the ages, that the First Ones are not in fact immortal; they simply live until someone seizes their power and takes their place. It is reasonable to conclude, then, that this is the natural order of things, and it would of course explain the different depictions of the First Ones that have passed down through history.*

My stomach turns and I slam the book shut. Why did my mother give me this drivel? The First Ones deserve our honor, our fealty.

Not this.

It's the middle of the night when I wake to a pulsing fire globe and Adriel's solemn face leaning over me.

"The queen has summoned you," he says apologetically. "You are to come at once."

He seems to have entered my cell in the non-manipulation-of-time way, and uses a key to let both of us out onto the long stair.

He leads me down and I follow, my feet slapping against the steps, my heart jangling in my rib cage. I realize that I am horribly, horribly afraid of the queen, of what she might do to me, of what she wants from me. In Tenebris, my terrors were known: falling to my death during my routine, Kallias drawing a knife across my throat and dumping me in the Sea of Bones. But here I don't know exactly what to fear, and that almost makes it worse.

I tell myself to breathe, breathe, that whatever it is, I can bear it.

The fire globe bobs ahead of us as we descend into the palace.

At the bottom of the stair, Brandr is waiting, his mouth set into a hard line.

"I'll take her from here," he snaps at Adriel.

The Violet Skapari bows to my brother and strides away.

Brandr grabs my arm, but I shake him furiously off, and he doesn't reach for me again.

We walk through the silent halls of Valrún's palace, vines running along the floor, Brandr calling more fire globes to light our way with a flick of his hand.

"I hear Mother came to see you," he says bitterly.

I clench my jaw, angry at his bitterness. "Valrún sent her."

I don't think I imagine that my iron collar cinches tighter around my neck than it did before.

I glance over at my brother and voice the question that has been itching at the back of my mind ever since I arrived at the palace. "Where are Drengur and Gróa?" His steward and scribe were with him in Tenebris last year, and I find it odd that I haven't seen them here in Iljaria. Drengur wielded White magic and Gróa Green.

Brandr avoids my gaze, staring straight ahead as we walk on through the dark palace. I'm not at all sure he means to answer me.

"You nearly ruined me when you locked my magic away," he says at last, his words tight and hard. "When I was finally able to unlock it again, I found that all of—all of my Prism magic was gone."

"You mean the Prism magic you murdered our father for?" I snarl. "Good!"

He curses at me and shoves his hands in his pockets. "I only had Ghost magic left. But I was still the Prism Master. And when I confessed all of this to Valrún, she helped me . . . gain most of the magic back."

I stare at him in utter horror. "What exactly are you saying, Brandr?"

He grinds his jaw and doesn't reply.

"They're dead, then. Drengur and Gróa are dead. You killed them for their magic, didn't you?"

He won't look at me.

"How many Iljaria did you kill?"

He stares resolutely ahead.

"Damn it, Brandr! How many?"

"Not enough!" he says viciously. "I don't even wield *half* the power I did before you ruined my life."

I laugh in outraged shock. "You are utterly *vile*."

"*You* should have stayed away," he retorts. "This is *my* domain. You had no business coming back here, and you have no right to judge me!"

"You don't own Iljaria," I return shortly, "and you sure as hell don't own me."

"Yes, I do," he retorts. "Or I will soon."

I stop in the corridor and turn to face him. "Do you think Valrún is going to make you her king?"

His eyes go hard and a muscle jumps in his jaw.

"You *do*!" I crow. "What a fool you are."

"She loves me."

I laugh. "That's absurd."

He seizes me by the arm. "She *does*."

"She's using you, Brandr. Why else would she let you go on pretending to be Prism Master when she knows your darkest secrets?"

My brother swears at me, and the iron collar grows so tight around my neck I can only breathe in shallow gasps.

"You talk too much," he seethes.

He pulls me along by the arm and into a small room that's surprisingly plain. A sofa and two armchairs face each other, a narrow table between. An honest-to-gods real fire burns in a real stone hearth on one wall. There are no floating plants, no displays of magic.

Valrún is standing by the hearth, and she turns at our approach. She's dressed simply, if evocatively, in a thin white robe that is mostly see-through. Her hair is unbound and unadorned, and she's not even wearing a crown. For a moment she reminds me, strangely, of Gulla, Ballast's mother.

"Leave us, Brandr," Valrún orders.

"My queen, I fear you will not be safe alone with my traitorous sister."

Valrún smiles at him in an indulging manner. She crosses the room and puts a finger under his chin, trailing her other hand along his shoulder.

He shivers, and I don't miss the way he carefully doesn't look at her.

"Do you doubt my power?" she asks him, sickeningly sweet.

"N-no, my queen," he stammers. His pale cheeks flood red, and then he does look at her, his eyes sweeping her appreciatively up and down.

Her smile deepens. "I will call for you in an hour, no more."

He bows and leaves us, the door closing behind him of its own accord.

Valrún comes over to the couch and lounges on it.

She waves me into one of the facing chairs, and I sit, tense, ready to spring away at any moment.

"Release her," Valrún commands.

To my surprise, Jóvin melts out of the shadows. He bends over me, breath hot on my cheek. He touches the iron collar and unlatches it, then tugs it none too gently off me. He sets it on the table between me and the queen. I don't miss how his eyes linger on her in the same way Brandr's did, and I wonder exactly how many men Valrún has at her beck and call. My stomach twists in disgust.

But she dismisses him, too, and then we are truly alone.

I try not to wince as my magic returns to me, flooding my veins, heady as wine.

"I hear," says Valrún conversationally, "that you possess the strongest Bronze magic to have graced an Iljaria in centuries. Is that true?"

I stare her down. "My mother told you it was."

"Is it true?" she presses. "Where is your brother right now?"

"Skulking in the corridor and—" I grimace with revulsion. "Thinking about you."

"And Jóvin?"

"Sitting just outside the door waiting for you to summon him to re-collar me, cursing the day I was born and wanting his power back so badly he thinks it might kill him, and . . . also thinking about you."

"Mmm," says Valrún. She studies me across the table, and I shiver, uneasy. "What about Finnur?"

I think for a moment. "He's reading in the library. He says hello."

Her smile is thin. "I will have a room prepared for you in the guest wing. You needn't return to the spire, and I won't make you wear the collar again."

She jerks up from the couch and curses at me as she realizes the words that just came out of her mouth were not hers.

I smile grimly. "I am surprised that the queen of the Iljaria has no barriers against Bronze magic in her own mind."

"I don't need them," Valrún spits.

"Because usually you are surrounded by your Skapari," I say. "The ones who wield most of the magic because you have so little of your own."

I expect her to lunge at me. I'm in a fighting mood; I want her to.

But she doesn't. She strides over to the fireplace, stares at the flames dancing on the stones. "If I asked you to serve me as one of those Skapari, Brynja Eldingar, would you do it?" She turns her head to mine, and there is weariness etched into her eyes.

"Could I ask for something in return?" I inquire carefully.

She laughs. "That isn't how it works."

She taps one elegant brown finger against the mantelpiece. A sprout appears and unfurls tender green leaves. A flower blooms, red as poison. It wavers there in an invisible breeze, and I catch the scent of it: strong and sour.

"How far away can you sense someone's mind?" Valrún asks me.

Without meaning to, I reach for Ballast. I feel a flicker of him, but nothing strong enough for me to latch on to.

"I don't know," I say honestly.

"Your magic is drawn to other magic," she says. "It must be easier to find an Iljaria than any of the barbarians in the West."

"They're not barbarians."

She curls her lip and draws her hand along the length of the mantel. More flowers appear akin to the first, their aroma turning my stomach.

"Will you serve me, Brynja Eldingar?"

"No."

She plucks all the flowers and throws them into the fire, one by one. "If you do not, I will have you killed. I will make your mother do it."

My heart feels dark and bitter. "She wouldn't care."

"Of course she would. She has been . . . hard to control since Brandr returned with news of you. She wanted to go to Daeros and fetch you back. That was before we learned of your treachery, naturally."

"Naturally," I echo.

I am not unaffected by this information, and Valrún smirks because she can see it in my eyes.

"What is your mother doing right now?" she asks me.

I reach out for her without thinking and am disquieted to find her in my childhood home, standing at the massive arched window she pulled up from the ground herself. She's staring out at the sea. She's crying.

Mother? I whisper into her mind.

She throws her head up, twists around. But of course I'm not there. She lifts her face, and I almost feel as if she can see me, as I can see her, though her eyes look past mine.

"Well?" Valrún demands.

"She is in my father's house on the edge of the sea."

Valrún nods, satisfied. "Tell her to come back to Regla City at once. I require her services."

I reach out for my mother again. *Valrún wants you to return to the palace.*

My mother's lips thin, and turning back to the window, she slams her hand against the glass. It shatters, and blood shows bright against her pale skin. But then she blinks, and the window re-forms itself. She stalks out of the room.

I refocus on the fire and the queen and the scent of poison flowers. I realize I'm trembling. I have never before stretched my mind magic out so far, or in such a tangible way. It scares me and excites me, all at once.

Valrún eyes me, as if considering something. "Where is the Violet Lord?" she asks unexpectedly.

I reach for him, because I am suddenly eager to test the limits of my power. I'm startled to find him immediately.

I stare at the queen in utter horror. "He's bound in iron below the palace," I whisper. "Deep, deep, beneath the earth."

I can feel his grief. His agony, which is not simply at being bound but held in one place, in one time. That is what pains him. It is against his very essence, a current of wind trapped in a bottle instead of being everywhere all at once.

I think about the Yellow Lord, imprisoned in the heart of Tenebris for centuries. And now the Violet Lord here.

"Is there a First One hidden in every city the Iljaria have ever built?" I blurt.

"No," says Valrún. She sighs, like this is a personal annoyance. "Alas."

I flick my thoughts toward the Violet Lord and feel his awareness of me. He is surprised, then hopeful, and then—

I gasp at the touch of iron at my own throat. Valrún has clasped the collar around my neck again, not caring that it burns her hands.

She steps back from me, studying the welts on her fingers. "That must hurt a lot," she says, nodding at the collar. "I nearly feel sorry for you."

"What do you *want* from me?" I demand.

"Will you serve me, Brynja Eldingar?"

I try to think past the iron at my throat and the wrenching awfulness of seeing my mother cry and my grief that the Violet Lord is bound beneath my feet in utter agony.

"It seems I do not have a choice."

She smiles. "Jóvin will take you to your chamber with my other Skapari. Good night, Brynja. This has been . . . enlightening."

Jóvin steps into the room, and Valrún relays her instructions. He jerks his head at me to follow and I do, every part of me numb and reeling.

FOUR MONTHS AGO

SAGA

Year 4201, Month of the Green Goddess

Skaanda—Staltoria City

My father's council chamber feels enormous without him or my mother or Vil to fill it.

Rain pours past the open window at the back of the room, and even though I'm sitting on the end of the table the farthest from it, a cool mist blows in and touches my hot face with soft fingers. All the lamps are lit in here against the gloom; I tell myself their brightness is what makes my eyes tear.

Elíndis, the head of the royal council, sits opposite me at the long table. To either side of her are Hildar and Nývard, my father's general and the palace physician, respectively. Flanking me are Pala and Leifur. The remaining half dozen seats are empty.

"It was poison, Your Majesty," Nývard says, setting his report on the table in front of me.

I thumb through the papers, the facts of my parents' deaths staring back at me in bald black and white. It sickens me to read that my mother was found slumped over her dressing table in the act of threading an earring through her ear, with foam at her lips and vomit all down the front of her dress. My father was found in his bath, thought drowned at first, but upon closer examination declared poisoned as well.

My stomach roils, and I glance sideways at Leifur, who looks as sick as I feel.

"What has—" I take a breath. "What has been done to find my parents' murderers?"

"We're conducting inquiries," says Elíndis, "but the assassin seems to have wholly disappeared."

"What of the attendants, the guards, the cooks, everyone who comes into the palace?"

"I have interviewed each of them," says Hildar, "and found no culprit."

"The poison is not native to Skaanda," Nývard adds. "I analyzed the traces of it that were found in . . ."

He trails off.

"No need to be delicate on my account," I say, though my twisting guts tell a different story.

"In the contents of your mother's stomach, if you'll forgive me, Your Majesty."

I fight down the overwhelming urge to be sick. "Where is the poison from?"

"I cannot be entirely certain, Your Majesty, but it matches the elements of a rare poison I have encountered only once before, made from a flower that grows in the mountains of mainland Aerona."

I jerk up from my seat and slam my hands on the table. "My parents were murdered by Aeronan assassins while my brother is in Daeros negotiating peace with the Aeronans?"

"We cannot be entirely certain, Your Majesty," says Hildar again, his voice irritatingly gentle, like I'm a horse he's trying not to spook.

I circle the table, trying not to scream or cry or vomit, or—gods forbid—all of them at once.

Vil doesn't know. Vil couldn't possibly know, could he? I've had disagreements with my brother before, but he wouldn't be capable of signing our parents' death warrants, would he?

A hand closes warm about my wrist, and I glance down to see that it's Leifur's. He looks up at me with a solemnity in his eyes that somehow grounds me.

I realize that I'm trembling, gooseflesh pricking all up and down my bare arms.

"Could someone shut the window?" says Leifur, his gaze never leaving mine. "Her Majesty is cold."

An attendant goes at once to fulfill the request while Elíndis tells another attendant to bring me a robe.

Leifur lets go of my wrist and I stand in the middle of the room, feeling wholly lost.

The window is closed, the robe is brought. Someone presses a mug of steaming tea into my hands, while someone else coaxes me back into my seat.

"Your Majesty," says Elíndis gently, "you need not fear for yourself. You will be guarded day and night, your food and drink tasted before it touches your lips."

I glance at Leifur again, and his solemn face goes all blurry.

Oh gods. Oh gods, I'm *crying*. In front of all these important, official people.

"Your Majesty," says Elíndis in my ear. "Let's resume this session when you are feeling a little better."

The tears come and come, like a raging river released from its dam.

I let Elíndis coax me to my feet, let her and Leifur escort me to my room, which was shut up in my absence and so smells a little musty, feels a little stale.

Leifur searches the chamber, checking under the bed and behind the curtains and in my wardrobe. He nods at Elíndis that it's safe for me in here.

She tucks me into bed like I'm a child.

"I need to send a message to Vil," I say frantically, sitting up. "I need him to come home. We can figure all of this out together. But he can't stay in Daeros anymore, not when it's crawling with Aeronans. Treaty with Daeros be damned. I need to tell him that—"

"You've had a shock," says Elíndis, pushing me back against the pillows. "You can send a message to your brother tomorrow."

"I can't *wait* until tomorrow."

"There will be plenty of time, Your Majesty. Rest."

"I'm queen of Skaanda," I say. "You can't tell me what to do."

She smiles faintly. "Rest, Your Majesty." Then to Leifur: "Commander, you are not to leave her side."

Leifur salutes smartly as Elíndis sweeps from the room.

He's silent for a few moments, and I watch him standing by the arched doorway, strong, assured, but weary.

"I can't wait until tomorrow," I tell him.

He flicks a smile at me. "I know, Saga."

He fetches paper and ink from my writing desk, and he sits beside me on my bed as I dictate my message.

When it's done Leifur blots the paper to keep the ink from smearing, then folds it into thirds and melts wax for me to seal it with. I affix the seal, an eight-pointed star, hissing as my hand slips and touches the scalding wax.

"Saga."

He catches my burned hand in both of his, stricken at the welt that's already rising.

I meet his dark gaze and we stare at each other, caught fast in this new grief.

"You are going to be an incredible queen, Saga Stjörnu," he says softly. "You will free Skaanda from the clutches of Daeros and Aerona alike, and usher us into an age of prosperity that we have never seen."

My chin wobbles, my damn eyes filling with tears again. "But my parents are *dead*," I say. "And they shouldn't have died that way. And—and I miss my mother."

I sob on Leifur's shoulder while he holds me tight against him, his hand warm and gentle on my hair.

When I have cried myself out, he places a whisper of a kiss on my brow, then strides to the door and calls for the attendants waiting in the hall. One he gives my message to, with instructions to have it sent to Daeros by royal courier without delay. The other he sends to Nývard, to fetch cream and a bandage for my burn.

Leifur tends my hand himself, when the supplies have come, and after that he sits quietly beside me, a warm and steady presence as the shadows deepen and night comes.

Somewhere in the space between waking and sleep, I wonder if it is Leifur's steadiness that brings me such comfort, or if it is Leifur himself. But then I think of Hilf, and guilt and shame and sorrow follow me into a haze of dark dreams.

CHAPTER ELEVEN

BALLAST

Year 4201, Month of the Red Lord

Iljaria/Daeros Border—the Galdur Skjöld

I am wrenched back into my proper body with a song.

I lie gasping on the grass, staring up at spinning stars, music ringing yet in my ears. I feel bitterly, bitterly cold.

Hands grasp my shoulders. They shake me, insistent.

My eyes focus on the vague outline of my mother, and I turn and am violently sick on the ground.

Water is pressed to my lips. I drink greedily, but the cup is drawn away before I'm ready.

I'm shaking. I can't get warm.

My arms are drawn into the sleeves of a coat that's too small for me, a blanket is draped over my lap. Except for these two things, I am naked.

She shakes my shoulders again, crouches down beside me.

I hear the rasp of her voice. She's trying to talk to me.

That's what shakes me out of my stupor, brings me wholly back to myself.

"Mother," I breathe.

The light of the Galdur Skjöld flickers like fire on her face. She's angry, fighting tears, and her fingers flash in my sight line. *You stupid,*

stupid boy. You could have lost yourself! What were you thinking? I could have lost you. I could have lost you! She curses with her hands.

"I'm sorry," I say. "I'm sorry, I didn't know what else to do. I thought that's what you *meant.*"

She slaps me hard across the face, and I suck in a breath and stare at her.

Then she's weeping like her heart is broken. She has never, ever struck me before.

My father was the one who hit me.

I wrap my arms around her. "It's all right," I whisper into her ear. "It's all right. I'm here. We're both here. We're safe. It's all right."

She pulls away from me after a little while, and I don't like the look in her eyes.

"Mother."

You scared me, she spells out with her finger speech, hands shaking. *You scared me.*

"I know."

She breathes, long and slow. *That magic is forbidden,* she says, *to all but the most highly trained Skepna. And even then it can easily go wrong.*

"Thank you for saving me," I say softly.

She nods unhappily, flicking her eyes to my face.

"It doesn't hurt that much."

Liar.

I smile and wince a little.

She takes a breath. *I suppose you'll be wanting this back. Carrying it through was an even stupider risk than changing your shape.*

My heart jolts as she pulls something from her pocket and lays it in my hand: my ring, the etched metal and polished blue stone no worse for its trip through the Galdur Skjöld, thank the First Ones.

I slide it onto my finger where it belongs, biting back the press of tears. "Thank you," I tell her. "I could never have forgiven myself if I'd lost it."

She shakes her head, her expression guarded. *It's just a ring, Ballast.*

I don't correct her.

It's a shame about the other two packs. My mother offers to go back through the Galdur Skjöld and fetch them, but she spent nearly all her magic wrenching me out of starling form. It's too risky, and I tell her so.

What are you going to wear? she wants to know. *You can't go walking through Iljaria in naught but your skin.*

I dig through our remaining pack and have to admit there aren't many options. I wind up draping the blanket around me and belting it with a strap I rip from the pack.

You look ridiculous, my mother helpfully informs me.

We walk on into the remnants of the night, the sun limning above the horizon and dazzling our eyes.

I miss Asvaldr. We will be far, far slower without him.

And we have quite a few miles left to go.

Year 4201, Month of the Red Lord
Iljaria—Regla City—the Blue Sector

I compel a dog to snatch a shirt and trousers off a clothesline and bring them to me outside the prismatic glass walls of Regla City. I am a little ashamed about using my magic for thievery, but I can't show up in Iljaria's main metropolis clothed in a blanket and part of a pack strap. I'm not even sure I'd be let in.

Are you ready? asks my mother when I've donned the purloined clothing in the shelter of a little copse of trees.

The shirt and trousers are not a perfect fit, but they're a whole lot better than nothing. "Ready," I tell her.

She gives me a hard smile and links her arm through mine. We approach the gate together.

Two guards stand watch, both women. One wears a black stone on her forehead, the other a polished bronze disk. I quickly shutter my thoughts in the way that Brynja taught me, to shield against her mind magic.

"What is your business in Regla City?" asks the wielder of Black magic.

I look her square in the face, like my mother instructed me. "Visiting friends in the Blue Sector."

The wielder of Black nods. "You have secured lodging?"

"Yes," I lie.

The Bronze magic wielder's eyes go a little distant, and I get the idea that she is recording my answers in a book somewhere in the city.

"And which First Ones bless you?" the Black wielder asks.

"The Blue Lady," the Bronze wielder says, glancing at me and my mother in turn, "and the White."

"Very well," says the Black wielder.

And then, to my utter relief, they wave us through the gate, and we step into the White Sector.

I feel like I am adrift in a world of snow, though the air is warm and fragrant, and filled with music. Absolutely everything here is white, from the intricately patterned tiles beneath our feet to the buildings we pass, which are made of polished alabaster. Some of them are so tall I have to tilt my head back to see the tops, some are single story; all of them are beautiful. Most incorporate decorative archways that lead to open-aired courtyards, where my mother tells me in her finger speech that choirs of Tónlist, wielders of song magic, perform great workings of magic together. She explains that the tallest building, topped with a great white spire, is the Tónlist Conservatory—White magic wielders are trained there.

We pass shops and street booths, hung with white awnings. Fountains bubble white water in corners, trees grow white trunks and white leaves and white flowers. Almost all the other people walking in this part of the city are dressed in white, the outliers clearly on their way to or from other sectors. The only variation is in people's skin tones, which range from very pale to very dark, though all are of course crowned with white hair.

My black-and-white hair and the nonwhite clothing my mother and I are wearing garner us more than a few suspicious looks.

But my mother doesn't seem to care. She looks about her in a daze, leaning on me as she closes her eyes, drinks in the magic that is as familiar to her as breathing. I wonder if she spent a lot of time here as a girl, if she attended the Tónlist Conservatory.

A cat winds around my ankles when we are halfway between the White Sector and the Blue, where my mother has determined we will find lodging. He's a scrawny ginger thing, missing half of his right ear and his entire right eye. I pick him up and let him rub against my face, trying not to let our matching infirmities move me to tears.

The cat sends images and emotions into my mind, a little scattered, a little random, but I understand him clearly. I don't send a return message, not yet, settling the cat over my shoulders and walking on through the city. He purrs and purrs and falls asleep, and I don't know that I can ever be parted from him.

My mother taps my arm, and I glance over at her. *I think it has fleas.*

"I'll ask them to leave, then," I tell her.

She rolls her eyes.

We pass through a high arched gate decorated with a mosaic of glittering cerulean stone into the Blue Sector.

My mother holds herself tall and proud, her eyes alight with joy. It feels odd and unsettling that she is at home here, while to me everything is foreign.

The streets here are paved in blue, while the buildings are still made of alabaster. Many are tiled with blue, or painted, but not all, and I find the variance refreshing. There are as many animals as people, from giant brown bears the size of Asvaldr to brightly colored finches flitting about through the air.

The buildings are a mix of housing and shops and open market stalls, and my mother squeezes my arm with excitement to point out the oblong blue structure that skewers the sky near the central hub of the city. *That is the Skepna Conservatory,* she tells me, *the school for wielders of Blue magic.*

I eye the place uneasily.

It's where you would have gone, she says, *if . . .*

She doesn't finish her thought. If we could have escaped my father earlier, she means. If she had stolen away with me in the night and brought me home.

I understand now why she didn't. But it is strange to think about the life I might have had. The life she is trying to offer me now. I wanted that life, once. Or I thought I did.

We slip into a street where a building with a blue door advertises *Lodging* in the window. I look to my mother for confirmation, and she nods; this place should do. Thank the Blue Lady, our pouch of coins was in the pack my mother brought through the Galdur Skjöld, so we're not complete paupers.

We step into the building, and I hail the woman who stands at a tall desk with a hound at her feet. She's young, her white hair bound in two braids, the gem on her forehead an unsurprising blue.

"We're here for lodging," I say.

She looks at me with blatant curiosity, and I watch her catalog my features, from my empty eye socket to the odd black-and-white mixture of my hair. The cat around my neck, though, seems to assure her that I am not a threat.

"Will it be one room or two, Mr. . . . ?"

"Heron," I tell her, using my middle name instead of my father's surname. I don't want anything of his, especially not that. "And one room is fine, thank you."

She grabs a book off the shelf behind her, and laying it on the desk, she pages through until she finds what she's looking for. She taps it with one finger. "Room 302. That will be forty drekar, twelve eyri a week."

I blink at her, feeling inordinately stupid. Turns out we are paupers, after all. Why in the Green Lady's name did I assume the Iljaria would accept Daerosian coin? It hadn't even occurred to me.

But to my surprise my mother opens our money pouch and counts out the proper amount of Iljaria currency on the desk.

Our new landlord swipes the coins into her hand and gives my mother a key, gesturing over her shoulder at the stairway behind her.

My mother leads the way, up to the third floor and room 302, the second door on the left. She has to jiggle the key a bit before it turns, but it does eventually, and then we step into our new . . . *home* is a bit of a stretch. Temporary living quarters, perhaps.

It's bleaker than the room above the bakery in Garran City, but at least it's clean. I see a window that looks out toward the palace, two narrow beds on opposite walls, a small chest of drawers, and a curtained doorway that, upon investigation, leads to a lavatory.

My mother looks about, drinking in our surroundings, and nodding like she's perfectly satisfied.

"What now?" I ask her. "And where the hell did you get Iljaria coins?"

Don't swear, she reprimands me. *I went to the money changer in Garran City before you came to fetch me. And right now we are going to go find a hot meal.*

I flick my eye through the window.

Her hand on my arm makes me look at her again. *Patience, Ballast,* she says. *All in good time.*

I just wish I believed her.

TEN MONTHS AGO

BALLAST

YEAR 4200, Month of the Black Lord

Daeros—Tenebris

Waking is agony. Sleeping is worse. Every night I relive the horror of my father taking my eye, the searing, shattering pain, half the world going suddenly dark, the sensation of my body being ripped apart by my own feral screaming.

But today my father doesn't let me hide in my bedchamber. He comes to see me in the late afternoon, barging through the door that connects my room to his. I rear my head up at his arrival, scrambling off the windowsill where I've been sitting, staring out into the never-ending darkness. I bow low before him, failing to keep myself from shaking.

He smiles his slick, satisfied smile, and steps up to me, grabbing my face with one hand and ripping the bandage off my empty eye socket with the other. I wince and ball my hands into fists, telling myself to be still, be still. I know he senses my unadulterated terror; I know it pleases him. I stand there and let him examine the wound, my heart slamming so hard inside my chest I am surprised it doesn't shatter all to pieces.

He nods and lets go of my chin. "Clean yourself up, Ballast. You will come to dinner tonight and court the Aeronan ambassadors."

I fight to breathe. "Father, I am not well enough—"

"You're well enough," he snaps at me. "Stop wallowing. Or do you not mean the things you swore to me when you came slinking back?"

"I meant them," I say fiercely. "I am loyal to you, Father. Always."

"Then you will come to dinner tonight."

I bow again. "Yes, Father."

He gives another nod and sweeps out the way he came.

He hasn't allowed me much time to get ready, as I'm sure was his intention. I bathe and dress in the silk and fur robes the attendants bring me. I put jewels in my ears and slide rings onto my fingers. I stare into the mirror at the horror of my missing eye. The palace physician gave me a box of silk patches, with ribbons in various colors to secure them with. I hate them, but I hate the raw, red empty socket more. I tie on one of the patches, adjust it to cover as much as I can.

I take a draught the physician made me to dull the pain.

Then my father steps back through the door. "Come, Ballast," he says, as if I am a hound.

Like a hound, I obey him.

The distance between my room and the dining hall has never felt so vast. My father doesn't say a word the whole way there. Outwardly, I am calm. Inwardly, I am an inferno.

We step into the dining hall, every seat around the long table occupied except for the two empty ones awaiting me and my father. The diners turn at our approach, and I hold myself stiffly, bracing for their whispers.

A woman sits to the left of my father's chair, dressed in violet, strands of gold adorning her short, dark curls.

A woman who shouldn't be here.

Why the hell is she here?

She's staring at me in bald shock, and I can't help but stare back at her. My gut twists in shame that she should see me like this.

It's Brynja.

CHAPTER TWELVE

BRYNJA

Year 4201, Month of the Red Lord

Iljaria—Regla City—the palace

The queen's Skapari live on a level of the palace that is laid out, yet again, like a wheel, the central round gathering room the hub, doors around the circumference leading to sleeping and bathing and dining chambers, a library, and what Salin refers to vaguely as a "training room."

There are no individual bedchambers. After Valrún's dismissal last night, Jóvin shoved me unceremoniously into the dormitory that all the female Skapari share. My aunt Dagfinna snapped a fire globe into existence with her Red magic so I could find my way to the empty top bunk at the back of the room. But she didn't speak to me, wouldn't look at me.

In addition to my aunt and Salin—the wielder of Black magic who came in the coach with me from Strönd City—the women's dormitory is occupied by Malen Ildjárn, who is twenty and wields Green magic, and Osa Hjaltalín, who just reached the end of her second century and wields Gray magic.

Malen has pale skin and light eyes, and her straight white hair is cropped to her chin. She's a cousin on my mother's side, though if I ever met her during my childhood, I don't remember.

Osa is head and shoulders taller than me, her skin a medium brown, her white hair bound in hundreds of long, narrow braids that skim the tops of her ankles.

It's Malen who wakes me from a fitful sleep and tells me it's time for breakfast.

I follow her blearily from the dormitory to the dining room, where a round table is centered beneath a dazzling chandelier filled with Prism magic; the chamber is a haze of rainbow light.

I sit between Malen and Salin, the collar heavy and itchy at my throat, a headache pounding in my temples. Aunt Dagfinna and Osa are on the other side of Malen. I am somehow surprised when the men file in: Jóvin and Adriel and Finnur. After they take their seats, there are still four empty ones.

There are eight of us here, representing Bronze, Prism, Violet, Black, Red, Green, Gray, and Yellow magic. Valrún needs only White, Blue, Ghost, and Brown to fill her twelve. My mother wields Brown magic, though, and my brother—for all he keeps it secret—Ghost. So Valrún is really only missing two.

It's strange, eating with so many people after my stint alone in the glass prison. The Skapari are easy in each other's company, alternatively teasing or arguing with one another, and casually using their magic to accomplish simple tasks. Malen grows some basil for Dagfinna's eggs and sausages. Dagfinna reheats Adriel's coffee. Adriel blinks back in time to stop Osa from accidentally knocking her own coffee mug off the table.

Finnur gets in on the fun, amusing himself by completely changing his breakfast from eggs and sausages to ham steak and steamed honey buns, then exercising time magic to keep Adriel from catching Osa's mug and letting it shatter all over the floor. Or, at least, I think that's what happens. Finnur and Adriel take turns going slightly fuzzy at the edges, and I know they are engaged in a merry battle over the mug.

Osa, possessing Gray magic, uses her power only once, blinking at a fly that's buzzing around her plate. It falls dead to the table.

Malen gasps in horror, resurrects the tiny creature with her Green magic, and then asks Finnur to compel the thing out a window.

Jóvin spends the entire time glaring at me, hardly touching his food. I wonder what he's even still doing here, with no magic anymore to wield for the queen. Or perhaps, with the way he was looking at Valrún last night, he stays because of her.

All in all, it's a very lively breakfast.

Afterward, the Skapari disperse. Dagfinna and Salin go to attend Valrún—I understand the women take this in turns—Malen to walk the palace and work her Green magic where the queen instructs. Osa says she will visit the bathing chamber. Finnur informs me he's to attend more training. Jóvin stalks off without a word.

This leaves Adriel, who acknowledges me with a nod as he leaves the dining hall.

I follow him to the library, watching as he selects a few volumes off the curved shelves in the partial circle of the room, and settles with them in a red armchair under a window.

"Did you need something, Brynja?" he asks me without looking up. He turns a page of his book.

"Did you know that the Violet Lord is bound beneath the palace?"

He raises his face to mine, his dark eyes sharp. "Yes." He returns his gaze to his book, turns another page.

I stand there gnawing on my lip. "Adriel, *why* is the Violet Lord bound beneath the palace?"

He turns yet another page, and I notice his edges have gone fuzzy—is he using his time magic so he can read that damn book while also condescending to talk to me?

He's suddenly standing next to me when I never saw him move; the outline of him in the chair is still visible. I realize he doesn't care to have anyone overhear this conversation.

"Valrún is collecting First Ones."

I go very cold. "Collecting First Ones? Why?"

He flicks his eyes toward me as he steps away from the chair, slipping between two overstuffed bookshelves, out of sight from the main door.

"Grab a book off the shelf," he instructs me. "Flip through it."

I do as I'm told, trying to think around the pounding of my heart.

"I don't know why."

I keep my eyes on the book. "How many does she . . . have?"

"Just the Violet Lord. And the Yellow Lord, or so she thought. She sent Brandr to collect him and she was . . . displeased when he came back without him."

I stare at the book, scrambling to rearrange my mental deck of cards in light of this new information.

"The Violet Lord was my fault," he says heavily. "I was beyond proud to be selected as one of the queen's Skapari—she only chooses the most powerful wielders of each particular discipline, and throughout her reign was never in a hurry to fill all twelve places. I knew I was powerful. I was top in my class in the Ári Conservatory. I even dreamed of the Violet Lord a few times."

"What did you dream?" I whisper. My hands tremble.

"That he was speaking to me, that he called me backward in time to see the world formed, and forward to see its ending. I arrogantly assumed it meant I was special."

"I think you are," I tell him. "I don't think they were dreams."

For a moment he doesn't answer, and I worry he's ceased using his time magic and gone back to himself in the chair again. But glancing aside, I see he's still there, anguish pressed into his face.

"Valrún interviewed me after I had offhandedly told an instructor about my dreams. She selected me as a Skapari before I even finished my training at the conservatory. I came to live here. She asked me all kinds of questions about my dreams, asked me to describe the landscape where I'd seen the Violet Lord, asked me if I thought I might be able to jump about in time and find him."

"You did," I said.

"Yes. Five years ago, now."

I don't want to know, but I need to, all the same. "How—"

"How was the Violet Lord bound?"

I nod.

Adriel shrugs, not meeting my glance. "I betrayed him."

"Why?"

His eyes go shiny with moisture. "Because Valrún asked me to."

Then Adriel's gone, and I'm alone among the bookshelves. I go back to his reading chair, but he's not there, either. I know I will get no more answers from him today.

"Finnur!" I hiss, peering through the doorway of the men's dormitory. "Finnur!"

He seizes my arm faster than I thought possible, and we creep out into the hub room, then through another door into the dark and empty bathing chamber.

Finnur snaps a small globe of Prism magic into existence, and we go together to the back corner of the room, away from the large circular pool of magically heated water. There are cupboards stacked with towels and soaps and lotions here, and stools for sitting on after stepping out of the bath.

Finnur and I perch on two of the stools, the Prism globe bobbing between us, casting multicolored shadows on his dark skin.

"We're not safe in here, you know," he says. "Adriel has memory devices in every one of these rooms. Everything we say can and will be reported to Valrún."

I lift my hands and use the finger speech that Gulla taught to all the children in Kallias's Collection: *I am not certain Adriel is wholly loyal to Valrún.*

Finnur squints at my fingers and replies the same way: *We still can't risk it. What was so important that you needed to drag me out of bed in the middle of the night?*

The Violet Lord is bound beneath the palace.

Finnur grimaces. *I know. I can feel him.*

Adriel says that Valrún is collecting First Ones. We need to know why.

Finnur jiggles his knee and won't quite look at me.

What's wrong?

I poke him and ask again.

Valrún is pressing me to find the Prism Lady.

Finnur, you can't do that.

The Prism Lady is more powerful than Valrún. Any one of us alone is more powerful than Valrún.

I sigh. *I don't like it.*

Neither do I, but we're stuck here, at present. We don't have a lot of choices.

I rub at my neck above the collar. *Can you get this off me?*

His eyes dart to the door of the bathing chamber, then back to me. *She would know, Brynja.*

Can't you make a magical key or something? So I can take it on and off myself?

He nods and, concentrating for a moment, pulls a glimmering prismatic shard out of the air. He presses it into my palm.

It should work, he says with his fingers, *but I wouldn't risk it here.*

I shove the Prism key into my pocket. *Thank you.*

Finnur stands from the stool then, and I do, too, grabbing him by the arm.

"Go back to bed, Brynja," he says aloud. "I don't think your second day as a Skapari will be as easy as your first."

But I squeeze his arm until he looks at me, and I ask one last question with my fingers: *Have you heard from him?*

His mouth goes tight. *Not here, Brynja.*

But my heart is beating triple time, and I find I cannot last a single moment more without knowing. *Have you heard from Ballast?*

Finnur gives me one sharp nod. *He's in the city.*

"He's here?" I blurt, heart racing. "In Regla City?"

Finnur doesn't answer, striding past me out of the bathing chamber, the prismatic globe bobbing along in his wake.

I follow him into the central room, desperate for more information.

Finnur pauses, glances back. *He's safe,* he tells me with his fingers. *Don't worry, Brynja.*

And then he returns to the men's dormitory, and I go numbly back to the women's, stumbling as I climb into my bunk. I use the key and pull the collar from my neck.

For the first time since I left Daeros, I sleep easily.

He's in the city.

I dream of him.

TWO MONTHS AGO

VIL

Year 4201, Month of the Prism Goddess

Daeros—Tenebris

The storeroom is freezing, but I chose it on purpose. No heating vent means less of a chance of her damn listening ears. She has seemed much involved with the one-eyed bastard, lately, but I can't take any chances. Not with this.

"Is there nowhere warmer we could meet?" says Junius irritably, tugging his fur-lined robe tighter about his shoulders. Sometimes—and this is one of those times—he doesn't seem exactly *imperial*, and it almost amuses me that I have to bow and scrape to him if I want my share of the power. Almost.

Hell, though. I'm cold, too. The mountain is always cold, even in summer.

But I don't have the time or the patience to prevaricate. "My parents were murdered, and my sister seems to think it was Aeronan assassins who killed them."

Junius barely reacts to this, a little muscle twitching in his forehead.

I have hardly absorbed Saga's message myself, though I've read it so many times since it arrived this morning I could easily quote it, word for word. When I first read it, I wanted to storm into Junius's chamber and take his head off. Subsequent readings cooled my temper enough to allow me to think it through. Saga's feelings, accusations, and orders were perfectly clear in her letter. But it was hard for me to learn of my parents' deaths and my sister's coronation in the same paragraph. Her commands make me balk: *Sign no treaty with Aerona. Come home at once.*

I want Junius to give me a reason to dismiss them. I *need* him to.

I don't want to think about my parents being dead or my sister sitting on the throne of Skaanda. I certainly don't want to go home. I want to stay in Daeros, help Junius make it a province of Aerona and drive the devil spawn of Kallias from the mountain; I want to be named viceroy, and be given the power that Junius has promised me.

But I relay to him the contents of Saga's message, and he barely reacts.

"Did you murder my parents?" I ask him coldly, when several long moments have passed and he still has yet to give me any reply.

The emperor of Aerona leans against the stone wall of the storeroom. A cobweb catches in his dark hair. "I didn't murder your parents, Vilhjalmur."

"My sister says the poison that killed them could only have been obtained in Aerona."

Junius's brows arch up. "How, exactly, would she know that?"

I shrug, caught between irritation at Junius for questioning Saga's theories and relief that they might be unfounded, that I won't feel honor bound to turn my back on everything I've been working so hard for. "Physician's report, she says."

"Hardly reliable. If you ask me, your sister is scared. Skaanda has depended on this ongoing war with Daeros to keep its people patriotic and inspired. Now that a peace treaty has been signed, and an alliance with Aerona is looking more and more likely, she is scrambling to keep her country independent. She doesn't want you to trust me. She wants you to go running back to Skaanda and bow and scrape to her. She will never rid herself of the insecurity of being chosen as Skaanda's heir, despite being the younger sibling. She's scared of *you*, Vilhjalmur, and she's scrambling to keep you under her heel. Because what is to stop you from returning to Skaanda with the claim that the First Ones have changed their minds, rejected your sister as ruler, chosen you? You Skaandans are so superstitious, it wouldn't be hard to make them believe that."

I clench and unclench my jaw. "You think she lied about my parents' deaths?"

Junius glances at me, and I can sense he's being careful here, like he's not sure how far I will let him manipulate me. "No. I think it likely that they are indeed gone, and you have my condolences. But what would stop her from having them killed herself, and pinning the crime on Aerona to make you come running home?"

Anger boils in my chest. I step toward the emperor, barely restraining myself from grabbing him by the collar and pinning him against the wall. "My sister is not a murderer."

Junius raises his hands in surrender and gives a forced laugh. "I mean no offense. But your sister *is* shrewd. Could you not see her using their deaths, however they came about, to her own advantage?"

I gnaw at his words, trying to find the meat of them, or ascertain if they are merely all gristle and bone.

"Yes," I admit finally. "I could see that."

His lips twist in a smile. "This leaves you with a choice, Vilhjalmur: to trust Saga, or to trust me."

"And what if I trust neither one of you?"

"Then you would prove yourself wise. But I would hate to have you in opposition to me now."

I don't know what to say to this. I feel all jumbled up. I'm not a fool—I know very well that Junius is using me for his own ends. But then I am using him for mine. Sometimes it's hard to assess whose ends we're actually striving for, and if they're even in conflict with each other.

"I mean everything I've said to you," says Junius, "everything I've promised. I only hope you can say the same."

I shift my weight from my left foot to my right.

"Can I count on you, Vilhjalmur?"

For a long moment we stare at each other.

"Everything you want is nearly in your grasp," says Junius quietly. "Are you really going to throw it all away on the strength of your little sister's hysteria?"

I should tell him not to disparage Saga, to show some respect to the new queen of Skaanda. But I don't.

I take a breath. "No," I answer. "I'm not going to throw it all away."

Junius nods, satisfied. "I am glad to hear it. Because tomorrow I am going to call an audience with the new little king of Daeros and demand he relinquish his throne or face execution."

I grind my jaw.

"Either way," the emperor continues, "the result will be the same. Viceroy."

He sticks out his hand, and we shake on it.

As we're slipping out of the storeroom, I hear a faint noise, the barest scrape of cloth against stone.

There's a heating vent in the ceiling that I swear on the Black God's bowels wasn't there before.

Damn, damn, damn.

She was listening.

CHAPTER THIRTEEN

BALLAST

Year 4201, Month of the Red Lord

Iljaria—Regla City—the Blue Sector

I really don't want to send the cat back to the palace with a message for Finnur. I've named him Hjarta, and he slept on top of me all night, and how can I not love a fellow creature missing an eye?

Send him, my mother tells me firmly. *He'll come back.*

She slips into the lavatory to change out of her sleeping shift and comes back wearing a white gown I've never seen before and didn't know she owned. She cinches it at the waist with a white leather breastplate and fastens a white gem on her brow. She wears a headdress to hold her tightly curled white hair back from her face.

It seems she was quite busy those few weeks she spent alone in Garran City.

"You look very Iljaria today," I tell her quietly.

She tilts her head to one side. *Ballast. That's what I am. That's what you are, too.*

"But I'm not. Not wholly."

None of that, boy. Now come here.

I obey her, let her bind a blue gem onto my own forehead. It feels heavy and cold.

"Where are you going today?" I ask her then, as she stoops to lace up her shoes.

She looks up at me. *Out,* she says vaguely.

"Why can't I come with you?"

Because you will be busy at the conservatory.

I grimace.

She finishes with her shoes and comes over to where I'm sitting on my bed, stroking a purring Hjarta. She puts her hands on either side of my face, her eyes going hard as she traces the curve of my empty socket.

You are going to be magnificent, she says. *Learn well. And send that cat to the palace!*

She kisses my brow, just above the gem, and then she turns and slips from the room.

By the time I go after her, Hjarta winding himself about my legs, she's already gone, lost somewhere in the sprawling streets of Regla City.

I sigh and crouch down to pet Hjarta. "You had better come back. You're more than a messenger cat, do you hear?"

Hjarta butts his head against my knee in clear assent. I flick images into his mind for Finnur and then watch regretfully as the cat trots off toward the palace.

My mother urges patience, but mine is quickly running thin.

I really don't want to be here, so I'm annoyed when I find it interesting.

Past the door of the Skepna Conservatory is a *forest.* Yes, a forest. Birds twitter from the tops of trees, rabbits scamper about, and I'm pretty sure I see a leopard peering at me from the underbrush.

The light has an eerie red tinge to it, like they ran out of Yellow magic light globes and had to resort to fire ones instead.

I'm so bewildered and disoriented that at first I don't notice the teenage girl lounging against a rock with her nose in a book, a deer curled up next to her.

"What do you want?" asks the girl without lowering the book.

I jump a little and walk up to her, fishing a piece of paper from my pocket and holding it out toward her. "Uh, I'm supposed to attend a class in here?"

She lowers the book and squints at the paper, then squints at me. Her skin is nearly as pale as Brynja's, though without the mesmerizing constellation of freckles, and her straight white hair pools all around her like water—it must be twice again the length of her.

"Who are you, exactly?" she asks.

"Ballast Heron."

"Is that supposed to mean anything to me? You look a little old for a twelfth-level class."

"My family is from the southern coast," I say, offering the lie my mother created for me. "They only just got around to sending me to Regla City for schooling. You know how southerners are."

She frowns. Apparently she doesn't.

"What is your heritage?" she wants to know.

My blank look causes her to roll her eyes in utter exasperation. "What magic is in your father's line, your mother's?"

Memory wrenches me backward, my father scraping the blue tattoos off my arm with a knife, trying to cut all traces of my Iljaria heritage out of me. I screamed and screamed, and I still don't know if it was because of the pain or the sight of my own blood, running down my arms and pooling on the floor.

"My father didn't have any magic," I say. "My mother has White."

She peers at me intently for a moment, then nods. "That explains the hair, though not the eye."

My gut clenches—I don't know how to respond to that, but thankfully she doesn't seem to expect me to.

She grabs another book and a pen from somewhere behind her, and jots down my answers. "Do you have the fee?"

I pull it out of my other pocket and hand it over.

"Right," she says, counting it out and then putting it in her own pocket. "Take two rights and then a left, and go down into the desert arena. Hurry, though, you're late."

I just stand there.

She sighs. "Anda will show you."

The deer beside her lifts her head and stands up, then walks off into the forest. I follow.

If there are any kind of actual paths here, I can't see them. Or maybe it's just that I'm distracted by the pulsing presence of so many animals. There are hundreds upon hundreds of creatures in here—it's overwhelming.

Anda leads me faithfully to a little pocket of desert, where three rows of plank benches face a tall Iljaria man who has vipers hanging off him, docile as kittens.

Six students occupy the benches, two per row, and they all swivel their heads to look back at me as I approach.

Not a one of them is over the age of ten.

The man with the vipers—clearly the instructor—looks intently at Anda for a moment, then nods and waves for the deer to trot away.

"Ballast, is it?" he says to me. "Have a seat. You're late."

I sit in the back row, a little Iljaria girl staring at me with wide eyes as she scoots over to make room.

After five minutes of listening to the instructor talk about the proper terms and techniques of animal magic, I realize I don't know half as much as I thought I did. After ten minutes, I begin to fear I don't know anything at all.

When he's finished with his introductory speech, the instructor, Rúrik, calls each student up to the front and asks them to manipulate the vipers.

I relax at this, though I have to fight not to be drawn back to my childhood, my father, a throne of writhing snakes.

None of the students have any trouble with the vipers. They are all able to do exactly what Rúrik asks of them. When it's her turn, my little seatmate smiles as one of the serpents coils up her body and winds about her hair, looking for all the world as if it means to choke her. But she compels the viper back onto Rúrik's shoulders and resumes her place on the bench.

Then Rúrik looks at me. "Ballast," he says.

I stride to the front of the class, feeling anxious and foolish and small, though when I reach Rúrik, I find I am several inches taller than him.

"I want you to use the first technique," Rúrik tells me.

I have no idea what the first technique is, but I'm not fool enough to tell him that. I snap my will toward the vipers, ask them to come, one by one, and wind about my legs and my torso, hang about my neck, crown my head. I hate the scaly muscle of them, the squeeze of their movement, and their cursed flicking tongues.

I stand there, clothed in snakes, and am rewarded with a near-deafening silence.

"First. Technique," seethes Rúrik. He rips the vipers off me with his hands, and they hiss in anger. "Go back to your seat."

I obey, resuming my place on the bench.

The little girl beckons me to bend close to her, and when I do, she whispers: "First technique is reaching out to the animal, understanding its will. He didn't want you to control them. Have you never been to any classes at *all*?"

I grimace, wishing it were possible for an adult to turn invisible in a class full of ten-year-olds.

The day doesn't improve much from there. After Rúrik's class I troop with the other students to the bank of a river, where more benches are waiting and our instructor, a short, dark-skinned woman whose age is impossible to guess, explains that different animals have different levels of comprehension and power of will. Fish, for example, are easier to compel than a lion, if less challenging and, ultimately, less rewarding.

The instructor calls us up one by one to make a fish jump out of the river. She's furious with me when I make seven of them jump out, twisting like acrobats in the air before sliding beneath the surface of the water again.

"You really need to stop showing off," says the little girl from the first class, who tells me her name is Geirfinna and has evidently made it her mission to keep me from embarrassing myself any further. She has medium-brown skin, like mine, and keeps her white hair bound in two puffs on either side of her head.

The next two classes are near the front of the conservatory, where desks are set up in a semicircle among the trees. Two Iljaria trade off lecturing about Blue magic, and I'm kept busy scribbling down terms I've never heard of while Geirfinna just listens and nods along.

Blue Lady, this is exhausting, and I am pretty sure I hate it.

We have lunch back in the desert arena, or at least the others do. I had no idea I was supposed to bring one. Geirfinna offers me half of hers, which I adamantly refuse.

"You're hungry, though," she says stubbornly. "All the birds are chattering about it. You ought to watch what sort of thoughts you send out at them."

Chastened, I humbly accept a piece of her ham and gravy pie.

By the end of the last class—another with Rúrik, who glowers at me the entire time—I am thoroughly exhausted. Geirfinna bids me a cheery farewell, and I trail along behind her and the others as they expertly make their way through the maze of forest toward the front door.

I am momentarily distracted by the fleeting thought of an animal that snags on me like a burr. I follow the spark of it, away from the door and farther into the forest. I wonder how many Iljaria wielding Green magic it took to make this place, and what kind of Prism or time magic was used to house it all within the conservatory's narrow exterior.

I glimpse a flash of blue through the trees, and I walk faster, determined to discover what it is.

I'm surprised when I step into a clearing and find myself at the door of a little stone cottage, bluebirds nesting in the eaves and a white fox peering at me from around the corner. But I don't think it was the bluebirds I saw in the forest.

I step up to the cottage door and knock, because that seems the thing I ought to do.

A woman opens the door, and the sight of her momentarily robs me of breath.

It's not merely because she is beautiful—though she is—but her presence is somehow larger, more real than other people's. That doesn't make sense. One person can't be more real than another.

But she is.

She's tall, with dark skin and light eyes, her white hair braided with blue and green and violet ribbons. Her gown is blue, and I know that's what I saw among the trees. Her feet are bare. She wears no gem on her brow. There's a hedgehog on her shoulder.

"Ballast," she says, smiling. "Come in."

CHAPTER FOURTEEN

BRYNJA

Year 4201, Month of the Red Lord

A Dreaming Place

Dream magic is tricky, and I am out of practice.

It takes a while to find him.

I pass through a forest, I climb over a mountain, I walk beside a sea made of glittering stars.

There is a pavilion on the shore some ways ahead of me, made of elaborate white arches open to a sky that shimmers with color. Joy sears down to my bones, because I know in that way of dreaming that he is waiting for me there.

I sprint across the sand and leap up the several shallow steps to the pavilion.

He stands with his back to me, his form tall and strong, a wine cup in one hand. Swirls of colored light catch in his black-and-white hair, gilding his skin in prismatic shadows.

He sets the wine cup down on the rail and turns to face me.

"Brynja," he breathes.

"Ballast," I whisper.

And then he's folding me in his arms and pulling me tight against him. In this dreaming place, he smells of wine and cedar, and I drink him in greedily.

There is a low divan on one end of the pavilion, draped with silk and strewn with pillows. We sink onto it, facing each other, mere whispers of breath between us.

He caresses my face with his warm hands, and I lean into him, tears slipping down my cheeks.

"I've missed you, Bal," I tell him. "I've missed you so much."

His remaining blue eye brims with moisture. Gently, gently, I brush a finger along the ridge of his missing one. He shivers, his breath catching.

"I've missed you, too, Brynja. I've been so worried about you."

"I couldn't reach you before," I tell him. "Evidently, dream magic doesn't work on the sea, and Valrún has kept me collared in iron."

He curses. "I'll kill her."

I shake my head. "This is bigger than me. Bigger than all of us. Valrún is collecting First Ones. The Violet Lord himself is bound beneath the palace."

"Collecting First Ones?" His brows bend together. "I don't like that, Brynja."

"Neither do I. You were right, Bal. I shouldn't have gambled everything on the Iljaria. I've been a fool, and you were right, and I'm so very sorry."

He presses a single kiss against my lips, making my body spark with awareness, wanting more.

"You have nothing to be sorry for," he says seriously.

A fragrant wind stirs through the pavilion, and I remember that dreams cannot last forever. Already this one is slipping away. Panic bubbles up inside me. I don't want to let him go.

"Finnur says you're in Regla City," I say urgently. "Why?"

He smiles, and I am mesmerized by his mouth, by the radiating heat of him. "I came to get you, obviously."

I choke on a laugh. "It wasn't supposed to happen like this."

"My dear little mastermind," he murmurs, "not even you can predict every outcome."

And then he tugs me against him and kisses me with a reckless passion, his hands tangled warm and wild in my hair.

Year 4201, Month of the Red Lord
Iljaria—Regla City—the Palace

I wake with a start, my magic an insistent, warning pulse in my mind.

I hear the voices, or maybe I sense the thoughts, but I am in time to lock the iron collar around my neck again and feign that I am still asleep when someone shakes my shoulder.

I look into the grim face of my mother. "Get dressed," she commands. "We are to wait on the queen this morning."

My mother is dressed already in a flowing gown the color of dark earth, cinched with a leather breastplate. My uniform is similar to hers, though both my gown and breastplate are bronze, the dress glimmering with metallic thread, the breastplate hammered, unyielding metal.

She doesn't speak a word to me as we leave the Skapari quarters and head toward the royal rooms. She doesn't even look at me.

I am still heady with the sensations of kissing Ballast, not quite able to convince myself it wasn't real. So right now I don't exactly give a damn about my mother.

I have never been formally instructed in Bronze magic. Part of me had hoped, when I got to Iljaria, that someone would mentor me, fill in the gaps in my knowledge. I especially want to be trained in dream magic, which I discovered by accident five months ago. Little chance of that now.

"Don't cross her, Brynja," says my mother in an undertone just before we step into Valrún's private dressing chamber.

The queen of Iljaria sits on a stool before an ordinary-looking vanity, clothed in a completely see-through shift, and nothing else.

Brandr lounges on the window seat nearby. He's wearing only his trousers, the laces tied in obvious haste, the prismatic tattoos that cover his arms and torso on full display. His ears turn bright red at the sight of our mother and me, but he's regrettably not embarrassed enough to get the hell out of the room.

"I will wear the green-and-yellow gown today," Valrún says. "The one with suns stitched onto it."

My mother nods me in the direction of the wardrobe on one end of the room, vines twining up the wood. I go over and open it, riffling through the gowns until I find the one the queen has asked for. It's immensely heavy, with layer upon layer of skirts, the suns stitched in what appears to be real gold thread.

The two of us dress the queen while Brandr looks indolently on. I want to grab him by the shoulders and shake him.

The gown is complicated, with countless hooks and laces and buttons, but at last it's on, and the queen looks in the mirror and nods in satisfaction.

"Put a shirt on," she commands Brandr.

And then she sweeps from the room, and my mother and I follow on her heels with Brandr coming behind, frantically buttoning his shirt.

We're joined by the other Skapari as we reach the throne room and mount the twelve steps up to the dais.

Valrún sits on her throne; the rest of us stand.

Everything becomes clear when petitioners flood into the room, stepping over the crawling vines and lining up before the dais.

Valrún calls them one by one.

Each petitioner climbs exactly six steps, then stops and bows before her and presents their request.

The first is a petty accusation of theft from the Regla City warden; he claims that one of the Skapari who stands nightly watch at the main gate has been stealing wine out of his cellar using Violet magic. (Adriel smirks at this, but even if the accusation is true, it feels rather beneath an illustrious Iljaria to present it before the queen and her entire court.)

A herder from the central plains of Iljaria asks for a team of Blue Skapari to come and help control the flocks and herds on shared grazing ground, as well as provide protection from increasing numbers of wolves.

There's a group of Regla City shop owners petitioning to have Red Skapari sent throughout the entire city to replace all the light globes filled with dying Yellow magic with ones filled with fire.

I am interested despite myself. Kallias did not rule this way in Daeros; he delegated it all to his governors. Ballast was attempting this level of involvement when he was king, but Junius and Vil ruined all of that.

Osa, Valrún's Gray Skapari and the oldest of anyone present, acts as her recorder during the petitions, and writes everything down by hand. She then confers with Valrún, who instructs certain of her Skapari to either go and deal with the requests or delegate them to others.

I learn that there is a host of lower-level Skapari who live in barracks just outside the palace. These are the queen's workforce, and they take orders from her personal Skapari.

By the end of an hour, everyone standing on the dais has been dismissed to do the queen's bidding excepting myself, Brandr, and Jóvin. Even my mother and Finnur have been sent off to deal with the many requests. Most of the petitioners have filed out of the hall.

But Valrún makes no move to get up, and so I stand there, uneasy, my foot starting to fall asleep.

I know we must be waiting for something, but I am still taken aback when more than a hundred people flood into the room, every single one of them wearing a yellow gem on their forehead.

I tense, and Jóvin smiles, and Brandr puts one hand possessively on the back of Valrún's throne.

The mass of former Yellow-wielding Iljaria crowd halfway up the dais steps. Jóvin strides down to meet them, turning to face the queen as their leader and spokesperson.

"Your Majesty," says Jóvin, "we humbly petition you to restore our light magic. We are cast out of our jobs, our homes. The Iljaria have no place for the powerless. We beg you, on the strength of our long and faithful service to you, to restore our magic, or, if it is possible, to bestow upon us another form of magic." He smiles at her, his eyes traveling all up and down her body, solidifying my impression that they are—or have been—intimately connected.

Brandr's hand goes to Valrún's shoulder, and he eyes Jóvin with a visceral hatred.

Valrún simply watches Jóvin from her throne, waiting.

Naked fear slices through me. I wish on the names of the twelve First Ones that I could rip this iron collar off my neck. Briefly, I consider Finnur's Prism key, tucked safely in my bodice. But if I use it now, I will be found out, and I know Valrún will make sure that Finnur is not allowed to create another. So I hold myself still and hope that this confrontation is not leading where I think it is.

"Thank you for bringing this petition to me, Jóvin," says the queen formally. "I am working toward a solution, but you must understand that it is no small thing to loose a First One, especially when he is bound to a celestial vessel. I will continue to seek to restore the Yellow Lord, and his magic, but it will take time."

"Forgive me, Your Majesty," says Jóvin. "But what are we to do until then? Where are we to work? Where are we to live?" His eyes go to Valrún's lips. "Who are we to love?"

Brandr's hand tightens on the queen's shoulder.

"I would advise you to attach yourselves to the magical discipline closest to your own," says Valrún. "Red magic. It may be that there is enough residual power in your blood from virtue of being Iljaria that you might learn to wield fire, as once you wielded light. I give you my solemn word that I will not forsake you in this. If it is possible for Yellow magic to be restored, I will see it done."

The Yellow wielders murmur to each other, perhaps uncertain if this is the answer they wanted, or if it is really an answer at all.

"Why don't you hold the one who bound the Yellow Lord responsible?" Jóvin demands. "Why must *we* suffer for her sin?"

My breath stills in my lungs, and I glance at my brother and the queen. I have no hope that they will save me. But Jóvin's words have a familiar quality to them, like lines he rehearsed for a play. That scares me more than anything.

The voices of the former Light wielders grow loud and angry, choruses of *Why must we suffer?* and *Who is responsible?*

"She is!" Jóvin cries, dramatically jabbing his finger at me. "She is the cause of all our suffering!"

I do not know if the sudden roaring in my ears is the crowd of angry Iljaria or my own frantic heart.

They rush up the dais toward me, and I am caught in the heavy tide of them, pulled down onto the floor, pounded with feet and fists.

The pain comes in bursts of heat, a trickle of blood at my temple, a sickening jab to my gut.

I can't breathe or see. I can only feel, and even that, at the last, turns to blackness.

TWO MONTHS AGO

SAGA

Year 4201, Month of the Prism Goddess

Skaanda—Staltoria City

I am anxious, waiting to hear from Vil.

The distance between Staltoria City and Tenebris is not short. I can't possibly expect an answer—or, please gods, Vil himself—before four months have passed, and that would be the fastest riders on the fastest horses, changed often.

It's been four months today.

Leifur tells me not to worry, that Vil will be home as soon as he can.

But I do worry. It feels as if that's all I do.

I sit on a balcony that overlooks the aviary, listening to the sounds of parrots squawking and finches singing sweetly from their trees. I asked for an hour's recess from the council chamber, because sometimes I cannot bear to answer another question, make another decision. Sometimes I need solitude, quiet, so I can hear myself think again.

I'm alone up here—well, except for Leifur, who stands guard in the archway that leads back into the palace, the sun gleaming on the warm brown of his skin and glinting off the gold bar in his ear.

Past the aviary and the walls of the palace, Skaanda stretches on into the horizon, undulating hills a glorious summer green. But my eyes are drawn more often to Leifur in the archway. I am struck by his beauty and my stomach twists, because what right do I have to think him beautiful, when Hilf is dead and gone?

"How much longer until I have to go back in there?" I say.

Leifur turns to me with half a smile. "The hour is nearly up, Your Majesty."

"I wish you wouldn't call me that."

His smile fades, but his eyes glitter. "What is it you want me to call you?"

"My name, for a start."

"The general would not approve."

"Lucky, then, that I outrank the general."

He grimaces.

"Will you come and sit with me?" My voice sounds petulant, even to my own ears.

But it softens him. "Saga," he says gently, "if you would like to make me more than your guard, you have merely to say the word. But it is not my place to do it for you."

My heart beats dully in my chest, and I can no longer quite meet his eyes.

The last two months have taken their toll. I have wept at my parents' graves and worn a crown on my head. I have climbed the hill in the city and petitioned at the temple for the Prism Goddess to guide me. I have made decision after decision after decision, doing my best to listen to my council's advice. But not all of those decisions have been correct.

I miss my parents. I miss my brother. I even miss Brynja. Sometimes I almost begin to understand her motivations: loyalty to her country, absolute conviction that what she was doing was right.

Leifur has been with me during all of it, just as he was with me on the long road to Tenebris, and through everything that happened there. Just as he was with me on the journey back. I am no longer quite certain I can bear to be without him. I certainly don't *want* to be without him.

But I doubt myself, because the last man I loved had his throat ripped out by a lion. I am not worthy to love again.

And yet.

"Leifur," I say, hardly able to think beyond my pounding heart. "Please come here."

He takes a sharp breath and strides toward me, but just as he steps up to the bench where I'm sitting, he pauses and looks past me.

I turn to see a sleek white falcon landing on the balcony rail, a roll of paper tied to its foot. It walks up to me, opening its beak to emit a kind of rasping *kack kack* sound.

Leifur sits beside me on the bench, and I am wholly distracted by the heat of him.

"Do you think it's from your brother?" he asks.

"I don't know how it could be. It would take Iljaria magic to send a message so far."

"Well, there *were* three Iljaria in Tenebris that we knew of when we left," Leifur says.

He means Brynja and Ballast and the boy who had Prism magic—Finnur.

The falcon *kack*s at me again. I reach for the paper.

"You had better let me," says Leifur. "In case."

In case it's poison, he means.

He unties the message from the falcon's leg and unfolds it. "Just ordinary paper," he confirms, and hands it to me.

I'm disappointed not to recognize the handwriting, and I realize I wanted it to be from Brynja.

I grip the page tight as I read:

Ballast has relinquished his crown. The Aeronan Empire is absorbing Daeros, making it into a province with your brother, Vil, as viceroy. I have reason to believe that the emperor will use Vil's appointment to absorb Skaanda as well, and he has plans to conquer Iljaria. Brynja is being sent back to Iljaria in disgrace, and I am to go with her as her guard. We will do what we can from there, but I don't know that we will be of any help to

Skaanda. I hope this message will reach you faster than a rider would. If the falcon flies true, it will be only a week since all of this has taken place. I was sorry to hear of your parents' deaths. —Finnur

I read it twice, then jolt up from the bench and hand the note to Leifur.

I walk back and forth along the narrow width of the balcony, and I am a little surprised that the entire country doesn't light on fire with the sudden heat of my rage.

"Viceroy!" I shout. *"Viceroy!"*

Leifur is beside me the next moment, his face drawn. "Perhaps your message to your brother went astray."

"It didn't. Otherwise Finnur wouldn't have offered his condolences."

"Saga, what are you going to do?"

I turn to face Leifur, tipping my head up because he's taller than me. "I am going to Tenebris to give my brother hell."

"I don't think that's a good idea. Skaanda is fragile right now, and if it's true that Aerona means to conquer us, we ought to put our energy into bolstering our army, strengthening our cities, doing everything we can to protect our people."

Tears burn in my eyes, but I don't let them fall. "I am not going to let my brother sell my country to the godsdamned Aeronan Empire."

Leifur puts his hands on my shoulders, leans his head down so we're eye to eye. "But leaving your country without a queen is not going to help."

I clench my jaw. "The Aeronans *murdered* my parents, Leif. I won't let them take my brother, too."

He takes a breath, nods, straightens up again. "What do you need me to do?"

CHAPTER FIFTEEN

BALLAST

Year 4201, Month of the Red Lord

Iljaria—Regla City—the Blue Sector

The woman in the blue gown in the mysterious cottage in the middle of the Skepna Conservatory's impossible forest makes me tea.

There are a startling number of animals in here, from the hedgehog on her shoulder to three gray cats lounging in the rafters, to a pair of enormous wolfhounds snoozing by the fireplace. Not to mention a cloud of butterflies that dart here and there in a seemingly random but mesmerizing pattern.

The more I look, the more I see: a doe and her fawn in the corner, a lion cub under the table. There is a bowl of water on a bookshelf that seems, somehow, to house a whale. I am uncertain, studying it, if the whale is small or if the bowl is really the sea, and only *looks* small. Songbirds chitter from the rafters absent of cats. An entire family of rabbits huddle together on the armchair in front of the fire, little noses twitching. There is a beehive in one corner, the little insects flying in and out, humming, industrious. The cottage smells of honey.

The woman watches me take all of this in, and though I have a strange nagging sensation in the back of my mind that I've seen her before, I can't place it. I don't know how I could possibly forget someone like her.

"Come," she says, pouring tea from a stone pot into a stone mug. "Sit."

I do as she tells me, taking a seat across from her at a narrow table.

"Who are you?" I ask. I sip the tea: It's clear and hot and sweet.

"Your instructor, if you wish," she says. "You have powerful magic."

"For a half blood," I say bitterly.

She cocks her head to one side like a bird, and the hedgehog on her shoulder makes a grunting noise in protest. "You have powerful magic," she repeats.

I stare into my tea, chastened.

"Would you like to know more?" she asks me. "Do more?"

I look up at her again, a longing stirring in my chest. "Yes."

She smiles. "That is well. Because I have called you here to teach you. You can feel them, can't you? Every creature in my house, from the wolfhounds to the dust mites?"

I reach out with my magic and nod. "Even the dust mites."

"You commanded an army of animals, I hear. Every one of them obeyed you."

"Yes."

"There is such power singing in your veins, Ballast Vallin, you could bring the entire world to your knees, if you wanted. But that isn't what you want, is it?" Her light eyes fix on mine. "What *do* you want?"

"Freedom for my country," I whisper. "Provision for my people. Peace between our nations."

She nods, her braids bobbing about her face. "And for yourself?"

I swallow past the lump in my throat. "I want her to be safe," I say.

The woman gives me a *look*.

"I want her back."

Her smile returns, and she runs one finger along the hedgehog's spines. "Then what is stopping you?"

"I don't want to have to rip the world apart to save her."

"But you will, if it comes down to it."

I feel the ghost of her hands on my back in the dark, the heat of her lips on my neck, my jaw, my mouth. "Of course I will." My voice breaks.

"Then I will teach you," the woman says, "exactly what you need to know."

She leads me from the cottage, the hedgehog on her shoulder, the wolfhounds and the cats following behind.

We step onto a grassy plain under a riot of stars, and I get the feeling we are no longer inside the Skepna Conservatory, or Regla City, or even Iljaria, but somewhere else entirely.

The wind blows and the stars shine, and the woman settles onto the ground, the wolfhounds plopping down beside her and laying their enormous snouts on her knees. The cats slink away to hunt in the grass, and I sit across from the woman, who smiles as she absently strokes the wolfhounds' great heads.

"My lady," I say in a hushed voice, as it seems wrong to speak overly loud out here, "what am I to call you?"

"You may call me Lady Villidýr," she says. "Tell me, Ballast. What creatures roam the field?"

I reach out with my magic. "The cats," I say, "a snake, her belly full of eggs."

She nods. "What else?"

I reach farther. "Moths, thousands of them. Crickets and beetles. Ants. A warren of rabbits. An owl and—" I shake my head. "Something vast and dark, with wings. I don't have a name for it."

Lady Villidýr smiles. "It is a winged leviathan you sense, many leagues from here. He is older than the earth, stronger than thought."

I look at her in awe. "A winged leviathan?"

"Call him closer," she says, "if you would like to see him."

I try for some time, sending out my will toward his. After a while I shake my head, return my gaze to Lady Villidýr. "I can't do it, my lady. He is far too strong."

"You cannot exert your control on so great a creature as that," Lady Villidýr tells me calmly. "The lesser creatures obey you because you have shown yourself trustworthy, because they know you will not harm them. But even with the smallest of insects, there is another way."

The wolfhounds climb suddenly to their feet and dart off into the grass, though I sensed no command from her.

"What other way?" I ask.

"Call the wolfhounds back," she returns. Then: "Wait."

I pause my magic, snap my eye to hers.

"Call them to you not by overpowering their wills, but by surrendering your own. Give up control, and you will strengthen it."

I blink at her. "I don't understand."

"Ask them, Ballast. Don't command. Ask. And let them know you are willing to go and meet them, if that is what they wish. You understand, I think, the power of a choice."

I feel suddenly sick. A choice is something my father never gave me.

I close my eye. I let the wind whisper across my skin. I reach for the wolfhounds. I send them thoughts of me and Lady Villidýr sitting in the grass, petting their heads, giving them food. I ask them to come, if they wish.

To my astonishment, they do, trotting through the grass in a cloud of moths, the cats trailing absently behind them.

"Well done, Ballast," says Lady Villidýr. "Will you call the winged leviathan now?"

I rub the head of the wolfhound who settles near me, praising him with thought and word. I close my eye again and stretch out my magic to the great dark creature who bends the world to his whims.

I ask him to come, if he wills.

He does not.

But Lady Villidýr isn't upset with me. "You asked him," she says. "That is all you can do."

It's late when I get back to the lodgings my mother and I share, my mind and body buzzing with magic.

I'm surprised to find the room dark and vacant. I clap for the Red magic globe to light, wondering if perhaps my mother is already asleep, but her bed is empty, the covers undisturbed.

Fear races through me. I don't have any idea where she is because she wouldn't tell me where she was going.

There's a scratch at the door, and I open it with relief, only to find Hjarta, the one-eyed cat, proudly holding a dead mouse in his jaw. I tell him firmly that he needs to get rid of the mouse before I let him in, and he trots back out into the hallway, pulsing dejection at me.

He returns a few moments later, and I scoop him up in my arms, grateful for his scraggly warmth. I ask him to go and find my mother, to bring her back to me as soon as he can. He rubs his head against my jaw and hops down, going to fulfill my request.

I am weary to my bones. I put out the Red globe and crawl into bed.

I sleep.

I dream of Brynja.

She comes to me in a pavilion on the shore of a star-filled sea. Her beauty takes the breath out of me, and I pull her tight against my chest. We speak a little. She's been locked in an iron collar, and the Iljaria queen is collecting First Ones. She says she is sorry, she says she's a fool. I tell her she has nothing to be sorry for.

And then I kiss her desperately, wildly, under the dreaming sky.

A voice pulls me away from her.

"You needn't have sent Hjarta after me, you know," a woman is saying. "I was about to come back anyway. You worry far too much."

The voice is wholly unfamiliar to me, though it has a singer's cadence, lilting and sweet.

"Ballast?"

I open my eye to see my mother standing in the center of the room, Hjarta winding proudly around her ankles.

For a few moments I don't understand.

But then she smiles at me, her eyes blazing with joy, and I realize it was *her* speaking to me, *her voice* that pulled me out of my dreams.

Her voice.

I know now where she went today, and why she didn't want to tell me.

She went to find a Vaxandi—a powerful wielder of Green magic—to give her back her tongue.

EIGHT MONTHS AGO

BALLAST

Year 4200, Month of the Ghost Lord

Daeros—Tenebris—the heart of the mountain

My cheek hurts where the wasp stung me, my skin still sticky with honey. The iron collar burns at my throat. I feel dizzy and sick, but that doesn't dampen my terror of whatever it is that waits behind the glowing blue vein in the wall: the powerful weapon the Iljaria buried long ago, the thing my father is about to uncover with his pickaxe.

The chamber is crowded with Daerosian guards, Vil and Saga and Brynja, and Brandr, the Iljaria Prism Master, who has condescended to being collared in iron but only, I think, because he is not threatened by it.

My eye slides to Brynja, who is standing next to my father. He's only just let go of her hand. He's been playing at courting her, a twisted game conceived to torment me. But I'm certain Brynja is playing a game of her own. Her whole body is tense, alert, her face bathed in rippling blue light. She knows more than she claims; I'm beginning to think she might know everything.

"Today you witness history!" says my father. "Today I uncover the power at the heart of the mountain and claim it for Daeros. Today you will crown a man among gods."

"That was not our agreement!" cries Aelia. "We were to all decide together what is to be done with the weapon."

My father just laughs. Of course he laughs. At a snap of his fingers, the Daerosian guards draw their swords, and set the points against the throats of everyone in the room except for me, and Brandr, and Brynja.

I know I'm not imagining the tight smile that appears briefly on Brynja's lips as she takes a step back, flicks one hand up to her headdress, and then returns it to her side again, quick as lightning.

My father swings the axe against the blue vein, over and over again, shouting with every blow. The rock cracks, and little by little the crack widens.

"FOR DAEROS!" he cries.

Then the rock shatters, and magic surges out with the force of a gale, nearly knocking the wind out of me. The collar around my neck seems to spark at the touch of the magic, and I hiss as the iron burns me anew.

I fight to breathe.

Brynja slips up to my father, and I don't know how he doesn't see the cold calculation in her eyes.

"I am ready to give you my answer," she says sweetly.

My father grins, triumphant, and slides a possessive arm around her waist. "At last you see sense."

Suddenly there is a knife at his throat, a trail of red running down his pale neck. Brynja's eyes flash fire.

I watch, numb, as Brynja orders the Daerosian soldiers to release the Skaandans and Aelia, as Saga announces herself and attempts to claim the mountain for Skaanda.

As Brynja drags my father away from the wall, her blade still biting into his neck, and brings him not to Vil, but to Brandr. She unlocks the Prism Master's iron collar in one swift motion. Brandr smiles at her and puts his own knife at my father's throat.

Horror knots in my gut as Brandr claims Tenebris for Iljaria.

As Vil lunges at Brandr in fury.

As Brynja stops Vil with her blade under his jaw.

As Brynja reveals that Brandr is her brother, that she is not Skaandan but Iljaria.

I blink at her, immune to the others' shock.

Part of me always knew it was her, the girl who almost brought down the mountain.

All those years, those agonizing, long years, trapped and tormented by my father.

It was her.

I think of colorful cards spread out on my bed, the games of War we played together, my suspicion that I only ever won when she let me.

I thought I could win the game against my father, but I was wrong.

I didn't even hold all the cards.

She did.

I look at her here, in the heart of the mountain, and I'm wildly angry. But I don't know if I'm angry at her betrayal and her secrets, or that I didn't prove myself worthy of her trusting me with them.

CHAPTER SIXTEEN

BRYNJA

Year 4201, Month of the Red Lord

Iljaria—Regla City—the palace

I wake on a white bed in a white room. I have the strange sensation that all my bones have been shattered and knit back together again, my lungs pierced and repaired, my heart, having strained itself beyond bearing, relearning how to pump blood through my veins.

I remember, in a wrench of horror, the mob of Yellow wielders rushing the dais, pulling me down, trampling me.

I jerk upright and register Malen sitting in a chair beside the bed, little wisps of Green magic coiling around her neck and shoulders.

She looks at me with concern. "How do you feel, Brynja?"

I blink at her. "You healed me."

"Brought you back from the brink of death, more like. But yes."

My chest feels tight. "Thank you."

"It was on the queen's orders."

An object lesson, then. Valrún showing me very plainly what happens if I do not bow to her will.

"Brandr carried you in here," Malen says, like she's commenting on the weather.

I hate how my heart jerks, how, despite everything, I still crave my family's affection.

"He looked . . . ill," she adds, watching me. "He was sick in the corner."

"Did my mother come?"

"No one was allowed in here but me, while I was healing you."

I nod, telling myself I'm not disappointed. "How long has it been?"

"A day," she says.

That means I was in *really* bad shape and she had to use a *lot* of magic on me.

"You didn't . . . *change* anything about me, did you?" I find I'm desperate to hear that I remain myself, that she did not transform me into a wholly different creature.

Malen looks at me like I have three heads. "I was a *little* busy knitting your organs and bones back together to do anything cosmetic, if that's what you mean."

Relief floods me.

"If you can stand," says Malen, "the queen wants you. That was her order: the moment you're able to stand."

I slide my legs over the edge of the bed and put my feet on the floor and push myself upright.

Without Malen, I would have slid sideways, but she catches me before I can fall and supports me under the armpits.

"Does this count as standing?" I muse.

Malen laughs, but there's a grim edge to it. "I think it had better. Come on, I'll help you."

We stumble together out of the white room, which I'm surprised is in the Skapari section of the palace. Malen tells me the room changes, depending on what it's needed to be: a training room, a classroom, an infirmary. She smirks and adds in a conspiratorial tone, "A private bedchamber. Osa and Dagfinna have never used it that way, or at least not since I've been here, but—"

"Malen," I cut her off. "I really, really don't want to know."

She sighs like I've ruined all her fun.

She brings me to a chamber that's rounded on one end, a marvel of glass curved to fit the room, making the whole back wall a window. It is nothing like the great hall in Tenebris, really. The room is much smaller, the ceiling lower. But the glass wall looking out on a starry sky makes my gut wrench.

Valrún stands in the curve of the window, next to a chair that seems to be made of Prism magic. It shimmers in the bobbing red light of the fire magic globes. There are leather straps on the arms of the chair, a leather collar on the back of it.

"Hello, Brynja," says Valrún, her smile as sharp as her gaze. "I am glad to see you on your feet again."

I'm barely on my feet, still leaning heavily against Malen. She helps me across the room and stops just short of depositing me in the chair. My heart beats quick and frantic in my throat. I wish on the First Ones and every moment of time that I had asked Ballast to come and rescue me.

"Put her there, Malen," says Valrún, indicating the chair. "Then you are dismissed."

If I weren't so weak, I would have fought her, but as I can hardly stand on my own, there's nothing for me to do besides allow myself to be half slid, half dropped into the chair.

Malen gives me a look that's a mix of regret and shame. But then she strides from the room and I am alone with the queen.

Valrún fastens the straps on my wrists, pulling them tight enough that they pinch. She releases the iron collar on my neck and binds me with the leather one.

All this time I am quiet, my heart pulsing out my terror.

Magic whispers back into my veins, flickers bright and strong in my mind. Valrún has restrained my body and released my power. Which means she needs it. Needs *me.*

I watch her, swallowing against the pressure of the leather collar, reaching out with my magic to see if I can find Ballast.

He's in the city, Finnur told me, and I feel him, but before I can slip into his mind, Valrún stoops to my eye level and grabs my chin, nails digging sharp.

"You're going to find something for me," she says. "Or I will call that mob of disappointed former wielders of light magic back in here to finish what they started."

Straight to the threats, then. "What do you want me to find?"

Her eyebrows tilt up—my answer surprises her. She expected me to resist. Perhaps she wanted me to. "The Prism Stone."

My thoughts jerk back to my conversation with Finnur in the glass prison. *". . . and if I'd ever heard of the Prism Stone and if I knew where* that *was."*

Valrún lets go of my chin and strides past the chair to the window. I can't turn my head to look at her, so I stare straight ahead, reaching for Ballast again.

"The stories say that all the First Ones put a piece of their power into the stone," I say slowly, "so that no single one of them could ever wholly dominate the other eleven. Other stories say the First Ones came from the stone, that it was used to make the world."

"There are many stories about it," says Valrún. "I don't particularly care which one is true."

I latch on to Ballast. I'm not entirely certain where he is, but he's near enough that I can slip into his mind and tell him—

"Find it for me," says Valrún, pulling me back to my current predicament.

"Find the probably mythical Prism Stone?"

"Yes," she says. "Tonight. This moment. If you don't, I'll execute your mother."

"I thought you already threatened me with trampling." I force a bored tone into my words that I don't at all feel. "Did the whole of Iljaria abandon the philosophy of pacifism while I was away?"

Valrún turns to me, her face twisted in anger. "Don't *mock me*, Brynja Eldingar!"

Her breath is hot and foul. She reeks of rotting vegetation, of bones decaying under cold earth.

"You command the strongest magic I have *ever seen*," she says, "of any discipline, and that includes your Gray Lady–damned dead father. Find me the Prism Stone."

Anger burns through me. "You could have protected my father," I accuse. "You didn't."

She scoffs. "No one knew what Brandr was about until it was far too late. And what use do I have for a Prism Master who makes such easy prey for his weakling son?"

Something feral rears its head inside me, and I strain against the straps of the Prism chair. I command them to release me and they do, and then I'm lunging at Valrún, knocking her to the floor.

She shrieks and flails and I tell the floorboards to curl up and bind her at the ankles and wrists and neck, like she bound me.

She lies still and looks up at me, tiny green vines growing up from behind her ears.

"What will you do now, Brynja Eldingar?" she says wryly. "Will *you* abandon Iljaria's philosophies and put a knife in my heart?"

"I've killed before," I spit at her. But I make no move. I stand there trembling, feeling anew the awful sticky warmth of Kallias's lifeblood, pouring out on my hand.

"I am surprised," says Valrún, "that you would rush to defend the father who sacrificed you like a goat, the brother who has always hated you."

My chest heaves. Tears prick behind my eyes.

The world washes violet, and I am bound in the chair again, Adriel standing along with the queen in the curve of the window. He wasn't there before, but of course he's not bound by the same laws of time as the rest of us.

"Find the Prism Stone," Valrún says, low and cold. "The chair—the Prism magic in it—will amplify your power."

"And if you need to reach back through time to find it," Adriel adds quietly, "I will help you."

Valrún bends over the chair so her face is at my eye level. "If you do not obey me," she says, "I will hurt everyone you love, destroy everything you care for. You are powerful, but you are only a tool. If you do not allow yourself to be wielded, I will break you in pieces and cast you into the fire. Find the Prism Stone."

I nod, as much as I can against the leather bond. I shut my eyes.

I let my magic fill every part of me, racing through my veins, blazing out of my mind.

Despite Valrún's threats I can't stop myself from reaching for Ballast.

I find him at last, standing on a high cliff under a rising moon, which puzzles me—I thought he was in Regla City. A woman stands beside him, dressed all in blue, and there is a deer pressed against her, a hedgehog on her shoulder.

Eagles soar below the cliff, moonlight glinting on their wings.

The woman in blue is speaking to Ballast, but I don't catch her words, struck as I am by the tall form of him, his beauty, his immense power.

He feels my presence. He turns. "Brynja?" he whispers.

Please come, I say into his mind. *Please come. I need you.*

The woman looks over Ballast's shoulder and somehow meets my eyes. *Beware, Bronze Lord's daughter,* she says. *Do not meddle with things you do not understand.*

I'm trying to make it all right, I tell her. *I'm trying to save everyone.*

Sorrow touches the lines of her face. *It is not possible,* she says, *to do both of those things. Rightness requires sacrifice. Salvation comes only at great cost. Which one will you choose?*

But aren't sacrifice and cost the same thing? I ask. *Haven't I sacrificed enough already?*

"Brynja?" says Ballast, a sudden wind whipping his coat about his knees. "Are you safe?"

Tears blur my vision. I wish I could reach out my hand and touch him.

Beware, Bronze Lord's daughter, says the woman on the cliff.

A stinging pain across my face jerks me back to the Prism chair and Valrún, just retracting her hand from striking me.

"I told you to look for the Prism Stone," she snarls. "Not your one-eyed lover."

I clench my jaw. "How did you . . ."

Valrún holds up a mirror that shimmers with prismatic color. "It shows me everything you see when you're sitting in the chair. *Look for the stone.*"

I nod and shut my eyes again.

I am not sure how to find something I've never seen before, a thing that could be anywhere in the world, and that might or might not exist.

But I reach out for power, for strength, for magic, all-consuming.

I snag onto Adriel's time magic, feel him willingly bind his power to mine.

Then I feel as if I am flying over a vast distance, a falcon on the wind. Darkness and light, color and cold pass beneath me, rippling out in waves of magic and time.

I reach, reach.

I glance past mind after mind. I soar over the earth, I delve into the ocean, I wander the labyrinth of history.

The chair hums around me, and I pull harder on the thread of Adriel's time magic. It is heavy, heavy, and yet it weighs nothing at all because it is nothing.

I see a mountain, so high it scratches the sky, tangles in the fingers of the sun.

I see the First Ones, all twelve of them, from Bronze to Blue, kneeling in a circle at the top of the mountain, their foreheads wreathed in cloud and fire.

In the midst of them is a stone: ordinary, smooth, gray.

One by one the First Ones stretch out their hands and touch the stone. One by one they give it a piece of their power. Color threads through the stone: blue and yellow, red and brown, green and violet, white and black, and bronze and gray. When the Ghost Lord touches it, the stone shivers, and begins to fade.

But then the Prism Lady scoops it up, clasps it between both of her hands, and whispers into it enough of her power that it banishes the Ghost Lord's negating magic. The stone becomes solid again and pulses with the magic of eleven. The Ghost Lord turns away from the mountain and strides down, first of all, and all alone.

The remaining First Ones stand to their feet on the mountain. A thunderstorm roils around them.

"Who shall keep the stone?" asks the Prism Lady, lightning caught in her white hair.

"I do not want it," says the Blue Lady.

"I will not take it," says the Green Lady.

And the Gray Lady, "Nor I."

The White Lady, "Nor I."

The Black Lord's cloak flaps about him in the rising gale. "I desire the stone. And so I shall not take it."

The Brown Lady says, "Earth and rocks belong to me. I will take it, if My Lady wills."

The Violet Lord says, "I can hide it in the marches of time."

The Yellow Lord says, "I will bind it in my heart."

The Red Lord says, "Fire cannot harm stone. I will guard it."

The Bronze Lord stands tall and stern, before ever he was maimed. "I will take the stone," he says.

The First Ones feel the pulse of his power, tugging at their minds, seeking to persuade them.

But the Prism Lady looks at them all as thunder shakes the very mountain beneath their feet, and her eyes are filled with sorrow.

"The Ghost Lord shall keep it," she says.

And she strides down the mountain after him.

I open my eyes to see Valrún gripping the mirror so hard it begins to crack. Adriel has vanished.

"Where is it?" she whispers.

I shake my head, gut roiling, head aching. "We're going to have to ask the Ghost Lord that."

ONE MONTH AGO

VIL

Year 4201, Month of the Bronze God

Daeros—Tenebris

"Viceroy."

I turn from the window in the council chamber to face Rafn, my adviser. His face is grim, his eyes apologetic. A muscle tics in his jaw.

"The army is demanding to return home. They are refusing to work in the mines any longer without a direct order from the crown and additional compensation."

I grind my teeth, flicking my glance to Aelia, who sits quietly at the table, sipping wine and watching to see what I mean to do. I know she is not as calm as she appears. I know there is a storm inside her.

"I *am* the crown," I grind out.

Rafn grimaces. "Your title was given to you by Aerona, not Skaanda. The army does not see why they ought to answer to you."

"I *need* the iron, Rafn. How much ore has been mined?"

He doesn't answer at first, just stands there worrying his lip.

"Damn it, Rafn. *How much?*"

"Less than a quarter of what the emperor requires."

Aelia rises abruptly from her seat, the wine that sloshes over the rim of her cup betraying a little of her unrest. "Vil," she says.

I glance at her, not missing the desperate edge to her voice. "I'll get it," I assure her. "I'll have the ore in time, if I have to mine the damn stuff myself."

She presses her lips together.

"How can I incentivize the army?" I ask Rafn.

He shakes his head. "Money, Viceroy."

I pace along the back wall. "Empty the Daerosian treasury. Give it to them."

"The Daerosian treasury is already emptied," says Aelia quietly.

I curse. "Then we'll levy a thirty percent tax on every Daerosian city."

"Thirty percent is . . . extreme, Viceroy," says Rafn. "Ten would be more palatable to the city governors."

"Ten won't give us what we need, will it?"

He avoids my eyes. "No, Viceroy."

"Levy the tax," I snap. "And have the ore that has been mined so far brought to the barracks in Garran City for manufacturing."

"And those workers, Viceroy? Where are they to be found? How are they to be paid?"

"Take them from the Daerosian army. They will be glad to have work."

"They require payment, too, Vil," says Aelia dryly.

I try to curb my frustration; I hope she knows it's not directed at her. Twelve gods, I wish she would offer to pay for all this out of her father's deep imperial pockets, but I understand why she doesn't. Why she can't.

"Make the tax forty percent," I say heavily. "Pay them out of that. Everything must be ready for the ships to launch by winter. We only need to hold out until then."

"If you're sure, Viceroy," says my adviser.

I curse at him. "Get it done, Rafn. You're dismissed."

He bows and quits the room, leaving me alone with Aelia.

I step up to her, take the wineglass from her hands, set it on the table. I wrap my arms around her from behind, tuck her warm and close against me.

"When the ore is mined and my weapons are made," I murmur into her hair, "when your father uses them to conquer Iljaria, he will be content to stay on the mainland. We will be free of him. *You* will be free. We can do as we wish, you and I. Rule the peninsula together. And when we are strong enough—"

"When we are strong enough," she says softly, "we take my father off his throne. Free the whole world from his . . . cruelty."

The word chokes her and I tremble with anger, pressing a kiss to her hair. "I will keep you safe from him."

She takes a breath. "I know." Then: "What about your sister? She was chosen by your gods. Doesn't it bother you to overrule them?"

Guilt twists in my gut, but I shove it down as far as I can. "She will learn to bear it. As for the gods—I don't know that I believe in them anymore."

We're both quiet a moment, remembering the extremely real Yellow God who almost burned the world to ashes.

"And Brynja? You wanted to share all this with her, not so long ago."

Her name is still a knife to my heart, but it isn't affection I feel for her. "Brynja is nothing to me. She won't survive the assault on Iljaria."

"You wanted her to rule beside you," says Aelia. "You asked her to be your queen."

I step around so I'm facing Aelia, the fire inside me impossible to quench. "I don't want Brynja to be my queen," I tell her, my voice low and rough.

And then I cup my hands around her face and tug her mouth to mine. I kiss her until neither one of us has any room left for thought, or breath.

CHAPTER SEVENTEEN

BALLAST

Year 4201, Month of the Red Lord

Iljaria—Regla City—the Blue Sector

"Why does it make you angry?"

I sit with my mother in a tea shop in the Blue Sector, the proprietor not minding at all that I've brought Hjarta with me, seeing as she has a pelican on her shoulder and a leopard cub at her heels.

I hold my tea bowl with both hands, letting the heat seep into my skin, watching the steam curl up.

"Ballast. Look at me."

Obediently, I lift my head.

It is only my mother's tongue that has been altered, but she looks wholly different than she did in Tenebris: Lighter. Healthier. Fiercer.

"Why does it make you angry?" she asks again.

There is a hard edge to her voice—the voice I have never heard in the entirety of my life. Is this what it sounded like, before my father cut out her tongue?

"It doesn't make me angry," I say quietly, and I don't think it's a lie. "It's just . . . a shock."

"I have been without my voice for more than two decades, Ballast. I could not teach you how to speak, could not sing a lullaby over your cradle, could not let on to *him* that he didn't cut me off from my magic—and so could not use it. I am free now. He has nothing of mine anymore. I am free."

Tears run down her cheeks, drip into her tea bowl.

"Be glad for me," she whispers. "Be *glad*."

I dip my chin. "I'm sorry, Mother. I'm glad for you."

She takes a breath, raises her tea bowl to her lips, drinks, sets it down again. "They can give you back your eye, too," she says then.

My gut twists. "My eye is gone, Mother. I cannot have it back."

"A new one. They can give you a new eye."

Hjarta puts his paws on the table and sniffs at my tea. I nudge him gently back into my lap, but instead of protesting he starts purring like a thunderstorm.

"I don't want that."

"Why? Why wouldn't you do everything you possibly can to erase all the scars he gave you?"

Grief tugs me down into the abyss. "If I tried to erase all the scars he gave me, I am not sure there would be anything of me left. I'm still—I'm still trying to figure out who I even am, apart from him."

"You are yourself. You have always been yourself."

"I didn't live a whole life before him, like you did," I say quietly.

She looks away.

I rub Hjarta behind the ears. He purrs, purrs, purrs.

"Are you ashamed of me?" I ask her.

Her gaze snaps to mine. "Of course not."

"Are you angry with me?"

"Ballast, why would I be angry with you?"

"For leaving you, when I ran away the first time. For leaving you with *him*."

She shakes her head, her eyes welling with fresh tears. "No, my dear boy. I was a little angry when you came back again. I wanted you to stay away. To be free of him. But it all turned out all right, in the end."

"Did it?" I swallow past the lump in my throat. "Did it really?"

"Yes," she says.

She grabs my hand across the table and squeezes tight.

"Promise me you will think about it," she presses. "A new eye."

I pet Hjarta with my free hand, and I don't promise her anything.

I want to storm the palace and rescue Brynja. My mother tells me to wait.

"Brynja knew what she was getting into," she says, humming a few careless notes of song magic that twists into her hair and binds it on top of her head with invisible fingers. She sits on the edge of her narrow bed and pulls her shoes on, tying them with more magic.

"She didn't, though," I protest, not tying my own shoes because Hjarta is batting at the laces. "She thought she would be welcomed, not . . ." I grind my teeth.

"She should have consulted me," says my mother. Then, eyeing me sharply: "You both should have consulted me."

I grimace.

She comes to sit beside me, putting one hand on my shoulder. "Patience, Ballast. Learn everything you can at the Skepna Conservatory while I make my arrangements. We will not face Valrún unprepared, you and I. Brynja will be fine. And it isn't like you owe her anything. Do you?"

I don't answer, digging my fingernails into the mattress.

So I continue with my schooling at the Skepna Conservatory.

Every morning I leave our lodging and walk the short distance to the strange oblong building that harbors a forest inside. Most days I take Hjarta with me, and though Rúrik scowls about the one-eyed cat, it isn't technically against the rules, so he doesn't forbid it.

The classes are . . . bewildering. Frustrating. Magic that has been as natural as breathing my entire life is prodded and dissected and labeled and reassembled into shapes I don't understand.

I am clumsy at this kind of magic. Students half my age laugh at me, spouting sacred tenets they learned before they could walk, wielding with ease ancient techniques that I can scarcely remember the order of, let alone put into practice.

I can command an entire animal army, but I don't have the patience—or perhaps the control—to compel an ant colony to build a structure made of sand, one agonizingly small grain at a time. I don't know how to get a snake to shed its skin, convince a parrot to spout a sonnet. And I *loathe* the sessions where students and animals are paired at random and pitted against each other, to see which student has the strongest control of their magic—and their creature.

The only relief I find is Geirfinna, who has befriended me in that fierce, unrelenting way of a ten-year-old child. She helps me as much as she can, shouts at her peers to leave me alone, and celebrates every last one of my accomplishments, no matter how small. She reminds me of my sister Rhode, and it makes me miss my siblings so much I want to kick something.

In the late afternoons, when the regular classes are finished, I go to the stone cottage in the wood for my private sessions with Lady Villidýr. There, I can breathe again. There, I feel alive.

Little by little she teaches me to relinquish my control, to meet the creatures where they are, to align my will to theirs. I speak with spiders and leopards and dragonflies. I glimpse the dreams of an ancient leviathan, slumbering in the depths of the White Sea, all water and darkness and power. Lady Villidýr sharpens my awareness of their minds, helps me to translate emotion and images into a more precise language than I have ever been able to before. I understand the creatures that I have always loved more fully than ever. I understand myself more fully, too.

And every evening I reach out for the winged leviathan and ask him to come. He doesn't, not yet. But I can sense him, after a while, listening. He hears me. Perhaps, one day, he will answer.

Some weeks into our sessions together, Lady Villidýr brings me to the edge of a clearing open to the moon—impossible, because we are still inside the Skepna Conservatory. I've grown used to the way that the world bends around her; I never know what awaits us outside her cottage door.

Tonight she instructs me to sit down on the grass, and I obey her. She settles across from me, her blue skirts pooling like water around her.

"It was reckless, what you did at the Galdur Skjöld," she says, looking me square in the eye. Her hedgehog is on her shoulder again, as it often is, and tonight it's fast asleep, snoring softly, little snout tucked into her neck.

"How do you know what happened at the Galdur Skjöld?" I ask her, shocked.

Humor touches her lips, but she doesn't answer me, gently lifting a caterpillar from the grass and cupping it in the palm of her hand.

In the space of a few heartbeats, it transforms into a chrysalis, and then a butterfly, unfolding bright wings and flying up into the moon.

"You should not take the shape of an animal," says Lady Villidýr, "until you are certain you can shift back into your true form again. You are lucky your mother was there."

I dig my hands into the grass, thrown back to the feeling of being the starling, the wind in my feathers, my quick-beating heart.

Lady Villidýr watches me.

"How can you be certain of being able to shift back into your true form?" I ask her.

She smiles. "There are a few ways. Some Skapari use a token, a shard of rock or glass or metal that they have poured a bit of their power into. Others go about in pairs, with only one Skapari shifting at a time so their partner can call them back as needed. Some would cut off a piece of themselves and preserve it with Green magic, so that there would always be something that did not shift to anchor them to their real body."

I grimace. "Like what?"

"A finger, a toe, an ear." She looks at me frankly. "An eye."

I turn away.

"And some," she goes on, "a very few, have the strength of will to not lose themselves within their animal shape, and so shift back and forth as they have need or desire. But even those few, if they remain in their animal forms for long periods of time, are at risk."

"Of losing themselves forever?" I ask her.

"Of becoming monsters."

I lift my eye to hers again. "Then it's true. The cave demons we fought in the tunnels—"

She bows her head, and I have my answer.

We sit for a while in silence on the hill. I sense a family of crickets nearby, hidden in the grass. I ask them to sing for us and they do, a lament for the Iljaria who went into darkness, and never again saw the light.

"I do not think you need a token," says Lady Villidýr, when the chorus of crickets has faded to a single voice. "Or a partner. And you have been mutilated enough already."

I look at her, my heart a wild thing in my chest. "What, then?"

"Before you shift," she says, "fix in your mind a moment in time where you felt great human emotion: joy, sorrow, rage, love. In your animal form, when you feel your humanity slipping away, grab hold of that emotion. It should be enough to bring you back. But I will tell you what I told the Skapari who dwelled in the labyrinth long ago: Do not linger in your animal shape. Do not trust in your own power so greatly that you forget who and what you are. Do not think you are different than all the others who went before you, that you will not stumble where they stumbled, that you will rise above their mistakes."

The lone cricket hops up onto my knee, and I catch its little cricket thoughts: *sky, stars, song.*

I send thoughts back at it and thank it for its music.

"Well," says Lady Villidýr. "What are you waiting for?"

I blink at her. "My lady?"

She smiles. "Fix an emotion in your mind. Then shift into the form of an animal. And after a few moments, shift back."

"Now?"

"Ballast Heron Vallin," she says gently. "This is the only thing I have left to teach you. What better time than now?"

I take a breath. I close my eye. I am not sure why, but my thoughts go to myself as a boy, to a box of vipers at my father's feet. I feel my fear, acrid, sharp. It isn't hard to fix this emotion in my mind.

"Now choose an animal," says Lady Villidýr, "and take its form. Choose one that calls to you in this moment."

There comes the faint howl of a wolf from somewhere deep in the forest, and I am decided. I reach inside myself. I ask my magic to change me.

I am wrenched apart and remade. For a heartbeat there is mind-bending pain, and then—

I stand on the hill, paws in the grass, a million scents caught in my wolf's nose that I have never encountered before. I blink one eye up at the night sky, and I lift my head to the moon. A howl pulls out of me, triumphant and bright. My heart is fierce and pounding. I will run down the hill to the other wolf; we will wrestle and snarl and snap. We will go hunting before the moon is down. We will—

Ballast, says a voice in my mind. *Have you forgotten yourself already?*

I turn and see a woman sitting beside me on the hill.

Remember, she says.

Then I do remember.

Fear, pulsing through me. The crack of my father's hand across my face. Pain, hot and red.

I reach for my human form. I claw my way back.

It hurts more in this direction. The wolf does not want to leave me. But I force it to.

I feel the shift, the stretch of bones, the shedding of fur.

And then I am shivering under the moon, myself again, my clothes in a ruined heap around me. I raise my head.

"Cover yourself, Ballast," says Lady Villidýr. "Then we will try again."

"Again?" I say, dizzy at the prospect.

"Yes," she says. "We will stop when it is easy for you."

I pull on my torn shirt and trousers, as best as I can, and spend a few moments hunting frantically in the grass for my ring.

"I will hold that for you, if you like," she offers.

I give it to her.

"Now," she says. "Fix an emotion in your mind. Shift into an animal. Shift back. Try and do it without me this time."

I take a breath, and I close my eye, and I try again.

And again and again and again.

CHAPTER EIGHTEEN

BRYNJA

Year 4201, Month of the Red Lord

Iljaria—Regla City—the palace

I sit cross-legged on the floor in the palace library, Valrún looming like the Gray Lady herself while Brandr sits opposite me, anger pulsing off him in prismatic waves. He is less than happy about my plan.

"Get on with it," Valrún snaps, vines coiling around her ankles and poison flowers blooming under her feet.

"My queen," says Brandr, failing to disguise the panic in his voice, "I don't like this. I don't trust her. There has to be another way."

I don't blame him, really. The last time I pulled us both into his mind, I locked his magic away. But it's also the place we saw the Ghost Lord, so it makes sense to look for him there first.

"Do it, Brynja," says Valrún, ignoring Brandr entirely.

Hurt sparks in his eyes, but he makes no further protest.

Leaning forward, I put my hands on my brother's temples, and as easy as breathing, I wrench both of us into his mind.

I blink and we're standing in the dusty library I remember from half a year ago, cobwebs in the corners, the books on the shelves brittle with age. Brandr watches me, tense, angry.

"What are you really doing here, Brynja? Why did you come back to Iljaria? I don't believe you truly give a damn about returning home."

I wander through the maze of shelves, running my hand along the book spines. My brother trails after me.

"It's my home," I say quietly, "or it was. If you were the one Father sent to Tenebris, wouldn't *you* have wanted to come back? Remind yourself what it was all for?"

He snorts. "What was it all for, Brynja?"

I shake my head, dust swirling up under my feet. "I'm still trying to figure that out. But"—I flick a glance back at him—"I do wonder who I would have become if I'd never gone to Daeros. If Lilja hadn't died. If both she and I had grown up here. With you."

"It would never have been 'with' me," he says viciously. "You only cared about Lilja, and Lilja only cared about herself. You had no thought for me."

I pause a moment and just stare at him. My heart cracks. "That wasn't wholly true," I say. "But I'm sorry for the part of it that was."

He doesn't answer.

"How many Iljaria did you kill for their power so you could keep playing Prism Master?" I ask him then.

"Does it matter?" he snaps.

"I'm sure it mattered quite a lot to them," I say wryly.

"It's your fault," he says. "If you hadn't locked my magic away, I wouldn't have had to kill anyone."

I wheel on my brother. "Don't you dare try and pin your guilt on *me*, Brandr Eldingar. You only had that power in the first place because you murdered our father, or did you forget?"

"I didn't forget," he says tightly.

I study his face and am surprised to see a flicker of remorse written there.

I don't know what else to say.

We go on.

We come to a section of the library that is blackened with fire, shelves and pages reduced to ashes that eddy in beams of pale light.

"What is Valrún planning to do with the First Ones?" I ask.

The space in which we find ourselves is not physical and so has no limits, no end. We go on and on, and the shelves of crumbling books do, too.

"Valrún will be queen of all the world," says Brandr quietly. "Queen of history and time. Queen of judgment and blessing. Queen eternal."

I glance back at him. "And she's promised you what, that she will make you king eternal, that you will rule beside her for all time?"

His face tightens at my mockery.

"She's using you, Brandr."

"She loves me."

I shake my head. "Love isn't dependent on usefulness. Love isn't power, isn't an exchange of services. It isn't manipulation, or harm, or shame."

He curses. "What do you know of love?"

"Love is a vow," I say quietly. "A bond, a sacrifice. Love is brokenness. Love is healing. Love is . . . no secrets. Love is light in the dark, warmth in the winter."

"Did you turn poet in Daeros?" Brandr scoffs. "And, anyway, I thought you ruined it all by meddling in *your* lover's mind. Made him give up his throne, his *country*. I'm surprised he didn't wring your neck. Damn fool thing to do, Bryn."

I continue picking my way through the disarray of my brother's mind. "You heard about that?"

"Of course we did. You didn't think you were the *only* spy in Daeros, did you?"

I try not to show how much this rattles me. I had guessed as much, of course. But it hurts. What *was* it all for, then?

"He's one of the Iljaria I brought with me," Brandr says. "He has Blue magic and sends messages to Valrún via falcons."

My turmoil eases a little. He *wasn't* there the whole time, then. My father didn't send me to Tenebris just to torment me.

"It didn't take this long before," says Brandr. "To find the Ghost Lord."

"Call him," I suggest. "I feel him near."

We've come to an opening in the shelves, paper and ashes scattered at our feet. I stand beside my brother, and together we look back the way we came.

"My Lord," says Brandr, hands clenching and releasing at his sides, over and over. "My Lord, I would speak to you."

A shadow detaches from one of the shelves, and then he is here: the Ghost Lord.

I find him as hard to perceive as I did the last time, neither young nor old, neither tall nor short, neither dark nor light. He is absence and presence, everything and nothing, all these things and none of them.

I blink and the Ghost Lord solidifies into the blurry form of a young man wearing robes of rippling . . . nothingness.

"Brandr Eldingar," he says in a whisper, in a shout. "If you have come to surrender your stolen magic a second time, I will not return even Ghost to you when next we meet."

Brandr shakes his head, somehow not the slightest bit awed at the sight of his patron lord. "I did not want to meet you again. She did."

He jerks his thumb at me, and I find myself fixed in the Ghost Lord's disconcerting gaze.

"Bronze Lord's daughter," he says, dipping his chin in acknowledgment. "What is it you wish?"

I go toward him, pages crumbling beneath my feet, dust billowing up with every step.

I kneel before the Ghost Lord. "My Lord," I say, "I seek the Prism Stone, which was given into your keeping long ago."

It shocks me when he kneels, too, his eyes somehow on level with mine. "He told me you would come and ask for the stone. I hardly believed him."

"Who told you?"

The Ghost Lord smiles, and I see a profound sadness in him, a deep, unbearable loneliness. "The Violet Lord, of course. He is very free with his prophecies, no matter how often we tell him we do not wish to hear them. Time is his burden to carry, and his alone."

"Did the Violet Lord tell you why I want the stone?"

He shakes his head, and I feel a chill wind breathe past my face.

"No. But he told me to give it to you."

I frown. "Just like that? I am not even asking for myself."

"The Violet Lord read the storms of time," says the Ghost Lord, "and he told me to give you the Prism Stone."

The Ghost Lord reaches one hand up to his face. He plucks out his right eye, but it is not an eye. He opens his hand to reveal the Prism Stone there on his palm, threads of every color running through it.

He folds it into my own hand, and it is so heavy that I tremble under the weight of it.

"Take care, Bronze Lord's daughter," says the Ghost Lord.

And then he is gone.

Brandr crouches in the dust. He reaches out for the stone, but I hold it back from him, cradling it against my chest.

"You will have to give it to her," he says roughly. "When we go back, you will have to give it to her. Why not let me hold it, just for a little while?"

I meet his eyes, and my heart is hot with sorrow. "I can't trust you, Brandr."

"I don't know how to *use* it," he protests. "Just for a moment. Please, Brynja."

But I shake my head. "Time to go now."

And I pull the two of us out of his mind and back into the Iljaria palace library.

To my surprise, Valrún barely looks at the stone when I hand it over. She sets it into a jewel case lined with green velvet and locks it. Then she sends me back to the Skapari wing of the palace. She doesn't dismiss Brandr. I hear the sound of rustling cloth as I stumble from the library, of lips on skin, and whispered words of desire.

I can't get away fast enough.

Malen and my aunt Dagfinna are sitting in the central hub of the Skapari rooms when I get there, my aunt sipping a glass of red wine, Malen reading, the couch where she sits littered with leaves. I feign going into our dormitory but slip back out into the main corridor when they're not looking.

Valrún forgot to collar me again after the Ghost Lord experiment, and I plan to take full advantage.

It's strange to be in a place I am so unfamiliar with, to not have a map in my head of every corridor, every vent, every storage room. I lose myself for a while in the maze of the upper level before finding a stairwell door and descending to the next level down. I reach out with my magic, carefully, sporadically, in case anyone is monitoring the palace.

This level is far more utilitarian than the upper one. The floors are bare stone, the walls unpolished steel. I nearly collide with an attendant carrying a mounded basket of laundry, and as she passes me, cursing, I am momentarily occupied pondering why this task cannot be or is not being accomplished magically.

When I find myself back at the initial stairway, I discover that the corridor down here makes a huge circle. I hum in frustration. I know there are more than two levels in the palace—there has to be a way down.

I make another circuit, checking every door and interrupting a lot of servants at their work. I see that they *are* using magic to complete their tasks—the cooks wielding Red magic, the two men and three women in the laundry using a fascinating combination of Gray and Green magic. One young woman uses Prism magic to wash dishes, another Violet.

I've been around this level of the palace three times before I realize that the stairway leads down as well as up—a green medallion to the side of the archway changes the direction.

Down I go to the third level, which houses wine cellars and storerooms. Down again and I find the attendants' dormitories, dining hall, and central gathering room. It echoes the arrangement of the Skapari quarters, but more worn and sparse.

Another level down boasts a lot of dusty study rooms and an abandoned library that reminds me far too much of the inside of my brother's mind.

The next level down is empty, and is not divided into any rooms.

I seem to have reached a dead end. The stairway will not descend any farther, and I can't find a door or passage that leads on from here.

I reach out with my magic and am drawn to the middle of the level, where, crouching down, I see the outline of a circle in the stone, with a faintly green medallion in the middle. I press the medallion and the circle slides into the floor, revealing a flimsy-looking rope ladder trailing down into darkness.

I've had my fill of being underground—three months in the Iljaria labyrinth beneath the Daerosian mountains will do that to a person—but I've come too far to stop now. So I step onto the top rung of the ladder and begin the downward climb.

The descent is not as long as I feared; my foot touches a stone floor after only a few minutes. I reach out with my power and sense lamps hanging dim on the walls. I ask them to illuminate, and they do, flaring to life.

"Hello, Brynja."

I jump at Adriel's voice. The Violet Skapari lounges in a chair near the back wall of the stone chamber. There's a book in his lap that keeps disappearing and reappearing every few seconds.

"I'm here to speak with the Violet Lord," I tell him, striding over to his chair.

"You can't." He doesn't look up from his book.

I don't know why Iljaria wielding time magic can't read in the ordinary way; this seems exhausting and unnecessary.

"Why not?"

"Valrún said you would show up eventually. She forbids it."

I set my jaw and lean in toward him. "I need to see the Violet Lord."

Suddenly he jerks his chin up, his dark eyes flashing. "You. Can't."

I curse at Adriel, and reaching out with my magic, I command the wall behind him to let me pass. Its molecules waver and widen, and I step through.

Beyond is a space that doesn't make sense to my rational mind: It is a room and it is a mountaintop and it is the ocean and it is a forest. The Violet Lord is suspended in the air, his hands and feet and neck bound in iron, though the chains don't seem to be attached to anything. His white hair hangs ragged into his eyes, and he's dressed in purple robes that are worn and moth-eaten. His skin is a dark, rich brown, and his eyes, which he lifts to meet mine, are violet.

"Bronze Lord's daughter," he whispers. "You should not be here."

I move toward him, the strangeness of this place making my stomach roil. "My Lord," I say, "you should not be here, either."

But before I can reach him and tear the iron from his limbs, Adriel appears beside me, grabs me by the arm, and hauls me through time and space away from the Violet Lord, on up through the levels of the palace. In the span of three heartbeats, we are sitting together in the Skapari's central room, Malen and Dagfinna hardly batting an eye at our sudden appearance.

"Adriel," I say, low and angry. "How could you leave him like that? How could you let your patron lord *suffer* like that?"

"It's my fault he's there," says Adriel, not meeting my eye. "I should be chained in his place. But our queen has a plan."

"What plan?" I fairly scream at him.

He grimaces, glancing at Malen and Dagfinna, who are clearly listening but pretending they're not.

"A plan to bring back the Yellow Lord," he says. "A plan to restore light magic. A plan to bring back the dark."

CHAPTER NINETEEN

BALLAST

Year 4201, Month of the Violet Lord

Iljaria—Regla City—the Blue Sector

"How is she, Finnur?"

We're sitting in a noodle shop in the Blue Sector, a few streets down from the lodgings I share with my mother. Finnur's grown since I saw him last, a few inches at least, and he's already devoured two bowls of noodles in spicy broth and is halfway through his third. I wonder if they're not feeding him enough in the palace, or if these are just the realities of being a sixteen-year-old male.

My head aches from my latest session with Lady Villidýr; I lost count of how many creatures I shifted into after the tenth or eleventh one. I called the winged leviathan, as I do every evening. This time he came, a vast dark shape riding on the currents of the wind, allowing me the briefest glimpse of his magnificent form before he flew away again, disappearing into glittering starlight.

"I don't see her very much," says Finnur, between bites. "I'm occupied with my training most of every day, and Valrún calls her at odd hours."

"But does she seem well," I press, "when you *do* see her?"

Finnur eyes me like he's not sure how to answer that question in a way that will make me happy. "She seems worried, Ballast. Drained. And you know she doesn't like being cooped up. There aren't any vents to crawl about in because everything is heated by magic, and most of the time—" He grimaces and stares into his noodle bowl.

"Most of the time?" I prompt him.

"Valrún keeps her collared in iron."

I have known this since the dream we shared, but still it makes me angry and sick, makes my hand go to my neck to feel the scars left there from when my father collared me.

"Go and see her yourself," Finnur says then, shoving another forkful of noodles into his mouth. "That's why you're here, isn't it?" The spicy broth is making his eyes water.

I shift a little in my chair, because I haven't told him everything. "My mother isn't ready yet."

"Ready for what? I know you've been training at the conservatory, but what has Gulla been doing every day?"

I stir my fork into my own bowl of noodles but don't eat any. "I'm not really sure," I admit. "She's gone to the Vaxandi Center to be treated with Green magic a few times; beyond that—" I shrug. "I think she is enjoying her freedom. Exploring the city. Perhaps meeting up with old friends."

Finnur studies me, and I hastily close off my thoughts. He doesn't *mean* to read my mind, but it happens by accident sometimes.

He looks away, sensing my mental barrier and clearly hurt by it.

"Are *you* well, Finnur?" I ask then, feeling suddenly guilty that I didn't think to inquire after him until now, when he's only here in the first place because of me.

"Well enough."

"What do you make of the queen?"

He shakes his head. "She is seeking the First Ones and means to use their power to . . . I'm not entirely certain. But I think she intends to secure her immortality. I think she plans to be queen of Iljaria forever."

My pulse throbs uncomfortably in my neck. "Is it all for nothing, then, do you think?"

"The things we choose, the actions we take—it's never for nothing, Ballast."

I nod and finally try a bite of my noodles. They've gone cold, but the spices in the broth still burn on the way down.

Finnur finishes his third bowl and scrapes back his chair. "I can't stay any longer before I'm missed," he says apologetically. "Shall I take a message to her?"

I am overwhelmed with a fierce and sudden longing to be done with games and secrets, to be back in her arms where I belong. "No," I tell Finnur. "I'll take it to her myself."

He smiles. "Good."

And then I blink and he's gone, the tang of magic sharp on the air.

Violet Lord, his power has gotten stronger.

Mine has, too.

I pay the proprietor and slip out of the noodle shop, half running down the few streets to our lodging. I open the window before I transform, slip out of my clothes, and fold them in a neat pile on my bed, making sure to tuck my ring into my trouser pocket.

I seize onto the emotion of kissing Brynja for the first time, down in the dark of the Iljaria tunnels.

Then I transform into a kestrel and fly through the window.

I miscalculated how easy it would be to get into the palace.

It's protected by guards *and* magic, and both would definitely notice a one-eyed kestrel gliding into the courtyard.

I circle for a while, flying around the glass spires, peering down at the activity below. I glimpse a few people I am sure must be the queen's Skapari; magic hangs on them stronger than the regular guards and attendants.

After some consideration, I land just outside the walls in an out-of-the-way corner, and take my human form again. I only wear it for a moment before I become a mouse.

I skitter along the base of the wall and run past the guard's feet and through the gate, my little mouse heart beating quick, quick. The tiles are shiny and slick, hard to grip with tiny paws. The courtyard seems horribly large. But I don't dare shift into myself—there is nowhere for me to hide, and no clothes for me to put on.

I was hoping, inanely as it turns out, that there would be laundry flapping on clotheslines for me to grab. But this is the palace of the queen of Iljaria. She doesn't have her washing on display for all to see.

I am only a quarter of the way across the courtyard when I am snatched up by a large hand. For a moment I wonder if the Green Lady has blessed me with luck and sent me to Finnur, but it isn't him—I look up into the face of a dark-skinned young man with solemn eyes and a violet gem on his forehead.

"Hello there, little friend," he says.

I sit quietly and regard him with my one eye—he clearly senses the magic in me, and it is no good pretending I am an ordinary mouse.

"You shouldn't have come here, you know. I have to take you to the queen."

I shake my head vigorously, but he just sighs and claps his other hand over top of me.

So I bite him.

He jumps and swears, dropping me, but before I can scamper away, I feel myself yanked violently backward to the moment he claps his hand over me, except this time he's wearing gloves, and my teeth can't pierce the leather.

Time magic. It feels like a needle shoved through my head.

All right, then. If this Violet joker is going to use *his* magic, then I'm sure as hell going to use mine.

I seize onto the emotion of kissing Brynja in the dark, and I stretch into myself again, tumbling naked onto the slick tiles.

"No," grunts Violet. "No, no, we can't have that."

Once more he yanks me back in time, and I am a mouse again, caught fast in a glass jar capped with an iron lid. The iron is enough to dampen my power, to stop me from trying to transform again.

I don't like it. Panic twists through this body that isn't mine, and I worry I will lose hold of my true self, that I won't be *able* to change back if I'm trapped here for very long.

"You're remarkable, you know," comes Violet's voice, warped by the glass and the iron and my mouse ears. "Not many Skepna dare shift shape very much these days, or even have the power required to do it. The queen will want you for her Skapari. The last few Blue ones she had were not strong enough for her.

"I'm sorry I can't let you go. If I did, her Prism Master would find it out, and she would get rid of me, and I have worked too hard and sacrificed too much to be here. But don't worry. She's not likely to hurt you."

This speech brings me little comfort. My mouse brain screams at me to escape, to hide, and before I can stop myself, I fling my body against the glass, trying desperately to break through.

Violet shakes the jar, but he does it gently. "Easy, my friend. You will do yourself a harm. We are almost there."

This whole time, he's been walking, carrying me through the courtyard and deep into the palace. My view is bent and skewed from the jar. I see walls hung with greenery and glittering floors, pillars and statues and arched doorways.

We approach one of the doorways, and Violet pauses just outside. Brandr looms large, and I am not sure if it's my mouse heart or my human one that quails at the sight of him.

"Her Majesty is not to be disturbed, Adriel," Brandr snaps.

Using more time magic, Violet hides me smoothly beneath his robes, so I am concealed before Brandr sees my jar. All is dark, but I still hear their voices.

"She will want to see me," Violet—Adriel, I suppose I must call him—insists. "I have found something that will interest her."

"She's with Brynja and Malen," says Brandr. "She is not to be disturbed. Not even by me, she said."

I go nearly feral at the mention of Brynja's name. Lord of Light, she's *here*. She's *right here*. I can't bear this. I slam against the glass with all my might, but I manage only the tiniest *tink tink tink*.

"What is that?" Brandr demands.

Adriel sighs and produces the jar.

Brandr peers in. "A one-eyed mouse?"

"A *shape-shifting* one-eyed mouse," Adriel explains. "The most powerful Skepna I've ever encountered. I didn't know how to contain him otherwise." He taps the glass.

Brandr grimaces. "You're right—the queen will want to know. But he can wait until she's finished. I'll take him from here." He holds out his hands.

Adriel doesn't relinquish the jar. "I found him. I'll bring him to the queen."

"Fine. But you might want to give him some air."

Is *that* why I'm starting to feel ill?

With one gloved hand, Adriel unscrews the iron lid and opens it a crack. I breathe greedily, in frantic gulps, until my dizziness starts to subside.

Just then there is the murmur of female voices from within the chamber.

Brandr moves out of the doorway as two women step past him, one with her white hair cut close against her scalp and a green gem on her forehead, the other—

The other is Brynja.

There is an iron collar about her throat.

And there is blood on her gown.

I go feral, hurling myself once more against the glass, shouting in my tiny mouse voice.

But she doesn't see me, doesn't hear me.

She stumbles as she goes down the corridor, and the other woman, tucked under her arm, keeps her from falling.

I slam my body against the sides of the jar, over and over, until it feels as if my bones have turned to jelly, and even my brain is bruised inside my skull.

Brynja passes out of sight, and I cease my frantic attempts at escape, my heart beating too hard, too fast.

"You ought to have saved your strength," Adriel tells me.

Then he takes me in to see the queen, with Brandr close beside him.

NOW

SAGA

Year 4201, Month of the Violet God

Daeros—Tenebris

Tenebris looms near, a shadow of dark, jagged rock against the sun. It's strange to see it bare of ice and snow, but there's no ignoring my jittering heart, the rush of bald terror in my veins. I was captive here. Hilf died here, in fear, in agony. Gods above, I never wanted to see this place again.

I sense Leifur's eyes on me, but I don't look at him. I can't.

"Kallias is dead," says Leifur quietly. "He can't hurt you anymore, Saga. You're safe. I swear it to you."

I gnaw the inside of my cheek until it's bloody and force myself to relax my tight hold on the reins. All I can manage in answer to Leifur's profession is a slight nod. I still don't look at him, not even as he nudges his horse a little nearer mine.

It's been a grueling two months since we set out from Staltoria City, Leifur and Pala and me. We've ridden hard all of every day and part of every night, eating as we ride, stopping only to change horses and catch a few hours' sleep.

Neither Pala nor Leifur approve of this journey, but both have been fiercely loyal all the same. Pala wanted to bring as many soldiers with us as could be spared; I wanted to be able to move swiftly, without the appearance of hostility. Part of me—a large part—hopes that Finnur was mistaken, that my fears of Vil's betrayal are unfounded, that something other than Vil's ambitions have kept him in Daeros instead of returning home to Skaanda as I asked. In the end, I got my way, and only Leifur and Pala accompanied me the long miles between my home and the site of my greatest trauma.

But looking at Tenebris now, I begin to think that I've made a huge mistake.

I have been queen of Skaanda for all of six months, and for the last two, I haven't even been there. I left my kingdom in the capable hands of Elíndis and General Hildar. I know they will guide Skaanda well in my absence, but the guilt of having more or less abandoned my country—even in appearance—gnaws at me daily.

But I have to see Vil. I have to know what's truly going on. I won't have any peace in Skaanda until I do, and part of me thinks that the spirits of my mother and father won't, either. Maybe I'm being selfish. Maybe all of this has only to do with my pride, the feelings of guilt and inadequacy that have plagued me ever since the gods named me heir instead of my brother.

"Saga," says Leifur, drawing me back to the present.

I blink and find that the gates are opening, two riders coming out to meet us.

"Commander," says Pala from my other side, "it would serve you well to use Her Majesty's formal title in the presence of others."

Leifur outranks Pala, but he doesn't rebuke her for this admonishment.

"Yes, of course. My apologies, Your Majesty."

At this, I finally look over at him. There is a storm of feeling in his eyes, in the taut way he holds himself. I'm thrown back to the balcony, right before the falcon messenger came. *If you would like to make me more than your guard, you have merely to say the word.*

"No apology needed, Commander," I manage.

He grimaces, but there is no time for further conversation. The riders have reached us: Rafn, a third cousin on my father's side whom Vil chose as his adviser before I went home, and Ebbi, one of my father's generals. Ebbi is near seventy, and though he's no relation, he's been like a surrogate grandfather to Vil and me. Rafn, on the other hand, I hardly know; he didn't grow up in Staltoria City.

"Your Majesty, hail!" says Ebbi, bowing to me neatly from his saddle. "I am glad to see you."

"Your Majesty," echoes Rafn, with the barest inclination of his head. "What errand do you have in Tenebris?"

From the corner of my eye, I see Leifur stiffen at Rafn's blatant disrespect.

"I'm here to see Vil," I say, trying to quiet the unease racing through me.

"You arrive at an inconvenient time," says Rafn. "His Imperial Highness Emperor Junius has just come back from Aerona. The viceroy will be in meetings with him all day, and will be much engaged elsewhere for the next few weeks."

"Are you turning me away?" I demand, half laughing in outrage. "My brother is yet under my command—as, I must remind you, are you. I have no quarrel with the emperor. Take me to Vil at once."

Rafn's jaw goes tight.

"Denying the queen of Skaanda entry to Tenebris is an act of war, as defined by the terms of the peace treaty with Daeros," says Leifur with a confidence that ought to surprise me but doesn't.

"The terms of the treaty have changed," says Rafn shortly.

Leifur draws his sword with a sudden scrape of metal. "Let us in, Rafn. Or have you turned traitor against your queen?"

"There is no harm in letting her speak with her brother," says Ebbi then. He looks extremely uncomfortable, his eyes jumping everywhere but my face.

Leifur sits in his saddle, outstretched sword unwavering. He is as obdurate as stone, in complete control of his anger, honed by it instead of wielded by it. I think I never want Leifur to be angry with me.

"Very well," spits Rafn. "But if the viceroy refuses to see you and leaves you to kick your heels in the hall, don't say I didn't warn you."

"Like hell he will," I mutter under my breath.

Rafn pulls his horse around and leads the way through the gates, while Ebbi nudges his mount between mine and Pala's.

"How deep is Vil in with the Aeronans?" I ask Ebbi without preamble.

"Deep enough that I am not sure he could climb out very easily," returns the general, "even if he wanted to." Ebbi grimaces. "Which, forgive me, Your Majesty, I don't think he does."

Gods, I feel sick.

"I was devastated to hear of your parents' loss," Ebbi goes on. "My sincerest condolences, Your Majesty."

I blink furiously to stanch the sudden press of tears, but they slip past my guard anyway. I turn away from Ebbi so he won't see, but this just means I'm facing Leifur now. It's not the first time he's seen me cry, but he still looks stricken, like it guts him.

And then we're through the gates and into the courtyard, where we swing off our mounts and hand the reins to waiting attendants.

I surreptitiously wipe my eyes. Leifur offers me his arm, and I accept it with an eagerness that alarms me. I soak in the heat of him beside me, the solid muscle of his arm wrapped around my own.

"You are the queen of Skaanda," he says into my ear. "Your brother, viceroy or no, doesn't have authority over you. Don't forget that, Saga. Don't let him cow you."

My skin pricks at the warmth of his breath. I shudder and he misinterprets it.

"Nothing is going to happen to you. I'll protect you, Saga. Do you trust me?"

It feels as if there is no air in my lungs, or at least not enough for speaking. So I just nod and squeeze his arm, and hope he understands that there is no one in all the green world that I trust more than him.

Up the steps we go and into the front vestibule, where more attendants take our filthy boots and hand us satin slippers to wear instead. They are soft but very thin, and do nothing to protect against the icy chill of the floor.

Rafn leads us through corridors that have far more warmth than they used to. The walls are hung with tapestries or painted with bursts of bright color. There are plants and potted trees—none of them orange trees, like the one that stood outside of my glass cage when I was a captive here. I know at once that all of this isn't Vil's doing. He wouldn't have known about the orange trees, and if he did, I'm not sure it would have mattered to him.

Ballast did this.

My gut wrenches as Rafn brings us into the great hall, past the place where Hilf died, his throat ripped out by Ballast's lion.

Leifur's hand finds mine and squeezes tight. I wonder if it's wrong I find comfort in it. I wonder if it's wrong to find comfort at all, ever, when Hilf is gone, and when he died in such a way.

The old grief rushes up to clog my throat. I pull my hand out of Leifur's. He doesn't reach for it again, but he doesn't put more space between us, either. His presence steadies me, gives me the courage to approach Vil and the man I assume is Junius, who stand on colorful carpets at the back of the room. I try not to look through the glass wall at the glacier sea, try not to ponder the fact that Hilf's bones are down there, somewhere, scattered across the ice.

Vil turns at our approach. His face is hard, not the slightest spark of affection or warmth in his eyes. My chest swirls with a storm of emotions difficult to identify.

I adored Vil in my youth in that way younger sisters tend to idolize older brothers. I had no thought to being named heir by the gods—the possibility never occurred to me before our visit to the temple on the hill, when I was marked by the priestess and Vil was not.

I was terrified he'd hate me after that. But he didn't seem to. He attended royal councils and strategy meetings along with me. He trained with the army, studied hard for his tutors, threw himself into project after project that would improve the lives of the Skaandan people, like housing for field workers, raising money to build hospitals, and proposing laws to our father that men and women would not be allowed to join the army without first receiving two years of general schooling. I worked hard, too, and if I ever needed it, Vil helped me.

But then I fell in love with Hilf, and went away to war, and got captured by Kallias. Everyone in Skaanda thought I was dead, so Vil assumed the role of heir, the role it seemed he was born to. Yet he relinquished it to me when Brynja brought me home again, and I thought—

I thought he truly loved and respected me above his ambitions. I thought I could reason with him. I thought his long silence, his not returning home when I asked—I thought it was all a mistake, that the moment I saw him again, we could reach an understanding.

But looking at him now, I know I was wrong.

My brother is here in the place of my greatest torment, playing at being king of the country I've endured so much for. The country our parents *died* for.

Anger boils inside me.

I stalk up to him, my fury so visceral he takes a step backward.

"Why the *hell* did you not reply to my message?" I demand.

Vil blinks at me. Leifur and Pala step up behind me, both literally and figuratively having my back.

But before he answers me, before he even acknowledges me, my brother looks aside at the emperor.

"This is my sister, Your Imperial Majesty," he says.

Gods, I want to slap him.

I glance at the emperor, who looks faintly amused. He folds his arms across his chest.

"I am Saga Stjörnu, queen of Skaanda."

"Yes," says Junius. "I heard."

He offers no further comment, so I turn back to Vil again.

"Explain," I say coldly.

"There is nothing *to* explain," Vil returns with a careless shrug. "You were needed in Skaanda. I was—I still am—needed here. I'm not sure if you're aware, but I have been made viceroy of the former country of Daeros, now the newest province of the Aeronan Empire."

"Yes," I say, echoing Junius. "I heard."

Vil frowns. "Aren't you going to say anything?"

"Aren't *you* going to say anything?" I throw back at him. "Do you care even a *little* bit that our *parents* are *dead*?"

He winces at this and suddenly can't quite meet my eyes. "Of course I care," he says to the floor.

"Well, you have a funny way of showing it."

He traces a circle in the carpet with his shoe and doesn't answer.

"Your brother has been extraordinarily busy these last few months, Saga," says Junius, drawing my eye again.

"Doing what?" I snap.

The emperor smiles. "Ousting evil kings, drawing up peace treaties, helping me to solve my Iljaria problem."

"Pretty sure it was Brynja who ousted Kallias, and I don't think absorbing an entire country into your empire is the same thing as a peace treaty. What's your Iljaria problem?"

Humor dances in the emperor's dark eyes. "We got rid of Kallias's son, too—and good riddance. The treaty between Skaanda and Daeros was signed and finalized far before Daeros was named Aerona's newest province. And my Iljaria problem is their magic, naturally."

I look between my brother and the emperor. "How exactly did Vil 'solve' Iljaria magic?"

"By finding a way to neutralize it on a large scale."

Vil drags his gaze up to meet mine, and there is a hard determination in him. Whatever has happened since I've been gone hasn't changed him, really, as much as focused him, shaped him into a weapon he won't hesitate to wield against me, if it comes to it.

I wish my mind weren't so damn slow in coming to this realization. I stare at my brother. "You sold our country to Aerona on the strength of this magic neutralization. Didn't you."

Vil's eyes slide over toward the emperor before finding mine again. He doesn't deny it, just shrugs.

"What did he offer you?" My voice is low and cold, though my anger is as sharp as swords.

"That doesn't matter," says Vil. "What matters is we are—or we soon will be—one unified whole, the mighty arms of the empire. And once we have ground Iljaria under our heels, we will be truly strong. Truly free."

"WHAT DID HE OFFER YOU?" I scream.

Vil blanches in the face of my wrath but otherwise stands his ground.

"I offered him what you never could," says Junius calmly, "what you never wanted to."

I look my brother square in the eye. "Viceroys don't wear crowns, you know."

"I never wanted a crown," he says.

I laugh at him. "Liar."

Junius looks between us, truly amused. "When Iljaria is part of Aerona, Vil is to wed my daughter."

"Aelia?" This shocks me. I spent quite a lot of time with Aelia last year, and I know she felt admiration for Vil, but I hadn't thought she was the sort of person who would allow herself to be bartered with. And I thought Vil was too hung up on Brynja to transfer his affections to someone else so soon. Though perhaps this isn't about affection.

"The oracle chose me instead of you," I say to Vil, "so now you've decided to reach for something bigger than a crown. Is that it?"

"I was going to rule Daeros, regardless," Vil snaps. "That was the entire point of our plot last year."

"The entire point of our plot last year was to *end the war with Daeros and pull Kallias off his throne*!"

"Same difference."

"And the fact that our parents were *murdered by the emperor*? Does that also mean nothing to you, Vil?"

"You have no proof," he says.

"The poison that killed them—"

"Just the coroner's theories," my brother interrupts, "according to *your* message."

"The poison didn't come from Skaanda."

"That doesn't mean anything."

"It doesn't mean *nothing*!"

"Why would I send assassins to murder your parents?" asks Junius.

Both Vil and I turn to look at him. The emperor studies his fingernails, yawning a little, like he's bored with this conversation.

"To weaken Skaanda," I say quietly, "to put a young and untried queen on the throne, to distract me while my brother sold my country out from under me."

Junius shrugs. "I suppose that makes sense. But do you really think I needed to do that to accomplish my goal? And at this point, what does it even matter?"

Leifur's sudden light touch on my shoulder is all that keeps me from lunging at the emperor and shoving him through the glass wall.

"It matters because my parents are dead," I say tightly. "It matters because you've stolen my brother and my country from me."

"That's a bit of an exaggeration," says Vil. "Skaanda has an alliance with Aerona. It remains an autonomous country."

I hear his unspoken *for now*.

"An alliance that *I did not consent to*. You had no right to pledge Skaanda to Aerona without me, Vil. *I* am the ruler of Skaanda. Not you."

"You left me in Daeros to work toward peace."

"Peace with *Daeros*!" I am so frustrated I could strangle him. Behind me, Leifur squeezes my shoulder.

"But we knew Aerona was a threat," says Vil stubbornly, with an apologetic glance toward Junius. "We knew that something would have to be done—"

"I am tired of your excuses," I tell him, low and cold. "You did not have the authority to offer up Skaanda like a goat on the altar of your lust for power. And you know it. It's time to come home, Vil. You've done enough damage here."

For a moment we stand there, bristling at each other, Leifur's hand warm on my shoulder, heart straining against the confines of my chest. I have suffered things Vil can't even imagine. I lost Hilf and Indridi. I lost Brynja, if not quite in the same way. Now it seems I've lost Vil, too.

"As viceroy to the emperor of Aerona," Vil says then, his words hard and brittle as ice, "I have the authority to depose you from your throne and seize control of Skaanda."

"LIKE HELL YOU DO!"

"You are unfit to be queen," he spits. "You abandoned your country, leaving it leaderless and aimless, and came here to Daeros simply, it seems, in order to shout at me. That is not the action of a queen. That is the action of a petulant little sister who can't stand to see anyone but herself offered a chance at power."

I howl and lunge at him, my hand connecting audibly with his face before Leifur grabs my arm and pulls me back.

"What an emotional creature she is," says Junius.

I wish I had Brynja's magic, though perhaps it's better that I don't. I would use it to rip them both limb from limb, and would only regret it later. Probably.

"Go home, Saga," says Vil, putting his hand gingerly to the place where I slapped him. "Play at being queen while you still can. You are not needed here."

For a few heartbeats more I stare at him, caught between devastation and rage.

Then I stalk from the great hall with Leifur and Pala at my heels.

But I don't go home. I go to find the one person in Tenebris who has any sense at all.

CHAPTER TWENTY

BRYNJA

Year 4201, Month of the Violet Lord

Iljaria—Regla City—the palace

I am eating lunch in the Skapari dining hall when Valrún summons me. Only Jóvin is here with me, the rest of the Skapari otherwise occupied, so I am not exactly sorry to be called away.

But when I step past Brandr and into Valrún's parlor, I see the Prism magic, Malen standing grimly beside it, and I would almost rather have stayed with Jóvin.

Valrún is wearing a filmy green robe, and little else. A vine curls round her shoulder. She steps up to me and unlatches my collar without ceremony.

"Sit," she orders, gesturing at the glass chair.

I obey, watching Malen. Her hands are in fists at her sides, and I sense her dread.

Malen fastens the restraints at my wrists and my neck, not looking at me as she does so.

"Find the Green Lady," says Valrún, taking a seat in a velvet chair and crossing her legs at the knees. "Draw on Malen's connection to her if you need to."

"Is this necessary, Your Majesty?" asks Malen quietly.

"You cannot seem to find the Green Lady on your own," Valrún snaps.

Malen twists her hands in front of her. "And will you bind her, too, beneath the palace?"

"Only until Soul's Rest. I've told you, Malen. It is all for the greater good."

The Green Skapari nods unhappily.

Valrún turns her attention to me. "Find her. Do it now."

I don't answer, just close my eyes and feel my magic waking up, sparking and eager under my skin.

"What plan?" I asked Adriel three days ago, when he kept me from freeing the Violet Lord.

"A plan to bring back the Yellow Lord," he told me. *"A plan to restore light magic. A plan to bring back the dark."*

But he wouldn't say more than that, and before I could delve into his mind to find the answer despite his reluctance, he locked the iron collar around my neck, cutting me off from my magic.

I've used Finnur's Prism key the last few nights to allow myself to sleep more easily, to reach for Ballast in my dreams. But I haven't been able to find him, and the worry of it gnaws me to the bone.

"Brynja," says Valrún, her voice low and cold. "Find the Green Lady. Bring her here."

I open my eyes at Malen's gasp. Valrún has thrust a vine through her heart, and a poison flower blooms from her chest. Blood drips onto the floor.

"I am not as powerless as you may think me," Valrún goes on, flicking some invisible speck of dust off the arm of her chair, seemingly impervious to her Skapari's suffering. "Malen should be able to keep herself alive with her magic for a while, but not forever. I suggest you hurry. I have no qualms in letting her die."

Sweat drips from Malen's brow. She pulses with magic, and the air smells very strongly of earth, deep and dark.

I close my eyes and I reach with my power, flinging it out wildly in every direction.

Malen's breathing is ragged and rough. I grip the square arms of the glass chair so tightly the sharp corners cut into my palms. Pain pricks hot.

I catch hold of Malen's thoughts, her frantic, wrenching magic that keeps the air in her lungs and her heart pumping blood, despite the skewering vine, the poisonous bloom.

I try to grasp her Green magic, try to trace it to its source, but it slips away from me, leaves blowing on the wind.

"Find her!" seethes Valrún.

I take a breath. I try again.

I seek beyond the chair, beyond the room, beyond the palace. I stretch my magic out farther than I ever have before, tendrils of thought, fragments of knowing.

A memory winks into my mind: standing outside the ancient walls of Skógur City, magic pulsing warm at my back, snow swirling white before my eyes. Vil came after me, or I would have slipped into the city, walked for a while in the fabled wood that was said to have been grown by the Green Lady herself. Some stories claim that she walks there still, that it remains her earthly dwelling.

Is she there? I ask Malen.

Her answer comes like a gasp of pain: *Yes.*

I open my eyes and glance over at Malen. Blood runs down her leather breastplate and stains the pale green of her dress. She is deathly pale, her forehead creased in pain.

"Heal Malen," I snap at Valrún, "and I will tell you where the Green Lady is."

Valrún frowns where she sits, examining her fingernails. As I watch, they turn a too-bright green, and each one drips a tiny leaf onto the floor. "Bring the Green Lady here, or I will let Malen die."

"I don't know how to bring the Green Lady here. I have neither Violet magic nor Brown—I cannot walk unscathed through time, I cannot shift the foundations of the earth to suit me."

"Oh, I am not certain that's true," says Valrún. "You almost brought the mountains crumbling to their knees, I hear, when your sister died. And you were just a child then. Have you never learned to properly wield your power? *Bring the Green Lady here.*"

"Heal Malen," I insist, stubborn.

There comes a sudden sharp pain through my side as Valrún stabs me with one of her vines. There is poison in it; I feel it seeping into my veins.

"Bring the Green Lady here," she says yet again. "Do not think yourself unexpendable, Brynja Eldingar."

I squeeze my eyes shut against the pain and the poison. I reach my magic out to Skógur City, to the ancient forest it protects. I sense the power in those trees and can almost hear the whisper of the wind in their branches.

My Lady, I call with my mind. *My Lady, where are you?*

In my mind I walk among the trees, trail my hand on rough and smooth trunks, crunch leaves beneath my feet. Magic teems around me, and I almost think that the very trees themselves are awake, and listening.

My Lady, I plead. *My Lady.*

And then I see her.

She treads the ground in the heart of the wood, no shoes on her feet. Her toes curl into the earth, and she cradles a seedling in her hands, young and fair and tenderly green. She has pale skin and long, straight hair that is not a true white, like the Iljaria and the other First Ones, but the color of sunlight on a pale spring morning. Her gown seems to be made of leaves and flowers, and she wears a crown of wood sorrel and wisteria.

Like a whisper of wind she kneels among the trees, scoops a hollow in the earth, and plants the seedling. She stands again and watches it grow, curling up, up, toward the light that seeps in through the canopy of the wood. It sprouts branches and leaves, it rains white blossoms upon the forest floor. Fruits grow, round and dark, with the sheen of purple: plums, I think they must be.

The Green Lady plucks two of them from the tree, which now towers over her, stately and mature. She turns toward me and holds out one of the plums. "Bronze Lord's daughter," she says. "Come and eat."

I go to her, aware of the hard planes of the glass chair where I'm sitting and yet somehow fully present with her here, in the wood. I take the fruit she offers me and bite into it. It is sweet and good, bursting with bright flavor.

"Why do you seek me?" the Green Lady asks.

A breeze stirs through the forest, riffling through her hair and her sorrel-wisteria crown and her dress of leaves and flowers.

"The queen seeks you," I tell her, my voice a thread. I find myself wishing I were here of my own accord. I want to learn from the Green Lady. I want to sit at her feet and listen to her stories of the beginning. I want to know if she grew all the world as she grew the tree that now bows and bends above her.

The Green Lady eats her plum, until only the stone remains. This she presses into my palm; it is smooth and hard and sparking with power.

"The queen means to bind you," I say. "I don't know why. But if you do not come to her, she will kill one who wields your magic."

"Malen Ildjárn," says the Green Lady. "Yes. I know."

"Then will you come?"

She considers this, touching the trunk of the plum tree, which is smooth in places and ridged in others. "It is very far," she says at last. "I do not like to stray from my wood."

"Then you will let Malen die?"

Her face grows sad. The flowers stir in her hair.

"Your sister will come," I say quietly, "if you do not."

I wonder if all the stories are true, if love and enmity both are bound between the Green Lady and the Gray, life and death, springtime and winter.

"I will come," says the Green Lady at last, very heavily.

And then I blink and I am once more bound in the glass chair, the plum stone lying in my palm, Valrún's vine skewering through me, poison seeping into my veins.

Malen has collapsed onto the floor, her eyes filmy and unfocused, the life gone almost wholly out of her.

A shadow steps out of the air, and with it comes the reek of rot and mold and dead things: the Gray Lady, here to collect Malen's soul.

The wrongness of it wrenches through me, and I open my mouth to cry out, but I make no sound beyond a wet, weak moan.

Valrún watches from her chair, which is covered in a tangle of vines and poison flowers. An iron collar rests gingerly on her knees, and cupped in her hands is the Prism Stone. Fear and pain and horror twist inside me.

The Green Lady comes with the scent of summer, on a road of shimmering leaves.

She kneels beside Malen as she knelt beside the plum tree. She puts one hand on Malen's heart and the other on Malen's shoulder and speaks words of life and growth and healing. The poison flower in Malen's chest drops its petals. The vine retreats. The blood soaking her breastplate and her gown turns to apple peels that fall to the floor.

An icy wind blows through the chamber, and the Gray Lady vanishes, Malen's soul no longer ripe for the taking.

Color floods back into Malen's cheeks. Her eyes focus on the Green Lady, and for a heartbeat joy and awe are written in every line of Malen's frame. "My Lady," she whispers, reaching out her hand to touch the First One's face.

I blink and Adriel is here in a swirl of violet. At Valrún's order, he snatches up the collar waiting on her knees and locks it around the Green Lady's neck. It shimmers with the magic of the Prism Stone, the only thing, I realize, strong enough to bind her. Then Adriel and the Green Lady are gone, and I know he's taken her down below the palace, to be chained beside the Violet Lord.

My head is going fuzzy. My vision blears.

I realize distantly that I am bleeding out. The Gray Lady will come for my soul soon.

"Get her up," Valrún barks at Malen.

The Green Skapari looses the restraints from the chair and puts her hand on my shoulder.

I feel magic flow into me as the poison recedes, and then I am strong enough to stand, though my wound is not fully closed and my gown is still heavy with blood.

With a look of apology, Malen re-latches the iron collar around my neck. She helps me from the room. I have to lean heavily against her.

We pass Brandr and Adriel at the door, and I wonder vaguely if Adriel gets dizzy with all his hopping about through time.

Somehow I make it back to the Skapari quarters before the world goes black.

NOW

SAGA

Year 4201, Month of the Violet God

Daeros—Tenebris

I find Aelia on an upper terrace, standing at the stone railing and looking out over Garran City. She is dressed in a sleeveless yellow gown, and a half-circle gold bracelet adorns her right wrist, connected to a cuff on her shoulder by delicate gold chains running up the length of her. The jewelry is meant to evoke the sun, I think.

The day is warm for the middle of autumn, and it's still hard for me to comprehend that there will be no Gods' Fall this year, that we will have light, even in winter.

Brynja's to thank for that. For a moment I allow myself to admit that I miss her, even if I don't know yet quite how to forgive her. I'm startled by the realization that I want to.

I step out onto the terrace, leaving Leifur to stand guard in the archway behind. "Aelia?"

She starts at my voice and turns. "Saga." Her brows lift in surprise.

I quash the urge to hug her, but grasp her arm in greeting. Her skin is cold, and I don't miss the lines creasing her forehead.

"Aelia, are you well?" It isn't what I was going to ask.

She looks back over the city and I join her at the rail, leaning against the sun-warmed stone.

"I will be well," she answers quietly, "when all of this is over."

I study her, trying to untangle the knot of her character. We were friendly last year. We both volunteered in the orphan house, we had tea together in Brynja's suite, we laughed. But even then she was guarded.

"Your father is here," I say slowly, working it out. "You would rather he not be."

She glances swiftly aside at me but gives no other confirmation.

"Are you really going to marry Vil?"

Her eyes gleam with sudden moisture, and she turns her back to the city, hopping up to sit on the railing and letting her feet dangle.

I echo her movements and settle next to her, though I am rather more wary of the drop behind us than she seems to be.

"I will wed him as soon as Iljaria belongs to the empire."

My stomach twists. "Why?"

She shrugs. "I am in love with him, and he is in love with me."

I shake my head. "Eight months ago he was in love with Brynja."

Aelia snorts indelicately. "Eight months ago, one of your gods was bound in the heart of this mountain. Things change, Saga."

The sun heats my shoulders, and I am glad of a little wind that breathes past my face, cooling my skin. I glance at Leifur in the archway, and his eyes catch on mine with such intensity I flush and look away.

"I have been under my father's thumb for the entirety of my life," says Aelia then. "My mother died giving birth to me. I have no siblings, unless you count the scores of bastards my father has sired."

I appreciate her frankness, but it still makes me want to squirm.

"There is only me," she goes on, "and my father's insatiable lust for power. He claims to be schooling me to be empress when he is gone, but that's just an excuse for his"—her jaw works, and she takes a sharp breath—"for his cruelty. He wants to conquer Iljaria to expand the empire, but I think it's more than that. I think he wants to find a way to claim Iljaria's magic for himself."

"What does the emperor of nearly half the world want with magic?" I ask.

She plays with her sun bracelet and hunches her shoulders. "If he could make himself immortal, he truly would have no need of me."

My heart jerks. I put one hand on her arm. "Aelia. Surely he wouldn't—"

She gives a bitter laugh. "Your parents loved you and Vil, or so he tells me. I can't expect you to understand my father's brutality."

I shut my mouth, chastened.

"Your brother is ambitious, too," Aelia says after a moment. "But he isn't cruel. I am more than happy to throw in my lot with him. He has been a solace to me."

I study my fingers, overly aware of Leifur in the archway; I am sure he can hear our conversation—we are not keeping our voices low.

"I am glad for you," I say, though I'm not entirely sure that's true. "But I can't let Vil sell my country to your father."

"He already has."

Anger is a lion inside me; it wants to leap at Aelia's throat, and I have to fight to wrestle it down. "He didn't have the authority. *I* am the ruler of Skaanda. Not him."

"Why?" she challenges. "Because some woman in a temple marked your arm? That's nonsense."

I grit my teeth. "I'm not going to let Skaanda become part of Aerona."

"That isn't up to you."

"Aelia, *why*?"

She looks at me, and the sadness in her eyes pricks my heart. "My father will not allow Vil to wed me until Skaanda and Iljaria both belong to him. Skaanda is easy. Her queen cares more about quarreling with her brother than ruling."

Rage burns through me, and I scoot off the railing and onto the terrace, turning to face the woman I thought was my friend.

"It's true, Saga. There was no reason beyond your anger to come all this way to Tenebris."

"I didn't leave Skaanda leaderless," I snap. "My adviser and my general are—"

Aelia waves her hand. "I don't care, Saga. That doesn't matter."

I take long, slow breaths, trying to get hold of myself. "What about Iljaria? Vil said he'd promised your father something to neutralize magic."

The hint of a smile touches her lips. "Yes. And it doesn't seem to have entered his head yet that we would keep it in reserve to use against *him*, if he attempts to claim magic for himself, like I fear."

"What is it?" I grind out, irritated that she's making me ask.

"It's no secret." She smooths her skirt across her knees, still sitting up on the rail. I think of working with her last year in the orphan house, imagining that I had found in her a soul akin to mine. But I realize now she showed very little of herself to me, that the kinship I felt was all in my own head.

"Vil calls it Skaandan Fire. It's clay jars packed with shards of iron. Our soldiers will launch the canisters at the Iljaria's magical barrier, and when that is broken down, at the Iljaria themselves. Upon impact, the jars burst and the iron nullifies magic, reducing the illustrious Iljaria to the level of ordinary humans. My father can deploy his army without fear that they will be torn apart by barbarian power. It's simple, really."

"Simple," I echo, trying to absorb it all. "My brother invented this Skaandan Fire?"

Aelia nods. "You know how his mind works. Always seeking solutions, coming up with innovative ways to improve the well-being of the people around him." There is pride in her voice.

"I am not sure that will improve the well-being of the Iljaria," I say dryly.

Her face hardens again. "I had not thought Skaandans had any ounce of feeling toward the people who committed genocide against their ancestors."

I clench my hands into fists and don't answer.

"My father intended to use the weapon that was buried in the heart of Tenebris to defeat Iljaria," says Aelia then, "little knowing that it was a god. Your brother has provided him with an alternative. If everything goes smoothly, in six months or so, I will never have to see my father again."

"You think he'll leave you alone to rule the peninsula with Vil?" I say.

"There won't be any need for him to come here once the peninsula belongs to the empire. He'll look to the east or the west to conquer other lands. He'll forget all about us."

I shake my head. "And if he manages to seize Iljaria magic?"

Aelia shrugs. "Then Vil and I will stop him."

I rub my face with my hands. "Aelia. Do you really mean to sacrifice three countries to your father's greed just to get him to leave you alone?"

"Yes," she says without hesitation.

"You don't object to being used like a playing card in his twisted game of War?"

"I will play the cards I need in order to win," she says. "You ought to do the same. Go right now and pledge Skaanda to my father. Bend your knee to him and become a province willingly. He will make you viceroy of Skaanda, as he made Vil viceroy of Daeros. We can all have what we want."

"That is not what I want," I say tightly. "I bend my knee to no one."

She sighs. "Then you are a greater fool than I thought. Go, then. While you still can. But I wish you would stay and ally yourself with us. I would like to have you for my sister, you know, when all of this is over."

I feel heavy and sick, and I glance back to see Leifur watching, his dark eyes hard.

"When will your father march against Iljaria wielding Vil's Skaandan Fire?" I ask. My stomach churns.

"By winter," says Aelia. "And he will not march. He will sail. The first assault will be by sea."

Leifur and Pala and I hold a hasty conference in one of Tenebris's store-rooms. It's close in here, the chamber crammed with sacks of grain and flour, jars of preserves, and wine barrels. I stand next to Leifur, my arm touching his. Pala faces us, a white falcon on her shoulder that she has yet to explain, though I hope I already know the reason for its presence.

"Do you really think this is wise, Your Majesty?" Pala asks, a grim set to her mouth.

I nod, drawing strength from Leifur's steadying warmth. "It is long past time for Iljaria and Skaanda to remember our shared history. It would be far better than to surrender the entire peninsula to the emperor's whims. But I don't know how to get to Iljaria quick enough to be of any use."

"Where did you find the falcon, Pala?" asks Leifur.

"He's been knocking on windows all morning," she returns, "trying to get in. I think he was sent to look for you."

My stomach knots. Word from Finnur, or Ballast, then. I wonder how they knew to find me here.

Pala holds out her arm and the falcon hops onto it, extending one of his legs toward me. There is a little roll of paper tied onto his foot, but it is empty.

"Why would Finnur or Ballast send a blank message?" I ask.

Leifur shakes his head, thoughtful. "Perhaps it is not a message meant for you, but a way for you to send one to them."

My heart races. "Pala?"

She pulls pen and ink out of her pocket.

When I've scrawled a hasty note, we slip out of Tenebris through a back door and stand at the foot of the mountain in the red light of the falling sun. We release the falcon; it wings east, without hesitation.

"What now?" asks Pala.

I work my signet ring off my finger and press it into the other woman's hands. "Return to Skaanda. Tell Hildar to ready our soldiers for war. If I am unsuccessful, Skaanda will have to face the empire's army before the year is out, I think."

"And you and Leifur?" says Pala carefully.

I glance at him. "We will go east after the falcon, in hopes that my message was received, and something faster comes to collect us."

CHAPTER TWENTY-ONE

BALLAST

Year 4201, Month of the Violet Lord

Iljaria—Regla City—the palace

There is blood on the floor of the queen's parlor, more blood on the strange glass chair that sits against a curved window. Fear skitters through my mouse body, paralyzes my human mind.

"Adriel. I thought you were below."

This from a woman who sits in a chair covered in vines and flowers. She has dark skin and white hair and she looks a bit like my mother—something about the curve of her cheek, the way she holds herself. She must be Valrún. The Iljaria queen.

"Am I?" says Adriel. "What am I doing there?"

"Has it not happened for you yet?" says Valrún. "Tiresome. At some point, when you find yourself unoccupied, do report to my parlor ten minutes ago."

"Ten minutes ago," Adriel repeats. "I will be there."

Time magic, I think. *Horrible.*

"Why are you interrupting me?" Valrún asks Adriel then.

"He brought you something," Brandr supplies, lounging against the queen's chair and trailing his fingers along her shoulders. "A one-eyed, shape-shifting mouse."

I find myself lifted in my jar into the queen's view. She takes the jar from Adriel, and at once unscrews the lid fully and dumps me out onto the floor.

I shift into my human form, but it isn't my magic—it is Brandr's, I think.

Then I crouch there, naked, in front of the queen of Iljaria. I feel as if I have been torn apart and reassembled a few too many times. Probably because I have.

"Ballast," says Brandr with utter derision. "I hoped I would never see you again."

I shrug in an attempt at nonchalance. "Sorry to disappoint."

Adriel winks out of existence, and I assume he's going to ten minutes ago—whatever that means—but the next moment I find him beside me, offering me trousers and a shirt, which I pull on swiftly. They fit badly, but I'm grateful for them.

"Adriel," says the queen, "do you really have nothing better to do?"

"Apologies, Your Majesty," he returns, and vanishes again. This time he doesn't reappear.

Valrún refocuses on me. "What exactly is the half-blooded short-lived king of Daeros doing skulking about my palace in the shape of a mouse? That sort of Blue magic is strictly forbidden."

This is slightly mystifying, seeing as I was trained in *that sort of Blue magic* in the Skepna Conservatory. "I came to speak with you, Your Majesty."

She raises her eyebrows. "Did you."

"He's a traitor," says Brandr, "worse than Brynja."

I flinch at the sound of her name, and Brandr sees it and smiles.

"How does it feel to be betrayed by your own lover?" he sneers. "And with the very magic *you helped her* get back?"

"Shut up," I snap, momentarily losing hold of my temper.

"What would you ask of me, half blood?" asks Valrún.

I look up at her and catch the scent of the flowers that twine about her chair. They reek of rot, of dead things. "I want an army," I tell her frankly, "to drive the Aeronans out of my country."

"It isn't *your* country anymore," says Valrún. "By all accounts, you gave it up."

"No, I didn't," I reply.

Brandr laughs. "Brynja gave it up for you."

I try my very best to not let him rankle me. Damn, it's hard.

The queen taps the arm of her chair. "What makes you think I would give you an army?"

"Tenebris," I tell her, "and the labyrinth that runs beneath the mountains. Have you ever seen the cities that our people carved out of the earth? They're beautiful, hardly touched by time."

"Do not claim to belong to the same people as I," says Valrún coldly. "My blood is not diluted, as yours is."

"Regardless, you wish to reclaim the places that once belonged to the Iljaria, do you not?"

She frowns and does not answer.

"We have no use for Myrkur," says Brandr, playing with a bit of Valrún's hair. "The Yellow Lord is no longer bound in the mountain's heart."

"I will send no army," the queen says. "Daeros and Aerona—they mean nothing to me."

"Except that Aerona is coming to conquer Iljaria," I say, playing another card from my hand.

Brandr laughs. "They will dash themselves to pieces on our magic."

"Not if they have found a way to nullify it."

Valrún jerks up from her chair, which causes Brandr to startle backward. She crouches in front of me, grabbing my face with one hand, the points of her nails sharp enough to cut me. "Iljaria magic is strong," she says, "omnipotent, eternal. It cannot be nullified, and you are the greatest of all fools if you think you can cow me with such a tale. You should not have come here."

She shoves me away from her, and I knock the back of my head against the glass chair. It thrums with magic, and I am not sure if it's that or the blow that makes me feel dizzy and sick.

"Adriel!" snaps Valrún to the air, rising to her feet like a towering wave.

The wielder of Violet magic wavers into view before her, and I can't tell if, sequentially, he is the precise version of Adriel who was most recently here.

"Take him to the spire," the queen commands him, gesturing at me with utmost disgust.

Adriel blinks at me like he's never seen me in his life.

"I was a mouse," I offer.

"Interesting," he says. "I look forward to finding out what that means."

Then he grabs my arm and we are somewhere high above the palace in a narrow room that seems to be made all of glass. There is a window that looks over Regla City, a bed, a table, a shelf on the wall. Nothing else.

Adriel vanishes without apology, and I am alone, trying unsuccessfully to unravel the disastrous encounter I just had with the queen. Bronze Lord's bile, I ought to have listened to Brynja. I ought not to have attempted that on my own.

There is no way out of this glass prison—it has no door, and neither walls nor window will break, no matter what I hurl at them. Not even the table makes the merest crack.

I sink onto the bed and tilt my head back against the wall—gently, because of where I whacked it before.

It's then I finally have the time to worry over the blood on Brynja's gown.

Why was there blood on Brynja's gown?

CHAPTER TWENTY-TWO

BRYNJA

Year 4201, Month of the Violet Lord

Iljaria—Regla City—the palace

I wake with the plum stone from the Green Lady clutched tight in my right hand.

Malen is sitting beside me, weaving long blades of grass together with a small loom that rests on her knees.

We are in the women's dormitory, and there is a blanket drawn up to my chin.

"How do you feel?" she asks without looking up from her weaving.

"Better," I say. "A little weak. What about you?"

"I was healed by the Green Lady herself," she says, "while you were healed by a novice. I feel newly made."

"I would hardly call you a novice," I tell her.

She smiles, but it fades quickly.

I sit up, careful not to hit my head against the upper bunk.

"Do you know how Valrún means to restore light magic?" I ask her quietly.

Spots of color appear on her pale cheeks, but she doesn't answer, just keeps weaving. The fibers shimmer with power.

"You should not defy the queen," she says after a while.

"Why doesn't she make Brandr use mind magic?"

Malen shakes her head. "His Prism magic is not strong in every discipline, especially after having it locked away and then restored. As far as I can discern, he has the smallest grasp on Bronze magic out of all of them."

My stomach turns. Perhaps Brandr hasn't found a wielder of Bronze magic to kill yet. Perhaps he means to take *my* power, when Valrún is done with me.

"I wonder why she keeps him around then," I muse.

Malen shrugs. She doesn't suggest it's because the queen loves my brother; we both know that isn't true.

"Malen."

She weaves with a flash of pale fingers, and her tapestry grows quickly, nearly long enough now to reach the floor.

"Would you obey Valrún unto death?"

Her hands still for a heartbeat before resuming their work. "She is my queen."

"But do you think her higher than the First Ones?"

"We are all First Ones," Malen whispers, "or we can become them."

I think of the book my mother put in my glass prison, the one conjecturing that it was possible to seize a First One's power, and concluding *that the First Ones are not in fact immortal; they simply live until someone seizes their power and takes their place.*

"Is that what she means to do? Make herself immortal? But what does that have to do with light magic?"

"You ask too many questions, Brynja Eldingar."

"Don't you see that this is *wrong*?" I plead.

She lets go of the loom and looks up at me. "What is wrong or right," she says, "except what we make of it? Who are you to decide who does or does not deserve power? It is the way the world was written, the way it endures. Is it wrong to seize power if you are powerless? Is it wrong to want something more?"

I think of my brother, sickly and weak, using his Ghost Lord power to steal our father's magic and call it his own.

"Valrún uses *you*," I say tightly. "Uses you to the extent of seizing your patron lady. Do you think *that* is right?"

"She is my queen," Malen repeats. "She is a First One."

"No," I snap. "She's not."

Malen tenses and resumes her weaving.

"Malen," I say, more gently than before. "Why do you follow her? Why do you obey her?"

She sets her chin, her eyes going wet. "I have a sister," she says quietly. "Aris. Her patron is the Ghost Lord and she—" Malen takes a breath, gets hold of herself, and tries again. "Do you know what happens to the Draugur?" she asks, using the formal word for the wielders of Ghost magic.

I think of Brandr, how when we were children my parents claimed the Red Lord as his patron, because they would not accept the Ghost Lord for him. "Only that Ghost magic is forbidden."

Malen nods and wipes her eyes with the palm of one hand. "Draugur are bound in iron and kept in an underground prison in the Ghost Sector. They live out their whole lives in the dark, and it's—it's rare for family members to be permitted to visit."

"Malen," I say, hurting for her.

"I protected Aris when we were younger. I was so strong with Green magic that I gave her some for her own—that's how Ghost magic works, you know. It doesn't nullify power. It absorbs it."

"I know," I say wryly.

"But we were found out a few years ago, and she was taken away." Malen says this dispassionately, like if she allows herself any kind of sentiment, it will break her.

"And because you serve Valrún, you're allowed to visit her."

"Yes." Malen's fingers work faster and faster on the loom. "And Valrún says if I serve her faithfully until she becomes Queen Eternal, she'll take Aris out of that place. We'll be a family again."

"But do you really believe her?" I ask. "Surely you see how cruel Valrún is."

Malen shrugs, closing in on herself again. "If there was even the slightest chance that you could save Lilja, wouldn't you take it?"

I blink and see my sister, hurtling to her death in the Sea of Bones. My breath catches. "Yes," I say quietly. "I would."

Finnur is in the main palace courtyard sitting under a tree, a white falcon on his shoulder and a plate of half-eaten miniature strawberry cakes beside him.

I want to plant the plum stone from the Green Lady, but this doesn't seem to be the right place, so I leave it in my pocket.

I plop down beside Finnur. "Please tell me that Valrún hasn't gotten her claws into you."

He glances aside at me, letting a tiny roll of paper fall onto his lap. "Ballast is here."

All the breath rushes out of me. "Where?"

"In the city. Possibly at the palace. He said he was going to come see you."

Longing knots in my chest. "Well, he hasn't."

Finnur smiles a little. "Chin up, I'm sure he'll be along soon."

I lean back against the tree and shut my eyes, thinking of his hands on my shoulders in the dark, drawing me close, close. With an effort, I shove the memory away. "What does Valrún want with the First Ones? Malen seems to think that—"

"Excellent," comes a voice behind us. "You're both here."

I look around the tree to find Valrún sweeping across the grass, vines and leaves trailing behind her.

Finnur shoots to his feet, and the falcon wings away. I don't miss how he steps on the little roll of paper, grinding it under his heel.

"Finnur," says the queen, and she smiles at him like he is the sun in the deep of winter. Then to me: "Brynja, get up."

I obey, rising shakily.

"Where is the Prism Lady?" Valrún asks.

"The Prism Lady dwells in Skaanda," says Finnur. "She is a priestess there, watching over the people whom the Iljaria cast out."

Valrún doesn't like this, a muscle tightening in her jaw. But she doesn't turn her ire on Finnur. She leans toward me, unlatching my iron collar and letting it fall to the ground.

"Call the Prism Lady," she commands me. "Do it now."

"Your Majesty, I cannot call the Prism Lady like a stray hound to heel."

"You will do it, or I will kill him."

My eyes flick to Finnur.

"Not him," Valrún scoffs.

It feels like the earth shakes beneath me, though all is wholly still. "Where is he?" I whisper. "Where is Ballast?"

She just smiles. "You show a great depth of feeling for the man you betrayed."

I am more than weary of the game I set in motion, but I must play it now until all my cards are gone. "I care nothing for him."

She laughs at my lie while Finnur grimaces—I have done a bad job selling it.

"Where is he?" I demand yet again.

"You have your magic," Valrún snaps. "See for yourself."

I draw a sharp breath and close my eyes, reaching out for Ballast's mind.

I find him almost instantly, stretched out on the bed in the glass spire. He jerks upright as he senses my presence. "Brynja?" he whispers.

"Bal—"

The sharp crack of Valrún's hand across my face brings me back to the courtyard. I pull away from her, heart stammering, cheek smarting. I ball my hands into fists.

"Call the Prism Lady," Valrún repeats. "Or he dies."

I glance up at the glass spire, easily visible from the courtyard. He is so close. *So close*, and yet—

"My patience is running thin, Brynja," says Valrún.

My eyes find Finnur's. There is sorrow and resignation in his gaze. "Will you help me find her?" I ask him quietly.

He nods and holds out his hand.

I take it, and we stride together through space and time, until we are standing in Staltoria City, at the gates of a white temple on a hill. Saga told me about this place once. About the priestess who chose her as the next ruler of Skaanda.

"Finnur," I say. "Must we do this?"

He looks stricken. Sick. "I saw it already," he says. "I looked into time and I saw us. Binding her."

"But it's *wrong*. What Valrún is doing is *wrong*."

He nods, the sunlight touching his face in a way that reminds me suddenly of Ballast. They are the same height, him and Bal. And nearly the same build.

"Yes," he says. "Yes, it's wrong. But the First Ones are allowing this to happen. Allowing Valrún's cruelty to endure. For a time, at least."

I put my hand on the temple wall, feel the magic running through the stones. "Valrún holds something over all of her Skapari," I say, "even my mother. Even me. I'm trying to find a way through this where everyone lives. Where everyone stays safe. But I'm not sure I can. And I'm beginning to think that going along with Valrún at all, for any reason, is the wrong choice."

"I'm trying to keep everyone safe, too," he says. "I'm trying to keep *you* safe. That's what Ballast asked me to do, you know, when he sent me to Iljaria with you."

My heart kicks.

"I think there's something more going on," says Finnur. "Something far bigger than us, some grand story being told that we are too small to understand. Valrún sent us to bind the Prism Lady. But before all that, for a long time now, I've felt the Prism Lady calling *me.* Valrún thinks she's the one in control. But she's not."

The Ghost Lord's voice slides into my memory. *The Violet Lord read the storms of time, and he told me to give you the Prism Stone.*

I wonder what else the Violet Lord read in the storms of time, what other prophecies he gave to the First Ones.

I take a deep breath. "You're right, Finnur. This is bigger than us."

He nods.

Together, we walk through the wall.

We find the Prism Lady in a courtyard by a twelve-tiered fountain, water splashing down and down and down again, until it is collected at the last in a wide white basin shot through with veins of every color I've ever seen, and some I have not. Her hair spills in a river of white to her bare feet, and she is dressed in a simple white habit, girded at the waist with a silver belt. She turns to us and smiles, and in her eyes I see the deep reaches of time: immeasurable, infinite, and wise.

"Well met, Bronze Lord's daughter," she says to me. "I am glad to see you again walking quiet upon the earth." She looks at Finnur with a smile. "And you, son of mine. You have come at last."

"My Lady," says Finnur, his voice cracking. He falls to his knees before her, but she reaches out her hands and pulls him up again.

A warm, fragrant wind blows through the courtyard, stirring through her hair and skirts, causing a mist to spray from the fountain.

"My Lady," says Finnur then, his body tight with agony, with awe, "we are bid to bring you to Iljaria. To our queen."

"Yes," says the Prism Lady.

"Then you will come?" I ask her.

"Yes," she repeats. "It is the way it must be. My kinsfolk cannot think to walk forever upon the world doing as we will without consequence."

"What do you mean?" I say.

Her eyes fix on mine, and I tremble before her. She could turn me to dust with a thought, or the tiniest movement of her finger. "We have watched over humanity," she says. "We have shaped them to our wills. For good. And for ill. I have told my kinsfolk. I have warned them not to interfere. But they have not listened. And so." She inclines her head, first at me and then at Finnur. "We submit ourselves to be bound, for a time. We will bow to the foolish queen's whim. But not forever. So do not despair. This will not be our end. Now lead on. I will follow you."

For a moment more we stand there, Finnur and I, in the peace and power of the Prism Lady's courtyard. Then Finnur again offers me his hand.

I take it, and we step back through time and space, into the Iljaria palace courtyard, which seems weak and grim and colorless now.

The Prism Lady comes on our heels, and she looks at Valrún with what I can only read as indulgence.

She allows herself to be bound with an iron collar that Finnur and I weave with powerful Prism and Bronze magic. Finnur weeps as he works his power. He doesn't look at the Prism Lady, like he can't bear to.

Adriel appears, and he and Finnur together bear the Prism Lady to the underground prison that awaits her.

I stand alone with Valrún, vines curling round her shoulders, winding in her hair. Her glance is satisfied, cruel.

I let her lock the iron back around my throat again, trying not to wince at the awful pain of it.

I know it is futile, but I ask anyway. "Can I see him now?"

Valrún laughs. "Your work is only just begun."

Then she seizes my arm and hauls me into the palace, back to her parlor, and the glass chair that is stained now with my own blood.

She looses my collar and summons Salin, the young Skapari who wields Black magic. She orders me to call the Black Lord.

I think of Ballast in the spire, and I take Salin by the hand, slip into her mind. I read her quickly: She is young and eager, flattered to have been chosen by Valrún as a Skapari. She is new to her post, she has had it only three months, and she longs to please the queen as much as she is terrified to anger her. She has heard rumors of the fate of the last Black Skapari, reportedly strangled with cords of his own darkness. She is determined to do better.

I follow the threads of her magic, down into the dark reaches of the earth. We find the Black Lord there, in a cave by a fathomless pool. There are other things in it than water, a tangled mass of shadows I cannot bear to look at.

I call the Black Lord and he comes, back into Valrún's palace.

Salin weeps bitterly as he is bound and taken away, and Valrún curses at her and sends her from the room.

I sweat in the bonds of the Prism chair, eyeing the queen as she grabs the casket containing the Prism Stone off a shelf. She flips the lid open and shut again several times in succession, then sighs and replaces it. Her eyes fix on me.

My aunt Dagfinna comes into the room, every line of her hard with fury. She doesn't look at me as the queen commands her to stand close enough for me to touch, and orders me to call the Red Lord.

I put light fingers on my aunt's wrist and flick into her mind, but she hurls me right back out again.

"Dagfinna," says Valrún coolly.

My aunt clenches her jaw and screws her eyes shut. She allows me into her mind this time, but only enough that I can catch hold of her Red magic and trace the thread of it to a land impossibly far from here, one I have never heard of. It is a land of dust and fire.

The Red Lord walks through the flames, but they do not burn him. There are creatures in the fire, and they are beautiful and terrible all at once: mesmerizing, but intent on devouring you whole.

I call him, and he turns to meet my gaze. Where his eyes should be, there is only fire.

He follows us back to the palace and allows himself to be bound while my aunt falls on her face to the floor, her horror too deep for tears. Smoke wreathes round me; my skin is chapped and burned.

But Valrún isn't done with me yet. She dismisses Dagfinna, and summons Osa, the Gray Skapari who has lived two centuries already, after the manner of the Iljaria.

Osa stands beside the Prism chair, her hundreds of tiny white braids whispering over her ankles, her face drawn, her eyes looking far away.

Valrún orders me to call the Gray Lady.

I slip into Osa's mind, and for a few moments she lets me read her: death and secrets, shame upon shame, all in service of the crown. Tears pour down my cheeks. I reach for the thread of her magic, and I follow it to a place that is eerily, horribly familiar.

The Sea of Bones.

But whereas the Sea I know is a barren wasteland of ice, here, amid the glaciers that claw blue up into a gray sky, are strewn bones upon bones upon bones, grinning skulls and splintered rib cages, scattered hands and feet.

Through it all the Gray Lady walks, a veil drawn over her hair, the hem of her skirt dark with blood.

Osa trembles at the sight of the First One, though I know this is by no means the first time she has beheld her patron lady.

We walk after her awhile, through the field of bones. My head spins and my heart cracks and I am weary, weary.

We come to a grave freshly dug into the ice, and here the Gray Lady kneels, bowing her head.

There is a weariness in her, a hopelessness, that I never understood from the stories told about her.

"My Lady," says Osa.

The Gray Lady looks up, and I see the impression of a skull beneath her veil, like she has no face at all.

"My Lady, will you come with us?" I ask her.

She looks at Osa, and I shudder and shudder, because for a heartbeat I glimpse the Gray Lady's mind: In it are rotten things, worms and beetles and dead, filmy eyes.

I cannot bear it, and I turn and lead the way back to Valrún. Osa comes. The Gray Lady comes, too.

Osa does not wait to see her patron bound. She quits the room before Valrún dismisses her.

I shake in the Prism chair, empty of all but fear and the horror of what I have done.

It's evening now, stars showing white through the window.

But when the Gray Lady is bound, Valrún still does not release me.

She smirks as my mother sweeps into the room.

My heart rages against my breastbone. I dart into my mother's mind; I beg her to look at me.

But she doesn't.

"Call the Brown Lady," Valrún commands.

Look at me, I say to my mother. *Look at me!*

She keeps her eyes fixed firmly on the floor.

"Do it now!" Valrún snaps.

I reach out to grab my mother's hand, and she stands stone-still and lets me more fully into her mind.

I see her weeping in the tower room of our house by the sea. I see her quarreling with our father. I see her fear of Brandr as he grows stronger and yet stronger, and I feel her despair when she realizes what is happening but is too late to stop it. I see her groveling at the foot of Valrún's throne, begging the queen to bring her husband back or, at the least, to protect her from Brandr.

I grit my teeth to hold back the tears, and grabbing hold of my mother's magic, I follow it to a wide plain, where stones are scattered among a sea of golden grass that ripples in the wind. A woman bends over a potter's wheel, her hands and the hem of her gown covered in a red-brown clay that almost perfectly matches her skin tone. Unlike the other First Ones, her hair is not white but gray, the color of the stones strewn around her.

"My Lady, what are you making?" I ask as my mother and I draw near.

"I am making a jar," says the Brown Lady, the wheel spinning, the clay forming in her hands.

"What will it hold?" I ask her.

She smiles, though she does not take her eyes from her work. "Perhaps everything," she says. "Perhaps nothing at all."

"Will you come with us?" I say then.

The Brown Lady sighs. "He did warn us. I didn't want to believe him. But he is always right."

"Who warned you?" says my mother.

The Brown Lady stills her foot and her hands. The wheel slows, the clay on it becoming quickly misshapen. "Daughter of mine," she says. "I did not expect to see you here."

"The Violet Lord warned you," I say.

The Brown Lady doesn't take her gaze from my mother. "We tell him not to look forward into time, but I suppose he cannot help it. And yes. I will come with you."

My mother bows her head, unable to hold the Brown Lady's gaze, and then I am leading them both back to Valrún. My mother is quiet the whole time her patron is being bound. But I am still in her mind, and I read her sorrow, her regret.

I try not to be bitter that she feels none of those things for me.

Valrún dismisses my mother and then, to my profound relief, unbinds me from the Prism chair.

For a moment I stand before her, my magic burning in my mind and my body, exhaustion weighing impossibly heavy.

Then she locks the iron back around my neck and orders me out of the room.

I go, collapsing on my bunk in the women's dormitory, but though I am weary, body and soul, sleep will not find me.

Half the First Ones are bound beneath my feet—I helped Valrún do it. I can't see past this, despite the Prism Lady's words, despite knowing I had no other choice.

There is no peace in Iljaria, no good, no right. Nothing is sacred, nothing revered. There is only power, the lacking of it, the grasping for more.

I think of my sister, Lilja, absorbed in her work of fusing Green magic with her marvelous machines. What would she have become, if she had lived? Would Valrún have made her a Skapari? Would Lilja have gotten wrapped up in this plot? Or even orchestrated it? I wonder where her ambitions would have taken her.

I wonder where mine would have taken *me*.

Those long years I spent in Kallias's Collection, all I wanted was my magic back; all I wanted was to go home. But if those things had never been stolen from me, if I hadn't spent half my life powerless, adrift—what would it have made me? What would I have wanted?

I've seen what power and ambition have wrought in Brandr, I remember a little what they made of my father. They seem to have broken my mother entirely.

And me?

I am not arrogant enough to believe that I am unaffected by the draw of power. Wielding my magic makes my blood sing; being cut off from it by the iron collar is agony.

But I have begun to realize it is not the most important thing to me, that it never was. I am not willing to spend my own or others' lives in pursuit of it. I would rather live without my magic than use it for cruelty, for harm.

The First Ones are allowing Valrún to bind them. The Violet Lord has seen it all. He knows what will happen, for good or for ill.

But that doesn't mean I should just sit back and do nothing.

I shift on the bunk, the iron collar biting into my neck.

Someone has to stop Valrún. Maybe that's why I'm here. Maybe that's what the Violet Lord saw.

It's too much for me alone, too much even for me and Ballast and Finnur.

But damn the earth and everything in it, I am going to try.

TWO DAYS AGO

SAGA

Year 4201, Month of the Violet God

Daeros—Garran City

It's strange, being alone with Leifur. Largely because it's not really strange at all. I am easy in his company, I feel wholly safe.

We left our horses in the stable in Tenebris—I didn't want Vil and Aelia to know where we were going, and I didn't trust them not to stop us if they found out.

Leifur reasoned we should pick up a few supplies in the city, and he has a pack of food slung over his shoulder now. It thumps against his right side, his sword of course at his left. I'm wearing my sword, too, despite Leifur objecting that I don't need one—that's what he's for, he says.

We leave through the eastern gate as the sun is swallowed up behind us. Leifur folds one hand over mine in the growing dark, and I hold tight enough I can feel the thud of his heart, or perhaps my own, pulsing between our palms.

"What are you thinking, Saga?" asks Leifur as we tread out onto the autumn grass, flattening it beneath our feet.

Clouds of gnats swirl up, and somewhere a nightingale begins to sing.

"I'm wondering if you think we should be heading back to Skaanda right now, instead of farther away from it. I'm wondering if you think I've abandoned our country. I'm wondering—" I slant a glance at him, but I can't fully see him in the fading light. "I'm wondering what you think of me."

He doesn't answer for a while, his stride sure, his hand warm. When he does, it's not the answer I expect.

"Ever since I could remember, I wanted to be in the royal guard," he says. "My father was, you know. He served your father until he was wounded in battle. He lost his leg."

My heart jerks. "I'm sorry, Leifur."

"It all happened before I was born. He was discharged with honor and was given farmland outside Saadone City. He grew wheat and raised horses. Your father came to visit him every so often. My mother would get all flustered and clean the house, and make me comb my hair and serve tea. I served your father tea; did I ever tell you that?"

I shake my head, leaning closer against him, entranced by this peek into his childhood.

"I didn't have any brothers or sisters. My mother wanted me to stay and take over the farm when I was old enough, but I wanted to join the royal guard and win renown like my father. He understood, but he also didn't want to upset my mother. So it was only after—" His voice catches, and my stomach drops to my boots.

"It was only after she died," Leifur goes on, "that my father brought me to Staltoria City, and asked your father to grant me a commission in the guard. Which he did."

"That was five years ago?" I say, trying to think back to the first time I remember Leifur being at the palace.

"Six," he says.

A shiver curls through me. I was a completely different person six years ago.

"I trained alongside Hilf, when he first came," Leifur adds. "I knew him, Njala too."

Grief pierces me like spearheads, and Leifur puts his arm around me and pulls me tight against him. Njala was my body double. She was killed in the skirmish that left me and Hilf captured and eventually led to Hilf's death at Kallias's feet.

"What about Indridi?" I ask then, craving to know more.

"We were friends," he says. "We were close in the two years we all thought you were dead." His voice wavers on that last word. "But she only had eyes for your brother."

"Damn Vil," I say.

Leifur laughs softly against my hair.

We sober the next moment, thinking of Indridi's death.

"She shouldn't have ended that way," I say.

He takes a breath. "No. She shouldn't have. But—but I can't help but thank the gods I didn't have to carry out your brother's command."

I feel suddenly sick to my stomach. "I thank the gods for that, too."

We walk on, into the darkness.

"You wonder what I think of you," says Leifur after a while.

He stops walking, turning suddenly to face me.

He is a shadow against the blooming stars, and I can't see the expression in his eyes.

"Saga," he says. "I think *only* of you. Your bravery and your wit. Your fierce desire to do the right thing. Your passion for our country, your determination to rule well, to keep Skaanda free. You have endured horror after horror, you have borne traumas and griefs you should not have had to bear. But none of it has broken you, and here you are, still fighting for Skaanda, undaunted, unwavering."

He lifts one hand to touch my face, and I shiver, something swelling inside me, pushing against my skin, yearning to be set free.

So I let it.

"Leifur." His name is a whisper, a prayer, a desire, a command.

His fingers tremble on my cheek.

"Kiss me," I say.

"Is that what you really want, Saga?" His voice has gone husky.

"You said back at the palace that—that if I wanted to make you something more than a guard, I have only to say the word."

I hear the crinkle of his lips as he smiles. "Well?"

"I'm saying it."

"What are you saying," he prods me. "Exactly?"

"That when we get home to Skaanda, I'll find a new guard."

He laughs a little. "But *why*, Saga?"

"Because that isn't a job fit for my husband."

His chest rumbles as he laughs and says again, "But *why*, Saga?"

I blink at him in the dark, and I think my blood is on fire. "Because I'm in love with you."

"Well," he says, "a new guard it is, then, in that case. But make sure you choose one who is not as handsome as me."

"Do you think yourself overly handsome?" I demand, to distract myself from my wildly beating heart.

"Do *you* think me overly handsome?"

I grasp his collar and tug him down to my eye level. "Not overly so."

His lips twitch. "And what if I told you you are the most beautiful woman in all the wide stretches of the world?"

"I would call you a liar."

"Then you would be wrong," he says. "There's a first time for everything, you know."

"The only thing I've been wrong about is not telling you sooner," I retort. "But you haven't said anything remotely suitable in return."

"Haven't I?"

He kisses me, long and slow, and when he draws back, he cradles my face with his hands, turning me ever so slightly so we can see each other in the light of the rising moon.

"I love you, Saga." His voice is rough and low. "Body and soul. Life and death. I love you. And I will stand beside you, always, if that is what you desire of me."

The words are part of a simple Skaandan wedding vow, and I tremble as he says them. "I love you, Leifur," I echo. "Body and soul. Life and death. I love you. And I will stand beside you, always, if that is what you desire of me."

He smiles, caressing my cheek, fingers grazing the springing cloud of my hair. "It is," he says.

And then he kisses me again, as long as before—longer—but not slow.

I drink him in. I breathe him as if he were air.

When we draw apart, sometime later, there are tears on my cheeks. He wipes them away with his fingers, and once more folds my hand in his.

We walk on into the night, and it feels as if we have strayed into a story filled with moonlight and magic, where nothing sad or cruel has ever happened, where a happy ending is promised, where love lasts forever.

I am content to dwell in such a story, for as long as I can.

The sun is rising when a—I'm not quite sure what to call it; a vehicle, perhaps?—comes toward us over the hills. It's narrow and sleek and looks vaguely like a small ship, the bottom made of metal, the top dome of glass. There are seats inside, and one of them is occupied by a familiar-looking white falcon.

The vehicle-thing stops in front of us, and a door opens out of the side, steps folding down. Leifur and I look at each other. The falcon *kip-kip*s at us, ruffling his wings. There's a scroll of paper tied to his leg.

Leifur climbs in first, with me on his heels, and when we're both inside, the door shuts behind us, and the vehicle starts to move. I blink and the landscape blurs beyond the glass. We are moving impossibly quickly, but I barely feel it.

The falcon sticks out his leg with obvious impatience. Leifur looses the paper and unrolls it. I tilt my head against his, and we read the message together:

This coach will bear you safely through the Galdur Skjöld and to Regla City, as you asked. Wait for me before you come to the palace. I don't know that the queen will receive you. —F

ONE DAY AGO

VALRÚN

Year 4201, Month of the Violet Lord

Iljaria—Regla City—the palace

I am weary near to death of Brandr, but he is still of use to me, so I cannot discard him just yet.

He lounges on the chaise beneath the window in only his half-buttoned trousers, the prismatic tattoos on his chest and shoulders glimmering in the light of the newly risen sun.

I am still in bed, and he looks at me as if he is thinking about returning. A slow smile plays about his lips.

It is enough to compel me to get up, to draw a thin robe about my naked body. His lazy eyes trace the shape of me. "Valrún," he murmurs, "come here."

But I am not in the mood this morning to indulge his overly confident and far-more-dull-than-he-realizes lovemaking. "Call Malen," I tell him. "I will get dressed."

He pouts a little but gets up to do as I ask, trailing his fingers along the curve of my neck. Irritated, I pull away from him.

Sometimes I permit him to stay as I dress, but today I don't want him. I send him out. It makes him pout rather more.

He was diverting when I initially allowed him into my bed to make his apologies after the havoc he wreaked in Daeros. He was young and eager to please, and confessed every last one of his secrets that first night alone. I realized I could use him. And so I have. His prolonged company is the bitter herb I must continue to swallow if I am to get what I want. But damn him, I grow weary.

I sit before my mirror as Malen works her magic on me, smoothing away any traces of exhaustion or worry or age from my face. When I am Queen Eternal, I will not need her to do this for me anymore. I will not even need to do it for myself. I will simply *be*. And I will no longer have to suffer Brandr's companionship. I will have who I want, when I want. No more and no less. I smile at myself in the mirror.

"What gown will you wear today, Your Majesty?" asks Malen, when she is finished with my face and my hair.

"White," I tell her, "with flowers on."

She brings it to me, a sleeveless white dress that cinches at the waist. When it is laced up, she grows the flowers, roses and lilies and asters, blooming fragrant from bodice to hem. I do not tell her to stop until I am a garden.

I can only seem to grow poison flowers.

I am clothed thus when Dagfinna knocks at my door. Malen waves her in to relay her message.

"There is a woman in the palace demanding to see you," Dagfinna says, the red gem flashing on her forehead.

"How did she get in?" I ask, annoyed. "It is not a petition day."

"She is very strong with White magic," Dagfinna tells me. "She says she will pull the palace down if you do not see her."

A sudden suspicion jabs like a dagger in my heart. There is no possibility. It has been too long. There are no more ghosts to come and haunt me.

And yet.

"What is her name?" I ask Dagfinna.

The Red Skapari looks me square in the eye and says: "Ísold Solstrøm."

The earth shakes beneath me, and I fear I will never again be still.

I am aware of Malen glancing between Dagfinna and me, curious at the mention of my surname.

Malen is far too young to know that I ever had a sister.

CHAPTER TWENTY-THREE

BRYNJA

Year 4201, Month of the Violet Lord

Iljaria—Regla City—the palace

Seven First Ones are bound beneath my feet.

Valrún has not summoned me to call more, and I live in dread of it. I can no longer slip my collar; Adriel found and confiscated the Prism key, and keeps a wary eye on Finnur, in case he tries to give me another.

Cut off from my magic, I feel stupid, dull. It isn't like it was during the decade I spent with my power locked inside me; I am hardly half myself, and at my throat the iron boils and burns. I scarcely sleep, and I cannot dream.

Once a week or so, since I have been here, Valrún calls the host of her Skapari to dine with her at an extravagant feast in her great hall. Tables replace the thrones on the dais, accompanied by straight-backed chairs carved with blade and magic, shimmering each in the color of the power wielded by their occupant.

At the dinners I have attended previously, Valrún sits at the high table with Brandr and my mother—if she is present—these seats of honor reserved for the queen's Prism Master and architect. For their part, the Skapari sit at a half-circle table that faces the high one, our chairs arranged around the curve.

But tonight, when I enter the great hall with the rest of the Skapari, bleary from lack of sleep, the pain at my throat almost too much to bear, Valrún sits at the high table alone. The dais and the half-circle table are larger than they were—most likely my mother's doing. She and Brandr are sitting on either end of the curved table, my mother tense and pale, my brother thunderous.

The two chairs on either side of Valrún are present, but empty. The queen is clothed in a gown of leaves that shimmer every shade of green imaginable; there are clusters of berries on her shoulders, and spiderweb-thin vines trace the curves of her cheeks.

I take my seat with the other Skapari, Adriel on my left and Malen my right. On Adriel's left are Finnur and Brandr. On Malen's right sit Osa, Jóvin, Salin, my aunt Dagfinna, and then finally my mother. All of us are quiet, even Finnur and Adriel.

The silence stretches on. Valrún doesn't call for the attendants to bring out our dinner. Neither does she address us. She just sits there, her face hard, the leaves of her dress rustling in a magical wind.

"In three weeks' time," she says suddenly, "in the moment when autumn turns to winter, we will all of us assemble on the hill outside the city, where the First Ones awoke in the time before time. Together we will call the Yellow Lord down from his prison and restore light magic to our people. Together we will have again Soul's Rest, that was so wrongfully taken from us."

I dig my fingernails into my thighs. This is wrong, wrong. We have the sun all the year round now—isn't that light magic as it should be? No. I will not let Valrún bring back the dark.

But the queen isn't finished. "My Skapari represent here every branch of magic but two, and the Green Lady has seen fit to fill out the missing number and restore to me members of my family I thought forever lost, all at once."

A suspicion stirs within me that is hope and dread together. My heart is a wild thing, bashing against my ribs.

"Rise now," Valrún commands, "and make obeisance to my sister and her son, the high princess and prince of Iljaria."

I stand with the others and turn toward the door. A woman strides in, a young man after her.

All the breath leaves my lungs and my knees turn to water.

Because it is Gulla.

And it is Ballast.

ONE DAY AGO

VALRÚN

Year 4201, Month of the Violet Lord

Iljaria—Regla City—the palace

I should have made sure my sister was dead before I abandoned her in Daeros. Regret is a bitter thing. So is mercy.

The ghosts you do not kill come back to haunt you.

I have recovered from the shock enough that when Ísold steps into my parlor, her hair braided back from her face, a stone bound white and shining on her forehead, I am able to regard her impassively, though everything inside me is alight with rage.

For a moment, after Dagfinna withdraws and shuts the door, my sister and I stare at each other.

"Release my son," she demands, her musical voice clipped, percussive.

This is not the first thing I expected her to say to me; I am not sure what it was, but not this.

I have wondered, of course, what became of her. I have even wondered if my lost sister and the Daerosian king's mutilated Iljaria wife were perhaps one and the same. I grilled my Prism Masters about it—both Brandr and his father. But she was called by a different name, and so I deluded myself into believing that it wasn't her, that I wasn't in danger of her returning and seeking her revenge.

"Your son? Oh. Ballast."

"Yes," she says fiercely. "Release him."

I dip my chin in the barest show of acknowledgment and stride to the window. Sunlight streams through the glass, and I scowl at it.

"Valrún," says Ísold. "I am here to claim my birthright, and my son's."

I jerk around to face her, poison flowers blooming among Malen's innocuous garden. "You will never sit on the throne of Iljaria."

Her fingers play with the dress of her skirt. "We were supposed to share it," she says. "You and I. Green and White. More powerful than one color alone." .

"But *you* got all the power," I spit at her.

She lifts her shoulders. "Not all of it. Not enough to save me when you tricked me and abandoned me and left me behind."

I curse, and her jaw goes tight.

"You could have used your magic to flee at any time," I scoff. "You hurl more blame at me than I merit. You make yourself a victim. It was your choice to stay there."

Her eyes have a haunted look to them, and she says quietly, "You have never been caught in the web of a wicked king, tangled in the strands of his power, no matter how you tried to wriggle free of them."

"Always excuses with you."

She raises her white brows. "Are you sure you do not speak of yourself?"

Fear and anger boil in my chest. "I will call my Skapari. I will bind you in iron. I will cast you out."

"No," says Ísold. "No, that is not what you are going to do. You are going to release my son, and you are going to restore to the both of us the inheritance you stole away. Ballast will be high prince, and if you are unwilling to call me queen beside you, I will accept the title of high princess, for a time."

"You have not the authority to demand such things of me," I spit at her. I sweep past her, ready to call for aid at the door.

She grabs me by the arm, freezing me where I stand with a single note of her song magic.

I hate her with everything that is in me. I curse my younger self for not killing her in the only moment in time when I could have overpowered her, and chose not to. Fool, fool.

"I am sure," she says. "I am *quite* sure, that you manipulated the previous Prism Lord, or perhaps a lover in possession of time magic, to . . . alter memory of me, to essentially erase my existence. But I have spent the last few weeks visiting old friends and acquaintances, people on the periphery who were untouched, or hardly touched, by your careless time magic. And I am remembered. Documented, even. The Vaxandi who aided our mother in the birthing of us holds the certificate from the day we were born. And do you know what it states, Valrún?"

I stare at the floor and wish my poison flowers could overpower her cursed music. Fool, fool.

"I am the older," she goes on. "By twelve minutes."

I clench my jaw and don't answer her. There isn't any point. Cruel that the number of the First Ones' perfection separates me from her.

"Release Ballast," she says. "And restore us to our inheritance."

I shut my eyes and think of the First Ones, bound in iron beneath us. I remind myself I need only to indulge my sister for three weeks. When I am Queen Eternal, I will slay her, as I should have done long ago, and all of this will fade to nothing more than an unpleasant memory.

"Very well," I say through gritted teeth. "I will do as you command."

She lets go of me, and I turn to face her.

We are not identical; we never were, and time and Green magic have worked to further differentiate us. Yet I still see myself in her eyes, in the bow of her lips, the set of her shoulders. I should have known, the instant Ballast shifted from mouse to human, that there was a bond of blood between us.

"*Now*, Valrún," she says. "Release him *now*."

I stride to the door and summon Adriel to go to fetch him.

CHAPTER TWENTY-FOUR

BALLAST

Year 4201, Month of the Violet Lord

Iljaria—Regla City—the palace

My gaze is riveted to her, like she is the only person in the room, in the world. I can see, even across the distance that separates us, that there are blisters on her neck from the iron collar, that her freckled skin is wan, her eyes dull. The cursed metal is poisoning her, cutting off her magic, draining her of life.

But there is no missing the bald shock on her face.

I would have warned her, if I could. I would have told her, but my mother didn't even tell *me* until after Brynja had already gone, and there was no way to get a message to her that wouldn't have been intercepted, save in the single dream we shared.

I am royalty twice over, a prince of Daeros and a prince of Iljaria.

Shed your father's surname, my mother told me with her fingers. *Claim your birthright and your true name: You are a Solstrøm, like me and my father and my grandfather before me, on down to the beginning of time. There is great power in you, and that is no accident.*

I told my mother I had no wish to claim the throne of Iljaria. She told me I would change my mind. So we traveled to Iljaria together. She sent me to the Skepna Conservatory to be trained. She bade me wait until the time was right.

But I didn't come to Iljaria because of my mother. I came for Brynja, and I couldn't wait any longer.

My mother was angry when Valrún had me brought down from the glass prison. She had wanted the both of us to storm the palace in a haze of triumph, her wielding White magic and me Blue, displaying our power for all to see.

Instead, she had to come and rescue me.

And now here we are, here *I* am, sitting at the right hand of the queen of Iljaria, who, as it turns out, is my aunt. My mother sits on her left, and I do not understand how she can be so calm.

I cannot be calm.

I half rise out of my seat, but my mother shoves me down again with a soft note of her magic.

I stare across at Brynja, willing her not to imagine I have betrayed her. I try to speak into her mind, as she taught me, but the iron around her neck makes my words bounce back at me like a handful of pebbles.

Blue Lady, I can't bear this.

You must, says my mother's voice in my head. I blink in surprise. She has always believed that all branches of magic are available to the Iljaria, beyond the particular one granted them by their patron lord or lady. But she has never spoken into my mind before.

Attendants sweep in with platters of food that they set on the tables before us. Brynja drops her gaze from mine and does not lift it again for the whole of the dinner.

I can't eat. I feel as if my skin is made of stinging ants.

"Be still, Ballast," says Valrún.

I don't know how to be still.

Brynja, I beg. *Brynja, please look at me.*

But she doesn't.

At long last, when the meal is over, Brynja leaves the hall with the other Skapari, while my mother and I are ushered to our rooms in the royal wing.

There is a guard posted at my door.

And it is barred with iron.

And I cannot go to her.

I am not a prince here—just another kind of prisoner.

I bang my hands on the door until my knuckles split.

NOW

VIL

Year 4201, Month of the Violet God

The White Sea

The emperor's warships flash and gleam in the sun as they are let loose from their moorings at the docks of Oram City. There are a hundred and thirty of them, and they glide east through the waves like a flock of white swans.

I stand beside Aelia in the foremost ship, my face lifted to the light. My blood is singing. The gods have smiled on us.

We rode hard for a day and a half from Tenebris to meet the ships, me and Aelia and her cursed father and our generals. The ships themselves sailed from the Port of Navis, where they were built, and down along the coast of the isthmus that connects mainland Aerona with the peninsula.

The warships were already filled with soldiers.

Now they're loaded with thousands of canisters of Skaandan Fire, ready to bring Iljaria to her knees.

It's nothing short of a miracle that the iron ore was mined and manufactured in time, a sign that the gods are with me. It was the gods, too, I think, who led me to the preliminary plans for the weapon among Kallias's scattered papers—why else would I have found them before anyone else? Blessing upon blessing, and this time my sister didn't take it away from me.

The Daerosian governors are furious at the tax I levied to finance the Skaandan Fire, but it won't matter soon. When Iljaria belongs to the empire and Junius goes home, I will be the ruler of the entire peninsula, a king above kings. I will appoint new governors if I can't soothe the current ones.

I will order my kingdom for the good of all, take power from those who don't deserve it, and give it to those who do. Junius thinks to claim magic for himself? I'll find a way to do it first. I will clothe myself and Aelia in power, and we will be strong enough, then, to take her father off his throne, to repay him in kind for all the cruelty he showed her.

Gods, this feels good.

Junius steps up to the rail on my left and I tense, flicking my eyes to Aelia. Drops of salt water cling to her cheek, and she is so beautiful it takes the breath out of me. But with her father here, I don't dare touch her.

"Well, Viceroy," says Junius, eyes gleaming as he leans into the wind. "What say you?"

"We will be victorious," I say confidently. "All hail the empire."

I glance at Aelia. Her jaw is tight.

"Your little weapons had better work," says Junius then.

"They will," I tell him.

He shrugs like he doesn't really have a stake in the game, though the one hundred and thirty warships belie him. "If they don't, Vilhjalmur, if we are unsuccessful in conquering Iljaria, I will shove a canister into your chest cavity and light it on fire. I imagine it will work on you, at least."

Hatred buzzes along my skin, but I do my best not to show it. "The Skaandan Fire will work, Your Imperial Majesty. A few weeks from now, Iljaria will belong to the empire."

Junius smiles, and I am struck suddenly by his similarity to Kallias; both men seemed to take great pleasure in the pain of others.

"I hope, for your sake, that you are not mistaken." He steps past me and puts one hand on Aelia's arm. "Daughter, come and serve me wine in the cabin. The day is too bright."

"Forgive me, Father," Aelia returns, "but I feel less ill out here. The wind eases my stomach."

Junius frowns, his grip tightening on her arm.

My every nerve is alight, but as much as I would like to grab the emperor of Aerona and shove him off the side of the ship, there are too many soldiers watching, and I'm not eager for a sword in my heart.

"I will only be sick if I leave the deck," says Aelia stoutly.

"Very well," says Junius.

He lets her go and stalks off down the deck in the manner of a man used to ships.

Aelia sags a little against the rail, and I let out a breath, trying to distill some of my tension. I want nothing more than to pull her into my arms and kiss her wildly, but I don't dare, with her father so close.

"We will be rid of him soon," I say quietly.

Her breath hitches.

The ships sail on.

CHAPTER TWENTY-FIVE

BRYNJA

Year 4201, Month of the Violet Lord

Iljaria—Regla City—the palace

Ballast is here.

He's *here*, and I can't get to him, and the iron is making me ill, and I don't know how much longer I can bear it.

I lie on my bunk in the women's dormitory, watched closely by my aunt Dagfinna. She sits in a green wicker chair with two baskets on either side of her. The one on her right contains empty glass globes that she methodically picks up, fills with Red magic, and then sets in the basket on her left. She refuses to either talk to me or look at me, yet any time I so much as shift, she's instantly beside me, both hands filled with fire.

Ballast is an Iljaria prince. Valrún's nephew.

Gulla is Valrún's *sister*. Last year I asked Gulla what her story was, where she came from. She told me she and her sister wanted to see Tenebris, that they snuck out of Iljaria and were found by Daerosian soldiers. She said her sister used Green magic to get away, but no one ever came back for Gulla.

I can fill in the gaps easily enough. Knowing Valrún, it wasn't an accident that Gulla was left behind. Gulla clearly has some sort of power over Valrún, else the queen would not have introduced Gulla and Ballast to her court with such pomp.

Ballast.

Here.

He looked so horrified at dinner, like he was afraid I would think he had kept this from me. I know he didn't. We told each other everything in Tenebris; there are no secrets left between us. Which means he has known for only a short while—Gulla is the one who has kept this close for years on end. I would rail at her for not telling the truth sooner if I didn't know exactly what it feels like to be a captive in Tenebris with a dangerous identity.

But I need to see him. I need to talk with him. I can't bear that he's here, so close and yet vastly out of reach.

"Aunt."

She jerks her gaze toward me, a glass globe in one hand, a flame of fire magic in the other. "You are confined to the dormitory unless Her Majesty sends for you," she says coldly.

"But I need to see Ballast."

My aunt shoves the fire into the globe, then sets the globe in a basket of already-filled ones with a *clink*. "You had your chance with him, and by all reports squandered it. You stay here."

I squeeze my eyes shut, trying not to feel the iron seeping into my skin. "At least let me loose," I whisper. "For a little while."

"I am not a fool" is her only answer.

"Aunt," I say again, shifting onto one elbow and studying her face, which is so like Indridi's it makes my breath catch. "Where is Uncle Kár?"

She fills another globe, tendons straining against her hands, and sets it with the others. "He taught in the Stjarna Conservatory, before light magic was taken from the world. He could not bear the loss of his power and the loss of our daughter in the same year. He went to the Deya."

The Deya are the wielders of Gray magic. Death magic.

There's a sick, awful twist in my belly. "I'm so sorry, Aunt."

She shrugs. A Red magic globe slips from her hands and shatters on the floor. There is a sudden, overpowering flare of fire, but one word from my aunt makes it vanish again.

"Kár's choice was his own," she says then. She bends deep into the basket and picks up another globe but does not fill it. She turns it over and over in her hands. "Indridi had no choice." Her sharp eyes fix suddenly on mine, wells of anger and grief. "You could have saved her."

Tears slip down my cheeks, and I shake my head, trying not to feel the cold burn of the iron. "I couldn't, Aunt Dagfinna. I'm so sorry. You can't know how much. But I couldn't save her."

Dagfinna clenches her jaw. Her eyes flare red as she sends magic into the globe.

"You could help me now," I say quietly. "Stand up to Valrún. Let's stop her. Let's fix all this."

"I follow my queen. I am faithful to her alone."

"But *why*?"

Once more Aunt Dagfinna lifts her eyes to mine. "When she is Queen Eternal, when she has brought back the dark—she will right every wrong. She will undo death and sorrow. She will bring life. Hope. Joy."

"Do you really believe that?"

She fills five globes in quick succession, the flashes of Red magic making me a little dizzy.

"What has she promised you?" I prod her.

Her hands still, but her shoulders shake. "She has promised me my Indridi. A host of Vaxandi, to bring her back to life."

Horror grips me. "But Indridi has been gone for more than a year. That isn't possible."

"Who are you to tell me what is possible and what is not? You, who as good as killed her!"

My heart breaks. "I miss her, too," I say. "I know it isn't the same as it is for you. But I miss her, too."

"She was away from home for half her life," Dagfinna cries, "away from *me*, serving my brother, your Lords-damned *father*. She never came back. I haven't seen my daughter since she was thirteen years old. Don't you dare tell me you miss her, too. Damn you. Damn you to the Skaandans' hell."

Tears prick behind my eyes, and I turn my back to my aunt. I cry as silently as I can. I had been holding on to hope that my aunt would remember our kinship, would ally with me in the end. I have no illusions about that now. But I cry for Indridi. I cry for Dagfinna. I cry for all the years lost because of my father, moving children about like game pieces on his Lords and Ladies board, willing to make any sacrifice to get what he wanted. Nobody won, in the end. Least of all him.

There is a shift in the air after a while, and I turn back to my aunt's chair to see Finnur sitting there instead. There's a white falcon on his shoulder.

I sit up so fast I make myself momentarily dizzy. "Will you take me to him?" I blurt, not bothering to hide my eagerness.

"I can't, Brynja. He's being watched—as am I. Dagfinna went to get a glass of water and will be back in a moment."

He's using Violet magic to even speak to me, then.

"I just wanted you to know that *I* didn't know about Gulla and Ballast. I don't think she told him before we left Tenebris."

Despite the burn of the iron at my throat and the lingering pain of my conversation with my aunt, I smile a little. "I figured as much, Finnur. I'm not angry with Ballast, just surprised. There's no need to defend him to me."

Some of the tension relaxes out of Finnur's body. But not all. "I need you to promise you're not going to do anything stupid, with Ballast here."

I grunt in annoyance. "Why would you think that?"

"Brynja."

"Fine. I won't do anything stupid. But—"

"Saga is here," he cuts me off. "In Regla City."

It seems this day will never run out of surprises. "Saga? What's she doing here?"

Finnur grimaces. "I think she's come to ask for an army to drive Aerona out of Daeros."

I don't know if I want to laugh or scream. "You should tell her to get in line."

"I told her to come to the palace," Finnur says. "I told her to make a formal request to Valrún."

"Godsdammit, Finnur, why? Valrún will tear her to pieces!"

His eyes go grim. "I don't think she will. She's still keeping up the pretense of pacifism, and with Gulla and Ballast here, she can't afford to look cruel or unstable. She doesn't want her subjects to start asking questions, to wonder if Gulla is the one who ought to wear the crown."

This gives me pause, and for a moment I wonder if Ballast means to angle for the Iljaria throne.

"I'm hoping all this will distract the queen from whatever it is she means to do with the First Ones. We have to stop her, and we have to do it now." Finnur sets his jaw, looking suddenly far older than his sixteen years. "It's time we spread all our cards out, Brynja, and see who holds the winning hand."

I don't like this at all. "Will you at least tell Ballast that I'm not angry with him? That I—"

Finnur is gone, and Dagfinna is just resuming her seat, a cup of water in one hand. She looks hard at me, fire flickering just under her skin. "Who are you talking to?"

I lie back down on the bunk, turn away from her, and shut my eyes. "No one."

I try to use my magic despite the collar, try to break it off me. I reach for dreams. But I cannot find them.

CHAPTER TWENTY-SIX

BALLAST

Year 4201, Month of the Violet Lord

Iljaria—Regla City—the palace

"Ballast."

My mother's voice rouses me from my place on the floor, where I fell asleep without meaning to, my hands aching and bloodied, all of me wrung out.

I open my eye, heart frantic, and I shove to my feet, cursing at my wobbly, cramped legs. I move to step past my mother at the door, but she stills me with a touch. I focus on her, tell my pulse to slow.

She's dressed formally, in a glittering white gown and etched silver breastplate, a circlet of white gems on her brow.

"You're to bathe," she tells me, "and get dressed. Valrún has sent clothes for you. There is to be dinner and a demonstration."

I eye her warily. "A demonstration of what?"

"Power, I imagine. My sister wishes to impress the Skaandan queen—"

"Saga's here?" I interrupt.

My mother frowns. "So I understand."

"But why—"

"Iljaria is where the power is," my mother says, "and, currently, Valrún holds the majority of it. Everyone wants a piece. Even Skaanda."

"But why would Valrún indulge Saga's presence?"

"To impress her, and to show all of Iljaria that *Valrún* is the one who sits on Iljaria's throne. Not me." She pauses, considering me. "Not you."

That feels like a kick to the gut. "I haven't changed my mind, Mother. I'm not here for that. I'm here for—"

She cuts me off: "I know. But Ballast, I need you to promise me you won't do anything . . . foolish on Brynja's account. There is far more at stake here than you understand."

My heart thrums and my hands ache. "I know what's at stake."

"Then you will let Brynja look to her own affairs, while you look to yours."

"I thought you cared about Brynja. I thought you were her friend. I thought you trusted her."

"Trust her? No. Not anymore." My mother lifts my injured hands in her own and sings her magic over them. I watch the blood fade, the cuts close up, the skin grow new again. The pain eases, then vanishes altogether.

"I was a friend to her and she to me, for a time. But that time has passed. She doesn't need me any longer, and she doesn't need you, either. Brynja is powerful. Ambitious. Like her father was before her. I am sure she's playing games of her own with Valrún, no matter what it might look like. *You* need to be sure in your own mind whose side you're on, and what exactly it is you mean to accomplish. You could do far more, my son, sitting on the throne of Iljaria than you ever could in Daeros."

There's a sick knot of anger in my belly as I think of my sisters, of Rute and Zenobia running the orphan house, of Melitta at her bakery, of my governors and generals—of an entire country I swore to protect, to lead, to live and to die for.

"You're wrong, Mother. On all counts. Daeros needs me. I promised to rule her well, to heal all the wounds my father inflicted, to pull her fully out of the darkness and into glorious light. And I still intend to. I won't abandon Daeros to the whims of an empire who cares nothing at all for my people."

"You've abandoned it already."

"No, I *haven't*." I pull my hands out of my mother's and stalk over to the narrow window. "I don't belong in Iljaria. I would make a very poor king of a country I care nothing for, and that cares nothing for me. I know whose side I'm on. I know what I'm trying to accomplish." I take a breath, my eye blurring a little. "And Brynja isn't playing games."

My mother sighs and steps up beside me. "Ballast. I know what her family is like. They were born into betrayal and lies and grasping for power. Nothing less, nothing more."

"That isn't Brynja. You're wrong."

"Brynja lied about who she was for a decade. She meddled in your *mind*, Ballast. Chose her will over yours. She *used* you."

The anger is hard to grind under my heel, but I do it anyway. "I don't care about that."

"You should. Why are you so willing to let yourself be manipulated by her?"

"She's never manipulated me."

My mother gives me a hard look. "Ballast."

I clench my jaw. "Brynja has never asked me to do or to be something I am not, unlike every single other person I have ever met."

Her chin trembles. "I should have taken you out of Tenebris long, long ago. As soon as I realized you existed, I should have fled."

I eye her, knowing what she suffered, because I suffered it too. "Why didn't you?"

"I was too afraid. Of your father."

I look away.

"Of my sister, too. I was accustomed to being manipulated and tormented and used. I didn't let myself imagine the possibility of any other reality."

"Until Brynja set the world to rights again," I say.

"It wasn't Brynja. It was you."

"Brynja saved all of us. And she did what I never could, what you never could, either."

"She killed him," says my mother.

My chest goes tight. "As she had every right to. There is far more evil in my family than hers."

"You are not your father," my mother says sharply, "just as I am not my sister."

I regard her unhappily. "What is it you want, Mother?"

"Freedom," she says. "Worth. The life that was taken from me."

"You have it." I grasp her by both arms and look into her face, and it is strange to see her scars smoothed away, like those years in my father's court never existed. "You have all of that."

"What Valrún is doing is wrong," my mother says. "Our race is blessed with power and long life, but not omnipotence, not immortality. She would reshape the world to her whims, and I won't let her. I *won't*, Ballast!"

"I'm not asking you to. I'm asking you to trust me. To trust Brynja. Like you did before."

Her eyes go hard, but I don't miss the sheen of tears. "Brynja is under the sway of the queen. You *cannot* trust her."

"She isn't. You saw her! She's bound in iron. Her will is not her own."

"We both know that Brynja is practiced at appearing weak, when in fact she is not."

I take a breath. My mother isn't entirely wrong. This is the downside to Brynja's cunning, covert plans—they build distrust that is not easily overcome. She has revealed her whole self to me, while showing only parts to everyone else. It's difficult to trust someone when you don't know everything. I understand that. But I also understand that, whole truth or not, Brynja is worthy of trust.

"We won't agree on this," I say. "No matter what you say against her, I won't doubt her, and I won't apologize for it."

My mother takes my chin in her hand, and I freeze because it's what my father used to do. I try to tamp down the visceral animal of my fear.

"Get dressed, Ballast," she commands. "And when you go to join the others—swear to me you won't do anything foolish."

I jerk away from her and go get ready.

But I make no promise.

CHAPTER TWENTY-SEVEN

BRYNJA

Year 4201, Month of the Violet Lord

Iljaria—Regla City—the palace

The queen parades out her Skapari like we're performers in a traveling troupe, each wearing the color of our particular magic in the most ostentatious display possible.

My sleeveless gown is made up of hundreds upon hundreds of tiny bronze scales, sewn together on a linen under-dress and almost unbearably heavy. A polished bronze disk flashes from my forehead. My cheeks and lips, brows and lashes, arms and shoulders, have all been painted with glittering bronze powder. My ears are weighed down with bronze earrings, and there are bangles on my wrists and my ankles. At my throat the iron collar burns.

The other Skapari are equally outlandish. Adriel is wearing deep-purple robes sewn with many thin, fluttering purple ribbons that give him a strange fragmented effect as he walks. His face is painted with glimmering swirls of violet, and there are violet gems wound in his hair.

Malen's gown is made of flower petals, with a girdle of braided leaves. Lilies and asters and jasmine cascade from her hair, and her cosmetics are all varying shades of green, giving her an eerie, unearthly appearance.

My aunt Dagfinna wears red and orange and yellow, the colors of shifting flame, and real tongues of magical fire flicker along her skin. She looks very like Indridi in the moments before she died. My stomach twists, and I have to turn my eyes away.

Osa is gowned and cloaked in pale gray, her cheeks and hands painted silver, her hem and hood traced with swirls of crackling ice.

Salin appears to be clothed in living shadow; perhaps she is. Darkness twists and pulses around her. A black gem sits cold on her brow.

Jóvin wears gold scales to my bronze ones and is crowned with a headdress shaped to look like the sun.

My mother's gown is the color of stone and deep earth, with steel spaulders on her shoulders and a stone headdress set with a brown gem on her brow. She has the appearance of a walking statue.

Finnur's robes are made up of tiny prismatic beads that bend the light around him as he walks. His white hair nearly glows, and his face is covered in glittering diamonds. He looks as if he's made of pure magic.

We file into the great hall, my mother first and me last, and I see that once again the shape of the hall has been altered to suit Valrún's purpose.

The dais runs the whole length of the room, and on it sit the carved and colorful chairs normally reserved for use while dining. The ceiling is higher, almost impossibly so, rising to a dome that swirls with stars and magic.

Facing the dais is Valrún's throne, with two other, lesser thrones to her right, and an elaborately carved chair to her left.

The floor is grass, dotted with flowers, and only some of them are Valrún's poisoned ones.

I follow the other Skapari across the room and up the shallow steps of the dais. My chair is in the middle, and I sink into it, fighting the urge to make another futile attempt at clawing off the iron collar. My heart is overquick in my ears; I feel dizzy and slow, like my mind is pushing through sludge.

Valrún sweeps into the hall and sinks into her throne. Her crown is one I haven't seen before: It's made of prismatic glass and set with twelve gems in every color of the First Ones.

Brandr comes at her heels and takes up a post behind her, his hands tight on the back of the throne. He is dressed similarly to Finnur, though without the gems on his face. I wonder if it bothers him.

After Brandr comes Gulla—Ísold—dressed all in white, and on her heels is—

Ballast.

The sight of him unravels every part of me. His eye catches mine, and I ache for the anguish in his face.

He is wearing trousers and a long, fitted robe that is sewn with feathers in every shade of blue. The feathers climb up his collar, and a few have been artfully arranged to cover his missing eye. He looks like a man caught in the middle of transforming into a bird.

Ísold and Ballast sit on Valrún's right, Ballast never breaking my gaze.

Tears blur my vision. I can't bear this.

And then two more people come into the hall, a man and a woman, both wearing dark cloaks with swords at their hips. I blink.

"Saga!" I shout, jerking up from my chair.

At least seven different forms of magic shove me down again.

Saga glances at me briefly before sinking into the chair on Valrún's left. The man with her is Leifur; he stands tall and grim at her side, right hand on his sword hilt. Both are changed since I saw them last year. Saga looks worryingly thin, with shadows under her eyes, weighed down by long sorrow. Leifur looks like he's ready to rip the world apart for her. That's an interesting development.

"I do apologize for my Skapari," says Valrún to Saga in an exaggerated whisper. "My Bronze one especially has not learned her manners. But please! Eat and drink and enjoy the spectacle. There will be plenty of time to discuss our countries' affairs later on."

Valrún claps her hands, and four young attendants dressed in black come bearing food and wine on mirrored trays to Valrún, Ísold, Ballast, and Saga. Vines grow up out of the floor, forming strong, leafy tables. The attendants set the trays down, then go to stand on the edges of the room in case they are needed again.

Brandr snatches the glass of wine from Valrún's tray and drinks the whole thing in a few swallows. I can see the anger in him, stronger than his magic.

Leifur takes a sip from Saga's glass, waits a moment, and then gives it to her. He tastes her food, too, before allowing her to eat it: squares of spiced meat, black rice balls, and desserts that look like flowers in vases but are really sugar work, artfully crafted.

Ísold doesn't touch her food. Ballast doesn't even glance at his.

Valrún claps her hands again, gesturing to all of us sitting on the dais. "Runa," she says to my mother, "show to our guest the power of the Brown Lady."

My mother eyes the queen coolly. "What would you have me do, Your Majesty?"

Valrún shrugs. "Change the room around us, and then put it back."

I am a child again, dragged from my cage in Kallias's Collection to perform at his whim, or be slain. The raw, animal fear that is so horribly familiar to me claws up my throat.

"This is not necessary," says Saga. "I know your power, Your Majesty. I do not need it displayed before me."

"Oh, but you do," Valrún returns, dismissing the objection. "Runa. As I commanded."

My mother nods and raises her hands. Her stone dress shudders and cracks, pebbles falling at her feet.

Beneath us, the ground begins to shake. There is an awful grinding, wrenching noise, and the room folds up around us, becoming a sphere that holds us inside it. The walls melt away; the city vanishes; the earth opens up and swallows us, drawing us deep, deep, into its heart. Veins of glittering ore stretch out from the sphere of the room. Lava traces the edges of our boundary but cannot reach us.

I sit gripping the arms of my chair.

Saga has jerked up from hers, with Leifur holding her tight against him, his sword steady in his hand.

But as quickly as my mother transformed the chamber around us, she changes it back again, the sphere shooting up to the surface, the city and the palace walls folding back around us, the great hall becoming what it was.

"Put the sword away," Brandr snaps at Leifur, "or I will throw you out of here."

Saga nods at Leifur, who sheathes his blade. She resumes her seat, the tray of food before her wholly forgotten. She's shaking, though I can see her striving to keep herself still.

"Salin," says Valrún. "Amaze us."

The Black Skapari stands, and with the merest whisper she clothes the room in living shadow, forming shapes and creatures out of the darkness. She recasts the room around us, the world around us, until everything we see and touch, hear and feel and know is shadow, oily and slick. It makes me think of slaying cave demons with Saga and Ballast in the long dark of the Iljaria tunnels.

"Stop!" comes Saga's voice. "Please stop!"

And all is as it was: color and light, breath and life, the only dark that remains whispering around Salin's shoulders.

On down the line the Skapari show off their powers.

My aunt Dagfinna wreathes the room with fire, forming creatures out of living flame that twist and dance through the air like bright fish in a pond.

Finnur makes a prismatic tree grow from the floor, hung with fruits made of ten different magics, excluding only Ghost and Yellow.

Malen raises a forest of real trees around the prismatic one and turns the tiled floor all to flowers.

Adriel displays his time magic by disappearing and reappearing in various places around the room, and undoing both Malen's and Finnur's creations, so that the forest grows backward until it vanishes altogether, and the flowers and prismatic tree disappear.

Jóvin has no magic to display, so the queen doesn't call on him, but he sits seething in his chair, staring at Valrún with unfettered desire.

To my relief, Osa wields winter magic and not death magic. Both are powers of the Gray Lady, but the latter is less than welcome in the court of the living. She weaves a world of ice around us, fills the room with gently falling snow. She claps her hands and it all melts away.

And then I am the only one left who has not displayed my power. I can't, of course, not collared in iron.

But it seems I am not to be let off so easily.

Valrún rises from her throne and crosses the short distance to the dais. She climbs the steps until she is beside me, and the rotting-poison scent of her fills my nostrils.

She gives me a slick, purposeful smile, and I realize that all of this was an excuse for her to wield me like the tool she thinks I am in a public setting, where she thinks I can't—or won't—refuse her.

"You will do as I say," she says low into my ear, "or Adriel will put a knife in his heart."

She doesn't have to specify whose heart. My gut clenches.

"Adriel is there," she adds, "blade poised at his chest, in a moment of time that you cannot see. Perhaps he has done it already; perhaps your lover lies dead in a pool of his own blood on my beautiful floor a few moments from now."

I feel her smile, and her breath reeks of poison.

She unlatches the iron collar, lets it fall ringing to the dais.

My magic floods back, and I drink it in like air, desperate, greedy. I hadn't known how close I was to drowning.

"If you do a single thing against my order," says Valrún, "Adriel will kill him. Do you understand?"

I give a little jerk of my chin, fighting to keep hold of my power and my terror and my rage, to keep from being consumed.

Valrún turns, beaming, to her audience of four. She jerks me up by the arm.

"I give you Brynja Eldingar, wielder of Bronze magic, strong enough to command the very First Ones!"

And I realize what she is going to make me do.

I look at Ballast, sending frantic thoughts into his head, but there isn't *time*.

"Amaze us, Brynja!" Valrún crows. "Call for us the Blue Lady, and the White, to honor all our guests."

"Wait," says Ballast, and his voice makes my heart trip.

"Call them, Brynja!" Valrún commands, descending the dais and resuming her seat. "Call them!"

I see a glimmer of Violet by Ballast's throne, and I have no choice.

I call them.

CHAPTER TWENTY-EIGHT

BALLAST

Year 4201, Month of the Violet Lord

Iljaria—Regla City—the palace

She radiates power, the bronze scales of her gown catching the light, turning her into a leviathan of old. She's imbued with magic. She's made of it.

"Brynja." Her name is brittle on my lips, and I can no longer bear the torment of just sitting here, watching her.

I jerk upright and take three steps toward the dais before I am yanked back on an invisible tether.

The shadowy form of Adriel is suddenly beside me, his eyes hard, his mouth unyielding. I realize he used time magic to erase my three steps from existence—no one else is aware that I even got up. He presses a knife against my throat, and though he winks out of view, I can still feel the point of his blade.

So I sit, gripping the arms of my chair, forced to watch the spectacle unfolding before me.

The White Lady comes like a whisper, with the scent of ice and the thread of a song. I glimpse a vast cathedral made of alabaster stone, open to a sky of whirling stars. Suddenly there is music, a great cacophony of it, like every note that has ever been played or sung or ever will be is raised together. It is deafening, and yet I do not feel the need to press my hands against my ears.

The White Lady is luminous and tall, with obsidian dark skin and straight white hair that reaches past her heels. Her lips are as frost-white as her hair, and her eyes are like pale fire.

The world bends around her, and the vision of the cathedral vanishes.

In the seat beside me, my mother trembles. Tears pour down her cheeks. "My Lady," she whispers. "My Lady, long I have wished to see you."

The White Lady steps up to my mother, bending over her like a tree that bows in the wind. She touches the stone on my mother's brow, touches her lips, her throat.

My mother sobs like her heart is breaking.

"Dry your eyes, my daughter," says the White Lady, and there is music in her words, in her very being. "Your hurts will yet be healed. All will be well. There is a song yet for you to sing."

Then she moves past my mother, and past Valrún, too.

She kneels at Saga's feet.

"Goddess," Saga whispers. She's shaking.

"Do not fear," the White Lady tells her. "You also are a daughter of mine, and I have put a song in your heart. Sing it, if you wish to honor me."

The White Lady smiles. Saga stares at her in awe. "What do you mean, My Lady?" Saga asks her.

But then the White Lady is gone.

For a moment the pressure of Adriel's knife is gone, too, and I realize he has taken the White Lady to be bound with the other First Ones. A sour knot pulls tight in my gut.

"It is enough, Your Majesty," says Saga, her voice breaking. "Please, no more. It is enough."

"Nonsense!" Valrún smiles, sharp as a tiger. "Brynja. Call the Blue Lady."

Please, I think at Brynja. *Please don't.*

He'll kill you, comes her frantic thought back, and I am aware again of Adriel, hovering between moments in time, the point of his knife sharp under my jaw.

On the dais Brynja shuts her eyes. I feel her reaching out for a thread of my Blue magic, and I give it to her.

The world warps, and I catch a glimpse of the impossible forest in the Skepna Conservatory, of Lady Villidýr's stone cottage.

I watch in bewilderment as the door opens and my tutor steps out, the hedgehog on her shoulder.

For a moment the palace falls away, and it is just me and Lady Villidýr, standing together in the starlight. I know her, as I should have known her when I first went to her cottage. I saw her last year in the realm of the First Ones, when the Yellow Lord was bound in the sun. How could I have forgotten her?

"My Lady," I whisper.

She smiles and grazes a finger across my brow. "Fear not, son of mine. All will be well."

And then I'm back in the chair in the palace, and the Blue Lady is standing barefoot on the golden floor, ribbons shining in her hair.

Valrún smiles like a jackal, and though she's my mother's sister, it's my father she reminds me of.

The Iljaria queen claps her hands and the Blue Lady vanishes, as does the prick of Adriel's knife.

Grief sears me.

Valrún stands from her throne and spreads her hands out wide. "And now my Bronze Skapari will call her own patron, the Bronze Lord, from his mutilation and exile."

Brynja stands on the dais in front of her chair, her whole body shaking. "No," she says, "No, I will not call him. It is too much. I will not do it."

Valrún steps toward her, radiating wrath. "I *command you*, Brynja Eldingar."

Brynja raises her chin. Her eyes flash and her magic pulses in visible Bronze waves. "I. Will. Not."

"You will! Or he dies."

She did not mean, perhaps, for her voice to carry so shrilly, but it does. Adriel's knife presses against my heart, but not hard enough to pierce my feathered robe. I stand, slowly, from my seat.

"You won't," says Brynja. "That was a lie. You need him. Just like you need me, just like you need all of us."

Valrún grabs her by the throat and shakes her, and I am across the room and up the dais steps almost before I am aware of my intent. I grab the queen's arm and yank her off Brynja, my blood hot with rage.

"Leave my wife alone!" I roar at her.

And then everyone is staring at me, the room still enough you could hear the scrape of a feather falling to the floor.

Brynja gives me a wry look. "Ballast," she chides gently, "that was supposed to be a secret."

SIX MONTHS AGO

BRYNJA

Year 4201, Month of the Green Lady

Daeros—Tenebris

"What if you don't go to Iljaria at all," Ballast is saying. "What if you stay here with me instead?"

We're alone in Tenebris's courtyard garden—the one I never knew existed before a few weeks ago. I'm on the grass with my back against a crumbling statue, while he has his head in my lap, his one eye closed. The late-afternoon sun gilds him in molten gold, and somewhere a bird is singing. I don't know what kind. He would tell me if I asked him.

I play with his hair, tangling my fingers in the black and white curls. "We've discussed it from every angle," I remind him. "I have to go, for a little while. But it's not forever. Nothing in all the world could keep me from coming back to you in the end, you know."

He sighs and opens his eye, scooting to a sitting position. His leg presses warm against mine. He takes my hand in his. I wish I had time magic, so we would never have to leave this moment.

"We don't have to," says Ballast quietly. "We can stay here forever."

I glance across at him, amused at how rarely I keep my thoughts to myself when he's next to me. "You know that isn't true."

He makes a face. "What good is magic if I can't use it to keep you close to me?"

"Bal." I press a kiss to his cheek, and he puts his hands on either side of my face, gently adjusting the placement of my mouth more to his liking.

We lose a bit of time, then, and when we finally draw back from one another, the light is low, and the garden has grown chilly.

But we don't go in, not yet.

He tucks a loose curl behind my ear, traces the curve of my cheek, touches my lips. He tilts his forehead against mine, and I shut my eyes, drinking in the feel of his breath on my face.

"Brynja," he says, low and rough, "will you marry me?"

"What?" I pull back from him, startled.

He studies me in the fast-fading light. "Be my wife, Brynja. Marry me before you go to Iljaria." He tilts his head to the side. "So you have a reason to come back again."

"Ballast." I shove his shoulder. "I will come back to you whatever happens. Don't you trust me?"

"Of course I do. It's just . . ."

"Just what?" My heart is clattering at my breastbone, and I am caught in a strange twilight of surprise and wanting. My blood family at best abandoned me, at worst sent me purposefully to be sacrificed on the altar of Kallias's cruelty. And yet here is Ballast, offering me a new kind of family, a belonging I have never truly had.

"I don't want to let you go," he says, "and I want—I want you to know that I mean it. Loving you. That I won't go back on it. I want to pledge myself to you forever. I don't want you to feel alone."

My throat catches. Gods, this man will be the death of me. I shift to a kneeling position, facing him, and put my hands on his shoulders. Without realizing it, I've asked the air around us to be warmer, and it has obeyed. It's not the cold that is making me shiver.

"Yes," I tell him.

His brows pinch together, like he was expecting more of a fight. "Yes?"

"Yes," I repeat, and I lean forward to kiss him again.

He raises his hand to my lips, stopping me. "Can we do it now?"

Panic lights within me as I begin to realize all the ramifications of marrying the king of Daeros. "Now?"

His smile goes lopsided. "What's the point of waiting? We don't have much time before you leave."

"We have a few months," I argue.

"Exactly," he says. "We have a few months."

His eye is a storm that liquefies my insides. I can't be steady under his gaze, so I stare past him, to the crumbled statue I was sitting against when we first came out here. I'm not certain what it was originally. The base of it could be the hem of a woman's gown or the tail of a monster; perhaps both. If I called for Finnur, he could use Violet magic to read the stone, spin a picture of what it used to be in my mind.

"I don't want Finnur, just now," says Ballast dryly.

My cheeks heat, and I find the courage to look at him again. I try to put my trepidation into words: "I don't want a wedding, Bal. I don't want a crown. I don't want Skaanda and Aerona to look at us and imagine a Daeros-Iljaria plot brewing against them. I want peace. And rest." I take a breath. "I want *you*."

He smooths his thumb across my cheek. "So we don't tell anyone. Perhaps the less public our connection, the better. Aerona doesn't need to know the real reason you're going to Iljaria. *Vil* certainly doesn't."

I laugh a little. "You don't have to say his name like that."

He makes a face. "I can't believe that bastard is still dithering around in my country."

"Peace treaties take time. Especially with the Aeronans nipping at our heels."

Ballast rubs his forehead. "Must we continue to talk politics when I'm *trying* to propose marriage?"

This pulls a grin out of me. "You're the one who brought up Vil."

"I hate him."

"I know. It's sweet."

He grimaces. "Stop avoiding the question, you ferocious creature."

For a moment I just look at him, watching as the last of the light slips away, as he's wreathed all in shadow. "Yes," I say at last. "Yes, I'll marry you now. Tonight, if you want. But we can keep it to ourselves, keep it secret, for as long as we need to?"

He dips his chin. "Yes."

"Even from your mother?" I ask him.

He tenses, and I read his reluctance, his sorrow, as easily as if he spoke those feelings aloud. "I trust my mother. With everything."

"She will want me to be queen," I say.

He grips my shoulders in the dark. "I would never force you to be something you don't want to be. But I am king of Daeros. And I intend to remain king of Daeros."

I bite the inside of my cheek. "I know."

"One day," he says, "I will ask you to be queen. To rule beside me."

"I know," I repeat. "But not yet."

He takes a breath. "Not yet."

He stands and tugs me up after him. He slips his hand around my waist and pulls me close. "I love you, Brynja Eldingar," he says softly into my hair. "With everything in me."

"I love you, Ballast Vallin," I whisper back, "with all I am, and with all I will become."

His next kiss is a promise, a token, a vow.

We leave the courtyard, his hand large and warm over mine.

Finnur catches us sneaking out of Tenebris, which is the only reason we take him along as a witness.

I feel giddy and nervous.

Ballast bends his head to whisper into my ear: "Don't be nervous."

I can't help but laugh. I don't guard my thoughts around him. It's a good thing there are no secrets left between us.

"Yes, it is," says Ballast, and kisses my brow.

"Come on," grunts Finnur from ahead of us on the winding street.

Garran City sparkles under the stars, as used to darkness as it is to light, its lanterns always shining.

It turns out to be a good thing that Finnur caught us. When Ballast explains his plan, Finnur gives him a look that clearly means *you idiot* even to someone who can't read minds.

"You can't go to the city clerk in the middle of the night and demand he perform a marriage for the king of Daeros and not expect him to blab about it in the morning!" Finnur cries, absolutely appalled.

I catch a wave of embarrassment from Ballast. "What do you suggest, then?" he asks, more humble than I would be in his place.

Finnur shakes his head in exasperation and tells us.

Only a quarter of an hour later, Ballast and I stand together on a rooftop garden in the midst of the city. It's beautiful up here, bathed in moonlight and watched over by quiet stars. A fountain bubbles in the middle of the garden. Flowers bloom fragrant from stone pots. At the north end of the rooftop, an archway shimmers with color and magic, framing the lantern-lit city below. This place is Iljaria-made, and it remembers still the hands of its former masters.

Finnur has been experimenting with the Violet branch of his Prism magic, and getting quite good at it. The city clerk, however, isn't terribly pleased to be spirited from his bed to a rooftop in the deep hours of the night. But he cooperates, telling Finnur what paperwork he needs to fetch to make the marriage legal. And he has Ballast and me stand facing each other under the archway.

I shiver in the starlight.

"Repeat these words to each other," says the clerk, sounding bored and annoyed and sleepy and a tiny bit invested, all at once. "'I join my hands to yours, to represent this union which I enter into freely, and where I will remain until we both agree to dissolve it.'"

I look at the clerk in utter horror. "That isn't a vow, that's a temporary business arrangement! I'm not saying that."

Ballast's lips twitch up, amused. He pulls a paper out of his pocket and hands it to the clerk. "We'll have these instead, if you please, sir."

His eye catches mine. *This isn't a farce,* he says, his words a little shaky in my mind, still unfamiliar using magic that doesn't come naturally to him. *I mean this. I won't go back on it.*

I know, I think at him in return. *I won't, either. But I'm not repeating that drivel and calling it a marriage vow.*

Ballast smiles. *I know.*

The clerk pulls a pair of spectacles from his pocket and peers at the paper, Finnur helpfully bobbing over a light globe so he can see it more clearly.

"'I bind myself to you,'" the clerk reads, "'soul and mind, heart and body. I will love and honor you every day that I live, though the earth crack, though the sun fall, though the dark is never-ending. I am yours, forevermore. To you and you alone I will be faithful, and only death shall part us.'"

Better, I think at Ballast.

He huffs a laugh. *Shall I go first?*

I shake my head. *I want to.*

I take his hands and step closer to him, gazing deep into his one blue eye. "Ballast Vallin," I say softly, "I bind myself to you, soul and mind, heart and body. I will love and honor you every day that I live, though the earth crack, though the sun fall, though the dark is never-ending." My heart beats and my breath catches. "I am yours," I whisper, "forevermore. To you and you alone I will be faithful, and only death shall part us."

Ballast's eye gleams with moisture. "Brynja Eldingar, I bind myself to you, soul and mind, heart and body. I will love and honor you every day that I live, though the earth crack, though the sun fall, though the dark is never-ending. I am yours." His voice breaks. He lifts one hand to touch my cheek. "To you and you alone I will be faithful, and only death shall part us."

"That will do, I suppose," says the clerk. "It's the paperwork that makes it all legal. The words don't really matter. Come and sign these, both of you."

Finnur has the papers waiting for us on a little stone table, the light globe floating over to illuminate them. I sign first, hand shaky on the pen, ink dripping over the pages. Ballast signs after me, then Finnur, as witness. The clerk affixes his official seal to both copies.

"Right then," he says. "I will file this copy in the recorder's office. This one you keep." He glances between Ballast and me, and Ballast holds his hands out for the offered certificate.

The clerk's eyes glitter—there's no disguising who we are, now that he's heard our names and seen them written out so plainly.

What should we bribe him with? I think at Ballast and Finnur.

Finnur grins at me. *Violet magic, remember? No need for bribes.*

"Thanks for your services, my good man," he says to the clerk. "What an odd dream you've had this evening. Come on then, back to bed we go."

He touches the clerk's arm, and the two of them vanish in a spray of purple sparks.

I blink and Finnur is back, alone. "I'll just go and file the certificate," he announces, then grabs it and vanishes again.

Ballast tucks me under his arm, laughing. "Time magic is disorienting."

"Very confusing," I agree, "hard to keep track."

He grins in the starlight, and we come down from the rooftop together, leaving Finnur to follow in his own time.

SIX MONTHS AGO

BALLAST

Year 4201, Month of the Green Lady

Daeros—Tenebris

There are a few hours yet before the sun rises. My bedchamber is dark, illuminated only faintly by the mingled light of stars and moon slipping through the window.

This was never my father's room. It is in the royal wing but was formerly a study—my father rarely came here. I had it repurposed, shelves moved, space cleared for a bed and wardrobe to be brought in. Not his, never his. I burned my father's furniture, and it made a merry bonfire. So my bedchamber is perhaps smaller than a king's would usually be, but it suits me. Because I would never, ever bring my wife to a place my father had fouled.

Her hand is still caught fast in mine as we step in, as I shut the door behind us. I tease her that coming through doors is the usual way people enter rooms, that she should try it more often, and she gives me a playful shove and walks over to the window.

My heart is a skittering, wild thing in my throat. I go to stand beside her.

She leans her head against my arm. "Ballast," she says.

My name on her lips makes me shiver. "Brynja," I mumble into her hair.

She wraps her arms around me and tugs me fiercely close. I hold her like that for a while, my every nerve alight.

At last she pulls away from me. She kicks off her shoes and hops up onto my bed, sitting against the headboard with her knees pulled to her chin. I unlace my boots and sit facing her. Her nervousness pulses into my mind, and I send my own right back into hers.

She takes a breath. "I am not . . . unmarred by my time here, Bal," she says quietly. "I am riddled with scars."

My chest squeezes. "I have plenty of scars of my own, you know."

She nods. She does know. The echo of our shared torment pulses heavy between us.

"I am sorry for what he did to you," I say. "I am sorry for what my father did to you."

She touches the ridge above my empty eye. "I am sorry for what he did to *you*."

"That was my own choice."

Her face creases. "No, it wasn't, Bal, *no, it wasn't.*"

I shove away the memory of the white-hot agony, the sudden half dimming of my vision, the awful raging fire of it. I was sick on the floor and passed out from pain and woke in the infirmary to the skewed sight of my father's sharp smile. *"Don't let him die,"* he'd commanded the palace physician, then strode away and left me to my suffering.

"Let's not think of him now," she says. "He's gone. He doesn't have power over us anymore. This is about you. And me. Until death parts us."

And she shrugs out of her shirt, sitting there in only a black bandeau and her tight-fitting trousers. Freckles spatter her pale skin like a spray of stars, but there is no missing the marks all over her torso, raised and jagged and white. The sight of them wrecks me because I know exactly how she got them.

I tug my shirt off, too, and she reaches out to trace the scars on my chest with whispering fingers. I tremble beneath her touch, mapping her own scars with my eye.

"Brynja," I say, in this moment scarcely possessing the power of speech, "can I kiss you?"

She grabs my shoulders, tugs me toward her. "Come here," she whispers.

I do.

I kiss her brow, her jaw, the curve of her neck. I kiss her freckles and her scars, every one of them.

She tangles her fingers in my hair, pulls my face to hers. She kisses me back, desperate, wanting, her mouth hot as lightning against mine.

We slip beneath sheets, lying on our sides and facing each other, a single pillow under our heads.

I need her like water, like air. She is all my world, the beginning and the ending and everything between.

She lies on my bare chest, later, the sheets drawn up to cover her. Her heart beats against mine, and I feel as if I am floating away in a haze. I trace lazy circles on her back, twist my fingers through her white curls.

"Do you really have to go?" I say petulantly. "A few months is not enough. Stay. Every day can be like this one."

She laughs, breath warm on my skin. "This was your plot all along, was it? Convince me to marry you and lure me into staying?" She kisses my jaw. "But there's still the as-yet-unsigned treaty with Skaanda. There's still the Aeronans knocking at our door. You're still the king of Daeros, and we still need the Iljaria army."

"Bah," I say.

She rubs my shoulder with her free hand and sighs against me. "I wish I didn't have to go. I wish you could come with me."

I squeeze her arm. "I wish I could, too."

She shifts onto her side so she can look down at me, her hair mussed about her face. "I'll come back, Bal. No matter what happens, I swear to you I'll come back."

I cup her face with one hand, smoothing my thumb along the soft curve of her cheek. "You had better, wife."

She smiles.

Red light slips through the window, the sun rising. It turns her all to molten fire.

"There's still a few months," she says.

"So there is," I agree. I give her a wicked grin and tug her down once more to meet me.

FOUR MONTHS AGO

BALLAST

Year 4201, Month of the White Lady

Daeros—Tenebris

"Vil's stalling."

I'm used to her sudden appearances in locked rooms by now, so only start a very little at her voice. I'm sitting at my writing desk in the library—one of the few places in Tenebris that feels largely untouched by the ghost of my father—poring over a list of improvements for the working conditions of the mine laborers. I have already vastly cut back working hours and pulled anyone under the age of twenty off the roster entirely—I've sent them to school in Garran City instead. My father well and truly made a mess of things, busy playing god of his own little universe. I'm shocked there was never an uprising, probably down to the tireless work of his governors. My governors now. I need to find a way to reward them for their faithful service.

"Yes, I thought we'd established that," I tell Brynja, without glancing up.

She shoves the papers to the side and sits cross-legged on my desk so I'm forced to give her my full attention. This is, of course, distracting in a completely different way, and she grins ear to ear as she snatches *that* thought right out of my head.

I fold my arms across my chest and lean back in my chair, trying to ignore how hot my face is. "What have you found out now, my devious little spy?"

"He's even more deeply embroiled with the Aeronans than we thought. He has no intention of signing the treaty with Daeros, or of going home to Skaanda."

I tamp down my frequent urge to bolt from the room and take Vil's head off with the nearest available weapon. "Don't keep me in suspense."

"He means for Daeros and Skaanda both to become the empire's newest provinces, and he's vowed to help Aerona conquer Iljaria." Her face goes grim, any hint of her teasing smile gone. "He expects the emperor to stay on the mainland, and for himself to rule the peninsula as he wishes, a king in all but name."

I digest this for a few moments before I give her an answer, and she sits there patiently, understanding the way my mind works. I need time to sort things out. Her giving me the space to do that is one of the things I love about her.

"How does he mean to conquer Iljaria?" I say at last.

She produces a piece of paper from her pocket and unfolds it for me to examine. "Vil has invented weapons he's calling Skaandan Fire," she says, "clay canisters filled with gunpowder and shards of iron, to be catapulted at the magical barrier, or used in open battle against the Iljaria. They explode on impact, designed to neutralize magic."

I am suddenly, wrenchingly ill, and I have to look away from her.

"Bal?"

"That isn't Vil's design," I say to the desk. "It's my father's."

"What?"

I flick my eye up at her. "My father was an inventor, remember? He was determined to conquer Iljaria, eventually, even if he couldn't reach the weapon in the heart of the mountain. Vil must have found the design among my father's things."

She chews on her lip. "Do these weapons work?"

My gut is roiling, my father laughing at me from beyond the grave. "They work," I say vaguely.

I don't elaborate and she doesn't ask me to, but I allow her to pull the memory from my mind: He tested them on me once. Not the full might of the explosive canister, but he commanded me to control a wild fox and then flung a handful of iron shards at me. He laughed when the iron burned me, when the fox attacked, snarling. I still have scars on my arm.

"Bal," she breathes, and for a moment tilts her forehead against mine, lending me strength, comfort, peace. She knows me, understands me, more deeply than anyone else ever could, and I soak in the solace that she offers without me even having to explain why I need it. Blue Lady, I love this woman.

She kisses my brow and then hops off the desk, pacing between bookshelves, her tread light on the carpet. "Vil is pushing for the amount of iron ore mined to be tripled," she says, "and he's already set up manufacturing operations in city storehouses. He's hiring workers. And that isn't even the worst of it."

I watch her from my chair, both humbled and euphoric that she is mine and I am hers. "What's the worst of it, wife?"

"Someone will hear you," she scolds.

I don't apologize.

"The worst of it is, the emperor has stopped prevaricating. He's coming to Tenebris with ten thousand soldiers at his back."

I curse. "When, Brynja?"

"They'll be here in a week or two. Maybe less."

"Then our time grows short."

"Our time is up, Bal. I need to go to Iljaria, and I need to go now. I trust that my family connections will have some sway over the queen, but word of Vil's weapon—Skaandan Fire, he calls it—ought to persuade her fully."

I get out of my chair and fold her hand in mine. Together we step up to a narrow window that overlooks the courtyard garden where I asked her to be my wife.

"Do you really think she will listen?" I muse. "Do you really think she'll send an army to help a foreign half blood keep his throne?"

"It is far less of a threat to Iljaria for you to be king of Daeros than for Aerona to seize it. The queen will have to see that. I'll *make* her see it."

Uneasiness gnaws at me. "You haven't been there in over a decade, Brynja. Are you sure that—that it's what you expect? Iljaria doesn't exactly have a history of helping other countries, and your father and Brandr—"

"My father and Brandr had their own agendas," she says tightly. "But the Yellow Lord is not bound in the heart of Tenebris anymore. *I* freed him. At the very least the queen will thank me for that, and perhaps allow me to name my reward."

"I don't like *perhaps*es," I say.

She looks up at me, and I am desperate to pull her into my arms, to hold her close against me, to not ever, ever let her go. "I don't mean it," I tell her, in case she's read my mind again. "I would never keep you here against your will."

"I know, Bal." She stands on her toes and kisses my jaw, and I tremble beneath the heat of her lips.

"But it's dangerous," I go on, refusing to let her distract me. "It's impossibly dangerous."

"I've been in danger before."

"That doesn't make it all right."

She sighs and scrambles up to sit in the windowsill, her back to the glass, her feet dangling. I stand beside her, leaning against the wall.

"Will Vil find it suspicious, you going to Iljaria, just as word of the Aeronan army is sure to have reached your ears?"

"That is something that occurred to me," she admits. "I know I move about the palace as I wish, but I've been more careful of late—I'm being watched."

"I don't like that."

She tilts her head to the side. "That's why I didn't tell you."

"I'll kill him."

"No you won't, Bal. That would create far more problems than it solved."

"It would solve a really *annoying* problem," I grumble.

She gives a huff of laughter. "You really, really don't have to be jealous of Vil, you know."

I am, though. He has both of his eyes, and his father didn't torture her for eight years.

"Bal," she says softly, and I know she's read my thoughts again.

I pull myself together with an effort. "Will he try and stop you going to Iljaria?"

"I think he will. He hasn't trusted me since—well, since I betrayed him."

I smile a bit at that. "What do we do, then?"

She leans around the window frame, and I find her face level with mine, her freckles a fury of stars I want to trace constellations in.

"Do you trust me?" she asks.

I can't deny that this question makes something cold awake in the pit of my belly, but I nod. "Always. I swore that to you."

Her eyes glitter. "Do you remember when we were children, and we played at War in your room?"

"Of course I do." The colorful deck of cards laid out between us on the bedspread. Her legs tucked up underneath her, the plate of snacks I made sure was ready at her elbow, because my father didn't feed her enough. "You always won."

"Not always."

"Nearly always."

"If I asked you to gamble, Ballast, would you do it?"

"Gamble what?" I say carefully. "Gamble how?"

"The game is won when your crown is secure," she tells me. "But Daeros is not prepared at present to face ten thousand Aeronan soldiers in battle. Not with Skaanda set to betray us. We would be caught fast between sea and shore, dashed upon the rocks and destroyed. I very much doubt that the emperor has any intention of allowing you to stay on the throne, and that is what it would take at this juncture—him allowing you. Aerona holds all the power. Daeros has none."

I grimace, but it's true. I have only been playing at being king, while the emperor saw fit to kick his heels in his palace. Now that he has turned his gaze this way, the game is likely to be drawn to a swift and bitter conclusion. "What then?" I press. "Do you have a Ghost God card up your sleeve?"

"I think I do. Allow the emperor to take Daeros from you, for a little while."

"What? *No.*"

She lifts and drops her shoulders. "The emperor isn't bringing his army here just for fun, Ballast. If the Daerosians face him in battle, they will lose."

"They may not," I say stubbornly.

Her eyes go sad. "I should have gone to Iljaria months ago. I could have had an army here for you, ready to drive Aerona into the sea. Now it is too late."

I rub the brow above my missing eye. "Just tell me your plan, will you?"

She hops down from the windowsill, grabs my hand, and tugs me deeper into the library. We settle on a mound of cushions piled against the far wall, her curling up next to me, my arm tight around her.

"We are going to do three things," she says softly against my heart. "We're going to buy time for Daeros and not shed a single drop of blood. We're going to make Vil and the emperor both think that you are not a threat to them. We're going to get them to send me to Iljaria of their own accord."

I shake my head. "Little schemer, how exactly are you going to accomplish that?"

"No one expects you to freely give up your throne," she says. "They would be suspicious if you did."

"So," I acknowledge.

"If you and I had a falling-out," she goes on, "if I use my magic to make you relinquish your crown in a very public setting, if you then react angrily, accusing me of manipulating you, giving Vil and the emperor good reason to fear my power, they would send me away to Iljaria—I will seed the thought in their minds without them knowing, to make sure of it. I will get the army from Iljaria and bring it here, secretly, so we catch the emperor unawares. We drive the Aeronans out, we kick Vil back to Skaanda. You are crowned anew, the autonomy of Daeros secured. Simple."

I touch her chin with one finger and tilt her face toward mine. "That isn't simple at all."

"Have you got a better idea?" she challenges.

"No," I admit. "But I don't like it, Brynja. I don't want to gamble with my country. I certainly don't want to gamble with you."

She shivers, though the room is warm. "I know," she says. "But facing the emperor in battle now would be gambling with *you*. I won't lose you, Bal. I refuse."

"What if I come to Iljaria *with* you?"

"The emperor is not going to allow you to go running into the arms of a foreign power. It has to be me."

"But what if Iljaria isn't what you think?" I press, returning to the part of all this that makes me the most uneasy. "What if you can't get an army?"

"Then I will find another way to put you back on your throne," she says fiercely.

I drop my hand from her face and lean my head back against the wall. "What is all of this even for? Perhaps I am not meant to be king. Perhaps I should give up my throne in earnest, and—and go off and live in the hills with Asvaldr."

"So dramatic," she teases. Then, sobering: "Do you think the people, the country you have fought so hard for, will be better under the emperor?"

"No."

She nods. "Well then."

We sit in silence for a little while, and then I glance over to find her studying me, like she is memorizing my every feature. My heart kicks.

"Do we really have to fight?" I ask her. "That sounds terrible."

"We have a little while to come up with something truly spectacular. A passionate shouting match, maybe, where I loudly express my concern for your safety and press you to give up your throne, and you scream at me that you would never do such a thing, and that I should mind my own affairs. That would set up my publicly forcing you to change your mind quite nicely."

"You've really thought this through, haven't you."

She quirks a smile at me. "I do my best."

I tug her into my arms and kiss her recklessly. Our months have dwindled down to weeks now, and I mean to make the most of them.

THREE MONTHS AGO

BRYNJA

Year 4201, Month of the Prism Lady

Daeros—Tenebris

"What I want to know," says Ballast casually as I slip through the heating vent and hop down onto his bed, where he's sitting against the headboard with a tray of wine and food at his elbow and an intriguing wooden box in his hands, "is how much of the emperor's demands were of his own invention, and how much were yours. Because it's worked out a little too conveniently if you didn't have a hand in it. Or a mind, as it were."

I grin. "Do you mean all of that 'Give up your throne peacefully or face my army and be executed when you inevitably lose, tell me your answer tomorrow' nonsense? The ideas were mostly in his head already; they just needed a bit of nudging to form the phrasing that would suit us."

"Cleverly done," he says, and warmth blooms in my belly.

"Is that for me?" I ask him, nodding at the box.

"For both of us." He gives me a *look*. "I suppose you know what it is already."

"Well, yes," I admit.

"Little spy, is nothing safe from you?"

I go to sit beside him, pressing my leg against his. He hands me the box, and I open it. My vision goes a little blurry.

The rings are a matched set. His is a little bigger than mine, but otherwise there is no difference between them. The silver bands are artfully engraved, and the central blue stones have been polished until they shine, no rough edges left. I think of pulling a handful of these stones from the river down in the Iljaria tunnels, when we first kissed in the dark. I think of kneeling in the snow before him, holding those same pebbles up to him in a desperate bid for him to trust me.

We have come a very long way since then.

"They're beautiful," I tell him. "Thank you."

I take the larger ring out of the box and slide it onto Ballast's finger.

He kisses me—softly, deeply—then takes out the other ring and fits it onto my finger.

We sit tucked together for a while, neither of us quite ready to engage in the agreed-upon shouting match.

This is our last night together for a long while. Tomorrow he will give up his throne, and I will be sent to Iljaria. I don't know when we will see one another again, except in the dreams I have begun to spin with my magic. It won't be the same.

We sip wine and eat the food on the waiting tray: cheese and pears and ginger cakes, until only crumbs are left and our fingers are sticky.

We spend a while with our bodies tangled together, slowly and reverently memorizing the hard and soft planes of each other, fixing them fast in our minds to remember when we are apart.

We clothe ourselves again, eventually, me in Ballast's shirt and him in just his trousers. He produces a battered deck of cards from his nightstand and deals them out on the crumpled sheets between us. His hair is messy, and it makes my insides wobble.

"We had better shout now," I tell him reluctantly. I lay down one of my cards.

He sighs. "Must we?"

"It will all be for nothing otherwise."

"Let it be for nothing."

"Ballast."

He flicks his eye up toward me, and I'm gutted to see the moisture brimming there.

"It'll be all right," I promise. "This is all temporary. We'll be together again before long. A month, maybe two, and I'll be back with the army. I swear it to you, Bal."

He takes a ragged breath, turning his head away so I won't see him wipe the tears from his eye.

"But what if it goes wrong?" He doesn't look at me as he lays a card down.

"It won't go wrong. I won't let it go wrong."

He curses softly, then leans across our card game and kisses me. "Let's shout then," he says. "If we must."

I quirk a smile at him. "They will think me a faithless lover tomorrow."

"I'll kill anyone who calls you that."

"No, you won't," I remind him gently.

He curses again. "No, I won't," he concedes.

We have our fight then.

It feels impossibly cruel to look him in the eye and shout vicious things at him, even if I don't mean them and he knows I don't mean them. He rages at me in return, and it's all I can do not to call it off, not to beg him to stop, please stop.

For a moment, after we've shouted all the things we planned to shout, we sit there staring at each other. His chest heaves and my heart breaks. But I can't fall into his arms. That would undo all our hard work.

I kiss him once more, quick as a heartbeat.

I make sure to leave via the door, and I slam it as hard as I can behind me, screeching a parting curse over my shoulder.

I pass Lysandra in the corridor, and I give her a full view of me clothed in nothing but her brother's shirt, my face a mess of snot and tears.

My own bed feels cold and lonely. I lie awake for a long, long while, staring up at the heating vent and daydreaming about climbing into it, making my way back to his room, his bed, his arms. I curse myself soundly for my stupid, stupid plan that will keep me apart from him for *weeks*, if not longer.

In the middle of the night, I start awake, pulse rabbit-quick behind my rib cage. I reach out with my magic and feel him trapped in a nightmare. I will not leave him like that.

I travel the paths in the ceiling between my room and his, and after climbing into his bed, I touch his cheek, I call his name, I pull him from the dark dream that keeps him captive. I give him water to drink, and he folds himself around me, hugging me close as he drifts back to sleep.

It kills me to extricate myself from his arms and slip away again, to retrace the route to my room.

But I can't turn back now.

I have a mission to complete. An army to secure.

When Ballast is established on his throne, when the Aeronans have retreated to the mainland, when the treaty with Skaanda is at long last signed—

Then I will go back to him.

But for now I screw my eyes shut, and steel myself to the awful reality that, in the morning, I will have to ruin him in order to save him.

CHAPTER TWENTY-NINE

BALLAST

Year 4201, Month of the Violet Lord

Iljaria—Regla City—the palace

"Your *wife*?" It's my mother who breaks the silence, but I don't look back at her. I can't tear my gaze away from Brynja, from the welts on her neck left by the iron collar, from the glittering spectacle of her, magic dancing along her skin.

"It's good to see you, Bal," says Brynja softly.

And then I'm pulling her into a fierce embrace, and *I don't care* that the queen and her court and my mother are watching. I kiss her, my hands caught fast in her hair. She holds tight to me, her fingers digging almost desperately into my back.

"That will be *quite* enough."

It's Brandr who yanks me away from Brynja, and I turn on him with my fist raised.

"Don't," says Brynja.

I lower my hand.

"Well," says Valrún dryly, straightening her gown, "I see reports of your lovers' quarrel have been somewhat exaggerated."

"Sit down, Ballast," my mother orders, her voice tight with hurt.

I stalk down the steps of the dais and obey, flicking my gaze to Brynja in panic. *What now?*

Her voice is a little shaky in my mind: *All the cards on the table, Bal.*

I recoil as Valrún locks the iron collar around Brynja's neck again and sweeps back to her throne.

Brynja staggers, half collapsing into her chair.

"Stay. There," my mother commands, gripping tight to my arm.

I shake her off. But I stay. *All the cards on the table.* I can do that.

I turn to the queen. "Your Majesty, the time for games has passed. Send an army to Daeros. Help me drive the Aeronans from the peninsula. Then I swear you'll never have to see me again."

Ballast! snaps my mother in my head. *That isn't what we agreed.*

I flick my eye toward my mother. *We didn't agree on anything,* I remind her.

Valrún, for her part, taps her fingers on the arms of her throne, ignoring Brandr, who has oozed up behind her and is saying something low into her ear.

"My dear nephew," Valrún says to me in a honey-sweet voice that is anything but sweet, "Daeros, Aerona—they are nothing to me. There is only Iljaria. You should heed your mother and find a place for yourself here. You won't be going back."

"I, too, would ask an army of you," says Saga, rising from her seat and coming to kneel before Valrún. She speaks with her head bowed to the floor. "My brother has sold my country to Aerona, and the emperor means to send ships to Iljaria, filled with soldiers and Skaandan Fire—a weapon that can neutralize magic. You will no longer have the advantage of power over the powerless. I beg you to remember the blood shared between your people and mine. I ask you to think beyond the magical barrier protecting Iljaria, the one that will soon fall, if you do not send an army to Daeros."

Saga chooses this moment to lift her head and look directly into Valrún's face, though she doesn't get off her knees. I have been on the opposite side of Saga's ire before, and I don't envy the queen.

But Valrún, after only a moment, laughs. "Get up, little lost queen. I will send no army. Run back to your brother and see if he will take you. Iljaria has nothing to say to the Forsaken."

Anger twists Saga's face. But before she can do anything reckless, Leifur is there beside her, tugging her to her feet.

"What of the gods?" Saga demands, twisting in Leifur's grasp to confront Valrún once more. "What blasphemy burns in your heart that you would so debase the first powers of the world? I know you have bound them, and I demand you release them, lest we all suffer the consequences of toying with things we have no right even to touch."

Valrún stands from her throne, vines writhing at her throat. She is eye to eye with Saga but seems to tower over her. "You speak of things you do not understand," says the queen, low and raging. "Get out. Now. Before I have my Skapari flay you alive."

"Your Majesty."

We all glance at Finnur, who is sitting in his chair on the dais with his hands behind his head and his legs stretched out, crossed at the ankle.

"What?" Valrún snaps.

"She isn't lying. About the Aeronans and their magic-neutralizing weapons. About the ships."

Valrún is a storm cloud, blooming with poison flowers. "What do I care about ships?"

"Because there are a hundred and thirty of them," Finnur answers, "and because they are already halfway across the White Sea."

"Your Majesty," says Brynja from her place on the dais, her eyes unfocused, sweat slick on her skin, "Daeros has much to offer Iljaria. We would relinquish Tenebris to you, which the Iljaria carved out long ago, and reopen the labyrinth of tunnels that wind west beneath the mountain range. There are underground cities hardly touched by time, treasures uncounted. We would give all of that back to you, allow the Iljaria to come and go as they pleased. Our borders would be open. There could be trade between our people, a peace that benefits Daeros and Iljaria alike. But none of that can happen if Aerona seizes the peninsula. The emperor will grasp power anywhere he can find it, and those Iljaria he doesn't kill, he will enslave, binding them in iron, forcing them to serve him. That is Iljaria's future if you do not help us."

I catch Brynja's gaze, and she flashes me a quick smile, though her brow is creased with pain. This is the speech she intended to deliver months ago, when she first arrived in Iljaria—she practiced it for me in the quiet dark of my bed, our heads tilted together, the covers drawn up over our shoulders. But everything went wrong. I had not realized quite how wrong until now.

Valrún sweeps past Saga and up the dais, yanking Brynja once more out of her chair.

I jerk upright but am held in place by my mother's magic before I can storm after the queen.

If you do not behave, says my mother in my mind, *she will bind you, too, in iron. I know my sister.*

You have more power than she does! I mentally shout back. *Why are you letting her do this?*

But she doesn't answer.

"You are a fool," Valrún hisses at Brynja, "aligning yourself with these barbarians instead of your own people. *You* will relinquish Tenebris. *You* will reopen the tunnels—who do you think you are?"

Brynja shrugs. "The queen of Daeros."

She looks at me again, and I feel a sear of pride.

"This is your little plot, is it," says Valrún, "promising your lover to get him an army in exchange for a crown? It's turned out rather poorly for you, in the end. Adriel?"

The Violet Skapari blinks into existence beside her in a tempest of purple ribbons. "Your Majesty?"

"Put her in the spire."

"Wait," I say, wrenching out of my mother's magical hold and darting toward Brynja. "Wait!"

"Bal—" she breathes, reaching out her hand.

But then she's gone, and Adriel is back in his chair, and hers is the only one that is empty.

Valrún turns to face the room. "Let the little emperor's ships come. Let him break through the Galdur Skjöld, if he can. He is dust. I am the wind. I cannot be defeated."

"Your Majesty," says Finnur, "a bit of caution may be wise. Send some of your Skapari to the border. Don't give the emperor the chance to use his weapons."

"This is not a council," says Valrún sharply, "and I am not here to take advice, not even from you. Everyone is dismissed. *Go.*"

She stalks out first, with Brandr at her heels. The Skapari file out next, with Finnur flicking a thought into my mind as he passes me: *I'll try and get you in to see her, but I can't make any promises. I'm sorry.*

And then it's just me, my mother, Saga, and Leifur.

Saga regards me with only a flicker of hatred rather than the usual raging wildfire. "Well, Ballast. You've gotten us all into a horrible mess. How are you going to fix it?"

Adriel is back before I can answer, ushering Saga and Leifur to one of the palace guest rooms.

"Your *wife*, Ballast?" says my mother again, her words pulsing hurt.

"Yes," I say. And I go to find her.

CHAPTER THIRTY

BRYNJA

Year 4201, Month of the Violet Lord

Iljaria—Regla City—the palace

I am not pleased to see the glass prison again, but the poisoning iron burns so cold at my neck I give the place only a resigned, cursory glance before collapsing onto the bed.

I can't sleep. My pulsing anxiety and the damn iron collar won't let me. Gods, gods, gods, what am I going to do? I'm glad, at least, that Valrún was forestalled in binding the Bronze Lord. He and the Ghost Lord are the only ones left, save the Yellow Lord, who burns at the heart of the sun.

If I can slip my collar, I can—

What? Loose the First Ones? Spirit Ballast away to safety? Face the emperor's soldiers with only the power of my own mind?

But why not? I have grown stronger since last I stood up to an army.

And this is all my fault. *I* told Ballast to gamble with his throne. *I* swore to him I would bring him the means to secure it.

The only thing I've accomplished is getting myself trapped in a different cage, and in turn helping Valrún cage the First Ones. I thought that—that they would resist my call, resist being bound, turn us all to cinders.

But none of them did. They allowed themselves to be captured, they're allowing Valrún to spin out her game to its ending.

Why? What is the use of earth-rending power if you don't use it to protect yourself? Why give it up?

It's what I did when I was a child. I let my father bind my magic away so I could go and be a spy in Tenebris. I wanted to avenge my sister. I wanted justice. Unconsciously, I wanted to prove myself worthy of my family's love.

I thought I would be a hero for my people.

But that's not what I was; that's not who I am. I'm just a fool risking everything, again and again, for a game of War I have no chance at winning.

Sleep claims me at long last. The blistering pain of my iron collar follows me there, refusing me the respite of dreams.

I wake to red light from a fire globe, bobbing some inches above my head.

My mother is here, still wearing her stone-and-earth dress.

I sit up too quickly—it makes my head spin, my stomach wrench.

"What are you playing at, wedding the king of Daeros?" she demands.

Anger roils in my chest. "What do you want, Mother?"

"Call the Bronze Lord. Bind him to *yourself*. Then you can wield his power as well as your own. It might be enough to stop Valrún."

I stare at her, shocked. "Since when do you want to stop Valrún?"

"She is no longer fit to rule."

I don't even bother biting back my laugh. "What exactly drove you to that conclusion? I know it wasn't Valrún locking your daughter in iron, or wielding your son like the fool he is, or collecting First Ones like playing cards. So what was it?"

"Don't mock me, Brynja."

I glare at her.

"I didn't think she would be able to bind a single First One," my mother grinds out, "and now she has nearly all of them. I—I fear what she means to do. I fear what happens if she's successful. Ísold being here complicates things further. A power struggle would tear Iljaria apart, and Ísold and her bastard son are no more worthy to sit on the Iljaria throne than Valrún is."

"Don't call him that," I snarl. "Don't call my husband that."

She doesn't even acknowledge this. "Bind the Bronze Lord," she says. "Wield his power against Valrún. Brandr squanders his stolen magic—he doesn't know how to use it, not like your father did. But *you* are strong, Brynja. You can do what none of us could. Take Valrún off the throne. Loose the First Ones you helped to bind. *You* must be queen." She gives me a haughty look. "Of *Iljaria*. Not Daeros."

"So *you* can rule behind the scenes?" I demand. "I don't want any more power, and I'm sure as hell not binding the Bronze Lord and wielding him like a weapon. Why would I? What for?"

"For Iljaria," she says. "For your country."

I snort. "Iljaria never wanted me. My own family never wanted me. Didn't know what to do with my magic. You were too scared to send me to the Huga Conservatory for training—so you sent me to be caged by a murderer instead. Did Father even want me to be a spy? Or was he just trying to get rid of me, and made up this elaborate ruse so I would go meekly to the slaughter?"

"That is *quite* enough, Brynja!"

"Answer the question, Mother!"

She stares at me, chest heaving, hands balled into fists at her sides. Then she turns and strides to the window she made in the spire.

I sit on the bed with my knees tucked up to my chin.

"It wasn't a ruse," she says at last. "It wasn't. I swear it to you. Why else would your father have trained you so diligently? Why else would I have erected the practice arena? No. It wasn't a ruse. We needed a spy in Tenebris. Your father swore to your resilience. But both of us forgot, I think, that you were only a child. I begged him to bring you back, almost as soon as you were gone. But he didn't want it all to be a waste."

My heart beats heavy in my chest. Far from relieving my mind, her words make me feel sicker and angrier than before. "But it *was* a waste, wasn't it," I say tightly. "It was all a waste."

She turns from the window, and her gaze locks hard on mine. "It doesn't have to be. Bind the Bronze Lord. Defeat Valrún. Save us all. But leave the little Daerosian king out of it."

"I will not be leaving *my husband* out of anything."

She sighs and walks back to the bed. "You are hardly more than a child even now, Brynja. Too young by far to have a husband. Dalliances can be diverting, but little more than that. A marriage—such as it is—performed in Daeros is not legal here. You are not truly bound to him. Forget him and his lies. You are a high daughter of Iljaria. When you marry, it will be to a lord of our people, and the children you bear him will command magic even stronger than yours."

"Get out," I say, low and cold.

"We have more to discuss. When you bind the Bronze Lord—"

"I SAID GET OUT!"

She steps back from me, her eyes hard. "Daughter of mine—you must learn to curb your temper. Emotions are an evil bedfellow to power."

I jerk up from the bed. "Get out," I tell her. "Get out get out get out."

"Brynja—"

"You're still afraid of me, aren't you," I say. "The only reason you're having this conversation with me right now is because I'm locked in iron. Why do you think you can control me? Why am I only a vessel to be controlled, a tool to be wielded? I am not a piece on a Lords and Ladies board, and neither is Ballast. Ballast, by the way, treats me like a person who has value, a person worthy of love."

"Oh, I'm sure he *values* you," she mocks me.

I grab her by the shoulder and haul her toward the wall. "Stop disparaging my husband," I spit at her, "and get the hell out of here."

For a moment she just stares at me, her face twisted in a confused mixture of anger and longing.

Mercifully, she mutters a word of her magic and pulls a hole in the wall big enough for her to step through.

Ballast is standing on the other side.

But before he can come in, my mother curses and wrenches the hole shut again.

I sit with my back against the wall, feeling raw, exposed. I didn't know my mother hated me so much.

"Brynja? Can you hear me?"

His voice lights a fire inside me, and I spin about and press my face to the wall, like if I pushed hard enough I could reach him.

I could, actually, if it weren't for the damn collar.

"Yes," I say. "Yes, Bal, I can hear you."

I press my hand flat against the glass, imagining him doing the same on the other side.

"I'm going to get you out of there," he says, "as soon as I can figure out how."

"Finnur could do it."

"He's being watched. He was only vaguely able to tell me how to get to the spire, but it's no good without a door."

A noise pulls out of my throat that's half laugh, half sob. "Adriel, then."

"Do you trust him?"

"Not in the least."

"Black Lord's Ghost, Brynja. I miss you."

My throat hurts. I squeeze my eyes shut against the tears, but they won't stop falling. "I miss you, too. I made a mess of everything."

"You didn't."

"I made you give up your throne and then failed to bring you the army I promised."

"Not on purpose," he says. I can almost see his shrug. "I failed to tell you I'm the queen of Iljaria's *nephew*."

"Not on purpose," I echo him. "You didn't know."

"Minor details," he says. "I really didn't, though. My mother only told me after you left."

"Ballast. I hope we're both far past imagining the other of betrayal."

He laughs softly. "Oh, I've missed you."

"What are we going to do?"

"Well," he says, "first, I'm going to batter down this wall and kiss you absolutely senseless, and then—then we try and save the world, I guess."

"That's a good plan, Bal. Especially the first part."

This earns me another laugh. "I thought so," he says. "See you in a minute."

I feel the sudden force of his body slamming into the wall—he must have thrown himself against it. The room wavers, but the glass does not break. He tries again and again, grunting with every impact. The wall stays firm.

"Bal," I say. "Don't hurt yourself."

He's breathing hard on the other side of the wall. "There has to be a way in."

His voice is tight with pain, and I hope to the gods he hasn't broken his shoulder.

My heart pounds, my mind reels, the iron is agony at my throat. I tilt my head against the wall, wishing I could stretch my hand through it and touch him.

"Sit with me for a little while," I say.

"I'm going to get you out of there."

"Please, Bal." Tears bite at my eyes.

"I'm here, Brynja. Of course I'm here."

"Stay with me."

"I'm not going to leave you."

I breathe, quick and sharp.

"I'm here, Brynja," comes his muffled voice from the other side of the wall, over and over. "I'm here."

ONE HOUR AGO

VALRÚN

Year 4201, Month of the Violet Lord

Iljaria—Regla City—the palace

It is all I can do to keep from snarling at my twelve-Lords-damned sister. "You need to control your son."

Ísold doesn't sit, like I asked her to, just eyes me from behind the sofa that faces my green velvet chair.

I sent Brandr away because I was weary of his face and his words, but now I almost wish him back again. His company is at least more diverting than my sister's.

"The days remaining before Soul's Rest are dwindling," I say. "I will not allow Ballast to ruin everything."

"Valrún," says Ísold, her voice as lilting and musical as I remember from when we were children. "It's time you told me exactly what you're planning."

"Why? So you can try and stop me? It is far too late for that, sister."

Her eyes go hard, and I rein in my temper. I cannot afford to match my power against hers, not here.

Not yet.

"I know you have the Prism Stone," says Ísold. "What do you mean to do with it?"

Something foul makes a knot in my belly.

"Father told me all the same stories he told you," she goes on. "Do you really intend to—"

"What if I do?" I snap. "Why did *you* even come back here? I do not believe for a moment you really want the crown. You are merely lost, Ísold, a lost little girl trying to find her way home, but it is not at all what you remember, is it?"

"I thought you loved me, once," says Ísold softly. "Even when you betrayed me and left me for dead, even when you made no attempt to rescue me—I hoped. When we snuck away from Iljaria, both our parents were living and we—we had a happy childhood, I thought, in the house by the sea."

I look away from her. Because that is where it started, of course. The king's twin daughters, raised by nursemaid Skapari far from the palace, unimportant, almost unnecessary, because Iljaria live for three centuries, more, and our parents were barely a hundred when we were born. I didn't want to be unimportant. I didn't want to struggle to make seedlings sprout when my sister could shake the earth with a few careless notes of her song magic.

White Lady's bones, I should have killed her.

But I didn't have the stomach for it then. I believed all the drivel about peace and life being the most important things to the Iljaria, to the First Ones, to the endurance of the world.

Power is far more important, and I am about to wield it all.

"I would gladly rule Iljaria," says my sister, "if it meant stopping you from ruining this country that I love. Ballast would be a far better option than me to take the crown, but he doesn't want it."

"That is your own fault," I spit at her, "for mingling our bloodline with a foreign barbarian."

Her eyes go wet, and I hate her for it.

"It wasn't my choice, Valrún."

The sick thing in my belly solidifies, but I will not feel sorry for her. *I will not.* "Control your son," I say sharply, returning to my original theme, "or I will do it for you."

She sighs. "Your games, your lies, your threats—they're all ended now."

She opens her mouth and begins to sing.

Her White magic would have neutralized my weak Green magic and overpowered me instantly, had I not taken precautions.

"I will make no apology," I say as Adriel materializes and locks my sister in an iron collar. "I warned you."

Ísold's eyes go wide with the pain of the iron; I do not apologize for that, either. The knot in my gut loosens.

"Enjoy your last few weeks alive, sister," I say, rising from my chair and stretching languorously. "I will kill you, when the dark returns, when the power of every First One runs blazing through my veins."

She looks at me, welts already forming on her neck around the collar. "It's just a story," she says, "just a child's story."

I shrug. "I suppose we will find out if it is true, or if it is not. Take her, Adriel."

"Where, Your Majesty?"

"I care not. Bind her below with the First Ones, if there is room."

"Valrún," she begs, "please."

I curse at her. "Your erstwhile husband had the right idea when he cut your tongue out. Take her now, Adriel!"

They are gone in a flash of time.

I sink back into my chair.

"Malen!" I call.

She pokes her head around the door. "Your Majesty?"

"I want Brandr now. Send him in."

She bows and goes to do as I ask, and I bid him not to speak as I pull him into my bed, as I use him to forget, for a while, all my anger.

All my guilt.

CHAPTER THIRTY-ONE

BALLAST

Year 4201, Month of the Violet Lord

Iljaria—Regla City—the palace

"What are you doing?"

I jerk awake to find Saga staring down at me, her arms folded disapprovingly across her chest, Leifur looming behind her like one of the Gray Lady's demons, sword loose in his hand.

I'm on the landing at the top of the stairwell to the spire, where I've been slumped against the wall separating me from Brynja for what feels like an eternity. I didn't realize I'd fallen asleep.

"You're pathetic," says Saga, in case I misread her body language.

I grimace and stand up, unconsciously rubbing at both of my eyes. The empty one still startles me, even after all this time.

"I was sorry to hear about your parents," I tell Saga.

Her face closes. "Thank you."

"What can I do for you?"

"We're going to free the gods," says Leifur. "Do you know how to find them?"

"All I know is they're somewhere under the palace. Finnur might know, but—"

"He's being watched," Saga supplies.

I nod.

She clenches her jaw, and I sense how hard it is for her to even be talking to me. I try not to think about why, but I can't stop the sudden wrench of memory: my command to the lion, the blood on the floor, the awful churning horror of Hilf's vacant eyes—dead because of me.

"Can you help us?" Leifur presses.

I don't miss the protective way he stands by Saga, looking ready and able to take my head off if he senses the barest threat to her.

"I can try. But—"

Saga glances at the blank wall. "Brynja?"

My heart jerks. "The only way in is with magic. But not mine, damn my luck."

She studies me, and I am thrown back to those months when it was just she and I and Brynja in the Iljaria tunnels, battling cave demons.

"I don't suppose you've tried iron?" she says.

"Iron?"

"It cancels out the effects of magic, doesn't it?"

"Yes, and it's horribly painful, Saga. I don't carry any on me."

She rolls her eyes. "Leifur?"

He steps past both of us. "Stand back, if you please, Your Majesty," he says. Then adds as an afterthought, "Your Majesties."

He sticks his sword straight through the wall.

There's a shriek from the other side.

"Brynja is *right there*!" I holler.

"I'm all right," comes her voice.

"Please stand back!" Leifur calls.

He pulls his blade—clearly made of iron—through the wall like a knife in softened butter, cutting out a doorway.

The next moment the wall falls inward with the shattering of glass, and I unlatch the iron collar from Brynja's neck and hurl it to the floor before wrapping her in my arms and pulling her close against me. "None of that, none of that!" says Saga. "We're here to plot, not canoodle."

But that doesn't stop me from kissing Brynja rather more thoroughly than I ordinarily would with an audience.

"Now," says Saga, "if you're *quite* finished, we need to—"

She's cut off by Brynja dragging her into a fierce hug. "I've missed you, Saga. I know we left things badly between us, but I want—"

"We don't have time for this!" Saga wails, but that doesn't stop her from returning Brynja's embrace with equal ferocity.

"I'm so sorry about your parents," says Brynja into her friend's shoulder. "They were so kind to me when I stayed in the palace, and I wanted to come back and thank them properly and—"

Saga chokes on a sob, and the two of them cry together while Leifur stands stricken and my heart breaks because Brynja's does.

When they've dried their eyes, the four of us huddle in the stairwell, my arm tight around Brynja. I never want to be parted from her ever again.

Saga explains her and Leifur's resolve to free the First Ones. Brynja tells her where the First Ones are being kept, and how to get to the underground levels of the palace.

"But I don't know how much luck you'll have trying to free them," she goes on. "Adriel is not bound by the same laws of time as the rest of us, and he's always on watch—even when he's elsewhere."

"Time magic is unnatural," says Leifur.

"Wholly unnatural," I agree.

"We have to try," says Saga stubbornly. "Between all of us, we ought to be able to think of something."

"I can shift into the form of an animal," I offer.

All three of them look at me.

"You *can*?" says Brynja.

Her admiration makes me almost giddy. "I can sneak down there, distract Adriel, keep him away from the First Ones."

"The rest of us can free the gods," says Saga, nodding.

Brynja is quiet, and I glance down at her.

"I can't come with you," she says.

My gut kicks.

"Why?" Saga's voice is sharp.

"I need to find the Bronze Lord before Valrún makes me draw him here to be bound. I think—I think he could help us stop her."

"Brynja?" I murmur.

"It's something my mother said—she wants me to bind his power to me, and I'm sure as hell not doing that but—if his power is like mine, only greater, he could set the First Ones free and stop Valrún with a mere thought. Maybe that's even what the Violet Lord saw."

"Why don't you call him?" I ask her. "Like you did the others?"

She shakes her head. "I don't think it will work with him. He's not *like* the others."

I remember the stories: the Bronze Lord, mutilated, alone, cut off from his fellow Lords and Ladies as punishment for misusing his power.

Dread runs cold through my veins. "How will you find him?"

Her eyes are far away, and I want to cling to her, to beg her not to go off on her own. Again.

"I don't know. Follow the thread of the magic, I suppose."

Saga frowns; she doesn't like this, either. "Are you so sure we'll fail in freeing the First Ones?"

"No," says Brynja. "But I am sure Valrún has planned for every possibility. And we have a little time yet before the first day of winter. No matter how many First Ones she has bound beneath the palace, I think she will try to enact her plan. And I think the Bronze Lord can help us."

"All right," says Saga. She glances between Brynja and me. "I suppose you can have a minute to say goodbye, but we need to do this *now*. Leifur and I will be waiting for you at the bottom of the stairwell, Ballast. Brynja, good luck. Don't betray me and—stay alive, if you can."

Brynja smiles. "I will do my best, Saga."

Then Saga and Leifur head down the stairs, and I am at last alone with my wife.

I cup her face in my hands, smooth her hair back from her brow. I whisper healing magic over the cuts and blisters left by the iron collar. I kiss her, wildly, tenderly, the promise of more to come.

It feels like someone is ripping off a limb when she steps back from me, her fingers still tangled in my shirt. Her eyes are wet.

"Don't be long," I beg her. "And Blue Lady's heart, be careful."

Her chin trembles. "You too, Bal. I couldn't bear it if anything happened to you."

I touch her face, brush away her tears with my thumb. "Nothing will happen to me."

"I love you," she whispers. "I've missed you so much."

My throat goes tight, and I draw her face once more to mine. "I love you," I say against her lips. "To the very depths of my soul."

And then an exasperated Saga is grabbing my arm and pulling me down the stairs, and Brynja stands on the landing like some divine creature, crafted all of glittering bronze.

It's all I can do not to yank out of Saga's hold, run back to Brynja, fold her once more in the circle of my arms, and never again let her go.

But I don't.

I follow Saga to the bottom of the stairwell, and I transform into a mouse.

CHAPTER THIRTY-TWO

BRYNJA

Year 4201, Month of the Violet Lord

Iljaria—Regla City—the palace

For a little while after Ballast has gone, I stand staring blankly down the stairwell, fighting to keep myself from following him.

With the iron collar off my neck, with my husband's whispered healing magic having erased the cuts and blisters, I should feel lighter and freer than I have since I got here.

But I've parted from Ballast *again*, and my heart is utterly sick.

I come back into the glass prison and sit cross-legged on the floor.

I know exactly where to look for the Bronze Lord, the place I met him before, when I was a child:

My own mind.

But I have a strong sense that it is urgent for me to physically go to where he is, that it will mean more to him, that way, that he will take me at my word, understand my need, and agree to help me.

How does one physically travel to a place of thought?

I'm not entirely certain, but with the collar gone, I can think far more clearly than when I was trying so hard to puzzle it out in the Skapari women's dormitory.

I shut my eyes and call my magic to me. I let it fill me up like snowmelt in a mountain pool. It sparks in me, bright and strong. Eager.

"All right, My Lord," I whisper. "I'm coming to find you."

In my head I see paths of labyrinthine stone. I smell deep earth. I taste the heavy, stale air.

Opening my eyes, I can still see those paths, glimmering in the space between molecules.

I take a breath.

I slip through.

I leave the spire and the palace and Iljaria behind.

I step out of this world.

Into somewhere new.

NOW

SAGA

Year 4201, Month of the Violet God

Iljaria—Regla City—the palace

This whole place makes my skin crawl, and it only gets worse the farther down we go.

I was relieved to be reunited with Brynja, however briefly, up there in the tower. Her genuine grief about my parents softened me in a way I didn't realize I needed. I was sorry to leave her behind.

It's weird to see her and Ballast together. I remember how angry even the idea of it made me last year, and the shadow of the anger remains, but—

They suit each other.

She can move things with her mind, and he—

Well, he's currently a mouse.

That's weird, too. I really don't know what the First Ones were thinking when they handed out magic to the Iljaria.

But I'm pretty all right with not having any.

I hold Leifur's left hand as we descend into the bowels of the palace; his iron sword is ready in his right.

Mouse-Ballast scampers ahead of us, darting back every minute or so to make sure we're following.

We descend stair after stair, pushing a creepy green medallion set into the wall to give us access to every new level.

There aren't as many Iljaria about as I worried there might be; we have to duck around corners or hide in doorways only a handful of times. It's funny to me that even in a country filled with magical people, there are still dishes to wash and laundry to fold.

I've lost count of the levels by the time we reach the lowest one.

I don't like it down here. There isn't enough light and it smells . . . old and foul with a tang of something sweet, slowly rotting.

It smells like dead things.

We come to the center of the bare room, and I see the outline of the door in the stones at our feet.

Mouse-Ballast sits in the middle of it, squeaking insistently.

When he realizes that we don't speak mouse, he shifts back into human form with the same impossible and disconcerting stretch-crack-pop thing he did to become a mouse, only in reverse, which somehow makes it *even more horrifying*.

Leifur, who was paying better attention than I, grabbed Ballast's clothes when he first changed form, and he throws them at him now with a panicked squawk.

Ballast doesn't put them on, just hastily covers himself and then says: "Open the door, Leifur, and I will go distract Adriel. Free the First Ones, if you can, but I would put that iron sword away."

And then he's a mouse again, scampering across the stones.

Leifur pulls open the trapdoor and Ballast disappears down the ladder, which dangles into darkness.

If Leifur weren't looking so harried, I would make a joke about seeing Ballast naked, but this doesn't seem to be the time. He sheathes his sword and turns to me with a resolve I don't at all like.

"Saga, you should go back upstairs."

"No way in hell, Leifur."

He squares his jaw. "It isn't *safe*."

"The gods are bound down there," I say, waving toward the ladder. "Of course it isn't safe. But I've come too far to turn back now. Please don't ask me to."

His eyes lock hard on mine. We both know he could keep me from coming with him, if he really wanted.

We also both know that he never would.

"Damn it, Saga," he breathes, and then he's kissing me like the world is about to end.

There's a flash of violet light from down below, sudden and strong enough to break us apart.

"I'm going first," says Leifur in a way that brooks no refusal.

He climbs down into the darkness, and I follow so closely I nearly tread on his hands.

Then I'm setting my feet on the stone floor and turning to face the room.

Leifur grips my shoulder.

For a moment that feels like it spins out for centuries, I don't know what I'm looking at. I can't even comprehend it.

There is darkness and—and colors, in the darkness. But the colors are worlds in and of themselves. No, the colors *are* the world. Perhaps that's more to the truth of it.

I am pulled to pieces and sewn back together. I am shattered and remade. I am erased and redrawn, over and over again.

And then Leifur grabs my hand, puts it on the hilt of his iron sword.

My vision flickers. The world reinvents itself into a thing I can begin to understand.

There is darkness, yes, a great echoing hall of it. But it is broken by spheres that pulse with light and color, suspended on nothing.

In the spheres, I see, bit by bit, are the gods.

Leifur and I walk together into the massive expanse, our hands still gripping the sword hilt.

The Blue Goddess kneels in her sphere, her throat and wrists and ankles bound in iron. A hound lies at her feet, and there is a hedgehog on her shoulder. Her eyes are shut, her lips moving, but I cannot hear what she says.

The sphere hangs far too high above us to have any hope of reaching. Loosing the gods, even if we could reach them—

It's impossible.

But we don't turn back. How could we?

We tread deeper into the echoing dark, and I'm not sure if I'm shaking or if Leifur is.

We see the Black God, the Red God, the Brown Goddess. The Green Goddess, the Gray Goddess, the Violet God. The White Goddess, on her knees with her wrists and ankles bound like the others, but she has an iron band around her mouth instead of her throat. Her eyes are open, and she looks down. She sees us. I am overwhelmed with longing, with grief.

"We have to try," I say. "We have to try to save her. To save all of them."

"I know," comes Leifur's answer. His voice is thick with tears.

He boosts me to his shoulders, hanging on to my feet while I stretch up with my hands, my fingertips almost but not quite grazing the bottom arc of the White Goddess's sphere.

I lose my balance and fall, Leifur grabbing me in such a way that I don't slam into the floor.

We kneel together, my hand caught fast in his, our faces tilted upward to the gods we cannot save.

Tears pour down my face. I shut my eyes, and I do the only thing I can.

I begin to sing.

CHAPTER THIRTY-THREE

BALLAST

Year 4201, Month of the Violet Lord

Iljaria—Regla City—the palace

I lead Adriel on a merry chase.

The Violet Skapari must be tired. He winks in and out of existence, wielding his time magic, but he's never quick enough to catch me. I dart through the darkness of the chamber that holds the First Ones, a speck of dust in the marches of eternity.

The First Ones are trapped away over my head, awaiting the queen's pleasure like—well, like the children in my father's cursed Collection. They are each of them in a cage, and the wrongness of it cuts past my mouse heart to my human one.

I run with all that's in me, tiny nails on the shadowy floor, muscles straining, blood pumping. Adriel dives to catch me and misses. I jerk about and run in the opposite direction.

He is not always chasing me. There are a few occasions when he disappears and doesn't return for long moments—summoned by the queen, I expect, pulled in so many directions it's a marvel he doesn't fracture himself in time.

I take a risk during one of these instances: I shift into my human self and then assume the form of a falcon. I stretch my wings. I leap into the air.

I flap about the First Ones' spheres, not knowing—or not understanding—how to help them. I try to batter my way into the Blue Lady's sphere, agonized that I spent all those weeks in her company and didn't know her. But the magic around her repels me; I am thrown backward again and again.

Ballast, comes her voice in my mind, gentle as a lion with her cub, *I meant for you not to know. I did not think you would receive my instruction otherwise.*

I hover near her, my wings wearied from trying to hold me in place. I wonder how she can speak into my thoughts, locked as she is in iron. I get the feeling she could flick her bonds away as easily as an ordinary human might swat a fly, that her restraints only have the power to hold her because she allows them to. *But what can I do?* I ask her, fighting to wrench words out of the falcon's mind. *How can I save you?*

Son of mine, she says, *that is not the task laid before you.*

But—

A flash of movement below me catches my eye: Adriel, stepping once more into the room, hauling my mother by the arm—there is an iron collar around her neck.

I give a harsh cry and dive, hurtling downward, striking the side of Adriel's head with my beak.

"Ballast," gasps my mother, "what have you done?"

I twist away as Adriel grabs for me. He curses, vicious, weary.

We are halted by a sudden thread of music in the dark. It is tremulous at first, then grows stronger and stronger. It's filled with grief, and with power.

But the odd thing is I *know* that voice.

My wings follow the sound of it. I see her, kneeling below the White Lady: Saga Stjörnu, queen of Skaanda. Singing.

There is magic in her song.

Potent magic.

It pours from her lips, pools around her, rises like steam. It touches the White Lady's sphere, and it cracks it. The White Lady steps down from her prison, kneels beside Saga, catches her chin with one finger, lifts Saga's face.

Saga opens her eyes, the music still spinning from her tongue. She gasps at the sight of the White Lady, and her song is at last cut off. The final notes tremble around her, humming with power.

"Goddess," Saga whispers. She lifts a trembling hand and takes the iron muzzle from the White Lady's mouth. The White Lady smiles at her, though the smile is sad.

"I thank you, my daughter," says the White Lady. "You have risked much to be here. And now you see that there is magic in your heart."

"I don't understand," says Saga, reaching out to grab Leifur's hand. He is kneeling beside her, staring at her in awe.

The White Lady wipes the tears from Saga's face. "The Iljaria are not the only ones blessed with our gifts. You just have to learn to see them. I wanted to show you that. I wanted you to know that you are not powerless. That you are strong, daughter. That your magic is strong."

"My magic," Saga echoes.

The White Lady kisses Saga's brow and then stands.

Saga looks up at her, reverent, dazed.

"Now," says the White Lady, "I must return to my prison for a little while. Remember your strength."

"But—"

The White Lady begins to sing, a mirror of Saga's melody. She rises into the air, and the sphere re-forms around her.

"Wait!" Saga shouts, her voice breaking. "Please!"

"Your time is up," growls Adriel, and he snatches me suddenly out of the air and hurls me into a barrel bound with iron. He jams the lid on top, and I am cut off from everything but the sounds of Saga weeping and the scrape of Leifur's sword being drawn from its sheath.

The barrel sways as Adriel carries it, jolts as he sets it down. There is no sound after that—he must have wielded his time magic and gone somewhere else. I throw my falcon's body against the lid, but he's set something heavy on top, and I can't move it.

I spend some moments panicking, running in circles around the bottom of the barrel. I can't shift into human form in here—the iron suppresses my magic—and I am terrified I will lose myself to the falcon. I focus on the memory of kissing Brynja, her hair soft against my cheek.

Light floods in all at once, Adriel sliding the lid off the barrel. I launch myself out of it with one flap of my wings and tumble human onto the floor.

Adriel has brought me to the glass spire and repaired the wall that Leifur cut through with his sword.

The Violet Skapari throws me a shirt and trousers, which I pull hastily on, unable to keep myself from glancing around the room, looking for any sign of Brynja. There is none besides the iron collar on the floor.

Adriel shoves his hands in his pockets, watching me. "I'm not sure what you think you accomplished down there," he says. His lips are pressed into a hard line.

"Why do you serve Valrún?" I counter. "You have enough power to stop her all on your own."

He shifts his gaze away from me, tension in his frame. For a moment I don't think he's going to answer, but then his eyes find mine again, and I see the sorrow in them.

"Magic is not the only measure of power," Adriel says heavily.

"What hold does she have over you?" I ask him.

"I lost someone. My father."

I shove the thought of my own father out of my mind. "You have my sympathies. When did he die?"

Adriel shakes his head. "He isn't dead. I *lost* him, accidentally, in my first year at the Ári Conservatory. I was wielding Violet magic far outside of my control, and I sent him into Time, but I don't know where. I have looked for him ever since, but I can't find him. That kind of misuse of magic is punishable by death, but Valrún showed me mercy in taking me as her Skapari. And she has promised, when she is Queen Eternal, to help me find him."

"The Violet Lord is bound beneath us," I say shortly. "Why have you not asked *him* to help you?"

Adriel drops his gaze to the floor. "I have asked him. Many times. He wouldn't do it. Do you revile me, Ballast? For serving an evil queen to save my own skin?"

I see a sudden flash of my father's cruel smile in the moment before he put out my eye. "No," I say. "No, I don't revile you for that. But you can still change your mind. You can help us."

"Help you do what?"

"Stop her."

Adriel gives a heavy sigh. "We can't."

"Why not?"

He lifts his eyes to mine. "Because time is written this way, and there are some things I cannot change."

And then he's gone, and I'm alone.

TWO WEEKS AGO

VIL

Year 4201, Month of the Violet God

The White Sea

The sun is rising when the first wave of Skaandan Fire is launched against the magical barrier that shimmers out over the sea.

For a few moments I'm gripped by sudden terror that the Skaandan Fire won't work, that all my plans and promises will amount to nothing.

I will have failed Aelia. I will have failed myself.

But then the canisters explode against the magical shield in a flash of orange, and the whole thing fractures to pieces. The shards fall like rain on the water.

A shout of triumph pulls out of me, and I thrust my fist into the air.

Junius and Aelia stand at the rail on either side of me, both wearing golden helmets that glisten in the light of the burgeoning sun. Junius gives a satisfied nod, and Aelia grips my arm, her pulse beating fast in my wrist.

"Thus mighty Iljaria falls," she says quietly.

I hear what she doesn't say: *Thus my father falls.*

The ship cuts through the water, the rest of the fleet coming behind like the long tail of a kite.

We reach the shattered magical barrier. We sail across.

There is little, now, that stands between me and a crown. Between Aelia and her freedom.

I grab her hand. I hold it tight.

The gods are with us.

I smile into the sun.

CHAPTER THIRTY-FOUR

BALLAST

Year 4201, Month of the Black Lord

Iljaria—Regla City—the palace

Seventeen days pass in agonizing solitude. No one comes to see me in the glass spire. Every now and again food appears on the table, and I scarf it down, ravenous, but that is the only variation in the monotony. I sleep fitfully, yearning to dream of Brynja.

I never do.

Worry gnaws at me. Where has she gone? Why hasn't she come back?

I walk the confines of my glass prison. I page listlessly through the books on the shelf. I practice shifting in and out of various animal forms. Twice I transform into an armored rhinoceros and charge the wall, but the magic is too strong, the glass does not break, and I am left with a sore head for my troubles.

Today is the last day before winter. In any year prior to this one, that would mean a single hour of sunlight before the long dark of Soul's Rest. But the midday light is strong through the window, and it will continue to be, unless Valrún succeeds in bringing back the dark.

"Ballast."

I jump and turn from the window.

Finnur stands there holding the blue-feathered robe, a haunted look in his eyes, raw blisters around his throat evidencing a recently worn iron collar. Ah. That explains why he hasn't come to see me.

"Finnur, are you well?"

He doesn't look at me as he hands me the robe. "You're to wear this. Valrún's orders."

"What's going on?" My heart drums frantically inside me. "Any sign of Brynja?"

He shakes his head and stands there, staring at the floor.

"Finnur," I say gently. "Please tell me what's happening."

"I've failed you," he says. "I've failed everyone."

I toss the robe onto the bed and grip him by both shoulders. "No, you haven't."

He raises his face to mine. "Yes. I *have*. I could have stopped her before, but it's too late now. She will perform the ritual today."

"What ritual, Finnur?"

Pain creases his forehead. "The one to bring back the dark," he says. "The one to destroy the world. She will make herself Queen Eternal and then—then there will be nothing. I looked forward in time, Ballast. All I saw was darkness."

Fear twists cold and sharp as a sword. "What of the other Skapari?"

"She's collared them all in iron. Even me." His voice breaks. "My collar is waiting for me as soon as I take you out of here. There's one for you, too." He pulls it out of his pocket with a handkerchief, holding it gingerly so it won't burn him. "I'm sorry, Ballast."

I set my jaw, wondering if I can stomach fighting him to keep him from collaring me.

"What about Saga and Leifur? What about my mother?"

"Saga and Leifur were in prison until yesterday."

My gut clenches. "Where are they now?"

"Valrún chained them up on the north wall of the city. She says they're to greet the Aeronan army when it comes."

"Red Lord's *entrails*," I swear.

"Your mother is collared with the other Skapari. Valrún has summoned them all for the ritual. We're to join her. So you have to get dressed now. And then I have to put the collar on you. I'm sorry, Your Majesty." His voice breaks.

He's never called me that before. "Why are you sorry, Finnur?"

"Because I couldn't protect Brynja, like you bade me. And I can't protect you, like I bade myself. And because all of Iljaria will fall, and the world with it."

I think of Brynja, her power strong enough, even as a child, to nearly bring a mountain crashing down around us. And she has gone to the one who holds the whole of that power. I trust her. This is not the end.

"Have a little faith, Finnur," I tell him gently. "The sun is yet shining. The dark will not overwhelm us."

He nods in answer, but his face is still grim.

He helps me into the feathered robe like he's clothing me in armor. He crowns me in blue feathers, binds a blue stone onto my brow. And then I bow my head, and he locks the collar around my neck. I shudder as my magic is cut off.

"Forgive me, Your Majesty," he whispers.

He pulls me with him through the wall to the landing, where Adriel is waiting, wearing an iron collar and holding another in his hands. Finnur meekly allows the Violet Skapari to put it around his throat.

And then the three of us go downstairs, to see what horror Valrún has in store for us.

Please hurry, Brynja, I think, reaching fruitlessly out to her. *Wherever you are, whatever you're doing, whatever is keeping you—please hurry. Please come back.*

Please come back to me.

CHAPTER THIRTY-FIVE

BALLAST

Year 4201, Month of the Black Lord

Iljaria—the Sögu Byrjun

I feel like I am caught in a children's rhyme.

Ten Skapari, all in a row, dressed in the colors of their magic:

Blue and White, Brown and Violet, Red and Black, Green and Yellow, Gray and Prism.

Ten Skapari, all in a row, bound in iron, the queen at their head, her Prism Master at their tail.

Ten Skapari, all in a row, pass through the city gates in the full bright glare of the afternoon sun.

Ten Skapari, winding up the stone steps carved into an ancient hill with an ancient name: Sögu Byrjun, story's beginning.

This is a sacred place. Some histories say it is where the world itself began, others that the First Ones awoke here, and others still that it is the place where magic came into being.

Whichever story is true, I can sense the power in the earth beneath my feet, feel the old, feral strength of it.

I sweat under my feathered robe, and the iron burns at my neck.

We reach the summit of the Sögu Byrjun, the hilltop flattened and paved with a broad, circular stone. It is divided into twelve pieces that meet at a narrow point in the middle and widen out to form the circumference. Every section is marked with the colors and symbols of each branch of magic, from Green to Ghost. It is a miniature version of Regla City, and I have the distant realization that the hill must have served as its model.

In the exact center of the circle is a plinth about three feet high made of flawless white stone. Valrún goes to stand beside it, a prismatic crown on her head, her gown adorned with dazzling gems in every color, the bodice tight-fitting, the skirt flaring out from her hips. She flashes and glisters in the light of the sun, impossible to look at for more than a few seconds. At her beckoning, Brandr joins her beside the plinth, his smile sharp.

I am drawn without conscious thought to the Blue slice of the circle, and I stand there like my feet are fastened to the stone. All around me, the other Skapari do the same: my mother stepping into the White section—which adjoins the Blue—Adriel into the Violet, Malen into the Green, and on until all the sections are filled except Bronze and Ghost.

Magic thrums beneath my feet. I look at the empty Bronze segment and am gripped by wild, frantic fear. Where is she?

Up the other side of the hill comes a mass of light magic wielders clothed in the color of their power, with matching yellow gems glittering from their brows. They crowd into the Yellow section of the wheel, with Jóvin—the only Skapari not bound in iron—at their head.

A hot wind stirs across the hill, ruffling the feathers of my robe and bringing with it the faint, sour scent of decay. I shudder and try to step out of the Blue section of the stone circle but find I cannot, a will other than my own holding me here. The fear bites sharper still.

I glance around the circle to see the other Skapari are likewise fixed in place. My mother's face gleams with tears, and opposite me Adriel is cursing. To my left, Malen's eyes are wide with terror, and just past her is Finnur, who shakes his head at my glance. There is no plan. No way out of this.

Valrún circles the plinth, looking at each one of us in turn. Her smile is as bright as the sun that gilds her.

"Faithful Skapari," she says, her voice ringing clear, "today we call the First Ones to heel. Today we loose the Yellow Lord from his prison in the sun and bring back the great darkness of Soul's Rest. Today we restore the power of the Stjarna that was so cruelly taken from them."

A raucous cheer goes up from the Yellow wielders, with Jóvin thrusting his fist into the sky.

"Today," says the queen, "in this place of ancient ritual, on the first day of winter, when magic runs strongest through the veins of the earth, we will seize the reins of power and wield them to our liking!"

Another cheer from the Yellow wielders, but the rest of the Skapari are silent.

I glance at my mother, who trembles where she stands.

Valrún draws a small jewel case from the folds of her gown and sets it on top of the plinth. She opens the case and takes out a stone about the size of her palm. It's a light gray, with veins of color running through it. It looks heavy, and she holds it in both of her hands.

I can feel the stone's magic; it pulses so strongly I wonder she can even touch it without being consumed.

"Faithful Skapari," she says again, "you have served me well, and when the ritual is complete, you may stay or go, as you choose. Forgive me, if you will, your bonds of iron. I had to be sure of you. I am already missing one out of twelve." She looks at me with vicious hatred. "I could not afford to be without any others."

"But surely you are missing two, Your Majesty," says Finnur, his dark eyes glittering. "There is no Ghost Skapari here."

"That is where you are wrong, Finnur," returns Valrún in a tone of fond indulgence. She turns to her Prism Master. "Brandr. It is time."

He smiles and throws his arms out, his prismatic robes melting away to expose ones made of formless, shifting shadows.

"I hereby reveal to you the true patron of my Prism Master," says Valrún. "He serves the Ghost Lord, and so tonight represents the eleventh branch of magic. Ghost magic is no longer forbidden in Iljaria, and those who are born to wield it will no longer be cast out."

A sob chokes out of Malen in the Green section on my left, and I glance over her to see a fierce hope in her eyes. Tears glimmer on her lashes.

Brandr looks to Valrún with triumph and pride, and she spares him a swift smile as he takes a step into the Ghost section of the stone wheel. He does not come as far out as the rest of us, though, remaining very near the plinth. He's close enough to the queen that he could reach out and touch her, if he wanted. His gaze is fixed on her.

But she has eyes only for the stone in her hands. She lifts it high. Lightning seems to crackle around her. She shouts a word of ancient magic into the sun.

The iron collar around my neck unlatches, falling to the stone, making sparks fly up. But though I feel the rush of my power returning, my magic does not answer me, and I still can't move—my will is yet bound.

All around the wheel it is the same: the Skapari loosed from their collars, yet held in place by Valrún's magic. No, I realize—by the magic of the Prism Stone in her hands. She is using it to control us, to quench our power.

Horror winds into my bones, and for all I am desperate to have Brynja back, I am glad she is not here. I could not protect her from this.

Still holding the Prism Stone high, Valrún walks around the plinth, the stone catching the sunlight, bending and twisting it, so it seems like a living thing. Perhaps it is.

"My Skapari!" Valrún shouts. "You are the most powerful wielders in all of Iljaria. I chose you and called you, knowing you to be strong enough to perform the ritual of binding. Now I call the First Ones, each to the Skapari who wields their magic. My Skapari, you will bind your patrons to you, and drawing on their power, we will all together call down the Yellow Lord from his prison in the sun, and restore to Iljaria the magic that was taken from it."

This is wrong, wrong, wrong. I fight to move from the Blue section. I claw for my magic, try to wrest myself into the shape of a falcon, a wolf, a mouse. My body writhes and rages, trying to obey my commands and Valrún's. It feels as if I'm being ripped in halves, and I cannot bear the strain of it.

The First Ones come, like wind, like fire, drawn each from their imprisoning spheres by the power of the Prism Stone.

They step onto the hill, their throats and wrists and ankles and abdomens bound in iron, the White Lady with an iron muzzle over her mouth. And yet even restrained as they are, the immense power of them crushes the breath out of me.

Valrún shrieks with an awful, wild joy. "Bind them!" she cries. "Bind them!"

The First Ones step up to us, joining us in our sections of White and Brown and Blue. Dimly, I am aware that the Ghost Lord is among them, though he was not imprisoned below the palace like all the rest.

The Blue Lady stands before me, fierce and unflinching, and I get the sudden sense that she is only bound in iron because she has allowed it, that she could shake free of her restraints if she wished to, as easily as one flicks away a fly.

"My Lady," I whisper, and I know myself to be broken and utterly wretched before her. "Stop this. Please. I know you can."

Her hair whips about her face in a sudden gust of wind, and she smiles at me, a little sadly. "Do not fear, Ballast Solstrøm. All will be well."

Around the circle of Skapari, I hear the echo of her words, the First Ones offering comfort to the humans who wield their magic, though they are the ones yet locked in iron.

"Please," I say. "My Lady. *Please.*"

"All will be well," she says again. "He has seen it, son of mine. What he has seen we cannot change."

"You mean the Violet Lord." I peer across the circle to where Adriel stands face-to-face with the Lord of Time, and he looks small and frail in contrast to his patron.

"What has he seen?" I ask the Blue Lady. "How does this end?"

But she shakes her head, and there is sorrow in her gaze. "Son of mine. I cannot tell you that."

"Skapari!" cries Valrún from the plinth. "Loose your patrons!"

Against my will, I lift my hand to unlatch the Blue Lady's collar. It falls with a clang upon the stone, and she stands there patiently as I unlatch the bonds on her wrists and her waist, as I kneel to remove the ones on her ankles.

She pulls me upright again when it is done.

The other Skapari have freed their patrons also. The First Ones stand now unbound, a refuse of iron littering the stones at our feet.

"Now," says Valrún, wind lashing her skirt about her knees, "the first binding!"

Lightning fractures the sky behind her, and the Yellow wielders, huddled in their slice of the wheel, start up a chant, quiet at first, growing ever louder until it seems to shake the earth.

Clouds knot over the sun, and it begins to rain in stinging, icy sheets. The rain bites my face, runs into my eye.

Valrún shrieks a torrent of ancient magic into the rising storm, the Prism Stone flashing and glittering in her hands.

Before me, the Blue Lady gasps and stumbles.

I reach out my hands to steady her. "My Lady. What did the Violet Lord see? What's going to happen? *What did he see?*"

But she does not answer, though tears gleam suddenly in her eyes.

And then I gasp at the sudden sensation of power that's like a strand of living fire winding about me, starting at my ankles and swirling up and up until it wraps around my legs and my torso, my neck, my brows.

I stare at the Blue Lady, and she stares at me.

"I am sorry, son of mine," she says, quiet amid the roaring world. "I did not want this for you."

And I realize that this is what it means to bind the Blue Lady. I am binding her to myself. Binding her power.

All at once the full force of her magic rushes into me. I stagger under the weight of it, the blinding, white-hot pain.

I am mortal. I cannot hold it all.

In another moment I will be consumed.

And yet—

Yet I am not.

I don't know if it is the power of the Prism Stone that sustains me, or the magic of the Sögu Byrjun, the ancient hill where we stand. Perhaps it's the Blue Lady herself. Freely, she pours her magic into me.

I am re-formed, from the inside out. I am made new.

Yet as I am filled, the Blue Lady is emptied. I watch in horror as the life drains out of her, more and more, until there is nothing left and she slumps like a corpse at my feet.

A scream rips from my throat, and the power that holds me in place relents enough that I am able to kneel beside the Blue Lady, grab her frail shoulders, try to shake life into her again. But her eyes are vacant. There is not the faintest spark of her left.

Her life, her magic, is in *me*. I have taken it all.

I lift my head and peer around me in the rain. The Skapari blaze like torches, forced to bind and drain their patrons, just as I have. Only Brandr seems unbothered by this, the Ghost Lord lying like so many shadows on the ground before him. He smiles at the queen, who still grips the Prism Stone with both of her hands.

I feel as if I am seeing two worlds, layered over top one another. One is filled with the queen and her Skapari, the dead First Ones, the cacophonous chanting of the Yellow wielders, the bitter, driving rain.

The other is nothing but color and power that is hungry, vicious, wanting.

"My Skapari!" cries Valrún in utter triumph. "My First Ones reborn! Claim your newfound power. Lift your eyes to the heavens! Call down the Yellow Lord!"

The Yellow wielders' chanting swells to a roar, and I find my voice raised to join them, ripped from my throat without my consent.

The Prism Stone shivers and pulses. Even now she is controlling us.

Magic eddies all around me, teeming with strength beyond my comprehension, beyond my endurance, and every bit of it is *wrong*.

I try to wrench myself free, but I can't. The magic has seeped into my skin, wound into my bones. It fills up my soul. Whether I will it or no, it is part of me, just as I am part of the foul sorcery that shrouds this ancient hill.

Some instinct causes me to tilt my face up.

Through the storm I see the sun, falling like a comet from the sky. It turns the rain to steam. It collects lightning like metal shards to a lodestone.

My heart jolts, my breath stills.

Because it is we who have done this.

It is me.

The sun falls, falls, and as it draws nearer, I see him: the Yellow Lord, blazing with light, bringing down the dark.

The chanting of the Yellow wielders morphs into a wild and eerie song, rejoicing at the imminent return of their power.

I am able, at last, to snap my mouth shut, to cut off the command pouring out of me.

But it is too late.

He is here, feet touching the broad stone of the hilltop. Darkness whorls around him. The rain is gone, but the day has turned to night, and the air holds the sting of sudden, bitter winter.

The Yellow Lord blinks, gazing around the circle in confusion. I forgot how young he looks, clothed in the form of a boy.

"My Lord," says Jóvin, walking up to him and sweeping a bow that drips with mockery.

"What is this?" The Yellow Lord's voice crackles with energy. "I chose the house she prepared for me. I obeyed her voice. I am not meant to be here." His brows narrow as he sees the shells of the First Ones, slumped dead on the stones. He gives a great cry of anguish at the sight of the Prism Lady and takes a step toward her.

"Ah, My Lord," says Jóvin. "You serve her no longer."

He grabs the Yellow Lord by the throat and yanks him into the Yellow spoke of the stone circle. The Light wielders crowd around him, eager to reclaim their power.

Valrún watches with a feigned disinterest, not noticing, or perhaps not caring, that Brandr steps over the corpse of the Ghost Lord and comes to stand beside her.

Jóvin's mouth twists into an unholy smile as he draws the Yellow Lord's magic into him. He takes, takes, takes, and unlike the Blue Lady's power, it is not freely given.

At last the Yellow Lord lets out a small, weak breath, and slumps to the ground, the light going out of his eyes.

Jóvin turns to face the Light wielders, Yellow magic sparking off him.

"Give us the light," chant the Yellow wielders, "give us the light! Give us the light!"

"Yes," says Jóvin, in a voice that is not quite his own. "Yes, I will give it to you." He claps his hands, and every single Yellow wielder blazes suddenly bright as the midsummer sun.

Then there is nothing left of them but ashes, and the wind blows them away.

I am sick to my core.

Alone in the Yellow spoke of the circle, Jóvin turns toward the queen.

"You see me now restored to my power," he says to her. "You see me now ascended. Is it enough, my queen?"

"Silence," snaps Brandr, sliding one arm possessively around Valrún's waist. "She has no need of you."

Darkness lives and breathes all around us. No sun, no stars. Only emptiness.

My heart beats in agony, the Blue Lady's power roaring in my veins.

"There is just one more thing," says Valrún to Jóvin, fixing him with a radiant smile. "As we discussed."

"Yes, my queen," he says. "Of course." Jóvin lifts his hands, holding the full, consuming power of the Yellow Lord's magic.

For a heartbeat his eyes catch on my single one.

There is the sudden feeling like a knife slashed across my throat, the hot, awful rush of blood.

And then—

CHAPTER THIRTY-SIX

BRYNJA

Year 4201, month: unknown

Place unknown

The Bronze Lord is not in the mountain.

I wander the paths of the labyrinth, searching for him, calling for him, reaching for his power.

But he isn't here.

So I find a door that leads out of the mountain, and I step through it.

I am on an unfamiliar plain beneath a strange sky. There are no stars here, no sun, no moon. Just swirls of color, punctuated by threads of glittering light.

I walk and walk toward the light. I sense a fragment of his power, that way. I follow it.

It's strange, being here, in this place that doesn't exist in the reality I have grown used to.

These are the paths of thought, the world of the mind. All is magic, all is teeming, consuming power.

It's horribly, overwhelmingly lonely.

There is no sense of time or space. There is no life and no death, no birds, no music, no growing things. There isn't even any fire, and so there is no heat. But there is no cold, either.

I walk and walk.

I grow impossibly weary of the unending plain, the impossible sky. I tell them to change and they do, becoming undulating green hills that spread out before me, a sun rising in a sea of pink clouds.

But I know these things aren't real, and so they do not comfort me.

I walk and walk.

I rehearse to myself, repeatedly, who I am and why I'm here and what I'm seeking.

I twist a silver ring set with a blue stone around and around my finger. I think of Ballast, moving with me in the dark, his hands caught in my wild hair.

Husband, I tell myself again and again. *He's my husband.*

But as I walk on, the word loses its meaning.

It occurs to me, after a long, long while, that the Bronze Lord rules here, that he made this place, that he commands it.

If he wanted to, he could keep me wandering for all eternity and never allow me to reach him.

Anger sparks, and I stand suddenly still, the air crackling around me, charged with my magic, my rage.

"My Lord!" I shout into the sky that is not a sky. "Let me through this labyrinth! I would speak to you!"

I know he hears me. The earth beneath my feet softens. The non-sky *shifts.*

A path appears before me.

I step onto it.

I walk yet a long way. Slowly, everything around me begins to change, and becomes more like the world I once knew. Grass flattens under my feet. The sky grows pale and is traced with wisps of cloud. I hear, as if from far away, the sound of gulls, the crash of waves against a rocky shore.

I remember the story of the Bronze Lord: He loved the Prism Lady, but she did not love him in return, and in his great anguish of emotion, he could not, or would not, contain his power. He moved mountains; he compelled whole villages of people to tear out their own hearts in order to display his love. The Prism Lady would abide it no longer. With the Ghost Lord and the Gray Lady to help her, she maimed the Bronze Lord in punishment, cutting off his hands and his feet, his ears and his nose, putting out his eyes. He withdrew to a solitary island, there to dwell alone in his agony and heartbreak until the world's ending.

The scent of a storm is on the wind; the air crackles with the promise of lightning. Clouds knit together, heavy with rain.

I come suddenly to a cliffside that crashes down into a black sea, the seething waves topped with foam. A narrow stair is cut into the cliff, treacherous and steep, with many of the steps broken or missing. I go up to the edge of the cliff and peer into the depths below. A boat bobs at the end of a dock, and far, far out in the dark water is a smudge of land: the Bronze Lord's island.

There is nothing for it but to set my feet onto the stair, press myself against the cliffside like a spider, and creep slowly down.

I am not certain if this place truly exists, or if it is another construct of the Bronze Lord's mind. But it *feels* real.

I slip on one of the broken steps and fall, scrabbling desperately for purchase as I slide off into empty air. My hand clamps on to a jutting rock and the momentum of my body nearly rips my arm out of its socket. I hang there for a moment in a haze of panic.

Then clarity comes into my mind, and I laugh at myself.

I tell the stair to widen. I tell the mountain to grow, to give me a solid place to put my feet again.

Stair and mountain obey me at once.

The rest of the journey is easier, and I reach the bottom of the cliff without further incident. I could have told the air to carry me gently down, perhaps, but I wasn't quite brave enough.

The ground here is white sand, fine as powder. I kick off my shoes and walk barefoot down to the dock and the waiting boat.

There are no oars, but that doesn't matter. I step into the little vessel, settling myself on the plank seat, and tell it to bear me to the Bronze Lord's island.

It does, cutting smoothly through the restless waves.

The storm hits then, lashing rain and glittering lightning, so close it dazzles the sea.

The island is not as far away as I thought. It looms steadily larger: a grassy shore, a stone path winding up to a stone house. Despite the rain, smoke rises from a rather ordinary-looking chimney.

The boat bumps against the island. There is no dock here, but with a thought I make one and command the boat to tie itself securely.

I climb onto the shore. The grass is cool and wet beneath my feet, the rain warm on my face.

I stride up to the house, the front stoop sheltered from the rain by an overhanging eave. There is a bronze knocker on the door. I rap it several times, then pause as I realize my foolishness: The Bronze Lord cannot hear me.

And yet the door swings suddenly open.

I step in.

The room is dim—I don't know why I expected it to be otherwise. The only light slips through a single grimy window, gray and pale.

The ceiling is crossed with dark beams. There is an empty hearth at the back of the room, a worn wooden table under the window, a frayed rug spread over the earthen floor.

He sits in a chair by the empty hearth, his lank white hair obscuring his missing ears, his handless arms in his lap, the stumps of his legs hidden beneath a moth-eaten blanket. But it's his face that wrecks me: his unseeing eyes, the scarred remains of his nose, the lines of grief and pain pressed deep into his brow.

I go and kneel before him. *My Lord,* I say into his mind, *I need your help.*

Daughter, he says, and his voice is like a sigh, *there is no help I could give to you. Yet it would gladden my heart to speak with you awhile. Sit. Eat.*

I find myself drawn upright and, glancing back, see a second chair and a little table beside it, laden with food and a pot of steaming tea.

I sit, facing the faceless lord. I pour myself some tea and raise a cup to my lips, sipping slowly. The warmth of it seeps into me.

Food as well, says the Bronze Lord. *It has been many days since you have eaten.*

I don't like the sound of "many days," but I realize I am indeed starving and set to work obeying my lord's command. I am not certain what the fare is—nothing I have ever eaten before, in either flavor or texture. But it is real enough to fill my belly, and I finish it gratefully.

Thank you, My Lord, I tell him when I'm done.

Now speak to me, he says. *Speak to me of the outside world. Tell me what is done there.*

Terrible things, My Lord. Your fellow First Ones are bound, and the queen means to take all their power for herself. She will remake the world to suit only her and kill all that stand in her way.

He sighs very heavily. *That is naught to do with me, daughter.*

You can help me unbind the First Ones, you can help me stop her.

To my surprise, the Bronze Lord stands from his chair. I glimpse shadowy feet beneath the stumps of his legs, the power of his magic enough to bear him.

He walks to a door at the back of the cottage and opens it with a shadowy hand, also born of his power.

He steps through and I follow, standing beside him as he stops at the opposite shore from the one I landed on. He lifts his face into the rain, shuts his sightless eyes, lets the rain wash over him.

My daughter. His voice is softer now. *You should not have come to me.*

You are the last of them, I return, *the last of the First Ones who have not yet been bound. You are strong, My Lord. Stronger, perhaps, than all the others save the Prism Lady alone. You have borne your punishment long enough. It is time now to reach for your redemption. Why else, do you think, did the Prism Lady leave you your mind? Your power?*

It is only my physical form that has been mutilated, says the Bronze Lord, *but what good is a mind alone? No good at all.*

That isn't true, I say. *You yet live, My Lord. You can do good, you can choose right, you can choose restoration.*

He turns his face to mine, and for a moment I see the memory of his eyes as they once were; almost, they meet mine. *I yet live,* he says bitterly. *If this queen of yours means to hasten the world's ending, I welcome it. Then I will have relief. Then I will have rest.*

He takes a step into the sea, lets the waves lap at his ankles.

My Lord, I say, *you cannot abandon the world.*

It abandoned me.

He wades farther into the water, and I go with him, the icy coldness of the sea mingling strangely with the warmth of the rain.

I am going back, I tell him, *with or without you. But I cannot defeat the queen on my own. I cannot save the ones I love on my own. My magic isn't strong enough.*

Love, he says, *love is empty, love is cruel. Love is meaningless.*

You're wrong, My Lord. That isn't love.

Farther out he goes, until the waves are up to his chest and up to my neck, lapping just under my chin.

What is love, then? he asks me.

I think of Ballast. I think of my parents, my brother and my sister. I think of Saga and Indridi. *Love is not keeping secrets,* I tell him. *Love is not manipulating the other person for your own gain. Love is sacrifice, freely offered.* I'm gripped with a sudden, wrenching longing. *Love is light in the darkness, when all hope is gone.*

Pretty words, daughter. But poetry cannot help me.

He moves farther into the sea, and I put a hand on his arm to stop him.

My Lord, if I go deeper, I will be drowned.

He sighs, the waves beating round him. *Then go back. I have nothing to offer you.*

I will show you, I say stubbornly, *that love is more than poetry.*

And I put my hands on the temples of the Bronze Lord and pour my memories into him:

Working with Lilja to rebuild the machine I caused her to break.

Manipulating my father into letting me go to Daeros.

Watching Lilja plummet to her death while Kallias smiled. Nearly bringing the mountain down around us.

Training to be an acrobat in the arena my mother pulled up from the ground. Pushing myself to be stronger, better, faster, fiercer. Breaking every bone in my body. Allowing my father to lock my magic away.

Traveling to Skaanda. Giving myself up to the Skaandan woman my parents hired to sell me to Kallias.

The cage in the great hall. Performing for Kallias, my knees shaking, my body slick with sweat.

My terror of falling.

Ballast, tormented and controlled by his father, yet keeping food for me in his room, playing cards with me, bringing me books. Ballast, my one and only friend.

Outside of my mind I feel the water cover my nose and my eyes and my ears, lap over the crown of my head.

I send the memories faster and faster: Hilf's death. My and Saga's escape. Ballast rescuing us in the tunnels. Our journey back to Skaanda. Leaving Ballast behind. Finding him again in Kallias's court after his father put out his eye. My betrayal. The battle for Tenebris. Binding the Yellow Lord into the sun. Marrying Ballast. Promising to get him an army. Valrún's cruelty.

I show the Bronze Lord all my longing and love: for my husband and my friends. For Daeros and Skaanda and Iljaria, too.

The world and the people in it are broken.

But they're worth saving.

That's what love means.

My hands fall away from the Bronze Lord's temples.

I can no longer touch the ocean floor, and it is too dark for me to see. Water floods my nose, fills my lungs. I choke.

The Bronze Lord bears me out of the sea.

I gasp for breath as he carries me through the waves and back to the shore, where he sets me on my feet again.

Humbled, I follow him into the little house and sink into the chair opposite his.

With a thought I light a fire in the hearth. Warmth and light fill the room. "Thank you, My Lord," I whisper.

The Bronze Lord gives no answer. He sits with his head bowed, unmoving as a stone.

The fire pops and cracks. Slowly, the chill seeps out of my skin.

I will help you, says the Bronze Lord after a long silence.

I look at him, hope beating sharp at my breastbone.

I will help you, he repeats.

He turns his face toward me, and his power transforms him to what he must have been before he was maimed: eyes, swift and dark, a strong straight nose, white hair cropped neatly behind perfectly formed ears, with the dusting of white stubble on his chin. He wears a bronze gem on his forehead, and there are rings on every one of his fingers, with tattoos in metallic designs tracing the lengths of his arms.

He rises from his chair and comes to bend over me. There is a scent about him like cinnamon and wild things, a lashing wind and devouring fire.

"Your magic isn't strong enough," he says, his restored voice strong and sweet as honeyed wine. "That is what you said to me, is it not?"

I nod, cold fear cutting through me. "That's why I need you, My Lord."

He shakes his head, a smile touching his lips. "You don't need me. You need my power. And so I will give it to you. Freely."

"My Lord, wait—"

But he presses his magically restored hands against my temples, just as my father did, so long ago.

And he pours his power into me.

ONE HOUR AGO

SAGA

Year 4201, Month of the Black God

Iljaria—the walls of Regla City

"Saga. What's that?"

Leifur's voice cuts through the awful fog of my headache, and I force my eyes open.

It was considerate of the queen, I suppose, to chain us to the wall right next to each other. I could stretch my foot out and touch his leg, if I wanted, though after nearly a day of being hung by our wrists, metal cuffs digging into our skin and arms being wrenched from their sockets, the effort is too much. For hours I scrabbled to find purchase with my feet in an attempt to ease the burden on my arms, but the walls are made of magic and glass—there are no cracks, no chinks.

"What's what?" I ask, forcing words past my impossibly dry throat. What a long and dull and degrading way to die.

"That," says Leifur, and jerks his chin northward.

I am gutted that he's here with me. I would step easier into paradise if I knew he was safe and alive and well, not chained to the wall beside me, punished for my sins.

I squint through the blinding glare of the afternoon sun, wishing there were enough moisture left in me to sweat and provide some kind of relief.

"I don't see anything," I say dully.

"Look," he insists. *"There."*

Then I see the line of dust to the north, the shimmer of light. I blink and it is a little closer.

We watch in silence for a few minutes, and as the dust and the light draw ever nearer, there can be no mistaking it.

"The Aeronan army," I whisper. They're marching *here*. To Regla City.

Leifur turns his head toward me, and I force myself to look at him, at the messy cut on his temple from when the queen seized us and he fought like a lion to save me.

"Saga," he says, "do you think you have another song in you?"

My chest hurts, and my eyes are itchy and hot, unable to produce tears.

I don't understand what happened in that strange chamber below the palace, when I knelt beneath the White Goddess's prison and sang with everything I was. Her glass sphere cracked, and for a moment she was free. She told me there was magic in my heart; she told me I was not powerless.

But even if that's true, I don't know how to reach for that power when the White Goddess is not before me.

"I've been trying, Leifur," I say through my dry and aching throat. "This whole time, I've been trying to sing."

Somewhere behind us there is an eerie rumbling. Clouds knit swift and sudden over the sun, where a moment before there wasn't even a thread of cloud. Wind whips cold; the air smells of rain. I shiver violently in the absence of the sun's heat, my body unable to regulate the abrupt change in temperature.

The Aeronan army comes nearer and nearer, inescapable as the Saadone River flooding in the aftermath of our violent summer storms, when the rain has gorged its banks and there is nowhere for the water to go.

They are marching to Regla City, bearing their Skaandan Fire, and here we are, chained to the wall. It will not be long before they reach us and launch their initial assault. *That* is how we will die.

It begins to rain, lashing against my exposed body, and I don't understand how I can be so very cold, when a few moments ago it felt as if I was burning alive. I can't stop shaking.

"Saga," says Leifur, a tenderness in his voice that utterly wrecks me.

He reaches out with one foot, hooking it around my leg, tugging me nearer to him. He can't hold me, and I can't caress him, the metal cuffs on our wrists cutting in deep enough that blood trickles down our arms.

He twists his head, straining toward me, and I stretch out to meet him.

He kisses me in the rain, his lips cold and yet somehow filled with fire.

"Let me sing with you," he whispers. "Let's sing together. A song to welcome the army."

"All right," I say.

His foot slips from my ankle, and I swing back to my original position, dangled from my wrists by the damn chain, feeling once again the full weight of my body.

Leifur opens his mouth and sings into the night, a child's lullaby that I haven't heard in years, meant to provide comfort in the long months of Gods' Fall. His voice is ragged, unrefined, untrained, but it gives me courage.

It is better this way, to stare into the face of your oncoming death with a song on your lips.

I open my mouth, and I sing with him:

"Don't fear the dark,
It'll be undone,
The light will come,
The light will come.

Don't fear the dark,
It cannot harm,
You're safe and warm,
You're safe and warm.

Don't fear the dark,
Just lift your eyes,
The sun will rise,
The sun will rise
again.

And the gods will keep you
until then,
Until then."

CHAPTER THIRTY-SEVEN

BRYNJA

Year 4201, Month of the Black Lord

Iljaria—the hilltop outside Regla City

The Bronze Lord pours his magic into me.

I feel it burning in my mind, blazing in my heart, seeping into every one of my cells. It is too much for me, and yet it does not consume me.

And then he is finished, and I blink at him out of new eyes.

He staggers back into his chair, once more wearing his ruined form: sightless eyes and hewn-off nose, stumps of ears and hands and feet.

I stand before him, teeming with his magic, and there are more colors in the world, I think, than there ever were before.

Go, comes his voice, faint and tremulous in my mind. *I have given you all that I can. Freely.*

My Lord, I say, *I cannot bear your power. Take it back and come with me.*

I do not want it back. It is a relief to be rid of it. I am free now, daughter. Free to find peace. Free to rest.

No, no, I say, nearly frantic. *You must take it back. I did not come here to rob you of your power!*

You did not rob me, says the shell of the Bronze Lord. *I gave it to you freely. This is my sacrifice. My act of love. Go now, or it will be for nothing.*

But My Lord—

Go. Time runs short. There is a change in the wind, in the world. It is already happening, a shift in power. Souls cry out—can you hear them? The Gray Lady will have much work, tonight, or she would if she, too, had not fallen.

Fallen? I say, alarmed. *What do you mean?*

Go, daughter. If you wish to save the ones you love, you must go now. Farewell.

My Lord. Wait. Please.

But he's gone, nothing left except his empty chair.

The island shakes. The stones of the cottage crack and fall.

I run from the house before it collapses on me. I run down to the shore.

The sea bubbles and boils. It pulls the boat down to the depths.

But there is much power in me; I do not need the boat.

I walk across the roiling sea.

I step into the cliff as easy as breathing.

And with a wrench of power, I pull apart the walls of the realm where the Bronze Lord once dwelt, and step back into the one I know.

The world is dark and hungry.

There is no light, no breath, no warmth.

There is only a whorling, devouring emptiness.

Inside me Bronze magic burns. I can no longer quite remember who I am, what I am, why I have left the safety and solitude of the Bronze Lord's realm.

A metal band weighs heavy on my finger. I begin to pull it off, meaning to drop it into the nothingness and continue on my way. But this thought distresses me so much I slide the ring back on, and the panic in my heart subsides. A memory pulses through me: a man with black-and-white hair, cradling my face in his hands, pressing his lips against mine.

Through the dark, a ways ahead of me, there is a hill that blazes with power like a torch. Even from a distance I can feel the awful strength of it. It is more, far more than even the magic I hold inside me. I am drawn toward it.

I think it is why I've come.

I glide through the darkness. I reach the base of the hill. I climb.

There is a star on the hill. No, not a star. A First One. The Yellow Lord.

I watch as from a dull, numb distance while a human with a bright gem on his forehead seizes the Yellow Lord, drains all his power from him.

A crowd of men and women press in behind him, straining to be given a taste of that power.

But the man who drained the Yellow Lord claps his hands, and a flash of light magic reduces them all to ashes.

I near the summit of the hill, awash with dread and horror, though I do not understand why.

I am made of magic.

There is nothing else.

But then I see him, a man with black-and-white hair and a single blue eye, clothed in feathers, fixed in the spoke of a broad stone wheel, a crumpled body at his feet.

I remember everything.

Ballast.

His name forms on my lips. Magic and longing and fury blaze inside me.

I move toward him.

Yet somehow I am sluggish, my limbs weighed down as if in a dream.

The man who drained the Yellow Lord—Jóvin—lifts his hands, a devilish grin on his lips.

I am dimly aware of the queen's Skapari, including my mother, fixed like Ballast around the circumference of a great circular paving stone. Valrún and Brandr stand at a plinth in the center, Valrún holding the Prism Stone high. It writhes and flashes in the whorling dark and Valrún says something to Jóvin, but I do not listen to what it is.

I have eyes only for Ballast.

It is a heartbeat, half a breath, half a thought.

That is all the time it takes for Jóvin to form nine blades out of glittering light, each appearing beside one of the queen's Skapari.

He jerks his hand sideways and the light blades echo his movements, slashing across the Skapari's throats. They gasp and slump and fall.

A feral cry rips out of me, and I am at Ballast's side in another heartbeat, catching him before he hits the stone.

But it is already too late.

His eye stares into emptiness; his blood pours red down the front of his feathered robe.

He is gone, gone, gone.

And though I am overflowing with the power of a god, it is not enough.

I cannot save him.

NOW

VALRÚN

Year 4201, Month of the Black Lord

Iljaria—the Sögu Byrjun

My Skapari fall beside their patron First Ones, whose power they stole at my command. The knives of light that slew them dissolve into yellow sparks and flit away like fireflies.

Jóvin turns to me with satisfaction and lust in his eyes, while beside me Brandr tightens his hand around my waist.

Fools, both of them.

"My queen," says Jóvin, stepping toward me. "My beloved."

There isn't time for this, and I give Brandr an almost imperceptible nod.

Jóvin doesn't see the knife until Brandr has shoved it into his heart, all the way up to the hilt. The Yellow Skapari gasps and sputters and slumps dead like the rest of them in a rush of red blood.

Now it is Brandr who turns to me, smiling, the only other soul left alive on the Sögu Byrjun.

No, that is not quite true.

Someone cradles one of the dead Skapari in the stone circle, a powerful being of glistering Bronze.

I frown. I had not reckoned on the Bronze Lord's presence. After Brynja vanished, Brandr assured me my plan would work with just eleven Skapari. We did not need all twelve, he said. We did not need the Bronze Lord.

Now he is here, but he is too late. I cannot use him—but neither can he stop me.

I turn my glance back to Brandr, who commands the full weight of the Ghost Lord's absorbing magic. He shuts his eyes and spreads out his hands. The darkness does not touch him, and his face seems to shine.

He really is beautiful.

I will almost regret him.

But for now I stand quiet and watch him use his power.

As my Skapari's souls flee the world, their magic—and the magic of the First Ones that they stole—lingers briefly about their corpses unfettered, unbound. Brandr, wielding the Ghost Lord's power, drinks all this magic in.

He drinks and drinks. He gorges himself on magic that is not his own, and still there is more and yet more. I shift the Prism Stone to my left hand, loosing the knife I have hidden in my right sleeve.

Brandr soaks in the last stray drops of magic. He lowers his hands, opens his eyes. Power clothes him, and the pit of my belly shivers with want.

"My queen," he says. His voice is thunder and snow, lilies and ashes. "I have done all you asked. Let me now give to you the power of the Ghost Lord, that you may drink all the magic from me that you wish, and become Queen Eternal at my side."

These last words rankle me, but I beam at him and hold out my hand.

He clasps it in his and pours Ghost magic into my veins. It is strange and cold, and yet it burns, like poison.

He pulls me toward him when it is done, desire in his dark eyes.

"Queen Eternal," he says, tracing his fingers along the line of my hip, "and I am your king."

He kisses me, mouth rough and hot and eager.

I stab him through the heart.

He gasps against my lips. He stumbles.

There is confusion in his glance as he slides to the ground, blood leaking out of him.

I step over his body, grip the Prism Stone with both my hands again.

With the combined power of the stone and the Ghost magic Brandr gave to me, I take all the magic he absorbed and draw it into myself.

It happens more swiftly than it did for him, because I bear the Prism Stone, as he did not. Power pours into me, fills every part of me, and I am strong, strong, for the first time in my life.

My gaze is drawn down the hill to Regla City, and in the swirl of living darkness that blankets the world, I see that it is burning.

My city is burning, Aeronan soldiers swarming it like ants.

Fury fills me. Magic strains against my skin, begging to be wielded against them.

I set the Prism Stone down on the plinth. I do not need it anymore.

I am remade.

And now I will remake the world.

My city is burning.

Its walls crack and shatter. The Aeronan army flows through like the tide, wielding canisters filled with iron shards. They roar as they come. They laugh.

Fire bursts in the dark, iron sprays like deadly rain, striking the Iljaria host, who stand their ground in the midst of the city. The Iljaria who are not torn apart by the explosions are hewn down by Aeronan swords, the iron shards having robbed them of their magic, making them as powerless as ordinary mortals.

The earth runs red with the blood of my people. Corpses litter the roads of my city, trod upon by foreign boots as if they are nothing more than rubbish on a scrap heap.

And the Aeronan army marches on, gleeful, exultant, swinging swords like scythes.

They launch their vile canisters at my palace, at my great glass spire. I watch it fracture, cracks splintering out. I watch it fall.

I am wrath. I am fury.

I am power omnipotent.

I am Queen Eternal.

And I will not stand for this.

I feel the branches of my power stretching out like I am a tree. There is Green magic, but I do not want life, just now. I want death and destruction. I want revenge. I want justice meted out by my hand. I want these Aeronan *insects* to pay for what they have done.

I see with the eyes of the Prism Lady, because I *am* the Prism Lady. I can feel every heart, every breath, every soul.

They are mine.

I tug on the Violet branch of my power—time magic. I halt the Aeronans where they stand, holding them still in a single frozen moment.

I hover near them, peering into faces, reading fear in bitter eyes.

It pleases me. I want more.

I wield the Black branch of my power—the magic of darkness. I form shadow creatures with too many eyes and too many teeth and too many claws. I hurl them at the Aeronan army. Their fear grows visceral, acrid as piss, but they do not scream because they cannot; they are yet frozen in time.

I wield Red and Brown and Blue—the magics of fire and earth and beasts. I burn the barbarian army. I bury them. I command wild animals to fall on them with teeth and claws.

And then I do wield Green—growing magic. I strangle the soldiers with vines, I pierce them through with thorns.

I release them, after a while, from the time magic. I let that power slide through my fingers.

I want to hear them scream.

I wield White next: song magic. I torment the Aeronan bastards with melodies that make them want to stop their ears or cut them off. Some of them do.

I wield Yellow—light magic. I shove stars into their eyes, blinding them.

They weep and curse and scream.

They beg for me to stop.

They beg for me to kill them.

But my fury is not yet sated.

Away behind me I am suddenly aware of a powerful presence in the dark. With the Prism Lady's eyes, I see that it is the Bronze Lord.

No.

A Bronze Lady.

Curious.

But she can't stop me.

I refocus my gaze on the miserable Aeronans, less than ten thousand of them now, as some have perished already from fear or pain.

I realize they are not worth all the magic I have spent on them. I have far better things to do as Queen Eternal.

I seize hold of the Gray branch of my power—death magic.

I kill them, every last one. I stop their hearts or choke off their lungs or make their brains swell to bursting in their heads.

They die, falling all into a vast, stinking pile.

There is silence now.

Silence and darkness.

And behind me, the Bronze Lady.

I turn to face her.

THIRTY MINUTES AGO

SAGA

Year 4201, Month of the Black God

Iljaria—Regla City

We are still singing when the rain stops.

When the sun falls.

When the darkness folds over the world.

When the Aeronan army reaches the city and launches the first volley of Skaandan Fire at the walls.

"Don't fear the dark, just lift your eyes

The sun will rise, the sun will rise again

The gods will keep you until then, until then."

There is power in the song. There is power in *me*. I can feel it swelling in my heart, blazing through my veins.

And I decide I will not die here today. Not like this.

"Don't fear the dark, it'll be undone."

The manacles on my wrists break open. I make sure Leifur's open, too.

"The light will come, the light will come."

I grab his hand, and we slide straight down the wall, just under the arc of Skaandan Fire.

"Don't fear the dark, it cannot harm."

There's a sear of red light as the canisters of Skaandan Fire explode against the wall. Glass shatters all around us, and Leifur and I hit the ground with a wrenching *thud.*

"You're safe and warm, you're safe and warm."

We're running away from the city, away from the fracturing wall and the oncoming army.

We're running into the darkness.

"Don't fear the dark, just lift your eyes

The sun will rise, the sun will rise again

The gods will keep you until then, until then."

We stand together on the plain outside the city, hand in hand, the coldness of the wind no longer touching me.

I let the song die on my lips, and I look up into Leifur's face. I can scarcely see him but for the distant glow of the Skaandan Fire.

The Aeronans pour into Regla City, and there are so, so *many* of them.

"Saga," says Leifur, tremulous and soft, "you are a marvel."

I lean my head against his shoulder. "It was a gift from the White Goddess, nothing more."

"I think you're wrong," he says into my hair. "I think it has been inside of you always. How many times have your songs saved you?"

I think back to singing for Kallias on the battlefield so he would spare my life; I think of singing in the dark of the caves, in the rain on the journey back to Tenebris. "Perhaps you're right," I say, wonderingly.

"Of course I am."

"Don't get used to it."

He laughs.

For a moment we stand quietly together, awed that we are still here, that the gods saw fit to keep us safe.

But what am I supposed to do now?

I can't save the city.

We watch it fall, hear the thunder of the Skaandan Fire, the screams of dying Iljaria, the Aeronans' harsh shouts of triumph.

My brother is out there somewhere, participating in this bloodbath. This is what his ambitions have wrought.

I am sick down to my core.

Gently, Leifur turns me away from the city so I do not have to view the unfolding destruction any longer.

We look up at a high hill that pulses with strange magic. It has stopped raining, and the darkness has grown malicious, grasping at us with cruel fingers.

Fear twists into me. "Leifur," I say, "what has happened to the sun?"

"I think she did it," he returns quietly, "the Iljaria queen. I think she brought back Gods' Fall. Only—"

"Only it's wrong now," I say. "In a way that it wasn't before."

The darkness slips over our feet and winds up our legs, coiling higher and higher. It means to drag us down, I think. It means to devour us.

So I pick up the threads of our song. I don't know how else to save him.

"Don't fear the dark, it'll be undone, the light will come, the light will come!"

The darkness recedes, slips away from us. Leifur's hand is cold over mine. I can feel the pulses of his heart, sharp and terrified.

And then—

Then a—I am uncertain what to call it. A being of all-consuming power cascades down the hill, singeing us as it passes.

It blazes toward the city, magic and fury, and something in me understands that it is Valrún as she wished to be: Queen Eternal.

And then it is no longer the Iljaria I am afraid for, in the ruins of the burning city, but the Aeronans.

There is a period of . . . strangeness . . . after that. Leifur and I stand together in the writhing dark. It feels as if time freezes, or like the world itself no longer exists in the proper sense of the word. I can see very little, just sparks of color before my eyes, and the only thing that tethers me to the earth, I think, is Leifur, his hand in mine, his quick-beating heart.

Then—

Motion. Flames, reaching up to the sky. The sound of screaming that turns suddenly to a profound and utter silence.

"She's killed them," I whisper. "She's killed them all."

"She'll break the world," he says, voice trembling.

I hold tighter to him. "I think she already has."

A sudden pulse of power causes me to turn my head. I see a woman striding down the hill, a woman clothed in—no, *made* from—Bronze magic.

She shines, she *glows*. Her eyes are flashing stars that could peer into eternity and not be undone. And yet her gown is heavy with blood, and there are tears on her glistering cheeks.

I let go of Leifur's hand, and I step up to her. Because I am not afraid. I know her. Or I did, once.

"Brynja," I whisper, not quite daring to touch her. "Brynja, what has happened?"

"He's gone," she says in a voice that rattles like metal in wind. "They killed him. They killed my Ballast, and I couldn't stop them."

Her grief lodges in my throat, nearly chokes the breath from me.

"You can stop Valrún now," I tell her softly. "You can keep her from causing any further destruction. She's slaughtered the Aeronan army, and I don't think that will satisfy her."

Brynja trembles like a leaf in a storm, like she herself is not made all of lightning.

"What am I, Saga?"

The tears that pour down her cheeks turn to curls of shining bronze.

"You are Brynja Eldingar," I say, and find the courage to put my hands on her shoulders. I am not burned. "You are strength and conviction. You are loyalty. You are kindness. You are, it seems, the gods-blessed Bronze

Lady. And you are my friend. Now go and keep the Queen Eternal from ripping the world apart."

Brynja blinks at me, dips her chin.

"I am sorry about Ballast," I say.

"She killed him," Brynja intones. "Valrún killed him."

"Don't let his death be meaningless."

She takes a shaky, human-seeming breath. "I have to stop her."

"Yes."

Brynja turns to where the city used to stand. It is a torrent of darkness now, with Valrún blazing at its heart.

"How do I do it?" she asks. "How do I pull apart the dark?"

I give her a grim, sure smile, reaching my left hand behind me and feeling Leifur fold his own over top of it.

"I'll help you," I tell her.

And once more I open my mouth and begin to sing.

"Don't fear the dark, it'll be undone, the light will come, the light will come."

CHAPTER THIRTY-EIGHT

BRYNJA

Year 4201, Month of the Black Lord

Iljaria—the ruins of Regla City

Song magic unfolds in the air, cutting a path through the darkness, toward the city, toward Valrún. I regard my friend with awe as she keeps singing, magic spilling from her lips.

"Saga," I say. "How did this happen?"

"Go, my lady," says Leifur beside her. "While you still can."

"Thank you," I tell my friend.

Then I turn.

I go.

Darkness coils around my ankles, but Saga's song magic and my own Bronze are enough to allow me to shake it off, to stride unhindered toward the remains of Regla City.

As I draw nearer, I see Valrún suspended in the air, protected by a sphere of roiling dark, her stolen magic flashing around her like multicolored stars.

I have to push through somehow. I have to reach her.

I think back to when I was a child, when my sister fell to her death and I nearly brought the mountain tumbling down in my anger.

Now my mother and brother are dead.

Now Ballast is dead.

And I have the whole of the Bronze Lord's magic boiling in my mind.

This is nothing to a mountain.

So I tell the darkness to part for me, and it does, the sphere cracking as an egg cracks, falling in pieces to the ground.

She turns to face me. She is hard to look at, colors writhing and whirling under her skin. Every kind of magic save Bronze branches out from her like she is the trunk of a tree: Green from her fingertips, Blue from her shoulders, Red from her toes and Brown from her heels. Prism whirls around her head, and White spiderwebs out from her mouth. Her eyes are flashing Yellow stars. Violet stretches out from one side of her heart and Gray from the other. Darkness pulls from her belly, and in the very center of her chest is a swirl of what I think must be Ghost magic.

She smiles, and the world trembles beneath my feet.

"Brynja." She tilts her head to one side. "Have you come to give me the only piece of power I do not yet possess?" Her voice is brittle and bright, a storm and a whisper. "How courteous of you."

"No," I say. "I have come to take back your stolen power and make you pay for murdering my husband."

"Husband," she muses. "Oh, it isn't worth it to have a husband. Lovers are all right, now and then. But a husband? Binding your heart to another? Only the most asinine of fools would so degrade herself."

She turns away from me, like I am no longer worthy of her notice.

"Valrún."

She lifts her hands and begins to pull on the strands of magic. Darkness rushes up around her, locking both of us in the sphere.

She wields Brown magic, drawing stones up out of the earth, erecting a crude room, with an empty wall that looks out onto the universe.

She wields Violet magic, opening windows to various points in time.

I see what must be Valrún's childhood pass swiftly before my eyes: Valrún and Ísold chasing each other through the gardens of the house by the sea where they grew up.

Valrún and Ísold playing Lords and Ladies in an upstairs chamber while rain rattles on the roof.

Valrún's anger at her weak Green magic, her jealousy at Ísold's impossibly strong White magic.

They are teenagers when Valrún attends Ísold's First Heir's Banquet in the palace. She is overlooked, overshadowed, while their parents praise Ísold to the Skapari and all the assembled guests.

Valrún convincing Ísold to sneak off with her to Daeros, slipping easily through the Galdur Skjöld, merry and laughing in the Daerosian hills.

I watch Valrún betray Ísold to Kallias, watch her flee home to Iljaria, not even once looking back.

The memories come faster now: Valrún sobbing to her parents about Ísold being lost, her manipulation of the then-Violet Skapari, who began to subtly erase Ísold's memory from time.

Valrún's frustration at not quite being able to wipe Ísold's existence from her parents' minds. Her discovery of Gray Skapari Osa's secret: the unsanctioned murder, via death magic, of the man who assaulted her sister. Blackmailing Osa into murdering her parents. Ascending the throne of Iljaria at the age of twenty.

A reign marked with blackmail and manipulation and her desperate thirst for power. A dalliance with Jóvin that resulted in a pregnancy. The birth of a child who possessed no magic, her order to Osa to kill him, and to the Violet Skapari to erase him, too, from the memories of the people. Having Osa execute the Violet Skapari, because Valrún could no longer trust him.

Stumbling upon old books in the library, the beginnings of a plan that would garner her, at long last, true power. Approving the plot to send Brynja to Tenebris to keep watch over the Yellow Lord.

Commanding Brandr to fetch the Yellow Lord and bring him back to her.

Her anger at Brandr's failure, his assurance that they could still make her scheme work.

My gut wrenches at this look into Valrún's story, because it so mirrors my own. I grew up in a house by the sea. My twin brother resented my power, while my parents feared it. What would I have become if I'd never gone to Daeros? Would I be in opposition to Valrún, here in the ruins of Regla City, or would I stand as Queen Eternal in her place? Was it only my experiences that shaped me into what I am, or would I have reached my same convictions in a different way?

My heart pumps Bronze magic through my veins, and I realize that it doesn't matter. What might have been is meaningless. There is only who I am now, and what is before me.

Ballast lies dead on the Sögu Byrjun.

I am going to avenge him and stop his murderer from ripping the world apart.

Valrún's memories are distracting her. I slip into her mind with my magic, grab hold of the Violet thread of her power, and tear it out.

She gasps and turns on me, but it is too late. I reach through the Black darkness of her storm, across the hungry void to the Sögu Byrjun, the ancient hill where the shell of the Violet Lord lies slumped upon the stone. I pour his magic back into him, every last bit.

Valrún shrieks, lashing out at me with a Green magic vine studded with poison thorns. They slice into me, and Bronze blood drips from my wounds. But I just laugh, because I am still in her mind. I yank the Green magic out of her, too, and send it into the body of the Green Lady away on the hill. I think I feel her stir, or I hope I do.

Valrún shoves me out of her mind before I can pull free any more of her stolen power. She clothes herself in fire and death, she forms ravenous beasts out of the dark. She pulls the corpses of the Aeronans and the Iljaria upright, puts bone swords in their hands. She sends the beasts and the dead at me, clacking and snarling.

I grasp at the remaining sparks of consciousness in the minds of the dead. They are fleeting, faint, but they are there. As the dead descend upon me, trampling me like the Yellow wielders did, I trace the sparks of their minds back to Valrún. I grasp at the branch of her Gray magic, and I send it hurtling into the Gray Lady on the Sögu Byrjun.

The dead fall on and around me, and I push up through them, flinging them aside with my Bronze magic.

There are still the Black magic beasts, screeching and diving, lashing out at me with teeth and claws and venomous tails. I fight to hold their wills at bay even as their darkness slides into my mind and begins to erode my control. I cannot quite grasp the branch of their power, cannot fling their magic into the Black Lord.

Valrún laughs, and suddenly there are real beasts among the ones made of darkness. I do not like reaching into the minds of animals. I do not understand them, as Ballast did. But I seize hold of them now, letting go of the darkness to trace the thread of Blue magic back to Valrún's mind, to yank it out of her and send it into the Blue Lady.

The real animals fly or run away then, and I am left battling the ones made of darkness that ooze in and out of my consciousness like oil.

I reach for Valrún's Prism magic, and to my surprise I cannot find it; it is already gone. I stretch my thoughts toward the Sögu Byrjun, and for a moment the Prism Lady's mind meets mine; I hear her thoughts: *You do well, Bronze Lady. Don't let go. Don't stop until she is defeated.*

My Lady! I think back at her. *Oh, My Lady, can you save him?*

But then a beast made of darkness slams into me, knocking me backward, pinning me down. Darkness floods my nose and my mouth, blinds my eyes. I choke on it, and somewhere outside of me, Valrún laughs.

"You think you are so clever! Yet you cannot take all my power from me. You cannot even fight against something as simple as darkness. Fool, you are!"

Tendrils of darkness bind my throat and my wrists and my ankles. I feel myself hoisted up into the air, where I dangle from nothing.

"You will pay for what you've done," comes Valrún's voice, distorted through the dark magic that stops up my ears. More Black magic drives like a knife into my heart, and pain splinters through me. But I am still able to reach into Valrún's mind, to pull the light magic out of her, to send it hurtling back into the Yellow Lord.

Valrún cries out at this last betrayal.

And then there is no more time for thought, for magic.

There is only pain.

NOW

Year 4201, Month of the Black Lord

Iljaria—the Sögu Byrjun

"Come," says the Green Lady to the Violet Lord, as, in the ruined city below the ancient hill named Sögu Byrjun, story's beginning, the Bronze Lady battles the Queen Eternal. "There is much to do."

The Violet Lord sits on the plinth in the middle of the stone circle, as he did long ago, when the world was made.

Some, but not all, of the other First Ones stand solemn and still around the Violet Lord. They are missing from their number the Black and Ghost and Red Lords, the Brown and White Ladies. These have not yet been restored, their shells lying still where they fell.

The Prism Lady takes the Prism Stone from the plinth and grinds it to powder beneath her heel. It will not be used against them a second time.

"I give you leave," she says to the Green Lady and the Violet Lord, "to restore the souls that were lost. Do it quickly, lest the world be unmade, and unless I do not see clearly, it is not yet time for that."

"You see clearly as always, Lady," says the Violet Lord. He hops off the plinth and goes to join the Green Lady.

It is strange, perhaps, to mingle the magics of growth and time, and yet neither one can happen without the other.

They bring back the lost of their number, first, the lords and ladies whose power is yet tangled in the mind of the human queen. These go to join the other First Ones in the center of the circle, watching in silence as the Green Lady and the Violet Lord perform their tasks.

The Green Lady kneels beside the body of a young woman clothed in leaves and flowers, with an emerald on her brow. The Violet Lord winds back the time she has lain there dead. The Green Lady calls her to life again.

Breath rushes into her lungs. The line of red at her throat vanishes.

She gasps and sits up, and the Green Lady draws her to her feet.

All down the line of dead Skapari the Green Lady and Violet Lord go, turning back time, restoring to life all those Valrún ordered cut down.

There is some discussion over the man who called himself the Prism Master, and of the Yellow wielder who murdered the Skapari on Valrún's command. But in the end they, too, are resurrected, along with the other wielders of Yellow magic who were burned to ashes.

The Yellow Lord looks with sorrow on the workers of light magic. He goes to kneel before the Prism Lady, bowing his head to the stone. "I did not choose this, My Lady," he says. "I was faithful to your order. I did not leave the great house you made for me of my own accord."

"I know you did not," says the Prism Lady and, reaching out her hands, lifts him to his feet again.

"I do not like this great darkness!" he says. He begins to weep.

"Nor do I," she returns with infinite gentleness. "I will bear you back to your house, if you will, but there is something I must first attend to."

The Prism Master is brought before her, the Gray Lady holding him by one arm, the Green Lady by the other. He twists in their grasp, his face a mess of snot and tears, blood still wet on his chest from where he was slain.

"Brandr Eldingar," says the Prism Lady, "you have been tried, and you have been found wanting. Ill you wielded the power given you at your birth, ill you wielded the power you stole. Ill you chose to aid the cruel desires of the queen who even now seeks to rend the world to pieces. Your life was restored to you in an act of great mercy. But no longer will you command any power. You are unworthy, and I strip it from you."

"My Lady!" cries Brandr, dropping to his knees. "Please don't take my magic from me. Please! I am nothing without it."

"Then you will be nothing," she answers calmly.

She touches a single finger to his brow, and he gasps as the power goes out of him, as the shell of the Ghost Lord steps up beside Brandr to gather it into himself.

"Please," begs Brandr, sobbing. "Please. I would rather be dead than live without magic. *Please.*"

But the Prism Lady has no further thought to spare for him. She takes the Yellow Lord by the hand and climbs with him up into the sky, where the hidden orb of the sun hangs still.

A moment passes and there is light again, blazing through the shroud of darkness, tearing it to shreds. The Yellow Lord has returned to his house; the sun is unveiled.

The only dark that now remains wheels around Valrún in her ruined city.

CHAPTER THIRTY-NINE

BALLAST

Year 4201, Month of the Black Lord

Iljaria—the Sögu Byrjun

I wake on the hill where I died.

My heart beats; breath fills my lungs. I open my eye to see the Green Lady and the Violet Lord looking down at me, and I understand that they are the ones who have brought me back to life. But before I can shape the words in my mouth to thank them, they have stepped past me, into the next spoke of the circle.

I lie dazed for some moments, peering up into the sky as the darkness is pulled apart and filled with a glorious light. My eye tears.

"Ballast," comes the whisper of my mother's voice.

I turn my head to see her lying beside me, her cheeks wet, blood bright on her collar, though the wound at her throat has been erased.

I lift trembling fingers to my own throat, reliving the searing pain of the light blade that slew me.

"Ballast," she says again.

I sit up enough that I crawl to her, pull her into my arms. We weep until our tears have run dry.

"Ballast," says another voice, one that holds sorrow, and great power.

I lift my head to see the Blue Lady, wind stirring through her gown.

My heart breaks. "My Lady—"

"Rise, Ballast Solstrøm."

I do as she commands, standing shakily to my feet. My mother gets up, too, clinging to my arm, her eyes flitting around the hilltop. She gasps and I follow her gaze to where the White Lady stands by the central plinth, her eyes vacant, her form frail as a leaf in winter. I realize there is no power in her; she is empty.

I turn my eye back to the Blue Lady, who stands patient and solemn before me.

"I killed you," I say. "I didn't mean to. I didn't *want* to."

"You did not orchestrate this piece of our story, Ballast Solstrøm. It was not time yet for my ending. Nor for yours." She brushes gentle fingers across my brow.

"How are you here?" I ask her quietly. "How are you restored when . . ." I flick my glance to the White and Brown Ladies, the Red and Black Lords, who stand staring into nothingness, unblinking, unmoving. "When they are not?"

"The battle for their power is still being fought," she tells me. Taking me by the arm, she draws me to the northern rim of the hill, and points to the place where, before I died, Regla City stood. There is nothing there now but a whorl of darkness, punctuated by flashes of—

Bronze.

I suck in a sharp breath. "Brynja."

The Blue Lady smiles. "She has saved me, as she has saved you. But the Bronze Lord's power grows heavy for her. Soon she will be lost to it. And Valrún is yet very strong. Go to her. Help her break the remainder of Valrún's power and heal the last First Ones. And then—"

"Then?" My heart wrenches.

"Then we will step from the shores of this world. We will have no more dealings with it. It is enough."

Grief clogs my throat.

She presses a kiss to my brow. "Go, son of mine," she says.

I glance to the snarl of magic where the city used to stand. The magic is a storm. Brynja is at the heart of it. "How? How do I reach her?"

"You know how," she says softly. "You have been made ready for this moment."

I am gripped with a sudden, wild fear. "The winged leviathan."

She dips her chin. "The winged leviathan. You have seen his form, beheld him in his majesty. You understand him enough to borrow his shape, for as long as you need it. Now go. Wield the power you were given. Free your wife from the Bronze Lord's last folly, before it is too late."

I bow to the Blue Lady, already feeling the magic buzz along my skin. Then I lift my head and stride down the hill, commanding my body to break, to shift, to change.

The form of the winged leviathan folds over me, the long sinuous body, the clawed feet, the sleek, many-toothed jaw, the gleaming horns, the wide, dark wings. I beat them and rise into the air.

I fly into the heart of the storm.

NOW

VALRÚN

Year 4201, Month of the Black Lord

Iljaria—the ruins of Regla City

I sit on a throne made of fire and song, reaching into the depths of the earth to shake it asunder, to rework it according to my will. I am angry that many of the branches of my power have been ripped away, but all will be well. I will get them back again. I will make her bring them back.

And then I will rip the heart out of her and laugh as she dies.

I keep the Bronze Lady bound in darkness, driving needles of Ghost magic into her while I try to pull her mind magic *out*.

But the Bronze Lady is strong. She fights back, sometimes grabbing hold of the darkness and unraveling it just a little; other times seizing my thoughts in a fool's attempt to thwart my purpose.

Yet she cannot get wholly free. I am stronger.

And the Bronze Lady is weakening.

I hiss in triumph as Bronze tears pour down her face. I bid the bonds of darkness squeeze yet tighter around her throat and wrists and ankles. Just a few moments more, and her magic will be mine. Then I will reclaim the magic that she stole from me and secure my reign as Queen Eternal.

Her chin sags to her chest. Drops of blood bead on her brow.

There comes an unearthly screech from outside my sanctuary of darkness and stone. I turn to see a great beast hurtling through. Foam drips from its ravening jaw, and the blue-black feathers on its massive wings gleam with knives' edges. Spikes as long as a man's arm protrude from its tail, and long, wicked horns curl back from its head. It opens its mouth and lets out another demon's call.

And then it slams into me, and I release the strands of darkness binding the Bronze Lady.

I lash out at the beast with fire and song and darkness. I draw stones up from the ground and hurl them at it. They shatter like ice against its thick hide, doing nothing at all to deter it.

Freed from her bonds, the Bronze Lady strides up to the beast, looks into its single, blazing eye, and puts one hand upon its great shoulder. And I understand that the beast is her lover in another form, the deposed king, the half-blooded disgrace. My own kin, called somehow to life anew.

That doesn't matter.

They cannot defeat me.

They are not stronger than the Queen Eternal.

I sing at the dark, I call it around me like a shield. I raise an army with my power, forming soldiers of earth and song, darkness and fire. They stand ready at my back, an innumerable host, the enactors of my victory. The crown of my eternal kingdom blazes upon my head, and I look at the Bronze Lady and the winged leviathan. I send my army to mow them down, to rip them into pieces, to restore the right order to the world: *my* order.

And I laugh and laugh and laugh.

CHAPTER FORTY

BRYNJA

Year 4201, Month of the Black Lord

Iljaria—the ruins of Regla City

I am thrown back to three years ago, battling cave demons in the dark.

Only now the demons are made of fire and earth and song as well as darkness, and I burn with all the magic of the Bronze Lord. And Saga is not here.

And Ballast is a winged leviathan.

His feathers are warm and sharp beneath my touch, his eye flashing with anger—and power. I have not gotten over the shock of seeing him, the swift rush of unlooked-for joy that he does not lie dead on the Sögu Byrjun, as I left him, that by some miracle of the First Ones, he has been restored to me.

But I do not like him in this form. I try to speak to him, to reach into his mind, but I read only darkness there, want and need and rage.

We fight Valrún's army together. He rips her magical soldiers apart with his jaws, bashes them to pieces with his tail, shreds them with his claws, skewers them with his horns. I wield a sword of Bronze magic, dancing and spinning as I cut through the teeming host, all the while reaching for the strands of magic connecting the soldiers to Valrún.

I catch hold of the White magic in her mind, and I pull it free, sending it swiftly into the White Lady, who waits on the Sögu Byrjun.

The song magic soldiers vaporize, and Valrún cries out in rage. She forms more soldiers of darkness, earth, and fire. She makes them stronger than before.

But Ballast rises into the air on his dark wings. He dives into the heart of them, crushes them to melodies and dust and ashes. Those few who escape his attack I hew with my Bronze sword, magic alight in my veins.

Still her soldiers come, and come. It doesn't matter how many we destroy, they spring up and spring up and spring up; all the air rings with the sound of fire and choking earth and Valrún's cruel laughter. Fire burns us. The ground splits open and pulls us down into its depths. Darkness burrows into my eyes and my nose and my throat, crawls into my mind, reaching, reaching for the magic that the Bronze Lord gave to me.

But the next moment I am wrapped round with a warm wing, borne upward again, out of the earth's suffocating grasp.

He sets me on my feet, and I stand against his massive shoulder, gasping for breath. I reach out to his thoughts, but he doesn't hear me, or doesn't know how to answer me in his beast form.

This isn't working. Valrún will send her soldiers at us until we are dragged down and no longer have the strength to fight. We must be united to defeat her. And that means I need to talk to him.

I call his name, and he bows his great head before me. I place my hands on either side of his ridged brow. I give no heed to the army of earth and fire and darkness that looms at my back.

I wrench both of us into his mind.

I am standing on a rock ledge jutting out over miles and miles of undulating green forest. The trees below teem with birdsong and the movement of a thousand unseen creatures.

Ballast stands beside me with his hands in his pockets, staring at the wood. Wind stirs through his hair, and I am startled to see that here, in his mind, he has both of his eyes.

I go to him, slip my hand into his. I think his mind is beautiful, and I tell him so.

A smile touches his lips, but he doesn't turn his head to look at me.

"I don't know how to save you," he says. "I don't know how to stop her."

"We're saving each other," I reply. "We'll stop her together."

"How?"

"If I can get into her mind, I can pull the rest of the magic out of her. Easy."

"That doesn't sound easy, Brynja."

"I got in here, didn't I? Don't you trust me at all, husband of mine?"

He does turn aside then, lifting his free hand to trace the curve of my cheek. "I've missed you, little schemer. And I let you in here, by the way."

I smile. "It hasn't been that long, has it?"

"Weeks," he chides me. "It's been weeks."

"Well. I'm here now." I brush my finger along the ridge of his eye that exists only in his mind. "I just need to get close enough to Valrún to touch her temples. Can you help me?"

"You'll be careful, won't you?"

"I'm always careful."

"Liar," he scolds.

He crushes me against him and kisses me, his magic, his longing, lighting a fire in my veins.

With an effort, I wrench the two of us out of his mind again, where his beast form folds over him and Valrún's army sears my shoulders.

I climb onto Ballast's back, and he flaps his wide wings, bearing me up, up, above Valrún's seething host.

She stands in the midst of them, hands raised, spinning out magic, more and more, like she doesn't ever mean to stop.

Ballast flies straight toward her, and when we are near enough, I leap from his back, slamming hard into Valrún, grabbing her head and pressing my fingers against her temples before she has a chance to react.

I pull her sideways into her mind.

We are in the wreck of a garden, flower beds choked with weeds, once-elegant stone columns and archways cracked and tumbled down, reduced to dust and rubble.

The sky overhead is a sickly green-gray, like a storm is coming that will break the world. Between the cracks in the cobbled footpaths poison red blooms grow, the originals of those Valrún sprouts with her paltry Green magic in the waking world.

"What are you doing?" Valrún spits at me, her eyes wild, her hands grasping. The branches of magic that are left to her are yet new to her; she does not know how to wield them in this place. And as I already pulled her Green magic out of her, she is essentially powerless here. "I am the Queen Eternal!" she cries. "I demand you take me back!"

"No," I tell her simply. "I will not take you back. Not until I have addressed a few things."

She curses and lunges at me, but I jerk out of her way. So she falls among the stones and poison flowers, scraping her arms.

"You cannot hurt me here," I say. "You can only hurt yourself."

Blood drips from her wounds. She swears at me, picks herself up. She does not try to attack me again.

I move through the ruined garden and up to the crumbled remains of an archway that looks out into a whorling void. I can't help but compare this place to Ballast's mind: his full of life and hope, despite everything he's suffered; hers decay and despair, despite everything she's been given.

Valrún follows me.

I can sense the cords of magic in her: Black and Red, Ghost and Brown. But I don't pull at them. Not yet.

"I mistook you for a being of power," she says, "someone like me, a worthy opponent. But I see you now for what you truly are."

"What am I, Valrún?"

She steps up beside me, but I don't look at her, my eyes fixed out into the void.

"A thief," she says. "You stole the Bronze Lord's power. You dared to make yourself the Bronze Lady. Dared to imagine you could stand against the Queen Eternal."

I allow myself a smile. "If I am a thief, what exactly does that make you, Your Majesty?"

She scoffs at me. "You have the power of one god; I have the power of eleven."

"Four," I remind her. "You have the power of *four*."

"Even so," she seethes, "how do you expect to defeat me?"

"I have already defeated you. I am not the one trapped in my own mind."

She snarls like a wolf and, leaping at me, pushes both of us through the ruined archway and into the emptiness beyond.

We fall, the void dragging at us with clawed fingers, pulling us down, down.

She screams as we fall, a high, keening terror, but I do not have time for fear.

I reach into the heart of her; I tug the cord of Red magic free and let it go. I reach again, with both hands, and grab Brown and Ghost. I think of my mother and my brother as I release these, too.

There is only darkness left.

It evades my grasp, slick and oozing, trying instead to slide into me, to overtake my will.

I do not know if we will fall forever. It seems there is no end to the void inside Valrún, no variation in her emptiness.

With the rest of her stolen magic torn away, Valrún grapples to take hold of the darkness, and she is the one who grabs it, in the end. She commands it to bear her back up into her ruined garden, and grasping her ankle, I am carried up, too, and so stand with her once more in the reek of poison flowers.

Darkness coils around her feet, crawls up her arm, drapes across her shoulders like a liquid-boned cat. She bares her teeth at me. "Little fool," she says, "there is nothing that can defeat the dark." Her words are steeped in shadows.

I shake my head. "You're wrong, Valrún."

I reach into the darkness and yank us out of her mind, into the ashes of the city she helped to destroy.

And the sun is shining.

CHAPTER FORTY-ONE

BALLAST

Year 4201, Month of the Black Lord

Iljaria—the ruins of Regla City

The Blue Lady herself calls me out of my leviathan form, clothes me in a garment formed from the dark feathers that made up my great wings. I lift my head to see the ruins of Regla City before me. Smoke curls up in shafts of sunlight.

"Is it done?" I whisper. I peer into the swirling ashes, searching for any sign of my wife. My bones ache and my throat hurts and my mind is a whirl of leviathan thoughts that overwhelm my human ones, making them hard to grasp.

"Very nearly," says the Blue Lady.

I turn to look at her and see we are not alone. The First Ones stand silently with us, all of them present save the Bronze Lord, the Yellow Lord, and the Prism Lady.

Behind them come the resurrected Skapari, my mother and Finnur leading them, the Yellow wielders following after. I glimpse Brandr, Adriel gripping his right arm, Dagfinna his left.

Between one pulse of my heart and the next, Brynja and Valrún tumble out of empty air and onto the ground. Brynja is all burnished Bronze, pulsing with power. Valrún is darkness and rage, her clothing in tatters.

Brynja raises her eyes. They catch on mine. And she smiles.

The Black Lord and the Green Lady come toward Valrún. They gently pull her to her feet.

She trembles before them, as well she should.

"My Lord," Valrún stammers. "My Lady. Glad I am to see you thus restored."

The Black Lord says nothing as he holds out one hand, drawing his darkness back to him. Valrún gasps as she is emptied of magic. Her face goes gray at the pain of it. When the power is all pulled out of her, the Black Lord turns on his heel and strides from this world into the other, where it is said only magic dwells.

Valrún lifts her glance to the Green Lady, her patron First One. I am shocked she doesn't fall to her knees, doesn't grovel, doesn't beg. She smiles, like she is indulging a wayward child. "I ask of you one thing only," Valrún says. "Give to me a greater part of the Green magic than what was allotted to me at my birth, and I will serve you faithfully and rule Iljaria well until the end of time."

The Green Lady frowns, and it is only then that fear lights in Valrún's eyes.

"My Lady," she says, suddenly desperate, "I did not intend for you or any of the First Ones to come to harm. I was only trying to fulfill a prophecy, to bring power fully to the world, to—"

"You wished to be Queen Eternal," the Green Lady interrupts, her voice an icy wind coiling through a glacier sea, "and so you shall be."

Valrún's body goes suddenly rigid. Her hands still, the skin on her face and arms hardens. Her hair turns all to trailing leaves, and her eyes and nose, mouth and ears, melt away, leaving in their place the rough brown bark of a tree. Her arms turn to branches, her legs and torso to a trunk. Sap leaks down from where her eyes once were.

Sunlight glints on her leaves, and at her roots grow a carpet of poison flowers.

"So she will stand," says the Green Lady solemnly, "until the world's ending."

I shudder, looking at the tree. I suddenly recognize that the First Ones didn't need to take part in any of this. That if they wanted, they could crush us all like insects between their fingers. And yet they haven't. They have allowed themselves to be debased. To be bound and emptied and refilled. They have shown us great mercy, unimaginable forbearance. But I understand in the deepest parts of me that it is all over now. That it will not happen again.

"You're leaving, aren't you," I say to the Blue Lady, who stands yet at my shoulder. "You aren't coming back. None of you are coming back."

"We are all of us done with the world," she answers me gravely. "With the humans in it, their whims and their torments and their tragedies."

"But what will we do without you to guide us?"

"Wield your power well, son of mine. And do not yield to the darkness."

I bow my head before her, pricked to the heart.

She presses one finger to my brow and then strides across the grass to join the other First Ones.

They leave one by one, stepping into the air and out of the world, shimmers of magic lingering behind them.

For a moment all is still, like every one of us is holding our breath.

Then there is motion again, gasps and sighs, quiet curses. The Yellow wielders weep on the ground while Jóvin throws himself at the roots of Valrún's tree, beating the trunk with his fists until blood bursts bright against his broken skin.

Brandr rips out of Adriel and Dagfinna's hold and lunges at Jóvin, the two powerless men grappling at the foot of the tree that was the woman both of them, in their own twisted ways, had loved.

I close the distance remaining between me and Brynja, folding her in my arms, holding her tight against my chest. I stroke her hair. I breathe her scent. She sighs against me, hands gripping hard to my arms.

There is tension in me because there is tension in her. "Brynja," I say softly in her ear. She looks up at me, and my heart fractures. "Brynja."

"I've work yet to do, Bal. I can't—I can't leave everything like *this*." She waves her hands to the twisted, smoking ruins at her back. "The Bronze Lord gave me all his power. I mean to use it until I can use it no more. I need to set the world to rights. It's why he gave it to me, I think."

She shines in the sunlight, like she herself is a star.

"You can't do it alone," I say.

"She won't be alone."

I turn to see Malen and Adriel coming up beside us, blood dark on their collars, their faces grim with determination.

"We have to go now," Adriel says. "Before we run out of time."

Brynja nods and goes to join him and Malen.

"Wait," I say.

She looks at me with the weight of worlds in her eyes. "I'll be back soon, Bal."

Then she takes Adriel's hand, and Malen takes hers, and the three of them wink out of existence.

CHAPTER FORTY-TWO

BRYNJA

Year 4201, Month of the Black Lord

Iljaria—the ruins of Regla City

Adriel opens a pathway into time, and Malen and I step through it with him. We walk into the destruction of the city; we see Valrún slaughtering the Aeronans; we see the Aeronans hewing down the Iljaria.

My heart twists, and the Bronze Lord's magic blazes like a comet inside me.

Adriel lets go of our hands as he and Malen kneel before an Aeronan soldier whose skull has been split open. Adriel touches the soldier, Violet dancing all along his body as the blood disappears and his wound knits back together. But he doesn't stir until Malen kneels beside him and calls him back to life. He sits up with a gasp, eyes wild, unfocused.

Then Adriel is pulling us on, to an Iljaria who was killed by a blast of Skaandan Fire, her body riddled with iron shards. He works his Violet magic and Malen her Green, and the Iljaria is resurrected.

But it is too slow. Thousands and thousands of souls have fallen here today. Not even Adriel wields enough time magic to restore them all.

I touch his shoulder as he moves toward a pair of bodies so marred it is impossible to tell if they are Iljaria or Aeronan.

Adriel glances back at me.

"I wield all the Bronze Lord's magic," I say. "I am going to help you."

Malen's face grows solemn and Adriel's sorrowful.

"Thank you, Bronze Lady," he says quietly.

I take a breath. I shove down my fear.

And I pull apart the very atoms of the air and pass into the infinitesimal expanse of the universe, where all things are connected: life and death, light and darkness, joy and grief.

I step into the mind of all things.

I blink and see the First Ones striding past me, taking the paths to their realms beyond the world. They do not look aside at me; I am not even sure they see me, because I am not certain I am in quite the same place as they are.

Then I am alone again in the mind of the world. It would be easy to get lost here, a single snowflake in a whirling storm. But I hold hard to the magic inside me, let it root me in place, let it hone me like a blade.

I focus on the minds of Adriel and Malen. I sort through the fibers of the world, and I see them, striding through the field of destruction, where the bodies of Aeronans and Iljaria alike lay scattered about like so much wheat, hewn down and left to rot.

I pour magic into Adriel and Malen to amplify their own abilities, to make them swifter, stronger. Adriel dances through time, drawing men and women back to the moments of their deaths while Malen dances after him, pouring Green magic into their bodies and sparking their souls back to life.

Magic writhes around me, and I harness it, command it. I send a piece of myself to walk through time with Adriel, another piece to wield Green magic with Malen. I can see two worlds: the one in the place between atoms, made all of magic and thought, and the one where

Malen and Adriel dwell, defying the destruction that Valrún wrought, making thousands upon thousands of sad things come untrue.

A piece of myself walks with Adriel to the time just before the first of the Skaandan Fire blasts broke Regla City's walls. I shelter a man and a woman beneath an overturned wagon, so they are not ripped apart by the explosions. Some distant part of me recognizes them as Vil and Aelia, but though the names spark familiarity in my mind, they mean nothing to me.

All is magic, the wielding of impossible power, holding together the building blocks of the universe. If I let go, we will all of us be atoms again, unbound into any sort of form, incapable of love or pain or thought.

So I hold the world together, and I walk with Malen and Adriel, and I help them restore every last soul that was killed—Iljaria and Aeronan alike.

And then the task is complete, and Adriel tries to find me, but he cannot reach me here. In this moment I realize I cannot reach him, either.

The magic is inside me and all around me. It is all there is.

I wove myself into the fabric of the universe, and I am afraid that if I attempt to unravel my mind from that of the world, I will fray to pieces until there is nothing at all of me left.

Not love or light or breath.

Not thought.

Not even memory.

NOW

SAGA

Year 4201, Month of the Black God

Iljaria—Regla City

The world is strange.

It was broken, and it was healed.

And now it feels new again.

I stand with Leifur, watching as, impossibly, Regla City remakes itself before our eyes. Its streets and buildings rise from smoldering ruins. Its towers thrust into the sky. Its wall re-forms and circles the city once more in glittering glass.

Corpses become living men and women again, standing to their feet in the light of the sun, the entire Aeronan army blinking before the wall, stripped of all their weapons. Those are the only things that are not brought back. The ground is littered with broken swords and snapped spear shafts, shattered canisters of Skaandan Fire empty of iron shards.

The Aeronans murmur in confusion, looking around for someone to command them. I wonder where the emperor is. I wonder where *Vil* is, and despite everything he's done, my heart wrenches at the thought of him, and I hope he is alive. I hope I will get to see him again.

In the space between heartbeats, Malen and Adriel step out of the air, weariness weighing on them like a burial shroud.

"You did this," I realize in awe. "You brought the dead back to life. You restored the city."

"Brynja helped us," says Malen quietly.

"I think Brynja rebuilt the world for us," Adriel adds.

"Where is she?"

Ballast comes up behind us, clothed in dark feathers, worry on his brow. He smells . . . *weird,* like the musk of some giant beast.

Adriel shakes his head. "She did something back there, I'm not exactly sure what. I've never seen anything like it. But—I think she stepped beyond the world."

"Can you take me there?" says Ballast frantically.

Adriel eyes him. "I can try."

He grabs Ballast by the hand, and both of them vanish, Adriel reappearing a moment later alone.

"Did you find her?" I ask.

"I'm not sure," Adriel returns. "But if anyone can reach her now, it's Ballast."

A sudden sharp cry rings out on the air, and the three of us turn to a crowd of people—the Skapari and a knot of Yellow wielders—who are standing near a tree I don't remember ever seeing before.

Brandr stands at the base of the tree, a knife in his hand dripping blood. A crumpled body lies at his feet.

Leifur, Adriel, Malen, and I stride toward the tree, and I see that the body is Jóvin, his face twisted in one last expression of rage.

Finnur is suddenly beside him, vanishing and reappearing several times in succession. He curses, tears sliding down his cheeks.

Malen and Adriel walk over to Jóvin's body, the two of them working their time and life magic. But Jóvin doesn't stir.

Malen stands to her feet again, placing a gentle hand on Finnur's arm.

"I'm sorry," she says. "He refused my call. He does not want to come back to a world where he wields no magic."

Finnur bows his head, and I don't understand his grief. The dead man was wicked, and cruel, and can't have meant anything to him.

Brandr, for his part, shakes off the hands of the Yellow wielders who attempt to seize him. He stalks away toward the city and doesn't look back.

I stand shoulder to shoulder with Leifur, as around and behind us the Skapari and the Yellow wielders gaze at the restored city, like they are trying to understand the new shape of the world. The wind stirs through the leaves of the strange tree, and the sunlight that glances upon my face is warm and good.

"What happens now?" says Leifur to no one in particular.

I think that's what all of us are wondering.

Finnur shakes his head, tears drying shiny on his cheeks. "A new beginning," he says quietly.

"What of Valrún?" I ask.

Finnur's jaw goes hard. "She's gone, though she got what she wanted, in a sense. The Green Lady turned her into a tree."

"A tree?" I say, dumbfounded.

"*That* tree?" adds Leifur, nodding toward it.

Finnur nods unhappily. "That tree."

Leifur curses. "I'll take an axe to it, shall I?"

"Don't do that." Finnur shoves his hands into his pockets, and my eyes catch on the dark stain that runs all down the front of his shirt. "As it turns out, she was my mother." He looks at Jóvin, dead in the grass. "And he was my father."

There is chaos, for a while, before the rebuilt gates of Regla City. The Aeronan army is restless, disquieted, putting hands to sword hilts and spear shafts that are no longer there, looking toward the walls and then over their shoulders, as if reckoning the long miles back to the shore where they left their ships. Their generals order them to reform their ranks, and then *I* am uneasy. Even without weapons, ten thousand soldiers can do a great deal of harm.

"They won't do anything without their emperor's command," says Leifur into my ear. "And he won't dare attack now, not without his iron canisters to wield."

Malen takes charge of the Skapari, dismissing the powerless Yellow wielders into the city to order things there. She sends Finnur onto the battlefield to find Junius. Then she turns to everyone else standing here and fixes me with her sharp eyes.

"You should call a council, Your Majesty."

I blink at her. "Me?"

She looks faintly amused. "There is no one here of higher rank, at present."

I feel very little like a queen, so far from my country and an army that would follow me, but I squeeze Leifur's hand tight and acknowledge Malen with a nod.

I glance around at the others: Brynja's mother, Runa, blood staining the front of her brown dress; Ísold, her white gown similarly sullied. I have a sudden flash of foresight: I will invite Ísold to Skaanda, ask her to tutor me properly in song magic. It will be the first step in bridging the chasm between our nations, in remembering that we used to be one people, that we can be so again.

Salin and Osa, Dagfinna and Adriel, are here, too, all of them watching me, waiting for my command.

"A council then," I say.

Malen smiles. "Where, Your Majesty?"

"Here," I tell her. I find I don't want to go into the city.

Quick as blinking, Runa makes chairs out of the earth, and Adriel vanishes and reappears with cushions for the seats. We all settle into them, Leifur close enough to me that I can continue to hold his hand with ease, which I appreciate.

The ranks of the Aeronan army part, and suddenly my stupid, infuriating, traitorous, beloved brother is coming toward me.

Aelia stumbles along beside him, with Finnur and the emperor just behind.

I'm broken at the sight of Vil. I hate him. I hate him so much. But I'm glad he's alive.

Leifur threads his fingers through mine, and I cling to the solidness of him, letting him tether me to the earth.

Vil doesn't look at me as he draws nearer. Neither does Aelia. Both of them are streaked with soot and blood. They stink of death.

Junius looks even worse, like his body was blown apart and put painstakingly back together again. I glance at Malen and realize that's exactly what happened.

Runa makes three more chairs. Finnur sits gratefully in his, while Vil slumps and scowls. Aelia remains standing, tension in every line of her frame.

Junius is not offered a chair. He stands there with his jaw set, eyes blazing fury.

"Right, then," I say, forcing my voice not to shake. The fates of four nations will be decided today, and the weight of it is too much for me to hold.

Leifur squeezes my hand.

"Where is Ballast?" I ask, realizing suddenly that he and Brynja have yet to return. "We cannot forge war or peace without him."

"I'm here."

He steps, it seems, out of empty air, and there is a scent of beast and storm and fire about him. He still wears his robes of blue feathers, with a sapphire stone on his brow.

But he is alone, and sorrow hangs on him like a sodden cloak.

CHAPTER FORTY-THREE

BRYNJA

Year 4201, Month of the Black Lord

Brynja's Mind

I have strayed too far into the place between atoms.

I cannot get out again.

I bleed into the universe. I become formless and nameless.

There is nothing left of me anymore. I am only magic, only thought.

Soon there will not even be that.

Yet he takes me by the hand.

"Let me in," he says.

So I do.

We step together into a low room with walls of stone and endless branching pathways.

I have been here before, I think, but I do not remember when.

I do not remember anything.

"Brynja," comes his quiet voice. "Brynja, you're crying."

"Who am I?" I whisper. "What am I?"

"You are Brynja Eldingar," he says. "You are my wife."

My heart beats and beats, and I remember the ring on my finger, the one I could not quite bear to throw away. I am not certain I am still wearing it. I am not certain of anything.

But I look down at my hand, tug it out of his. And the ring is there, the blue stone pulsing with a magic all its own.

I fling my head up. "Ballast," I breathe.

He throws his arms around me, crushes me into him. I sob on his neck, and he tangles his fingers in my hair.

"All is well, little schemer," he whispers into my ear. "All is well, all is well."

I lift my face after a while, peer into his fathomless blue eye.

"Hey," he says, smiling at me as he cups my cheek with one hand and tucks a stray curl behind my ear with the other.

My heart hurts because he thinks that it's over, and I know that it's not. The Bronze Lord's magic blazes and boils inside me. There is nowhere for it to go.

"Will you walk with me awhile?" I ask him.

"I will walk with you forever," he returns.

He folds his hand over mine, and we stray through the caverns of my mind, very like the labyrinth beneath the mountains we traveled in what feels like another lifetime.

There is a little door that leads out of the caves. I wrest open the latch, and we step through onto a hill under glittering stars.

We stretch out on the grass, facing each other. I trace the ridge of his brow above his missing eye, and he draws a ragged breath and pulls me into him, his fire-hot mouth finding mine. And then we're shedding our clothes because we do not need them just now. We need only to be closer, closer than skin, than breath, than beating hearts. We meld into each other tenderly, reverently, lying bare in this place that is real and yet not real, cherishing the precious thing between us that we know we cannot keep.

When the fire has waned, we still lie there for a while, tangled together, and Ballast cradles my head to his chest as my tears leak out onto the ground.

"Brynja," he says quietly. "Why are you crying?"

"Because I can't come back with you."

He strokes his thumb against my brow. "Why can't you?"

Power swirls inside me, worming into my brain and my heart, seeking to unravel me from the inside out. The tears come faster, and I tremble in his arms.

"The magic is too much for me. I can't hold it all, Bal."

"You are the strongest person I've ever met."

"Not stronger than this."

He tightens his grip on me, his hands warm on my bare shoulders. "What do you need to do?" His voice shakes, though I can tell he's fighting to keep it steady.

"I need to return the Bronze Lord's power."

Ballast kisses my hair. "Easy enough. You found him once. You can find him again."

I choke on a sob, and Ballast pulls away enough to look into my face. "Brynja, what is it? What aren't you telling me?"

I glance away, but he grips my chin, tugs my gaze back to his.

"The Bronze Lord is dead, Bal. His power was the only thing sustaining him, and he gave it all to me."

I hate the feral panic that lights in Ballast's eye, the stubborn determination creasing his face. "Then we find a way to help you control it," he says, "or we—we bind it."

"Would you keep your wife locked in iron?"

"No," he says viciously.

I pull away from him and he releases me, allows me to untangle my limbs from his. I slip back into my clothes, and after a few moments he does, too.

We sit together, gazing out at the fathomless stars.

He glances over at me, and I try not to feel my heart breaking.

"What will you do, Brynja?"

"Hope that I am mistaken," I say, "hope that the Bronze Lord yet lives, and will take his power back."

"And if not?" His quiet voice is like a knife to my belly, twisting and sharp. It eviscerates me.

"I will go to the First Ones and throw myself upon their mercy."

"Can't I come with you?" he asks.

I turn my head, meet his piercing eye with both of mine. "You have a throne to reclaim, Bal."

"I don't want to be a king without you."

I try to smile but can't quite manage it. "You'll be all right without me."

"No, I won't, little liar."

I blink back fresh tears. "I will come back to you. If I can."

"You had better," he says. "A king is nothing without his queen."

I choke on a sob as I grab his shoulders, as I tug his mouth once more to mine. I kiss him desperately, pouring into him all my longing and love, all my hope and agony, every beginning and every ending and all the things between.

When we break apart, I study him a moment more, memorizing the shape of him. "Goodbye, Ballast."

He takes a shuddery breath. "Don't be too long," he says.

"I love you, Bal," I say, because there is no other promise I can make him.

His eye goes shiny with unshed tears. "I love you, Brynja." His voice cracks.

I blink and rip open a doorway in my mind. I send him through it.

And then I am horribly, irrevocably alone.

CHAPTER FORTY-FOUR

BALLAST

Year 4201, Month of the Black Lord

Iljaria—the walls of Regla City

"I'm here," I say, stepping onto the grass in front of the restored city walls, where Saga and Leifur sit facing the assembled host of the Skapari.

Belatedly, I notice Junius, Vil, and Aelia.

It takes a monumental effort to not grab Leifur's sword and run Vil and Junius through with it, one after the other. Black Lord's bowels, I hate them. Vil has the audacity to glare at me, but Junius stares steadily past me, like he is doing his level best to not be here at all.

My blood boils, and Brynja isn't here to keep me from doing something really stupid. I stand there seriously considering Leifur's sword.

"Ballast," says Saga, and I jerk my gaze to hers.

She shakes her head, not needing Bronze magic to read my mind.

I sigh and sink down into the empty chair on Saga's right. My mother sits on my right, with Finnur on hers.

"Now," says Saga, her sharp eyes flitting around the circle and fixing on Junius. "The first thing that is going to happen is the Aeronan army is going to march back to their ships and return to their country."

The emperor sets his jaw but says nothing in answer.

Aelia sits straight-backed and regal, her face hard, one hand playing anxiously with the folds of her skirt. "Aerona acknowledges," she says formally. "The army will retreat."

Saga nods.

A storm brews on Junius's brow, but he still doesn't speak.

Vil's glance darts between Saga and Aelia, all anxious, fearful energy.

Saga doesn't even look at her brother. "Ballast," she says, raising her brows at me.

I give her a little acknowledging bow and stand from my seat. "Daeros will no longer be a province of the Aeronan Empire. There will be no viceroy, and Aeronan soldiers will no longer be permitted on Daerosian soil. In the presence of you all, I reclaim my title as king."

Vil curses at me, and I eye him coolly, thinking about Leifur's sword with renewed regret.

Again, Aelia is the one who answers. "Aerona acknowledges and accepts your claim and your right, Your Majesty. Aerona will withdraw from Daeros."

"And pay remonstrations," I press.

Aelia glances aside at her father, but when he says nothing, she echoes: "And pay remonstrations."

This is a bridge too far for Junius. He jerks to his feet with a violent oath and grabs Aelia's arm, yanking her roughly from her chair. "How dare you answer for me, for the empire, you traitorous, unfeeling *whore*."

He strikes her hard across the face, but the next moment his eyes go wide and a strangled, burbling noise comes out of his mouth. He slumps to the ground with Vil's blade in his back, dead for the second time today.

Aelia's breathing has gone ragged, but she stands there with her hands balled into fists, looking dispassionately down at her father. The mark of his hand shows clear on her cheek, already purpling against her bronze skin.

I feel tight and sick.

Vil pulls his sword out of Junius and wipes it clean on the grass before sheathing it. Then he takes Aelia's hand and leads her back to her seat. She leans against him, and he wraps a protective arm around her shoulders. I study him, realizing that at least part of his motivation in wresting my country away from me was an endeavor to shield Aelia from her father. Clearly Junius was cruel to her, as my father was to me, though Junius hid it rather better until today. I respect Vil for this. But that still doesn't give him any right to Daeros. And I sure as hell don't have to like him.

A cool wind breathes suddenly through the circle, and everyone shifts uneasily, staring at the dead emperor. I glance at Adriel and Malen, but neither of them moves to resurrect Junius.

Osa and Salin, the Gray and Black Skapari, rise after a few moments. They lift the emperor's body between them and bear him out of the circle, laying him down on the grass before taking their seats again.

I clear my throat. "Iljaria," I say. For a moment I can't continue; the word feels too thick and heavy in my mouth. I take a breath and forge ahead. "Iljaria is left without a ruler. I make no claim to the throne, though I have a right by blood."

I look sideways at my mother, who sits steady and serene, the wind blowing her white skirt about her knees. "I make no claim to the throne," she says, "though I also have a right by blood."

I am surprised and relieved in equal measure. But Iljaria cannot be leaderless, and I am suddenly worried that this is my mother's way of maneuvering me into the job.

"There is another who has a right by blood," says Saga unexpectedly.

I look at her in sharp confusion. *"You?"*

A surprised laugh pulls out of her. "No, dumbass. Your cousin."

I blink at her. "I don't have a cousin."

"Yes," she says. "You do. Although to be fair, *I* didn't know until a few hours ago."

"Know what?" I press. I am so damn tired of critical information being fed to me a little at a time.

"That Valrún was my mother," comes Finnur's quiet voice.

I stare at him. "Your mother?" I'm just stupidly repeating things now.

"When I was born, she thought I didn't have any magic. So she had her Violet Skapari erase the memory of me from time. Then she had him killed."

Osa, the Gray Skapari, stirs in her seat, and I understand that she must have acted as Valrún's executioner.

"She ordered me killed, too, only—" Here Finnur's eyes catch Osa's. Hers are wet, and tears drip down her brown cheeks. "Only I was saved instead," he continues softly.

Osa bows her face into her hands, her shoulders shaking as she weeps.

"The glass boat," I muse. "That's what you told me when you were my steward in Daeros. You were found in a glass boat, washed up on the shores of the White Sea." I don't say the rest of his story out loud: brought to the orphan house in Garran City. Found by Kallias. Locked in an iron cage.

Finnur's fingers are nervous about his knees. "That's all I knew then, Ballast. I swear it on the Prism Lady. I would never have lied to you."

I rise from my chair and step over to him, my mind working to reorder my understanding of the world.

"Finnur," I say softly. My voice catches.

He looks at me. "You're not mad?"

I throw my head back, howling in laughter, and then pull him out of his seat and into a crushing embrace.

"Mad!" I gasp when we pull back again, laughing so hard I can hardly talk. "Why on the Green Lady's earth would I be *mad*?"

And then Finnur is grinning, and my joy is sharp as swords.

"Are we finished here?" snaps Vil, *still* not understanding how perilously close he is to losing his head every time he opens his mouth, excellent impulse toward regicide notwithstanding.

I resume my seat, anger settling over me again like a well-worn coat.

"Are we in agreement?" asks Saga, completely ignoring her brother. Her eyes pass from Aelia, to Finnur, to me. "Do we strike an accord for peace? Skaanda wills it so."

"Daeros wills it so," I say.

Finnur takes a breath. "Iljaria wills it so."

Aelia lets a moment pass before she says, last and quietest, "Aerona wills it so."

The four of us rise and step to the middle of the circle, grasping one another's arms in turn to seal our verbal oaths.

It is an ending, and a beginning, and I wish with everything I am that Brynja were here beside me. Her absence is as keen and piercing as my missing eye.

"What about me?" says Vil, stepping up just behind Aelia. There is a hard twist to his mouth.

"What about you?" Saga repeats. "You betrayed me, Vil. You betrayed our country. Our parents." Her eyes go wet.

"But I didn't," he says. "I was trying to—to unite the peninsula, to strengthen it. I couldn't run back to Skaanda just because—"

"Just because your little sister asked you to?" says Saga quietly. "Vil, Junius *murdered* our parents."

"You don't know that," Vil returns. "And anyway, he's dead now."

Saga presses her lips together.

"He did," says Aelia quietly. "My father did murder your parents. That poison—he likes using it." Her eyes flit to the still form of the body outside the circle. "Liked using it," she amends. "I would have stopped him, if I'd known in time."

Vil drops his gaze from his sister's. "I'm sorry, Saga," he says roughly.

Tears slide down Saga's cheeks, but she holds herself up straight and still. Leifur comes and folds her hand in his.

"We still need to discuss Daeros," Vil says. "After everything we went through last year, I won't relinquish my role of viceroy just because the one-eyed bastard has decided to call himself a king again."

"Daeros doesn't belong to you," I tell him coolly.

"It doesn't belong to you, either," he retorts. "Your little Iljaria spy made you give it up, or have you forgotten?"

I glare at him. "Don't disparage my wife."

His eyes go as wide as an owl's. "Your what?"

"You heard me."

"She *married* you?"

"Yes, Vil. Try and keep up."

He gives a howl of outrage and lunges at me, slamming me to the ground just shy of the place Junius died. I punch him in the jaw and twist out of his grasp before he can return the favor.

And then Leifur and Saga grab Vil's arms and haul him upright while Finnur's voice darts into my mind: *He's not worth it, Ballast. Let him go.*

I realize I inadvertently called a wolf up from its den, an eagle down from its aerie, a serpent from its hole. I pick myself up, brushing grass from my knees. I was spoiling for a fight, and I'm sorry I didn't get to finish it. But I send the wolf and eagle and serpent home again. Finnur's right—Vil isn't worth it. And Brynja would be disappointed in me if I caused him any real harm.

Very undignified, Your Majesty, says Finnur.

I grimace.

Vil shakes free of Leifur and Saga and glares knives at me.

"What will you do, Vil?" Saga asks her brother. "Will you come home now? Honor our parents' memories by helping me to guide Skaanda well?"

Vil takes a breath, his eyes catching on Aelia's. "No," he says. "No, I'm not going back to Skaanda."

The barest scrap of a smile touches Aelia's lips. "He's coming with me," she says.

And that's the end of it.

Aelia and Vil depart with the Aeronan army, the rearguard scarcely visible by the time the sun is down and the stars are out. They take the emperor's body away with them.

I go with Finnur and my mother and the rest of the Skapari into the palace, which feels neither so sinister nor so grand as it did when Valrún lived.

Finnur tells me I'm to sit with him at his first dinner as Iljaria's king, but I can't quite face that now. I am far too weary.

He finds me a room that has no iron binding the door, and I throw myself onto the wide bed and fall into a deep sleep.

I dream of my father, of a viper in a box, of the sharp crack of a cruel hand across my face.

It is not Brynja who wakes me; of course it is not. She isn't here.

But I stir in the night to find that somehow Hjarta, the one-eyed cat, has found me. He curls up on my chest, purring like a thunderstorm, and sleep folds once more over me. It is easier now, but I feel the gaping emptiness of her, the place she's meant to be, the place she's not.

I search for her in my dreams; we've met there before.

But I cannot find her.

CHAPTER FORTY-FIVE

BALLAST

Year 4201, Month of the Black Lord

Iljaria—Regla City—the palace

Saga and Leifur are anxious to return to Skaanda, but Saga wants to speak with Brynja first.

"Tell me *exactly* what she said to you," Saga says over breakfast, spreading jam on her toast like this is a perfectly ordinary day. "About where she's going, about when she's coming back."

I shift in my seat, overly aware of Finnur and my mother and Brynja's mother, Runa, watching me. Runa disconcertingly resembles Brynja; she's just a little older, a little taller. I can't bring myself to think charitable things about the woman who sent her ten-year-old daughter to be caged and tormented by my father. So I do my best not to glance her way.

"She said she was going to find the Bronze Lord and give his power back." I push bites of sausage around on my plate with my fork. I don't tell them that she also said the Bronze Lord was already dead, that she said she'd come back to me if she could.

"She was gone a few weeks, before," Saga muses. "Can we afford to wait a few weeks, Leif?"

Leifur is sitting beside her, and he smiles at her, his eyes soft. "If His Majesty will agree to lend us a coach for the journey home, then yes, I think we can."

Finnur scratches his jaw, embarrassed by his new title. "Of course I'll lend you one," he says.

It's only later, when I'm wandering listlessly through the courtyard, Hjarta winding about my ankles, that my mother catches my arm and asks if we can talk. She tugs me onto a stone bench overshadowed by a vast evergreen tree, and I sit with her. Hjarta hops up onto my lap and kneads me happily with his needle-sharp claws.

"When are you going back to Tenebris?" she asks, looking square into my face.

I am still not used to the sound of her voice, but it heals something that was broken in me to see how much lighter she looks now, how contented, how free. I hate that my father robbed her of those things for so long.

"I'll go when Saga and Leifur do. Our journey lies the same way, for a while."

She nods and strokes Hjarta, who has thankfully left off his kneading and curled up on my legs, head tucked under his tail.

"You don't think Brynja is coming back."

"I need her to."

"That isn't what I asked."

I turn away from my mother. I don't want her to see my tears.

"Will you go to the Vaxandi for a new eye before you leave?" she asks me.

I refocus on her, the ghost of old pain shivering through my skull. "Why is that so important to you?"

"I let him hurt you," she says, her voice small and trembling. "I let him hurt you, and I could have stopped him, but I didn't. I *didn't*, over and over and over again."

I turn and grip her by the shoulders, lowering my face so it's even with hers. There is a crack inside me that I feel down to my soul.

"He got what he wanted," I tell her. "He *did* what he wanted. His cruelty was his own. You couldn't have stopped him. No one could have. And I have never blamed you, not even once. Do you hear me, Mother?"

She nods but won't meet my gaze, tears sliding down her cheeks.

"You cared for me," I say quietly. "You protected me, the best way you knew how." I take a breath. "It is easy to erase a physical scar but impossible, I think, to undo the deeper hurt of it. The painful things of my past are still part of me, they made me who I am. And even with the deepest of wounds, there can be healing. I've found it. I hope you are finding it, too. So, no. I will not be going to the Vaxandi for a new eye."

She shakes as she weeps, and I pull her into a hug, kissing her forehead and marveling that the woman who gave life to me should feel so small in my arms.

"I'm not coming with you," she says when the tears have gone out of her. "I can't go back to Tenebris. There is too much . . . grief there."

"Even though he's gone?" I ask her quietly.

She gives me a wan smile. "It's like you said, love. Easy to erase a physical scar, impossible to undo the deeper hurt."

I nod, though I do not like that I will have to leave my mother here, along with my newly found cousin. *And your wife,* says my brain, unhelpfully. I dig my fingernails into my palm.

"I'm sorry, Ballast," says my mother softly. "I belong here. In Iljaria. Finnur has asked me to be his adviser. He is, after all, very young."

"He will rule well with you to guide him," I say.

Her eyes fill again, and she touches my face like I am something precious. "You won't reconsider trading the Daerosian throne for the Iljaria one?"

"Finnur is more than capable," I admonish. "My place is in Tenebris. I was born, I think, to try and heal the deeper hurt. And I am uneasy about the state of Daeros. I've been gone too long."

"Oh, my boy," she whispers, "oh, my dear boy. How I ached for you. How I wished every day for a way out."

I kiss the top of her head. "I am only sorry it took so long to find it."

We weep awhile together, Hjarta purring in his sleep between us, and when we lift our heads and dry our eyes, we are a little freer of my father's ghost than we were before.

There is a chill in the air as Saga and Leifur and I bid our farewells in the palace courtyard. Clouds knot over the sun, and I think it will snow soon. The weeks have passed slowly and swiftly all at once—neither Saga nor I can delay returning to our countries any longer.

I embrace Finnur, telling him sternly to take care of my mother.

I hug Geirfinna, too, who is skipping her classes at the Skepna Conservatory this morning specifically to see me off. I've asked her up to the palace several times since the city was restored—the first time to make sure she was all right, and subsequently because I realize I'll miss her when I'm home in Daeros. I've told Finnur she will make an excellent King's Skapari, if she likes, when she's older.

Before I can bid my mother farewell, I have to wait for her and Saga to finish their conversation. The two of them have bonded over their mutual song magic, and there are even plans for my mother to visit Saga in Skaanda before the year is out. There are no such plans for her to come see me in Tenebris, and I try my best to understand; my father's presence doesn't haunt the halls of Saga's palace.

"Don't despair," says my mother in my ear when I at last get the chance to hug her goodbye. "I believe Brynja will come back to you."

And then I climb into the coach after Saga and Leifur, lounging along one wall with my feet on the seats while they occupy the opposite side. Leifur puts his arm around Saga's shoulders; she snuggles into him.

The door slides shut and the coach whirs into motion and we're off, the city and then the Iljaria countryside blurring past the glass.

It isn't as uncomfortable as I thought it would be, sharing the coach with Saga and Leifur. Saga is the easiest around me she has ever been. She talks a lot about Brynja and asks me to tell her exactly what went on with Vil and the emperor after she went home to Skaanda last year.

"I'm so angry with Vil," she says when I've told her everything. She clenches and unclenches her jaw. "But I'm not sure I'll ever stop missing him."

The hours pass swiftly. I doze for a while. When I wake up, Saga and Leifur are lying half on top of each other in order for both of them to fit on the narrow seats, and I miss Brynja so much I can hardly breathe.

Hjarta hops up to join me just then, purring smugly at having successfully stowed away. I laugh and pull him onto my chest and fall asleep again.

I part with Saga and Leifur just outside the Bone City, in Daeros. They are to continue on in the coach the most direct way to Staltoria City from here, while I go to Tenebris alone.

Well, not wholly alone. Hjarta drapes himself around my shoulders, and Asvaldr is waiting for me when I step out of the coach. The great bear yawns at the sight of me to let me know how *long* he's been waiting and how undignified it is for a magnificent creature such as himself.

I turn back to Saga and Leifur.

"Send word," says Saga, "the moment you hear anything from Brynja."

"Of course I will. And if you need any support in securing your throne, please know that Daeros will come."

Saga gives me a smile, soft and a little sad. I'm not sure she has ever smiled at me before. "Thanks, Ballast. I suppose I'll have to see you again at some point. Give Brynja my love."

I nod. "Farewell, Saga. Leifur."

The coach door shuts, and the vehicle speeds away, quick as blinking.

Asvaldr yawns again pointedly, and I go over to him and throw my arms around his great white neck, Hjarta squirming in protest. "Missed you, you great oaf," I tell him fondly.

I let the cat and the bear sniff each other, both sending flashes of indignation at me while I open myself to their wills and allow them to feel my thoughts of safety and friendship. They decide not to murder each other—though both are sure to tell me that they could if they wanted.

And then Asvaldr projects images into my mind of his den near Tenebris, of his mate, waiting for him. My heart kicks, and it's ridiculous to envy a bear, and yet here I am. Doing exactly that.

I climb onto his broad back, Hjarta between my knees, and Asvaldr lopes happily westward, toward Tenebris, which is the beginning and ending, it seems, of every one of my journeys.

I could, of course, transform into a creature and take myself home, but I do not think Hjarta would like it overly much, and besides that it is difficult for me to remember to carry my human things when I'm in animal form. I cannot bear to lose my wedding ring.

And it's good to be reunited with Asvaldr, to let the wind rush past my face, to think human thoughts and prepare myself for my return to the throne I still can't help but think of as my father's.

I spend one night out on the winter plain, curled up against Asvaldr with Hjarta tucked against me, the soft-falling snow not able to dispel our joined heat.

It's still snowing late into the next afternoon, when Tenebris comes into view against the gray sky. I feel relief unlooked for, the solid sense of being home again where I belong.

So I am more than a little miffed when the Daerosian army rides out to challenge me, my half brothers Zopyros, Alcaeus, and Theron leading them. All three wear coats of scale armor, with swords at their sides and helms on their heads. The extra gold band on Zopyros's helm tells me everything I need to know. Gray Lady's bones, I was afraid of this.

Hjarta drapes himself across my shoulders and asks me in his animal way if I would like him to claw out the eyes of the entire army. Asvaldr offers to rip everyone's throats out. The two of them seem to approve of each other's bloodthirsty tendencies. I tell them both to calm down.

"Ballast," says Zopyros, his tone clipped and cold. "You are not welcome here."

I sigh, flicking my eye down the ranks of the army, amused that my brothers brought mounted soldiers to face me. Do they not realize I could compel the horses to shake them out of their saddles and dash their heads open with their hooves? It would be as easy as breathing. I accidentally catch all the horses' consciousnesses. They shift uneasily, waiting for my command. *Be calm,* I tell them. *All will be well.*

They are still again.

"Zopyros," I say in a bored voice, distracted by the impatient flick of Hjarta's tail against my neck. "Do you know, every single governor advised me to execute the lot of you when I took the throne? It's what you would do to me, I'm sure, if you were in my place, though I see you were not quite brave enough to enact such justice on Alcaeus and Theron."

"We are His Majesty's generals and top advisers," Alcaeus snaps.

"We support his rule," adds Theron haughtily. "He is the eldest, after all. It never should have been you."

I rub my temples. What a headache. "I see you have been busy since the Aeronans went to war."

"The emperor didn't leave enough of his soldiers to keep us subdued when he left," says Zopyros. "He forgot, to his ruin, the loyalties of the Daerosian army."

"Yes," I say, amused. "He certainly did."

Zopyros frowns. "You are hereby banished from Daeros. By order of the king."

I snort. "You're not a king."

"If you do not leave at once, I will be forced to arrest you. You will be tried and executed."

"For what?" I scoff.

"Treachery," he says tightly. "You sold us to Aerona."

"No, I didn't. That was just a bit of gambling." I look past him and raise my voice a little. "Rhode, are you here?"

A very slight-looking soldier rides out of the ranks and takes her helmet off, shaking out her dark hair and revealing herself as my fourteen-year-old half sister. "Hi, Ballast," she says shyly. "I thought you were never coming back."

I smile at her. "Sorry it took so long. Is everything in order?"

She nods. "I did just as you said. Paid the generals off, with the promise of more to come on your return, if they play along with our brothers and hold Daeros secure in your absence." She smiles, bright as the sun.

"What are you *doing*, Rhode?" demands Alcaeus. He nudges his mount toward her, but I nudge it back again and am petty enough to compel the horse to dump him onto the ground while I'm at it.

"You forgot about me," Rhode informs our three half brothers. "You couldn't *imagine* that I had any sort of merit, was any kind of threat to you. You were wrong."

"Thanks, Ro," I say, and beckon her over to join me, soothing her mount in Asvaldr's presence and telling the bear severely to be *nice* and not snap at it.

"Demetria, Nereus, Iason," I call, naming the three generals I hand selected during the first part of my reign. "Arrest my brothers. Then you may return to the garrison. Any chance of an early dinner, Ro?"

My generals are suddenly beside my brothers, knives held to their throats, no time for Zopyros and Theron and Alcaeus to do anything besides curse.

Rhode and I ride past them, me snatching the gold-circled helm from Zopyros's head as we go.

I climb off Asvaldr, and she dismounts from her horse as we near Tenebris's gates, and then we're stepping into the mountain palace and Hjarta is coiling round Rhode's ankles and there is a good, warm hum of contentment in my body.

There is only one thing missing.

I try not to look for her around every corner, my eye flicking often to the heating vents.

But she isn't here.

I twist my wedding ring around my finger again and again as I go with Rhode to the dining hall, where her mother and sisters are waiting for us.

For the first time, I truly allow myself to examine the possibility that Brynja is never coming back.

CHAPTER FORTY-SIX

BALLAST

Year 4202, Month of the Yellow Lord

Daeros—the Sea of Bones

I watch the first sunrise of the year in the place I saw the last one: on the edge of the Sea of Bones. But unlike last year, I am alone.

Leviathan's heart, I miss her.

The work of ruling Daeros, of undoing all the harm Vil and the emperor wrought here—and my father before them—keeps me busy enough. It is good work, steady and sure. I like doing it. I am bringing my country to life again.

But I miss her.

Rhode and her mother and sisters don't live in Tenebris, though I ask them to every time they come to dine with me, which is once a week or so. They are happy in Garran City, Rhode tells me, her and Xenia at school, Pelagia with her seamstress work and caring for little Charis, who grows like a weed.

We don't use the grand dining hall my father preferred, when we eat together, but a small, cozy tearoom, with carpets on the floor and tapestries on the walls and plants in hanging baskets.

Charis has started to toddle around after Hjarta, who is infinitely patient with her overenthusiastic love for him. One evening she pulls his tail, and Pelagia is horrified. She apologizes to me frantically, again and again, like she's worried I'll get angry, but I just kneel on the floor beside Charis and, coaxing Hjarta back over, take her little hand and show her how to pet him gently.

I glance up at Pelagia to see tears in her eyes, and it guts me to understand that she will always be a little afraid of me, a little uncertain, because of my father.

But despite all that, she continues to bring my half sisters to dinner, and these nights are precious to me. Surrounded by family, I feel Brynja's absence more keenly, and yet it is also easier to bear.

My generals—Demetria, Nereus, and Iason—don't wholly like these little dinner parties, and they *heartily* disapprove of my not executing Zopyros, Theron, Alcaeus, and Lysandra—the latter having attempted to make herself queen while her brothers were occupied taking charge of my army. I send all four of them to be servants in Lady Eudocia's household in the Bone City; she has promised to keep me apprised if they get out of line.

I miss Finnur dreadfully, having realized without him here how indispensable he was as my steward. I still haven't found a replacement for him. We communicate via animals, which we send back and forth every few days. Sometimes he includes a prismatic memory bead with a message from himself or my mother, so I still get to see her, too. She is settling well into life at the palace and her role as Finnur's adviser. I am glad for her, for both of them, but I can't deny it makes jealousy pinch at me.

Finnur has reordered the palace, along with Regla City. He has destroyed the underground prison that housed countless Draugur—wielders of Ghost magic—and liberated all its inmates. Ghost magic is no longer forbidden, and he is working with the Draugur to establish safety regulations, as well as building up the Ghost Sector of the city.

He has retained only a few of Valrún's Skapari in his service—most he has dismissed, at their request. Dagfinna has gone to live in Runa's house by the sea, the house that used to belong to her brother, Brynja's father.

Malen has left to start a new life with her sister Aris, one of the liberated Draugur. Adriel has vanished somewhere in time, looking for his father—Finnur is confident that Adriel will find him eventually. Runa lingers at the palace, waiting for Brynja. Osa has gone to meet her patron, the Gray Lady, for the last time, surrendering her life freely, when she could have lived a full century longer. Only Salin, the young wielder of Black magic, seems to have no current plans to leave the palace.

Valrún's tree yet grows on the plain outside the city, and what has become of Brandr, Finnur doesn't know.

He has seen nothing at all of Brynja.

I send animal messengers to Saga, too, commanding them to return to me when she bids them. Saga has crowned Leifur king beside her, and they are to have a child. This news stirs in me a deep, unquenchable ache.

I have sent a falcon twice to Aelia in Aerona. She replied to the first with the news that Vil had quarreled with her about wanting to try again to conquer the peninsula. She refused, and he stormed out of the palace. She said there was unrest in the mainland provinces, that she had her hands full trying to hang on to the empire her father built. And though she didn't state it in so many words, it was clear she was disappointed in Vil for wanting more power, for not being content with what she had given him. I don't know if he ever returned, or if they healed the breach between them, or if the empire is set to fracture—Aelia never answered the second falcon.

Out on the edge of the Sea of Bones, the sunlight dazzles my eye, glinting off the translucent blue peaks of the glaciers, touching my face with warm fingers.

"Good morning, My Lord," I say to the sun. "Happy New Year."

For a moment I think I hear the Yellow Lord's laughter in my ears.

Then the sun is over the rim of the Sea, climbing up the arch of the sky.

"He says hello," comes a sudden voice.

I jump and, turning to the right, find Brynja settling beside me, easy as you please.

Her hair has grown past her hips, dark curls weighed down into long waves. Her freckles look dark against her pale cheeks, and she's dressed simply, in tight-fitting trousers and a shapeless shirt. A heavy-looking medallion rests against the hollow of her throat, and there are scars yet on her neck, where the iron collar burned and blistered her.

"The Yellow Lord," she explains, as I have done nothing whatsoever besides stare at her. "He says hello. I visited him. I visited all of them, actually. I'm sorry it took me so long—there was no way to send a message, and I couldn't come back until it was done."

Her form blurs before me, and I forget how to breathe.

"Ballast," she chides. "It hasn't been *that* long. Has it?"

"Three months," I say. "An eternity."

She leans forward to kiss my brow, but I tilt my head up so her lips meet mine instead. I sigh against her, drinking her in like wine. Her mouth is warm and wild. She tastes of magic, of unbridled things.

The sun rises higher, and Brynja stands to her feet, tugging me up with her. I study her in the light. She is softer, somehow, than she was before.

She looks out over the Sea of Bones, fiddling with something in her pocket. "There's something yet I need to do," she says. She glances aside at me. "Can you take me down there? Into the Sea?"

I trace her cheek with one hand and nod, slipping out of my clothes and letting the form of the winged leviathan once more fold over me. She gathers my clothes and my ring, and climbs onto my back.

I bear her down to the Sea below, where the snow and ice have given way to sucking mud. I shake free of the leviathan and tug my shirt and trousers back on. She hands me my wedding ring, and I slide it onto my finger, comforted by the sure, solid weight of it.

She stands on her toes, and I bend down to kiss her again. I pull back when I feel her tears touch my skin.

"Brynja," I whisper, smoothing my thumbs over her damp cheeks. "What is it? What do you need to do?"

"I missed you," she says, but I know it's more than that.

She takes me by the hand, and we walk awhile in the Sea we cannot name *Bones* any longer. Death is giving way to life here. All things are becoming new.

There is a place in the boggy earth where a spray of white flowers grows, bright against the dark soil. Here she kneels and digs a hollow in the ground. She pulls something from her pocket and lifts it into my view.

"A plum stone," she tells me. "The last gift of the Green Lady. I think I'm meant to plant it here."

She sets the stone in the hollow and folds the earth gently over it. Then she glances up at me.

I finally realize what is different about her: Her hair is wholly dark, not a strand of white in it at all.

She watches me register this. "My magic is gone. All of it."

My heart is beating fast enough to make my head spin. "The Bronze Lord took it away from you?"

I kneel beside her, my leg touching hers.

She shakes her head. "The Bronze Lord is dead, Bal, like I told you. He's truly gone. I went back to his island, but it broke to pieces around me and fell into the sea. I knew I could re-form it, that the easy path before me would be in allowing myself to be remade, to become in truth the Bronze Lady and take my seat among the First Ones."

I am stricken as I study her, though her eyes are on the place where she planted the plum stone. Already, a tiny sprout pokes its green head above the dark earth.

"But I didn't want that," she says. She turns her head to meet my eye. "I wanted you."

She slips one hand into mine, and I can feel her heart beating in our joined palms, quick and erratic.

"Tell me," I say softly. "Tell me everything."

And she does.

BEFORE

BRYNJA

Year and month, unknown

Beyond the World

The Bronze Lord's house falls into the sea. I weep, for I am all alone, and his magic is eating me from the inside. My mind and my body are not strong enough to hold it all.

I want to go back. To step out of this nonplace and into the world, to fold myself into my husband's arms.

But I can't.

Not like this.

I let the waves lap over my shoulders. I shut my eyes in utter despair.

There is only one path I can see before me, but I recoil from it, because it would keep me from Ballast for all of time, and what comes after, and I cannot lose him now. I will not lose him now.

I pick up my head. I seize hold of the Bronze Lord's magic and tell it to bear me beyond the world, to the place where the First Ones are.

I climb into the sky and above it. I walk through storms and stars. I trod the fractured paths of lightning, and I come at last to the dwelling place of the Prism Lady. She walks in a garden made of color and light, the very air around her teeming with magic.

I go and kneel at her feet. I beg her to take the Bronze Lord's magic from me, that I might return to the place my heart dwells.

"Bronze Lord's daughter," she says, putting out her hands and drawing me to my feet again, "you have been bestowed with great honor. You alone of all humankind may shed your first form and be counted as a First One among the twelve. Become the Bronze Lady, and the magic will no longer burn you."

I weep in this place of power and light. "Please," I beg her. "Please, take it from me. I do not want it. I cannot bear it. Please."

She is stricken as she looks at me. She traces her finger across my brow. "You would be immortal. Wield power beyond reckoning."

"I don't want that."

"Are you certain?"

I think of Kallias, the king of his own little universe, using his power for cruelty while drilling into the heart of the mountain in pursuit of more. I think of Brandr, who murdered our father for his magic and still wasn't satisfied. Of Valrún, who betrayed her own sister, who killed and manipulated over and over again to crown herself Queen Eternal. I think of my father, pushing me past my breaking point, honing me into the tool he needed, locking my magic away. I think of Ballast helping me find my magic again, trusting me with everything that he was. I blink and see a vision of myself as I might have been if my father had never sent me to Daeros: cold and exultant, eager to take the gift the Prism Lady offers me, hungry to order the world according to my whims, and my whims alone.

But that isn't what I am.

And it never will be.

"Are you certain?" asks the Prism Lady again.

I tremble before her, hope hot in my heart. "Yes."

"Very well. Go to the Brown Lady. Tell her to make this for you, and then return to me." She plants an image in my mind of a medallion.

So I trod the paths around the world to where the Brown Lady dwells, in a place of rock and earth. Here magic glows in veins of gray stone, and water splashes in clear pools.

The Brown Lady crafts the medallion with molten rock and the sharp sear of her power, and when it is finished, she hangs it around my neck.

"When you have done all you need to do, Bronze Lord's daughter, return to me, and I will seal it."

I bow to her and make the long journey back to the Prism Lady.

"Are you certain?" she asks yet again.

"Yes, My Lady. I want it gone. Please."

Then her hands are at my temples, and she is drawing it out.

But only a piece, not all.

She channels the magic she took from me into the medallion at my neck.

"You must go to all of us," says the Prism Lady then, "every one of my brothers and sisters, and you must petition them to each take a little part of the Bronze Lord's magic and pour it into the stone. Go to the Brown Lady last, and when she has taken the final bit of magic, she will seal the medallion, and all of the Bronze Lord's magic will be gone."

I nod and turn, eager to complete my task and get home to Ballast.

"Little one," says the Prism Lady then.

I look back at her.

"There is no difference between the magic you were born with and the magic the Bronze Lord gave to you. When his power is taken out of you, yours will go with it."

My heart beats, and tears bite at my eyes.

"Do you understand?" the Prism Lady asks me.

I nod. "Yes."

"And you are still fixed on your purpose?"

"Yes."

She smiles, but there is a sadness in it.

I leave the realm of the Prism Lady and walk the paths beyond the world to visit every First One and make my requests of them.

The Brown Lady, when she has taken the last bit of magic and sealed the medallion with iron, pulls open a doorway into the world and sends me through it.

Here I find Ballast, sitting on the edge of the Sea of Bones.

The sun is rising.

CHAPTER FORTY-SEVEN

BALLAST

Year 4202, Month of the Yellow Lord

Daeros—the Sea of Bones

Down in the place we can no longer truly call the Sea of Bones, I gaze at my wife through my one eye in humility, in awe. "Brynja," I whisper, and my throat constricts. "You fought so hard to get your magic back. How could you give it up again?" I can't help but think of last year, her kneeling in the snow, begging me to help her unlock her magic.

"There is magic in the world," she says, "in the sun and the sky, in the beats of my heart and the breath in my lungs. There is magic in just being alive. I don't need anything more."

I touch the medallion with one finger and snatch my hand back with a hiss of pain. The iron burns me. "Could you use it, though? If you wanted?"

She lifts one shoulder. "If I were to ever open the medallion, all the power would rush into me again, and I would become the Bronze Lady in earnest. I couldn't undo it a second time."

"But—"

"Why do I wear it?"

I give a huff of laughter. “It seems you don’t need magic to read my mind.”

She smiles. “It seems not. I wear the medallion because I would not relinquish such a task to another; it is my burden to bear, and I will bear it gladly, if it means I get to be here with you.”

She lets out a breath and nestles against my shoulder. “The First Ones aren’t ever coming back, you know. They are finished watching, and doing, and interfering. They have left their magic here for now, but I wouldn’t be surprised if it were to fade bit by bit. In a hundred years or so, perhaps there will be none left.”

I digest this, pondering an existence where I cannot commune with animals, or take their forms. I wonder what will happen to Iljaria, a people and a culture that consists entirely of magic, when that magic is gone. A worry for another day. I will discuss it with Finnur. Being full-blooded Iljaria, he will certainly still be alive in a hundred years. Maybe I will be, too.

“So it won’t matter, then,” Brynja is saying, “that I gave mine up a little early.”

I laugh a little, cupping her face in my hand. “I am in awe of you, Brynja Eldingar. You are an astonishing woman.”

She looks at me sideways. “You’ll still have me, then?”

“Have you? My dear little schemer, the world would need to be remade in a completely different way for me to not have you.”

Her smile turns shy, and I pull her onto my lap and she wraps her arms around my neck and crushes my face to hers. And then we’re divesting ourselves of our clothing, and I am not sure, after a while, where she ends and I begin. Both at once, I think.

I am certain, now, that I hear the Yellow Lord laughing.

By the time we are ready to fly back up out of the valley, the sun is high in the sky, and in the place Brynja planted the Green Lady’s stone, a tender sapling unfolds new leaves, straining toward the light.

EPILOGUE

Three Years Later

BALLAST

Year 4205, Month of the Yellow Lord

Daeros—the Sea of Memory

The glaciers in the Sea of Bones are all but melted. The frozen ground has metamorphosed into a wetland bog. There are frogs here now, tangles of plants, ducks and herons and water snakes, although these last I could do without. I will never love snakes.

It is fitting, though, that the five of us stand here together to pay homage to all the souls my father killed and threw down into this Sea.

The king of Iljaria himself found and read all the bones, slipping back in time to garner their names and their stories. We have written all the names on a single stone, and it will stand here watching over their grave for all of time, lending them more honor in death than they were given in life.

Not my father's bones, though. Those we burned and scattered, shutting our eyes so we would never know which way the wind blew him. He, we will not honor. He, we will do our best to forget.

But here, now, Brynja and Saga and Leifur and Finnur and I utter eulogies over these precious souls. We fold cool earth over them. We lay their grave with flowers.

We won't call this place the Sea of Bones any longer, but the Sea of Memory.

Leifur holds Saga tight against him; Hilf's bones are here, with all the rest, and I know that part of her will always mourn him, as will part of me. I still dream about him sometimes, of the wild look in his eyes in the moment before I compelled the lion to tear out his throat.

Saga and Leifur's daughter, a squirrelly little nearly three-year-old named Ásta, waits with her nurse back in Tenebris, and Saga's belly is swollen again with child. Children, actually. When Finnur and his envoy arrived from Iljaria, he took one look at her and informed her she is having twins.

There has, of yet, been no child for Brynja and me. We both begin to suspect we are unable to conceive one. But that sorrow does not belong to this day.

When the ceremony is over and the flowers laid, Saga and Brynja talk together quietly for a while. They have exchanged numerous letters in the last three years, and while I am not certain their friendship will ever be quite the same as it was before Brynja's true identity was revealed, it is perhaps stronger now. I am grateful for it. And Saga no longer seems intent to kill me on sight—I am grateful for that, too.

Finnur and Leifur walk up to me, and the three of us watch in a companionable silence as the women converse, a warm wind stirring over our shoulders.

"Your mother sends her regrets that she couldn't be here," says Finnur to me then.

I nod, tamping down my flash of hurt. I'm not quick enough to hide it from Finnur, though. His eyes go sad.

"She misses you," he says.

"Not enough to come and see me." There's no sense in trying to disguise my bitterness, so I don't.

"There is still too much pain for her, here."

I sigh and kick at a clod of dirt. "If she came, if she saw how much I have transformed Daeros, how I've unraveled and rewritten everything my father touched—she might find healing."

"I think she will come," Finnur says. "In time."

We lapse into another little silence, and then Leifur says, "What do you think they're talking about?" He nods over at Brynja and Saga.

Saga is gesturing wildly with her hands, and Brynja is laughing so hard she chokes.

Contentment curls in my belly; I am glad to see my wife so happy.

"Us, probably," I say.

Leifur smiles. "Probably."

My suspicions are all but confirmed when the two of them glance over at Leifur and me and double over with laughter again.

A cloud passes across the sun, and Saga realizes she's ravenously hungry, and our time in the Sea of Memory has come to a close.

I compel my faithful owls to fly Saga and Leifur back to the surface. Finnur tells me and Brynja sternly to not be long—they won't hold breakfast for us—and then vanishes.

For some moments Brynja and I stand together in the Sea, where it feels as if everything ended, and where everything began.

There are many beginnings left to come. I am grateful for that, too.

We stride hand in hand to the Green Lady's plum tree, which towers far over our heads now, as if it has lived for a hundred years instead of three.

We kneel at the base of it and dig a hole between the roots. There Brynja places the medallion that contains the Bronze Lord's magic. We bury it together.

When it is done, we stand to our feet again, brushing the dirt off our fingers.

She looks lighter with the medallion gone. Freer. It has been weighing on her, year by year. We thought the Green Lady's tree was big enough to watch over it now.

The cloud passes beyond the sun again, and light shines through the leaves of the plum tree. It speckles her with yellow, dazzles in her eyes. I get the feeling she can be whole now, without the burden of the Bronze Lord's power. I hope she can be.

"Brynja," I say quietly, looking down at her. "Are you content here with me, so far from your home and everything you always wanted?"

She smiles at the echo of the question I asked her years ago, when the Yellow Lord was first bound into the sun. She reaches up to brush a gentle finger over the ridge of my missing eye, and I go wholly still at her touch.

"I am more than content," she says. "I have everything I want. *You* are my home. I am glad beyond anything to be here with you, Bal. Here in the light."

Joy blazes hot inside me. "In the light, Brynja," I whisper.

She wraps her hands around my face. She pulls my mouth to hers.

I call the owls, and they bear us up into the morning. We stride into Tenebris, her hand caught fast in mine, and we join the others at the breakfast table, awash in love and laughter.

When the light returns, the darkness cannot come back again.

GLOSSARY

The First Ones & Their Powers

The Black Lord (darkness)
The Blue Lady (animals)
The Bronze Lord (minds)
The Brown Lady (the earth)
The Ghost Lord (nothing)
The Gray Lady (death and winter)
The Green Lady (life and growing)
The Prism Lady (all things)
The Red Lord (fire)
The Violet Lord (time)
The White Lady (song)
The Yellow Lord (light)

Places

AERONAN EMPIRE—the occupied territories on the mainland, north of the Gray Peninsula

Port of Navis—Aeronan seaport where the empire's ships are built

THE GRAY PENINSULA—region comprised of the three countries Daeros, Iljaria, and Skaanda

DAEROS—country in the north of the peninsula, bordered by mountains and the great Saadone River

The Bone City—city on the bank of the Sea of Bones

Garran City—capital of Daeros, just outside Tenebris

Oran City—city on the eastern coast of Daeros, from which the emperor launches his ships

Myrkur—Iljaria name for Tenebris; also the name for wielders of Black magic

Sea of Bones—massive glacier valley in Daeros

Skógur City—walled city around an ancient forest

Tenebris—mountain palace originally built by the Iljaria

ILJARIA—country in the east of the peninsula, bordered by the sea and a magical barrier the Iljaria erected

Regla City—capital city of Iljaria

The Sögu Byrjun—ancient hill outside Regla City

Strönd City—city on the northwestern coast of Iljaria

SKAANDA—country in the west of the Gray Peninsula, bordered by the Saadone River and the sea

Saadone City—city built on the banks of the great Saadone River, on the Skaandan side

Saadone River—massive river that borders Skaanda and Daeros

Staltoria City—capital city of Skaanda, location of the royal palace

Other Places

Draugur Isle—island in the White Sea

Ohreinindi Isle—island off the eastern coast of Iljaria, between the Green and Violet Seas; likely named after wielders of Brown magic

Terms

Galdur Skjöld—magical barrier that cuts Iljaria off from the rest of the peninsula

Skapari—Iljaria magic wielders, specifically those who serve the queen

Skaandan Fire—Grenades filled with iron shards that neutralize Iljaria magic

The Twelve Branches of Iljaria Magic

Ári—wielders of Violet magic (time)

Deya—wielders of Gray magic (death/winter)

Draugur—wielders of Ghost magic (absorbing magic)

Eldi—wielders of Red magic (fire)

Gyŏja—wielders of Prism magic (all magic)

Huga—wielders of Bronze magic (mind)

Myrkur—wielders of Black magic (darkness)

Ohreinindi—wielders of Brown magic (earth)

Stjarna—wielders of Yellow magic (light)

Tónlist—wielders of White magic (song)

Vaxandi—wielders of Green magic (life/growing)

Villidýr—wielders of Blue magic (animal)

POV Characters

Ballast Heron Vallin—king of Daeros, son of Kallias and Gulla; has Blue/animal magic

Brynja Eldingar—daughter of the late Iljaria Prism Master; has Bronze/mind magic

Saga Stjörnu—queen of Skaanda, Vil's younger sister

Valrún Solstrøm—queen of Iljaria; has Green/life magic

Vilhjalmur Stjörnu, Vil—Skaandan prince, Saga's older brother

Other Characters

AERONA

Aelia Cloelia Naeus—imperial crown princess of Aerona

Junius Valens Aelius Cloelius Naeus—emperor of Aerona

DAEROS

Alcaeus, Lysandra, and Theron Vallin—children of Kallias and Elpis, half siblings of Ballast

Charis, Rhode, and Xenia Vallin—daughters of Kallias and Pelagia, half sisters of Ballast

Elpis and Pelagia Vallin—Kallias's Daerosian wives

Kallias Vallin—deceased former king of Daeros, Ballast's father

Zopyros Vallin—son of Kallias and Unnur, half brother of Ballast

Daerosian Nobility

Lord Damianus—overseer of the mines

Lady Eudocia—governor of the Bone City

Lord Galenos—governor of Skógur City

Lord Phaedrus—overseer of the greenhouses

Lord Seleukos—governor of Garran City

Lady Thais—head arborist

Other Daerosians

Demetria, Nereus, Iason—Ballast's generals

Dion—guard at Garran City's gates

Kyrillos—ship captain

Melitta—baker in Garran City

Rute—former child of Kallias's Collection, now works with Zenobia at the orphan house

Zenobia—head of the orphan house

ILJARIA

The Queen's Skapari

Adriel Tonje—Violet (time magic)

Dagfinna Aarhus—Brynja's aunt, Indridi's mother; Red (fire magic)

Jóvin Reynir—Yellow (light magic)

Osa Hjaltalín—Gray (death/winter magic)

Malen Ildjárn—Green (life/growing magic)

Salin Norodahl—Black (darkness magic)

OTHER ILJARIA

Aris Ildjárn—Malen's sister; Ghost (absorbing magic)

Brandr Eldingar—Brynja's twin brother, the Prism Master; Ghost (absorbing magic)

Finnur—Former child of Kallias's Collection; Prism (all magic)

Geirfinna—Ballast's classmate in the Skepna Conservatory; Blue (animal magic)

Gulla Vallin—Ballast's mother; White (song magic)

Indridi Aarhus—Brynja's cousin, who served as a spy in Skaanda and died by her own fire; Red (fire magic)

Kár Aarhus—Dagfinna's husband, Indridi's father; Green (life/growing magic)

Runa Eldingar—Brandr and Brynja's mother; Brown (earth magic)

Rúrik—Skepna instructor; Blue (animal magic)

Lady Villidýr—Ballast's private tutor; Blue (animal magic)

SKAANDA

Aasgier Stjörnu—Vil and Saga's father, former king of Skaanda (deceased)

Ebbi—Skaandan general who stayed with Vil in Daeros

Elíndis—Saga's adviser

Hildar—Skaandan general

Hilf—Saga's former bodyguard and boyfriend, killed by a lion on Kallias's command

Nývard—palace physician

Leifur—Skaandan commander who journeyed with Saga to Tenebris and back; her companion and friend **Pala**—Skaandan soldier

Rafn—Vil's adviser; Vil and Saga's third cousin on their father's side

Unnur Vallin—Kallias's Skaandan wife

Valdis Stjörnu—Vil and Saga's mother, former queen of Skaanda (deceased)

ACKNOWLEDGMENTS

I am kind of in awe that *When the Light Returns* exists. It was such a privilege to be able to finish telling the story begun in *While the Dark Remains*, and I'm incredibly grateful to be meeting you here in the acknowledgments.

Huge thanks to Marilyn Brigham and the whole team at 47North for giving the Winter Dark duology such a wonderful home.

Many thanks to my wonderful agent, Sarah Gerton, who worked with me on revising an outline for *Light* before I started drafting. (I abandoned the outline entirely as soon as I started writing, but what can you do. Sorry, Sarah!)

Thanks to RJ Anderson, who read the first draft of *Light* as I was writing it, and brainstormed with me through some particularly thorny bits!

While I was drafting *Light*, I was blessed to participate in two writing retreats that were hugely helpful in getting those initial words down on the page! Thanks to Pinetop retreat buddies Karyne Norton and Erin McFarland, and Tulsa retreat buddies Hanna C. Howard, Rosamund Hodge, and Claire Trella Hill for the fabulous company and inspiration!

Huge thanks to Lindsey Faber and Marilyn Brigham for their brilliant editorial insight—*Light* would not have achieved its final form without you both!

Thanks to my author friends near and far, especially the Writing Friday crew, the Pod, and the Thing with Feathers, whose passionate discussions about story craft, K-pop, theology, medieval siege warfare, totally-normal-and-not-at-all-unhinged Adar-is-Celeborn theories, and everything between, constantly encourage and inspire me. You are all profoundly weird and brilliant and wonderful.

Thanks to my husband, Aaron, for being my life buddy—you're my home. And thanks to Arthur, who has finally agreed that writing books might be a real job after all. 😃 Love you guys!

To my readers, old and new: Thanks for coming along on the journey.

Soli Deo gloria.

ABOUT THE AUTHOR

Photo © 2024 Vanessa Rose Holman

Joanna Ruth Meyer is the author of *When the Light Returns* and *While the Dark Remains* in the Winter Dark series, as well as five young adult fantasy novels, including the critically acclaimed *Echo North*. She lives in Mesa, Arizona, with her husband, son, two orange cats, and a giant grand piano named Prince Imrahil. Joanna loves forests and rainstorms and stories that make her feel things, and in all likelihood, she's drinking tea right now. For more information, visit www.joannaruthmeyer.com.